About the author

Ian McFadyen was born in Liverpool and has enjoyed a successful career in marketing. He lives in Hertfordshire with his wife and has three grown-up children.

The Murky World of Timothy Wall is the ninth in the series featuring DI Carmichael, all published by The Book Guild.

By the same author:

Little White Lies, Book Guild Publishing, 2008. (Paperback edition 2012)

Little White Lies (large print edition), Magna Large Print Books, 2010.

Little White Lies (Czech edition), Allaboutbooks, 2020

Lillia's Diary, Book Guild Publishing, 2009. (Paperback edition 2012)

Lillia's Diary (large print edition), Magna Large Print Books, 2014.

Lillia's Diary (Czech edition), Allaboutbooks, 2021

Frozen to Death, Book Guild Publishing, 2010

Frozen to Death (large print edition), Magna Large Print Books, 2014.

Frozen to Death, (Italian edition), Bibi Books, 2018

Deadly Secrets, Book Guild Publishing, 2012

Deadly Secrets (large print edition), Magna Large Print Books, 2014.

Deadly Secrets (Italian edition), Miraviglia Editore, 2014

Killing Time, Book Guild Publishing, 2015

Death in Winter, Book Guild Publishing, 2016

The Steampunk Murder, Book Guild Publishing, 2018

Blood on his Hands, Book Guild Publishing 2019

IAN McFADYEN

THE MURKY WORLD OF TIMOTHY WALL

The Book Guild Ltd

First published in Great Britain in 2021 by
The Book Guild Ltd
9 Priory Business Park
Wistow Road, Kibworth
Leicestershire, LE8 0RX
Freephone: 0800 999 2982
www.bookguild.co.uk
Email: info@bookguild.co.uk
Twitter: @bookguild

Typeset in Baskerville

Printed and bound by CPI Group (UK) Ltd, Croydon, CR0 4YY

ISBN 978 1913913 441

British Library Cataloguing in Publication Data.
A catalogue record for this book is available from the British Library.

To Chris – my perfect 10!

Chapter 1

Friday 31st July

Faye Hemmingway looked at her watch; it was a minute to five.

She shut down her computer, pushed back her chair and stood up, straightening down the back of her pretty floral skirt as she got to her feet.

The door to her boss's office was a matter of a few paces away, so it took her no time at all to arrive. After knocking gently, she popped her head around and smiled at her employer; a man in his mid-fifties looking intently at the screen of his laptop.

"I'll be off now, Tim," she remarked with a broad, friendly smile.

Timothy Wall raised his head and grinned back at his PA. "Have a lovely evening," he replied. "Say hi to…" her boss paused as he struggled to recall the name of Faye's latest boyfriend.

"Richard," she replied.

"Yes," Tim remarked, as if he had remembered at about the time she reminded him – which of course he hadn't. "Say hi to Richard. I'm looking forward to meeting him," he added before turning his attention back to his computer screen.

Faye smiled again before exiting the room, pulling the door shut behind her.

"You can leave my door open," Tim remarked, "I've a new client coming in about twenty minutes. If the door's open when he arrives, I'll stand a better chance of hearing him."

With a puzzled expression on her face, Faye stopped in her tracks, opened the door and stood at the threshold of her boss's office.

"There's no appointment in the book for you this evening, Tim," she said.

"Did I not tell you," her boss replied, "a guy called Haverstock-Price called me this morning and I agreed to meet him at twenty-past five. He wants to talk to me about a new case for us."

Not wanting to be late for her rendezvous with Richard, Faye just smiled, nodded and, leaving the door ajar, exited the room grabbing her jacket and handbag before heading out of the office. Closing the door behind her, with the heavily embossed nameplate which read 'Timothy Wall, Private Investigator' in large, black letters, Faye made her way down the narrow, noisy wooden stairs and out onto the high street.

In her haste to meet her boyfriend, Faye didn't notice the figure in the window seat of Maria's café across the street, peering out over the coffee-stained menu. Faye had no idea how keenly she was being observed as she crossed the high street and disappeared out of sight. And, of course, had no way of knowing what was about to unfold in the next thirty minutes.

Chapter 2

Sunday 2nd August

Carmichael had felt restless all weekend, his mind continuously fixated on Lucy Clark, now DS Martin, who he'd had a brief dalliance with when he'd arrived at Kirkwood. Newly married to the local MP, for some unfathomable reason she had decided to come back to Kirkwood and, despite his attempts to prevent her return, was set to join his team on Monday.

No matter how hard he tried, Carmichael couldn't see why she'd want to return to Kirkwood other than to cause mischief for him, even though that theory didn't sit particularly well with the image he had of Lucy; a young, ambitious officer, but one that hadn't ever demonstrated any signs of being either vindictive or devious.

Surely, she had as much to be worried about as him, he thought, given that she was recently married and by all accounts already destined for further promotion before too long. Why on earth would she want to come back here?

In truth he'd thought of little else since Chief Inspector Hewitt had confirmed her re-appointment a few weeks earlier, but the fact that she'd returned from her honeymoon and her first day back in his team was on Monday, had made him even more preoccupied with the fall-out that her return could bring with it.

What had made his weekend even worse was the strange mood his wife, Penny, had been in. In all the years they had been together, he couldn't recall her being so irritable with him and the rest of the family; despite a few attempts on his part, she'd been unwilling to shed any light on why she was so sullen.

All in all, Carmichael was mightily relieved when DC Rachel Dalton called him early that Sunday evening to advise him about the body that had been discovered by a cleaner in one of the offices on Kirkwood high street. This was a perfect excuse to get out of the house for a while, and hopefully a chance to think about something else other than Lucy Martin.

As his black BMW disappeared out of the drive, Carmichael didn't see his wife staring out through the upstairs window, her eyes fixed on his car but her thoughts clearly elsewhere.

* * *

DS Marc Watson and DC Rachel Dalton were already at the crime scene when Carmichael entered Timothy Wall's small first-floor office.

"What have we got here?" he enquired.

"Evening, sir," replied Watson. "We believe it's the body of a private investigator called Timothy Wall."

As he spoke, Watson turned to his right which allowed Carmichael a better view of the dead man slumped over a desk, his hands in front of him in a pool of congealed blood.

Crouched next to the body, was the unmistakeable stout figure of Stock, dressed in his full white forensic outfit.

"Nice of you to join us," Stock remarked sarcastically.

"Evening, Stock," replied Carmichael. "What's your initial thoughts on this one?"

4

"As always, Carmichael, I'm not going to make any judgements until I've managed to conduct a proper examination," he remarked, "but judging by the massive blow this man received to the back of his head, I'm ruling out suicide."

Carmichael smiled. In all the years he'd known Stock he'd never managed to get much out of the forensic scientist at any crime scene, so he wasn't at all surprised by his guarded response.

"Have we any idea what he was struck with?" Carmichael asked.

Stock looked up at Carmichael. "This looks the most likely weapon," he replied, holding up a plastic forensic bag with a large, round brick-coloured stone inside.

Carmichael took the bag from Stock and looked carefully at the item.

"Looks like something you see on a seashore," he remarked before handing it back to Stock.

Stock placed the bag on the floor next to him. "With the naked eye, I can't see any traces of hair or blood on it, but it was on the floor just by the body, so it's likely to be the murder weapon," he added before turning his attention back to the body slumped across the desk.

"What about the time of death?" Carmichael asked.

"Again, impossible to tell," replied Stock unhelpfully, "but I'd say he's been dead at least twenty-four hours; possibly as long as three days."

Carmichael nodded and turned to face his two officers.

"Who found him?" he enquired.

"It was the cleaner, Irena Badowski," replied DC Dalton. "She's been taken next door by PC Twamley, who's taking a statement from her."

"And has she confirmed that this is Timothy Wall?" Carmichael asked.

DC Dalton shook her head. "No, she maintains she's only worked for the cleaning company for two weeks and has never seen anybody at the office. The company she works for is called Mid-Lancs Scrubbers. I was just about to call their owner, a man called Gerry Monk, when you arrived."

Carmichael nodded. "Well done, Rachel," he replied, "get on and do that now. Then go and check if there's anyone in at any of the neighbouring premises. At this hour on a Sunday, it's unlikely, but you never know."

As he spoke, he made a movement of his head to confirm that DC Dalton could go, and dutifully the young DC left the room.

"There's another desk through there," Carmichael commented to Watson, "which suggests that he had a partner or a secretary. Have a look to see if you can get a name and a contact number for whoever owns that desk."

DS Watson nodded and headed towards the adjoining room.

"Looks like our poor victim spilt his drink in all the commotion," remarked Stock. "There's a broken glass tumbler under his chair. And by the smell, I'd say it had whiskey in it."

Carmichael turned back, took a few paces towards the dead man and looked down at his feet.

"You're right, Stock," Carmichael replied. Then after spying the bottle in the deep, half-opened desk drawer added, "And no ordinary whiskey, either."

Stock carefully removed the bottle and placed it onto the desk.

"Gelston's fifteen-year-old Irish whiskey. Is that a good whiskey?" the pathologist enquired.

"At about a hundred pounds a bottle, I'd say it's pretty good," replied Carmichael, "although I prefer Scotch whisky myself."

Stock nodded as if he somehow approved of the victim having such expensive tastes.

"If this man is Timothy Wall, as we suspect," continued Carmichael, "then all I can say is that his business must be doing quite well for him to pay that sort of money for a bottle of whiskey."

"Either that or he had some very rich and generous friends," remarked Stock.

Carmichael nodded. "Anything in his pockets?" he asked Stock.

Stock shrugged his shoulders. "I don't want to move him yet," he replied, "and with him bent forward like this I can't get access to his trouser pockets. I'll look when I'm ready."

"What about the desk drawers?" Carmichael enquired.

Stock tutted loudly, before sliding open the top drawer.

"Here you go," he remarked as he handed a bulging black wallet to Carmichael. "Hopefully, that will tell you all you need to know."

Carmichael snatched the wallet from the pathologist's hand and quickly opened it.

"Ninety pounds in cash, several bank cards in the name of T. Wall," uttered Carmichael as he searched through the wallet, "a photo of a woman aged about forty with shortish blonde hair and a broad smile, a couple of business cards with the name T. Wall on them and…" at this point Carmichael paused as if to add some drama to his words, "Mr Timothy Wall's driving licence, complete with a picture of our dead man's face, and his address."

"Happy now, Carmichael?" Stock enquired.

"Very," replied Carmichael.

As he spoke, Watson appeared at the door clutching an empty crumpled-up Jiffy bag.

"Faye Hemmingway," he announced triumphantly. "This envelope was addressed to her, here; I'm assuming she's his secretary."

"And this is Timothy Wall," responded Carmichael. "We

found his wallet in his desk drawer and it's got his driving licence in it with a very clear picture of him."

Carmichael handed the wallet to his sergeant, who opened it up.

"She's a good-looking woman," he remarked as he spied the photograph behind the thin Perspex film. "His wife maybe?"

Carmichael nodded in agreement. "She looks a fair bit younger than the dead man, but I'd agree she's more likely to be his wife or girlfriend than his daughter."

At that moment Rachel Dalton remerged into the office.

"That was quick," Carmichael remarked, his brow furrowed with a look of bewilderment. "Did you do a thorough check of the shops and offices down the road?"

Rachel shrugged her shoulders. "They're all shut," she replied. "But I managed to talk with Gerry Monk. He was really shocked, as you'd expect, however he maintains that he can't come over tonight as he's away in a hotel in Chester with friends. He reckons he's been drinking all day, so he won't be fit to drive until the morning."

Carmichael smiled. "Well we don't need him, as we've established that this is Timothy Wall from his driving licence that we found in his wallet."

"And we know his secretary here is a lady called Faye Hemmingway," added Watson, who reaffirmed his finding by passing over the Jiffy bag to his colleague.

"I know Faye," remarked Rachel. "We went to the same school and she attends the same gym as me."

"Really," responded Carmichael. "Do you know where she lives?"

Rachel Dalton shook her head. "I don't know her that well, she's a fair few years younger than me," she replied. "I think she lives here in Kirkwood but I'm not exactly sure."

Carmichael thought for a few seconds before heading over towards the door.

"You come with me, Marc," he said to Watson. "Let's get over to Timothy Wall's house. If the address on his driving licence is right, it's literally just around the corner."

"What about me?" enquired Rachel.

"Contact the gym," replied Carmichael. "Get Faye Hemmingway's address and get over to her house. Find out when she last saw Timothy Wall and find out if he had any enemies."

"Will do, sir," replied Rachel.

"Call me when you've spoken with Faye Hemmingway," Carmichael added.

He was just a few paces from the door when Stock raised his head and shouted over at the DI.

"You might want to take these if you're going to the deceased's house," he remarked, proudly holding up a large bunch of keys which he'd just seconds before extracted from the same drawer where he'd earlier found Timothy Wall's wallet.

Chapter 3

Timothy Wall's house was located on Aughton Place: a smart row of terraced dwellings in a small, cobbled cul-de-sac. The houses looked well over a hundred years old, and in their day had probably been the homes of workers from the old brickworks, long since gone. However, in the past twenty years, the houses in Aughton Place had almost all been developed into attractive, desirable properties. And, due in part to their location close to the town centre and the mainline railway station, these houses now got snapped up quickly if they ever came up for sale.

Carmichael rang the doorbell and waited a few moments. When nobody answered, he turned the key in the lock, pushed open the front door and walked inside, with Watson following on just a couple of paces behind him.

The first thing that struck Carmichael as they entered was how neat and tidy the house appeared. From the polished wooden floor in the hallway through to the orderly lounge-kitchen, the house looked spotless.

"He's either a neat freak or he's got himself a good cleaner," remarked Watson.

"That's assuming he lives alone," Carmichael added.

Watson looked carefully around the room. "I think he lives alone," he replied. "This is incredibly tidy, but it doesn't give me the sense it's occupied by a woman. There's nothing feminine about it, at all."

Carmichael could see where Watson was coming from but was not about to leap to any quick conclusions.

"Why don't you take a look upstairs," he told his sergeant. "I'll take a look around here."

Watson nodded and headed back into the hallway.

Carmichael stood in the middle of the room and slowly looked around.

Although it was very tastefully furnished and uncluttered, what he noticed almost immediately was the total absence of any photographs or anything else that would provide some insight into the life of the man who lived there.

Carmichael walked into the kitchen area, which despite being decked out with an expensive-looking cooker and shiny, silver fridge, had only a small breakfast bar and one tall, metal-framed stool, presumably where Timothy Wall would have eaten alone.

Carmichael must have been studying the room for longer than he thought as, in what seemed like no time at all, he was joined by Watson holding a thick, red photograph album.

"Look what I've found," remarked Watson with excitement in his voice.

Carmichael half turned to face Watson as his sergeant placed the album on the breakfast bar.

"What is it?" Carmichael enquired.

Watson smiled broadly. "It was on top of his wardrobe. I'm not exactly sure what you'd call it," he replied, "but it appears to be a record of Timothy Wall's girlfriends, going back decades, with photos, dates and a score card against each one."

Carmichael frowned. "You're joking," he said.

Watson shrugged his shoulders and opened the book at the start.

"Anne Draper," announced Watson pointing to a picture of a smiling teenage girl with the date July 88 to Sept 89 written neatly in pen next to the photograph.

Carmichael continued to read the notes written underneath the photograph.

"Looks eight out of ten, personality nine out of ten, sex seven out of ten," he said.

Turning the page revealed Clare O'Hara, another smiling young woman, with the date of August 89 to March 90 against her name.

"Seems to have been an overlap between these two," Carmichael remarked.

Watson sniggered. "She scored less in the looks and personality department than the first one but gets nine out of ten for sex."

Carmichael didn't reply but carried on turning the pages.

"As you say, Marc, there must be dozens of women in here," he remarked as he pored over the pages.

"I can't believe any of them knew about Wall making a record like this," Watson commented. "It's a bit sick if you ask me."

"Bizarre and juvenile, maybe," Carmichael replied, "but it's not illegal."

Watson nodded. "But a bit of a weird thing for a grown man to be doing," he added.

"What about his current partners?" Carmichael asked. "Let's take a look at them."

As he spoke Carmichael flipped the pages to the most recent entries.

* * *

Despite an initial reluctance to divulge the address of Faye Hemingway, Rachel eventually managed to get the duty manager at her local gym to agree to give her the information she needed. Then, accompanied by PC Twamley, Rachel made her way across town to Dickinson Road, where Faye Hemmingway lived.

The two female officers had not expected the door to be opened by a young, blond, athletic-looking man in shorts and a tight T-shirt, which took them both by surprise.

"Does Faye Hemmingway live here?" enquired Rachel, who at the same time brandished her identity card.

The young man looked shocked and concerned.

"Yes," he replied nervously. "Is anything wrong?"

Rachel smiled as if to reassure the man in front of her.

"Is she in?" she enquired.

Before he had a chance to answer he was joined by a bare-footed young woman with long auburn hair wearing shorts and a baggy yellow top.

At first Faye Hemmingway didn't recognise Rachel, but within a couple of seconds she twigged who she was.

"I didn't know you were a police officer," she remarked. "Is there something wrong?"

"Can we come in?" Rachel asked.

* * *

"I see Timothy Wall's habit of dating multiple women at the same time hasn't diminished with age," observed Watson. "If his dates in here are right, he was seeing these last three at the same time... and the crossover lasted for about three months."

Carmichael checked the dates. "There's a name for that," he remarked.

"Expensive and exhausting, I'd say," Watson replied. "How on earth did he mange that without these women knowing?"

"Maybe they did know," Carmichael suggested. "And the word I was looking for is polygamy. Maybe this was some sort of polygamous set of relationships that they all were happy with."

Watson thought for a short while before shaking his head. "Nah," he replied, "I reckon it was more likely to be him just wanting his cake and eating it. Dirty old bugger."

Carmichael laughed. "I never had you down as a prude, Marc. Or are you just jealous?"

Watson smiled. "Whether they knew or not, you've got to hand it to him, our Mr Wall could certainly pull the ladies. And good-looking ones, too."

Carmichael nodded. "Yes," he concurred, "these are all attractive ladies, and have you noticed anything else about them?"

Watson looked again at the last entries in Timothy Wall's red book.

"They're all at least ten years younger than him, some maybe nearer twenty."

"That's true," continued Carmichael. "But there's something even more noticeable."

Watson turned back the pages slowly but shook his head.

"They're all blonde," Carmichael remarked. "Every single one of them."

"I bet there's a word for that, too," said Watson with a wry smile.

Chapter 4

Faye Hemmingway remained motionless and silent on the small blue sofa, her hand tightly gripping her boyfriend's wrist as she attempted to absorb the news about the death of her boss.

"Can you tell me when you last saw or spoke with Mr Wall?" Rachel enquired.

"Friday evening," Faye replied, her eyes staring down at the polished wooden floor. "It was at about five. I left early as I was meeting Richard at The Lamb."

"That's the pub around the corner from the office," Rachel confirmed.

"Yes," replied Faye. "I'd normally stay at least half an hour later than that, but we wanted to eat before going on to the cinema."

"And how was Mr Wall when you left him?" Rachel enquired.

"Fine," Faye replied. "Chatty, as usual. Asked after Richard, but just his normal self."

"And did he say what he was going to be doing that evening?" Rachel asked.

Faye Hemmingway shook her head slowly. "No," she replied quietly. "Actually, he did," Faye quickly announced, her head now raised and her eyes looking directly at Rachel. "He said he was going to meet a new client. A man called…"

Faye paused as she tried to recall the name.

"Haverstock-Price," she said loudly. "He said he'd called him that morning and he was due to come into the office at five-twenty."

"Did he say anything more about this man, Haverstock-Price?" Rachel enquired.

Faye shook her head. "No," she replied.

Rachel thought for a few seconds.

"Did he have any enemies, to your knowledge?"

Faye shook her head again. "No," she replied. "He was a really nice guy. Very friendly, very sociable and a really good boss."

"What about people from his cases?" Rachel enquired.

"There may have been some people in some of the old cases he'd worked on before I arrived who weren't happy with him," Faye conceded, "but I can't think of anyone from any of his more recent cases. No, I can't think of anyone who would want to harm him."

"What sort of cases was Mr Wall working on at present?" Rachel asked.

"It's a bit slow at the moment," replied Faye. "We're working on a few jobs for HMRC, we get a fair amount of work from them. Then there's the Poulter case, but apart from that it's quite quiet."

As she finished talking, Faye Hemmingway burst into tears.

"What sort of cases are these?" Rachel asked.

Faye took a few seconds to compose herself.

"The HMRC cases are mainly fraud investigations; in the main checking up on people who are claiming they can't work due to some illness or injury," Faye replied. "The Poulter case is a missing person case. An old lady, Agnes Poulter, wants to trace her daughter who went missing twenty years ago. She is terminally ill and is desperate to see her daughter before she dies. Tim was quite excited about that one, as after months of looking, he thought he might have found her."

Smiling sympathetically at Faye's boyfriend, who had now put his long arm around Faye's shoulders, Rachel stood up.

"We'll need a statement from you," Rachel said. "And we'll need you to help us with the details of the cases Mr Wall was working on. But that can all wait until the morning. Obviously, you won't be able to go into the office just yet, but if you could come into Kirkwood Police Station in the morning that would be really helpful."

"What time?" Faye's boyfriend asked.

"As early as possible," Rachel replied. "Shall we say about eight-thirty? Is that alright?"

Faye's boyfriend smiled up at Rachel. "We'll be there at eight-thirty," he confirmed.

Neither Faye or her boyfriend accompanied Rachel and PC Twamley as the two officers walked towards the door. Both remained on the sofa engulfed in each other's arms.

Before she reached the door, Rachel turned back to face the sobbing young woman.

"Did Mr Wall have any family or a partner?" she enquired.

"No family that I know of," replied Faye. "And I think his relationship with Cassie may have been over, too."

"Cassie?" enquired Rachel.

"Cassie Wilson," Faye said. "She's a fitness and wellbeing blogger. She lives out near Hasselbury. Cassie and Tim were together for quite a while, well a long while for Tim. But I think they must have split up as she hasn't called for several weeks now and Tim hasn't mentioned her for a while either."

"So, I take it Mr Wall has had a few female friends since you've worked for him?" Rachel asked.

Faye smiled. "I've worked for him for about three years now," she replied. "And I'd struggle to name all the female friends Tim has had in that time; and I probably never knew them all."

"A ladies' man then?" suggested Rachel.

"He was absolutely that," replied Faye. "He never treated them badly, as far as I could see, but he was never with them long. I think he was just one of those men who had an issue with commitment, and he had a dreadful roving eye. As soon as any of them appeared to get even remotely serious they were out of the picture."

"But Cassie Wilson was with him for quite a long time?" Rachel asked.

"Yes," replied Faye. "I actually thought at one time that he may settle down with Cassie, they seemed so happy together and he seemed to like her a lot, but as I say she's not been around lately, so I assumed she'd gone the same way as all the others."

Rachel smiled back at Faye and her boyfriend.

"You've been very helpful, Faye," she remarked. "I'm so sorry to have had to give you this dreadful news. We'll let ourselves out."

Chapter 5

It was almost nine-thirty by the time Rachel Dalton and PC Twamley clambered into Rachel's car.

"I better call the boss," she said as she grabbed her mobile.

Carmichael and Watson had just arrived back at Timothy Wall's office when the call came through.

"Rachel," Carmichael said loudly, "how did you get on?"

"We talked with Faye," Rachel replied. "She's clearly upset, and I asked her to come into the station in the morning to give a full statement. But what she did say was that she last saw Wall at about five on Friday evening and that he was expecting a potential new client to come in at five-twenty. A guy called Haverstock-Price."

"Did she say anything else about this man, Haverstock-Price?" Carmichael asked.

"No," replied Rachel. "He'd called Wall that morning. Until he mentioned it to Faye as she was leaving on Friday, she had no knowledge of the appointment and has never met or spoken with Haverstock-Price."

Carmichael thought for a moment. "Anything else?" he asked.

"She reckons that Wall was a nice guy," continued Rachel. "Very sociable and Faye says he was a bit of a ladies' man. Loads of girlfriends."

19

"Yes," replied Carmichael. "We've worked that one out, too. Anything else?"

"She mentioned that the last person he was dating, to her knowledge, was a lady who lives in Hasselbury called Cassie Wilson, a fitness and wellbeing blogger," Rachel added. "Faye reckoned it was quite a serious relationship, but she thinks it may have fizzled out now."

Carmichael looked down and opened the red book that he and Watson had taken from Wall's house.

"I think that relationship ended a month ago," he remarked as he looked at the picture of Cassie Wilson, the last entry in the book.

"How do you know that?" Rachel enquired.

"I'll explain in the morning, Rachel," he replied with a wry smile.

Despite being curious and confused, Rachel decided not to ask anything more.

"Do you want me to come back to Wall's office?" Rachel asked.

"No," replied Carmichael. "Get yourself home. There's not much more you can do tonight, but can you get into Kirkwood station early tomorrow as I'd like to get the team together first thing."

"What time?" Rachel enquired.

"Seven," replied Carmichael. "We'll have a team briefing then."

"Will do, sir," said Rachel, just before the line went dead.

"Now she's a looker," remarked Watson as he glanced at the red book over Carmichael's shoulder. "And she got three straight tens from Timothy Wall."

Carmichael shook his head gently.

"Well, it's your lucky day, Marc," he replied, "because we're going to go and interview her tonight before we call it a day."

Watson glanced briefly at his watch.

"Tonight?" he enquired. "But we don't know where she lives."

Carmichael smiled and shut the red book.

"According to Rachel she lives in Hasselbury," replied Carmichael, "so, it's not far out of our way. I'll drive and when we're on our way you can talk to the office and get them to check where exactly in Hasselbury Cassie Wilson lives."

"What about my car?" Watson asked.

Carmichael smirked. "Don't worry, Marc, I'll drop you back here afterwards," he replied.

It was clear from his expression that Watson would have preferred to drive, but he said nothing.

"We'll leave you to it, Stock," remarked Carmichael. "I'll await your report."

As he spoke, Carmichael picked up Wall's red book, placed it under his arm and headed for the door.

"Good night, Inspector," replied the stern-faced pathologist, "you'll have it by tomorrow lunchtime."

Chapter 6

It was exactly ten o'clock when Carmichael pulled up outside Cassie Wilson's cottage in the tiny hamlet of Hasselbury.

"The lights are still on downstairs," observed Carmichael, "so at least we won't be waking her."

The two officers walked up the short concrete drive and passed a gleaming white Tesla sitting on the drive.

"She must be doing well," remarked Carmichael. "Those Model S Teslas are over fifty thousand pounds new."

As soon as Carmichael pressed the doorbell, the unmistakeable sound of 'Greensleeves' echoed down the hallway inside and seeped through the crack between the door and doorframe. Watson just managed to suppress a chuckle. He was fond of unusual door chimes but had been banned from having one at his home as his wife, Sue, thought them a bit naff.

The outside light suddenly came on and the door opened, but only a few inches, the chain on the latch preventing it from opening fully.

One eye and half a blonde fringe came into sight. "Who is it?" the owner of the fringe enquired, her tone one of nervous suspicion.

"It's the police," replied Carmichael who held his identity card up close to the one visible eye.

"But it's ten o'clock in the evening," replied the woman. "What do you want at this time of night?"

"I'm sorry to call on you at such a late hour, Ms Wilson," replied Carmichael. "But we need to talk to you about Timothy Wall."

At the mention of his name the gap between the door and the door frame closed slightly and the two officers could hear the chain being released.

Suddenly the door opened wide and a perplexed-looking Cassie Wilson stood before them, dressed in a tight green T-shirt and loose-fitting grey joggers.

"What's the issue with Tim?" she asked, the concern on her face already suggesting that she feared bad news.

"May we come in?" Carmichael asked.

* * *

After a large, late Sunday roast and the best part of a bottle of Malbec, Trevor Baybutt had just nodded off in his favourite armchair when his mobile rang.

He picked up the phone and gazed down at the name on the screen.

"Bloody hell, Si," he said irritably as soon as he put the phone to his ear. "I was just having a kip. What's up?"

"It's Wall," Si remarked in almost a whisper. "He's been murdered."

"What!" exclaimed Trevor. "Are you sure?"

"Absolutely certain," replied Si, his voice still quiet.

There was a pause in the conversation before Simon Baybutt spoke again.

"I hope you're not mixed up in any of this, Trevor?" he remarked.

"What are you saying," replied Trevor Baybutt, furiously. "Do you really think I'd get caught up in a murder?"

Simon again paused before answering.

"I'd not put it past you," he replied.

"Well this is the first I know of it," continued Trevor, "and I can assure you, little brother, that it's got nothing to do with me."

"It better not," remarked Simon. "It's one thing lying to your Sarah and fiddling the tax man but I'm not going to start lying to the police about you."

"What are you on about," snapped Trevor. "I'm not going to pretend that Wall being out of the way isn't good news, but I won't need any help from you. I don't need an alibi as I didn't do anything. So, thanks for the news and the vote of confidence little brother, but can you just bugger off and leave me to enjoy the rest of the evening."

Trevor Baybutt ended the call, put his phone down on the small table by his chair and sighed deeply.

"Who was that?" shouted his wife, Sarah, from the room next door.

"It was just our Si," replied Trevor.

"What did he want?" Sarah asked, her voice loud and shrill.

"Just some news he wanted to tell me," replied Trevor. "Nothing for you to get excited about."

Trevor Baybutt poured more Malbec into his empty wine glass, took a large sip, eased himself back into his comfy chair and smiled broadly.

Chapter 7

"No, he was a lovely man," said Cassie Wilson. "Crazy and annoying as hell at times, but he was a really nice guy. I can't think who would have wanted to kill him."

With her hands clasped on the kitchen table in front of her, Cassie stared across at Carmichael and Watson, totally stunned by the news they had just delivered.

"How exactly did he die?" she added.

"At this stage, I'm sorry but I can't say," replied Carmichael quietly.

"Shall I make you a cup of tea?" Watson asked, seeing just how pale and shaky the young woman looked.

"Yes please," replied Cassie, "no sugar though."

Watson rose from his seat and walked over to the kettle.

"Can you tell us when you last saw Timothy Wall?" Carmichael enquired.

Cassie stared deep into Carmichael's blue eyes.

"It was about four or five weeks ago," she replied. "He came by to pick up some stuff he had here."

"How long were you and Mr Wall together?" Carmichael asked, even though he knew from Wall's red book that it was thirteen months.

"Just over a year," replied Cassie.

"And why did the relationship end?" Carmichael continued.

25

Frown lines suddenly appeared on Cassie's forehead. "You don't think I had anything to do with Tim's death, do you?" she enquired irately.

Carmichael shook his head. "Absolutely not," he replied. "We just need to get as much background as we can about Mr Wall, so any information about him and his life, particularly in the last days and weeks before he died are important."

His words seemed to reassure Cassie, who nodded gently.

"I ended it," she replied. "It had basically run its course and I wanted my independence back."

Carmichael nodded. "And was Tim happy that the relationship ended?"

Cassie pondered over her answer for a few seconds. "He'd rather it hadn't ended, I think, but he was fine with it," she replied. "I imagine he'd already moved on by now."

"What do you mean?" Carmichael asked. "Was Tim already in a new relationship?"

Cassie nodded. "Tim wasn't short of female friends," replied Cassie with a wry smile. "In fact, I know for certain he was seeing at least one other woman when he was still with me."

"And you were happy with that?" interjected Watson as he placed the steaming drink in front of Cassie.

"No, I wasn't," replied Cassie firmly. "Despite his assurances that he would stop seeing this other woman, once I found out what Tim was really like and that I couldn't trust him fully, it was never going to work. I value my freedom, and self-respect means everything to me, so it was best to end it."

Carmichael paused for a few seconds while Cassie took a sip of tea.

"Did you know that Tim kept a book of information about his previous relationships?" he asked.

Cassie put the mug down on the table and again looked directly at Carmichael.

"Oh yes," she replied despondently. "His scorecard. Have you seen it?"

Carmichael nodded. "Yes, we have."

"And what score did I get?" enquired Cassie, her inquisitive words delivered with a hint of bitterness.

"Straight tens," replied Carmichael. "Did you not know that?"

Cassie shook her head gently. "No, I didn't. Apparently, he only gave scores once a relationship was over," she said disapprovingly. "Well that's what he told me when I confronted him about his horrible, demeaning book."

Carmichael remained expressionless. "Did Tim have any living relatives?" he enquired.

Cassie Wilson shook her head immediately. "No," she replied, "he was an only child and his parents died some time ago. I think they must have been quite old when he was born, but they had passed away long before I knew him."

Carmichael nodded and paused for a few seconds before asking his next question.

"I have to ask you this," he said. "We need to know where you were on Friday evening?"

Cassie answered instantly. "I was here, alone all evening," she said. "My mum called me at about seven, and we spoke on the phone for about an hour, but other than that I was here alone all evening and all night."

Carmichael smiled. "As a matter of procedure, we'll have to check that out," he advised her. "It's just a routine thing, but before we go, we'll need you to give us your mum's contact details, and we'll need to know your mobile and landline numbers."

Cassie Wilson seemed unfazed by Carmichael's request. She picked up a pen from the table, scribbled down the particulars Carmichael had just asked for on the back of an envelope and handed it to the inspector.

"Anything else?" she then enquired.

Carmichael smiled, shook his head and stood up.

"No, that will be all," he said. "I'm sorry to have to call on you so late Ms Wilson and am even more sorry to have to give you such bad news."

As the young woman showed the two officers to the door, Carmichael tried to work out whether Cassie Wilson was genuinely sad to hear the news about Timothy Wall's passing, or whether it was an act. He still hadn't quite come to his verdict when the front door closed behind them and they were once again outside on Cassie Wilson's concrete driveway.

Chapter 8

"So, what do you make of Cassie Wilson?" Carmichael asked Watson as the two men headed back to Wall's office to collect Watson's car from Kirkwood.

Watson considered the question for a few seconds before replying.

"She didn't seem overly upset about his death," he replied, "but she was really unhappy about Wall's red book, even though she got top marks."

Carmichael rolled his eyes and shook his head gently. "I suspect her score was irrelevant," he remarked. "I doubt getting three tens made what he was doing any more palatable."

Watson shrugged his shoulders. "But she still asked what score she'd got," he replied. "Maybe we should have told her she got three threes."

Carmichael didn't answer. He didn't want to perpetuate that particular train of discussion but had to admit that Watson was right; Cassie Wilson had asked and clearly did want to know her score.

For the next ten minutes the two officers drove back to the crime scene in silence; Carmichael's mind once more preoccupied with the arrival of Lucy Martin at Kirkwood Police Station in the morning, whereas Watson, on the other hand, was wondering what he was going to have to eat when he got home.

"See you at seven in the morning, Marc," remarked Carmichael as he drew up next to Watson's car.

"Do you want me to call Lucy and let her know we're starting early?" Watson asked as he opened the car door.

"Good idea," replied Carmichael, "she needs to be at the debrief too."

"I'll call her now," said Watson.

Carmichael forced a smile. "I'll see you in the morning, Marc," he said.

Watson returned the smile and climbed out of the car.

As soon as Watson shut the door, Carmichael headed off on the thirty-five-minute drive back to his house in the quiet Lancashire village of Moulton Bank.

* * *

When Carmichael arrived home only Penny was still downstairs, their three children having either gone out or ensconced themselves in their rooms.

Angry that Lucy was now back on the scene, Penny had spent the first hour after her husband had headed off to Kirkwood in the foulest of moods; so much so that Jemma, Robbie and Natalie had made themselves scarce at the earliest opportunity.

However, once Penny was alone, she had managed to calm down and think more logically about her situation. Penny had always been a pragmatic person and despite being very annoyed about Lucy's return to her husband's team, once she was able to reflect on what was happening, she started to feel more at ease.

Firstly, she recognised that she had no real concerns at all about there being a repeat of what had happened in America.

Of course, she didn't know all the details of their sordid encounter in Winston Salem, but she knew enough to know that it had been no long romance. She had also seen just how uncomfortable Steve had been since he'd found out about Lucy coming back to Kirkwood; a sure sign he didn't want her around either. And then, of course, Lucy was now married, so surely any designs she may have once had on her husband would be well and truly over.

As far as she knew, he was still totally unaware that she knew something had gone on, and she still could recall the look on Lucy's face when she'd confronted her at the airport; both facts that gave Penny the feeling that she was still very much in control of the situation.

So, after mulling it all over and with her practical head on, Penny decided she didn't need to do or say anything… not yet at any rate.

"How did you get on?" she asked when her husband entered the living room.

Carmichael slumped down on the sofa next to her.

"It's a private investigator called Timothy Wall," he replied. "He's been murdered."

For the next thirty minutes, Carmichael outlined the case to his wife, who, as she always did, listened intently and asked the sort of questions Carmichael would normally only expect from a seasoned detective.

"He sounds the sort of man that women should give a wide berth to," Penny said once her husband had finished talking.

Carmichael shrugged his shoulders. "But ironically a man that didn't seem short of female company," he replied. "In fact, if that red book of his is anything to go by, I'd say finding attractive women certainly wasn't a problem for our Mr Wall."

Chapter 9

Monday 3rd August

Carmichael hated being late for anything; so much so that it was a standing joke at home and well known at the station that if he set a time, he'd be at least half an hour early. That morning was no exception.

Having arrived at the office at just after six o'clock, Carmichael had already made a few headings on the whiteboard before the first of his team arrived.

"Morning, sir," announced Rachel Dalton cheerily as she put her bag down by her desk and placed a coffee cup on the table.

Carmichael glanced up at the clock before replying.

"Morning, Rachel," he responded with a smile. "I hope the others are here promptly, too."

Rachel had yet to meet Lucy Martin, but for her sake Rachel hoped her new colleague would be on time. As for Marc Watson, as far as Rachel was concerned, he knew the score so if he was late, he'd only have himself to blame.

As it happened, Rachel had no need to worry as within a few minutes, a good fifteen minutes early, Marc Watson and a woman, who Rachel assumed to be DS Lucy Martin, arrived together; all smiles as if they'd just shared a joke before entering.

Carmichael heard them arrive but didn't immediately turn around, choosing instead to finish writing the last few notes on the whiteboard.

When he did turn, the first thing that struck him was how well Lucy looked, and well tanned too, no doubt from her honeymoon in Antigua.

"Morning, sir," Lucy remarked, just as Rachel had done earlier, but with much more conviction.

"Morning, Lucy," replied Carmichael. "Welcome back to Kirkwood."

The fact that he didn't receive any greeting from the boss didn't seem to even register with Watson, but Rachel noticed. Rachel also saw something in both Carmichael and Lucy Martin's eyes as they greeted each other that suggested this was more than a normal meeting between two old colleagues. She didn't know what but there was certainly something.

"Thanks for coming in so early and on time," Carmichael proclaimed. "Let's recap on what we know so far."

Carmichael half turned and pointed to the notes he had made on the whiteboard.

"Our murdered man is Timothy Wall," he said. "A single male in his mid-fifties who worked in Kirkwood as a private detective. He was found yesterday evening by the cleaner, slumped over his desk. We believe he was killed on Friday evening, but we've not got the report back from Stock yet."

"Do we know how he died?" Lucy asked.

Carmichael shook his head. "Again, we need this confirming by Stock, but it looks like he was struck hard on the back of his head."

Carmichael then pointed to the name Faye Hemmingway, which he had written on the whiteboard in red.

"From Rachel's conversation last night with Wall's assistant, this young woman called Faye Hemmingway," as he spoke Carmichael then moved his still outstretched arm and pointed to another name which was also written in red on the whiteboard, "she maintains he told her he had a meeting with a man called Haverstock-Price, which was due to happen at around five-twenty on Friday evening."

"Faye told me that Wall had said he was a potential new client," added Rachel.

"Clearly, we have to find this man, Haverstock-Price, as a priority," continued Carmichael.

"Shall I pick that one up, sir?" enquired Lucy.

Carmichael thought for a few moments before answering. "No," he replied, "I'd like Marc to get onto that one. I've another job I'd like you to focus on."

Watson nodded. "Fine with me," he remarked.

"Start with checking all of Wall's incoming calls on his mobile on Friday," continued Carmichael, "and his office phone, too. According to Faye, she hadn't made the appointment, so whoever this Haverstock-Price is he must have spoken directly to Wall."

"Will do, sir," replied Watson.

"Also, check to see if there are any CCTV cameras around Timothy Wall's office."

"No problem," said Watson.

"What do you want me to do?" Lucy asked.

"There are actually two things you can do," replied Carmichael. "Firstly, reacquaint yourself with Stock and chase him up for his report, then I want you to start contacting all the ladies in this book."

As he spoke, Carmichael pushed towards her the red photo album that he and Watson had found in Wall's house the evening before.

As Lucy started to open the book, Watson smiled wryly.

"What is this?" Lucy remarked, her forehead now wrinkled as she looked at the pictures of Wall's previous girlfriends.

"It would appear to be a record Timothy Wall kept of all his partners from the last thirty-odd years," replied Carmichael. "With scores against them."

Lucy Martin's mouth opened wide, as did Rachel Dalton's, who had moved over to stand behind Lucy in order to see what the dead man had written.

"What a creep," Lucy said loudly.

"Start with the most recent and work back," instructed Carmichael, who appeared oblivious to the looks of condemnation on the faces of his two female officers. "You can skip Cassie Wilson though, as Marc and I have already spoken with her. It's a long shot but any one of them could be our killer, or at least they may know if Wall had any enemies."

"Too right they'll be suspects," concurred Lucy. "I think I'd kill someone if they put scores against me in a book like this."

As she spoke her gaze moved up from the book and made direct contact with Carmichael, a look that Rachel Dalton couldn't help noticing.

"Especially if you didn't get top scores," remarked Watson glibly.

"What about me?" enquired Rachel, who had moved away from Lucy. "What do you want me to do?"

"You're with me today," Carmichael replied. "We're going to focus on Timothy Wall's cases, specifically his current ones and any that he's concluded recently."

Rachel smiled; she always liked working alongside the boss.

"But remember, I've got Faye Hemmingway coming in at eight-thirty to give her statement," Rachel reminded him.

Carmichael nodded. "I know," he replied. "We'll need her to help us get to grips with his cases, so that's ideal."

Carmichael looked up at the clock. "Let's reconvene at two this afternoon for a catch-up on how we're all progressing," he said. "Hopefully, by then we'll have made some headway."

DS Martin and DS Watson both rose from their chairs and made their exit, leaving Carmichael and DC Rachel Dalton alone in the office.

"Faye's not going to be here for almost an hour," Rachel remarked. "What do you want me to do in the interim?"

Carmichael smiled. "Why don't you go and grab some coffees from the canteen, then check to see if either Timothy Wall, Cassie Wilson or Ms Hemmingway have any criminal records," he remarked. "I'd not expect so, but you never know. And while you are getting the coffees, I want to make a call."

Rachel smiled and stood up. "Do you want anything to eat?" she enquired.

Carmichael shook his head. "No, a coffee will be just fine."

Chapter 10

When Rachel returned from the canteen Carmichael was still in his office, on the phone.

"Are you sure?" she heard Carmichael say. And when she put a coffee next to her boss he added, "Well, as always, you've been very helpful, George."

Rachel knew immediately who her boss was talking to. It was his pal Norfolk George, the proprietor of the town's local newspaper.

Carmichael ended the call, placed his mobile down on the desk and picked up his coffee.

"Now, that was interesting," he remarked before taking a sip.

* * *

"So, what's it like to be back?" Watson asked Lucy as they sat facing each other across their respective desks.

Lucy shrugged her shoulders. "Early days but an hour in and so far, so good."

Watson smiled. "I guess you must have missed me," he remarked.

"Absolutely," replied Lucy sarcastically. "You can't imagine how much I missed you, Marc."

Watson's smile grew even broader. "And the boss, too, of course," he added.

Lucy turned her gaze back to her computer screen.

"Yes, him too," she replied curtly, her Geordie accent sounding even more pronounced than usual.

* * *

"I take it that was Norfolk George on the phone," remarked Rachel.

"Yes," replied Carmichael. "According to him, Timothy Wall was a prominent member of Kirkwood Rotary Club, and some fifteen years ago was engaged to the daughter of a local doctor, a man called Scruton. George couldn't remember her first name, but he says that it was a big story here at the time, because she took an overdose when they split up. He reckons she didn't die but after that whole episode she went away somewhere, and then a few years later Dr Scruton and the rest of the family suddenly left the area."

"Really," Rachel said, her eyes wide open. "Do you want me to follow that up?"

Carmichael shook his head. "No, I want you to check for any criminal records for Wall and the two ladies, then we'll talk with Faye Hemmingway. I'll get Lucy to follow up on Dr Scruton's daughter, no doubt she's in the red book, scores and all."

"And the Rotary Club?" Rachel asked.

"That will have to wait, for now," replied Carmichael.

* * *

Lucy had just put the phone down to Stock's assistant when Carmichael appeared at the door.

"Stock says you'll have his report in the next couple of hours," she told him.

"Good," replied Carmichael, who walked over and sat on the vacant desk next to his sergeant.

"I've just been speaking to Norfolk George about Wall," continued Carmichael. "He informs me that Wall was once engaged to a woman called Scruton, the daughter of a doctor here in Kirkwood. She tried to kill herself when they split up."

"Really," exclaimed Lucy, who quickly grabbed the red book and started to turn the pages to find the young woman.

"Here we go," she added as she found the page with the picture of a smiling, fresh-faced young woman with shoulder-length blonde hair.

"Nikki Scruton," Carmichael read out loud. "She looks really young doesn't she. How old would you say she was there?"

Lucy thought for a few seconds. "I'd say very early twenties," she replied.

Carmichael looked at the dates that Timothy Wall had written against her name.

"So, he was seeing her for ten months," he said, "and that was sixteen years ago. He'd have been in his late thirties then."

Lucy put her hand on her chin. "At least ten years older than her and by the look of her, I'd guess nearer twenty than ten."

Carmichael nodded. "I agree," he replied.

"Shall I start with her?" Lucy asked.

"Yes," replied Carmichael. "See if you can find her, I'd like to get her opinion of our Mr Wall. And try to find her father, too. I know it's a long time ago, but he could well want to harm the man who was the cause of his daughter trying to kill herself."

"He'll have waited a fair amount of time to do it," Lucy remarked.

"True," Carmichael responded, "but we still need to talk with them both, if only to rule them out."

Lucy nodded. "I'll get on to them straight away," she replied.

39

Chapter 11

Trevor Baybutt was behind his large desk, his fingers tapping away on the keyboard in front of him, when Fat Malc, his long-serving, aptly named associate entered the office.

"You wanted to see me boss," Fat Malc remarked as he approached Trevor Baybutt's desk.

"Yes," replied Baybutt. "Are you on the pitch at Mount Rush Park tonight?"

Fat Malc nodded. "Yes, it's me and Mary," he replied.

Baybutt smiled. "Well you won't need to worry about Wall," he said. "He won't be coming this evening. In fact, he won't be coming any evening."

Fat Malc frowned. "Why's that, boss?"

Trevor Baybutt's smile widened. "Put it this way, Malc," he replied, "someone's just done me a big favour."

* * *

Faye Hemmingway and her boyfriend arrived at eight-thirty on the dot and were ushered into interview room 3 by the desk sergeant.

"Would either of you like a drink?" he asked them.

Both Faye and Richard Cox shook their heads.

Five minutes later, Rachel and Carmichael entered the room.

"Morning, Faye," Rachel said. "Thanks so much for coming in."

She then turned and moved her arm in the direction of her boss, who was standing a few feet behind her.

"This is Inspector Carmichael," she announced. "He's heading up the enquiry."

Richard Cox stood up and shook Carmichael's hand.

"I'm Richard," he said confidently. "I'm Faye's boyfriend."

Carmichael smiled back at Cox, shook his hand firmly then put his hand out in Faye's direction.

Still seated, Faye limply took hold of Carmichael's hand and shook it for a few seconds before releasing.

"We'll need you to provide written statements, which DC Dalton will help you with," announced Carmichael with a gentle smile, "but before you do, can you tell me how long you've known Timothy Wall and what sort of person he was?"

"As I told your colleagues last night, he was a really nice person; sociable, kind and friendly. A really good boss," Faye replied. "He was always great with me and I loved working with him."

Carmichael nodded. "Last night you told DC Dalton that you couldn't think of anyone who'd want to harm him. Now that this is all sinking in, has anyone come to mind that may have disliked Timothy Wall?"

Faye shook her head. "I honestly can't think of anyone," she replied.

"That's fine," continued Carmichael, in a reassuring tone of voice.

"And how long have you worked for him?"

"About three years," Faye replied. "I came in to replace Rene Rothwell, who was with Tim for years. We had a couple of months' handover then she retired."

Carmichael smiled and looked across at Richard Cox.

"What about you, Richard?" he enquired. "Did you know Timothy Wall?"

Richard Cox shook his head. "No," he replied. "Faye's talked about him, but we never met."

Carmichael nodded gently and turned once more to face Faye. "I'll leave you now with DC Dalton, but when you've finished giving your statement, I'd like us all to go back to the office and go through the files relating to Timothy's current and most recent cases. Are you happy to do that?"

Before she could answer, her boyfriend spoke.

"I'm not going to be able to go with you back to the office," he remarked gently to Faye before turning his attention in Carmichael's direction. "I'm due to meet a new potential buyer at ten."

Faye Hemmingway looked over at her boyfriend and squeezed his arm.

"That's OK, Richard," she replied. "I'll be fine by myself."

"That perfectly fine with us, too," Carmichael assured him, before rising from his chair and leaving the room.

* * *

Lucy Martin waited patiently for someone to answer the phone. She was just about to hang up when a slightly hoarse, male voice suddenly said "Hello."

"Good morning, is that Dr Scruton?" Lucy enquired excitedly.

"Yes," came the reply, "this is Dr Scruton; who's calling?"

Chapter 12

Timothy Wall's office still showed signs of forensic activity when Carmichael, Rachel and Faye arrived.

Although Wall's body had long since been removed and the blood stains on his desk had been eliminated along with any obvious testimony that a crime had been committed, the smell of chemicals and the sprinkling of white powder on numerous surfaces were tell-tale signs that these were offices that had been investigated thoroughly by Stock's small army of white-clad scientists.

"Shall I make us all some coffee?" Faye suggested.

"I'll do that," replied Rachel with a smile, before walking towards the small kitchen area.

"Talk me through Tim's current cases?" said Carmichael.

"As I told DC Dalton yesterday, we're working on a few jobs at the moment," Faye replied. "Some for HMRC and the Poulter case."

"Tell me about the Poulter case?" Carmichael asked.

"It's actually a case that Tim took on for free," replied Faye.

Carmichael's perplexed expression showed some surprise at what he'd just been told. "He wasn't charging anything," he remarked, just so he was clear.

"Yes," replied Faye. "He'd done that a few times before with people; when he felt they needed some help but couldn't afford the normal fees."

"And that's what he thought about this one," Carmichael remarked.

Faye nodded. "He was introduced to Mrs Poulter by Cassie," she replied. "I think Cassie's mum is a friend of Mrs Poulter. I'm not totally sure, but with Mrs Poulter being so ill I don't think Tim had the heart to charge her. He was really soft like that."

"So, what sort of case was it?" Carmichael continued.

"It's a missing person case," replied Faye. "Agnes Poulter's about eighty and wants to trace her daughter who went missing twenty or thirty years ago. As I just said, she's now terminally ill and is desperate to see her before she dies."

"And how was Tim doing with that case?" Carmichael asked.

Faye's eyes widened and her face seemed to light up on hearing Carmichael's question.

"Really well, I think," she said. "He told me on Friday that after months of looking, he thought he might have found a link to her."

"Really," remarked Carmichael. "Where is she?"

Faye's elation quickly waned.

"I don't know," she replied. "He didn't give me any details, but he told me he'd located someone close to her who was going to arrange a meeting."

"Did he give any indication of who this close friend was?" Carmichael asked.

Faye shook her head. "He didn't say," she replied despondently.

"Could this Haverstock-Price have been that person?" Carmichael asked.

Faye shrugged her shoulders. "Maybe," she replied, "but Tim didn't say he was, he just said he was a potential new client."

"What about the other cases he was working on?" Carmichael asked.

"They're all HMRC cases," replied Faye. "They're mainly fraud investigations. You know, checking up on people who are claiming they can't work due to some illness or injury. They are our bread and butter cases."

"Which presumably Tim charges for?" Carmichael added.

Faye nodded. "Oh yes," she replied, "and they pay really well, and on time."

* * *

Lucy Martin eased herself back into her chair, put her hands behind her head and smiled smugly in her colleague's direction.

"How are you getting along?" she asked Watson.

"With the CCTV footage, not bad," Watson replied, "but with Haverstock-Price I'm getting nowhere. I think he's just a made-up name. So far, I can't find any male in the UK with that surname."

Lucy frowned. "There must be," she said. "Have you checked Facebook and LinkedIn?"

Watson shook his head slowly.

"I may not be a rising star like you, Lucy," he replied, "but I do know how to trace someone."

Lucy tilted her head slightly to the side and smiled. "Touchy aren't we," she remarked. "I'm sorry I spoke."

Watson let out a sigh and pushed himself back into his chair. "I suppose you've been making great strides this morning," he remarked.

"Well, as a matter of fact," replied Lucy, before pausing dramatically, "I have."

* * *

"Can you go through the cases that Tim was currently working on with HMRC?" Carmichael asked.

Faye Hemmingway sat down at her desk and switched on her computer.

"There are three," Faye replied, as she waited for the desktop to spring into life. "They're all documented in my HMRC file."

As they waited for the file to appear, Rachel came over with a tray of drinks, which she placed on the desk.

"Who's your contact at HMRC?" Carmichael enquired. "And where are they based?"

"It's a lady called Turnbull," replied Faye as the screen suddenly opened with the case details. "She's based in Newcastle."

"Newcastle!" exclaimed Rachel. "I thought they would be nearer than that."

Faye shook her head. "No, all tax returns and claims for this area are managed there," she replied. "I think it's so that people at the tax office don't get to work on cases of people they know."

Rachel nodded. "I guess that makes sense," she remarked.

Chapter 13

Having spent the best part of an hour looking at the details of the three HMRC cases being worked on by Tim Wall, Carmichael felt he'd heard enough.

"You've been really helpful," he told Faye. "If you can send DC Dalton a copy of all the case information you've shown us and also give us Ms Turnbull's contact details at HMRC Newcastle, that would be great."

Faye nodded. "And am I OK to stay here?" she enquired. "I'd like to make a few calls and tidy a few things before I shut up the office."

Carmichael hadn't expected her to want to stay but saw no reason to refuse.

"Of course," he replied. "We've finished here now."

"Take care, Faye," remarked Rachel sympathetically.

Faye forced a smile, before turning her attention to her computer screen.

Carmichael had just reached the door when he stopped and turned back to face the lonely looking figure behind the desk.

"There's a few more things I meant to ask you about Tim," he said, his hand now rubbing his chin as he spoke.

"Oh yes, what are they?" Faye replied.

"The forensic team found a large red stone on the floor near Tim's body," Carmichael announced. "Did that belong to either Tim or you?"

"That sounds like his paperweight," replied Faye immediately. "Is that what killed him?"

Carmichael shook his head gently. "It's far too early to tell, but it's possible."

Faye looked shocked. "It was here before I arrived," she continued. "I'm not sure where it's from. I never asked him."

Carmichael smiled back at Faye before continuing his questioning.

"Also, we know he didn't have any relatives, but what about any close friends?" Carmichael enquired.

"He had loads of friends," she replied, "always talking to people on his phone, but I never met any. Nobody ever came here to see him socially, other than Cassie, of course. But as I told DC Dalton, she hadn't been here for ages either."

"And out of work," continued Carmichael. "Did he have any specific hobbies or interests?"

Faye thought for a few moments. "Not really," she replied. "Well, none he talked to me about. I know he did a lot with the Rotary Club, so maybe they can help you, but we never really talked much about stuff he did out of work."

"He had a nice bottle of Irish whiskey in his desk drawer," Carmichael added. "I take it he liked a drink."

Faye smiled. "I don't think he was a big drinker. And that bottle in his desk had been in his drawer for a long time. I think it was a gift from a client."

"So, he wasn't in the habit of drinking in the office?" Carmichael enquired.

Faye shook her head. "No," she replied, "but he'd always pour himself a small glass at the end of the day when he'd successfully concluded an important case. It was a sort of ritual he had. He could be a bit OCD about some things."

"So, had he concluded a big case on Friday?" Carmichael asked.

Faye shook her head. "He said he'd made a breakthrough in the Poulter case, but it wasn't completed by any means, as far as I know."

Carmichael smiled. "Thanks Faye," he remarked before turning back and walking out the door.

The two officers were halfway down the steep wooden steps that led out to the high street when Faye appeared at the top of the staircase.

"He never talked about it," she said, "but I think he may have been a bit of a gambler."

Carmichael stopped and looked up at Wall's young assistant.

"Why do you say that?" he enquired.

"Well I've a friend, Caitlin, she works at Mount Rush Park racetrack. She works part-time on a Monday night on the champagne and oyster bar. She told me that she regularly saw Tim at the races. Her bar's outside, near where the bookies have their pitches. Caitlin said she saw him there on most Monday evenings in the summer, placing bets."

"Really," Carmichael replied. "Did your friend say whether he was with anyone?"

Faye shook her head. "No," she replied. "But I didn't ask."

"And I take it that this couldn't be to do with any case he was working on?" Carmichael enquired.

Again, Faye shook her head. "No," she replied. "I don't recall any case he'd worked on recently that would need him to go to the races."

Carmichael smiled up at Faye, then still pondering what she had said, continued his journey down the stairs.

* * *

"There's nothing earthshattering in Harry Stock's report," Lucy remarked having read it for a second time. "He was killed by a single massive blow to the back of his head and he estimates the time of death was between five and ten on Friday evening."

"Was he killed with that stone Stock found?" Watson asked.

Lucy nodded. "Stock's not definitive on that," she replied, "however, they found some of the dead man's skin cells on the stone, so he's suggesting it is the likely murder weapon."

"Have they found anything else?" Watson asked. "Fingerprints or any DNA belonging to the killer?"

"They've identified several fingerprints on the front door and on the door leading into the main office, but none have a match on the police database."

"So, it suggests our killer is either someone we've not had dealings with before or he wore gloves," Watson remarked.

"You are, of course, assuming it was a man," Lucy said.

"Well, with a made-up name of Mr Haverstock-Price, I'd say that's a fair bet," Watson replied.

Lucy shook her head. "As I'm sure Carmichael would say," she replied with a smile, "you may be jumping ahead there. Our Mr Haverstock-Price may prove to be totally innocent."

"He may have nothing to do with Wall's death, I grant you," continued Watson, "but I'm certain it's a made-up name. There's nobody I can find in the whole of the country called Haverstock-Price."

Chapter 14

Carmichael's team briefing began at two that afternoon, exactly, dead on time.

"So, who wants to go first?" he remarked, looking across at his three colleagues.

"Why don't I kick off," replied Lucy enthusiastically.

Carmichael nodded. "Yes, you go ahead," he replied.

Lucy passed across a printout of Stock's report.

"Forensic are saying that Wall was murdered between five and ten on Friday evening," she announced. "He was killed by a single massive blow to the back of his head. They are suggesting the stone they found is the murder weapon as it has Wall's skin cells on it, but they are not prepared to be definitive about that. Also, they say they have found several fingerprints on the front door and on the door leading into the main office, but they haven't come up with a match to any of these on our database."

"It suggests our killer is either not someone we have had dealings with before or is someone who wore gloves," Watson remarked as he had done earlier to Lucy, but this time without inferring the killer was male.

Carmichael nodded. "And the front door is the only way our killer could have gained access into Wall's office?" he asked.

"Well, in the report Stock does mention a fire door tucked away off the hallway," replied Lucy. "But his team checked it, and it had no prints on it, can't be opened from the outside and hadn't been forced open either."

"Anything else?" Carmichael enquired.

Lucy shook her head. "Not from Stock's report."

"How are you getting along chasing up Wall's old girlfriends?" Carmichael asked.

"I've made quite a bit of progress," replied Lucy, with confidence. "I managed to locate Dr Scruton and have had a good chat with him on the phone about Wall and his daughter, Nikki."

Carmichael raised his eyebrows. "What did he say?"

"He said that he actually liked Wall," Lucy replied. "He and his wife were both very sad when they split up, and he seemed really shocked and upset when I told him Wall was dead."

"I'm surprised to hear that," remarked Carmichael. "From what Norfolk George told me I'd expected him to be quite anti-Wall."

Lucy shook her head. "Not a bit of it, sir," she added.

"What about his daughter and his wife?" Carmichael asked.

"He informed me that his daughter was alive and well and now lives with her husband and a couple of kids in San Francisco," said Lucy.

"What about her mother?" Carmichael asked again.

Lucy shook her head. "Apparently she died a few years ago."

"And what about the attempted suicide claim from George?" Carmichael asked. "Did you talk with Dr Scruton about that?"

"I did," replied Lucy, "and he said it definitely happened and that Nikki was unsettled for a good few years after, but that she's now fine and has moved on. In fact, he joked that had it not been for Timothy Wall dumping his daughter, as he did, she'd never have met her husband. Apparently, he was one of the psychologists that helped her through her 'dark period', as he called it."

Carmichael thought for a few seconds.

"I take it you'll be talking with Nikki Scruton at some stage later today when they're awake in San Francisco?" he remarked.

Lucy nodded. "It's just about eight in the morning there, so I'll call her once we've finished this debrief."

"Good work, Lucy," said Carmichael. "Any joy with any of the other ladies in Wall's red book?"

Lucy grinned again, as if she had even more positive news for the rest of the team. "I've talked with another two of them so far on the phone and have left messages for two others," she replied. "The ladies I've managed to talk to were Kelly Underwood and Heather Jones."

"And what did they have to say about Wall?" Carmichael asked.

"Apart from the fact they both said he was a neat freak, really fastidious about certain things, like being orderly and tidy, they had very different views about him," replied Lucy. "Kelly Underwood thought he was marvellous. Funny, loving, caring, great company; it was quite unnerving to be honest as she talked about him as if he were the best guy that ever walked the earth."

"And the other one?" Carmichael enquired, having temporarily forgotten her name.

"Heather Jones," Lucy reminded him. "Now she hates his guts. She described Wall as an untrustworthy cheat and in her words, a danger to women."

"A woman clearly scorned," remarked Watson flippantly.

"And how did they react when you told them he was dead?" Carmichael asked.

"To be fair they both sounded stunned and in Kelly's case really upset," replied Lucy. "But the thing that struck me was, despite both being ex-partners of Wall, their opinions of him couldn't have been further apart."

"And the red book?" Watson added. "Did they know he kept a record of them and gave them scores out of ten?"

Lucy shook her head. "No, neither maintained they knew," she replied. "Kelly seemed really shocked and said she couldn't believe he'd do a thing like that; but still didn't have a bad word to say about him. Heather, however, said that she wasn't surprised as it was typical of him. She then went on to call him devious, unpleasant and immature."

"Do you think Heather Jones hated him enough to be responsible for his death?" Rachel asked.

Lucy shrugged her shoulders. "Hard to say based on just a telephone call," she replied, "and their relationship ended about three years ago, so if she was going to kill him, I'd have expected her to have done it before now, but she's certainly not a fan of his."

Carmichael took a few seconds before he spoke again.

"That's great work so far, Lucy," he remarked. "Make sure you speak with Nikki Scruton later and keep contacting Wall's other girlfriends. If there are any who you feel might still hold a grudge against him, like Heather Jones, find out where they were on Friday evening."

"Do you want me to interview them face-to-face?" Lucy asked.

"You're going to have to use your judgement at this stage," Carmichael replied. "If they're local I'd certainly want you to try and meet them, particularly if they express some hatred towards him, but I'll leave you to make that call as I know there's quite a few ladies you'll need to make contact with."

Lucy nodded. "Will do, sir," she replied.

Carmichael then turned his attention towards Watson.

"How about you, Marc?" he enquired. "How've you got on?"

Watson took hold of his notes and smiled. "I'm certain that this man Haverstock-Price doesn't exist," he replied. "I've not been able to find anyone on social media or through any of our normal sources with that surname. Either Faye Hemmingway heard it wrong or it's a made-up name."

Carmichael nodded. "I guess that shouldn't be a shock, as if he is our murderer, he was hardly going to give his real name."

"But it does suggest that he's our man, whatever his real name is," suggested Watson.

Carmichael shrugged his shoulders. "I agree he's probably our prime suspect at the moment," replied Carmichael, "but I'd not want to pin our hopes solely on him at such an early stage of the investigation. What about the CCTV footage? Is there much for us to look at around the murder scene?"

"Yes and no," replied Watson obtusely. "There are some good cameras located across the road from Wall's office, and about two hundred yards either way from Wall's office door. However, there's nothing on the premises and unfortunately nothing that covers the office entrance. I've not started to look at the images yet, but I plan on doing that as soon as we've finished here."

"That's a blow," Carmichael replied with a dismayed expression on his face. "That would have been a real help if we'd had better CCTV; but we need to look at it anyway as a priority."

Then turning his gaze on Rachel Dalton, he added, "I want you to help him with that, Rachel."

Rachel nodded. "Will do, sir," she dutifully replied.

"Anything else?" he asked Watson, his eyes now firmly back on the only other man in his team.

Watson picked up a pile of A4 sheets of paper he'd printed off from his computer earlier and passed them over to Carmichael.

"Those are the activity reports from Timothy Wall's mobile and from the office phone for Thursday and Friday," he remarked.

Carmichael took the sheets from Watson and started to look through them.

"No calls made or received and just a few messages on his mobile," he remarked. "This person Sara-Jane could well be his latest girlfriend, by the look of their conversation."

Watson nodded. "Yes, that's what I thought," he replied. "Her final note to him on Friday saying, 'Can't wait to see you on Tuesday', signed off with a kiss, suggests they are more than friends."

"Not necessarily," Rachel remarked. "Lots of people put a kiss at the end of messages. It just says to me that they are close friends."

Watson shrugged his shoulders. "If she's under forty and has blonde hair my money is on her being his latest girlfriend."

Lucy shook her head. "I agree with Rachel," she said. "And she's not in his red book, so I'd say she's just a friend rather than his girlfriend."

Watson still wasn't having any of it. "Not true," he said firmly. "If she's not in the book that just means it's on-going. Cassie Wilson told us that."

"Whether she's just a friend or something more we need to find this person Sara-Jane," Carmichael remarked. "I'd like you to do that Marc, after you've finished looking at the CCTV."

"I'm happy to do that," interjected Lucy, "as I guess that's tied in with what I'm doing."

Carmichael thought for a few seconds before answering.

"No," he replied, "you stay focused on contacting the ladies in the red book. I'm comfortable with Marc picking up the Sara-Jane lead after they've looked at the CCTV images."

From the frown on Lucy's face it was clear to her colleagues that she was not happy, but she said nothing. Carmichael, however, didn't seem to care, electing to look at the record of the calls coming in and out of the office phone line on Thursday and Friday.

"They didn't get that many calls," was his initial observation.

Watson nodded. "No," he replied, "and I'd say about fifty per cent were from that number ending 7855."

Carmichael nodded. "Who does that number belong to?" he enquired.

Watson smirked, which signified he, for once, was ahead of Carmichael.

"It's a guy called Cox," he said. "Richard Cox."

"That's Faye's boyfriend," remarked Rachel.

"Really," replied Watson. "Well it must be love as he's called her countless times from just after eight to around four on both days. There has to be at least half a dozen calls a day."

Carmichael nodded. "What about the other calls?" he enquired. "Could any of those be from our Mr Haverstock-Price?"

"They might be," replied Watson. "I haven't managed to identify the other numbers yet, but all of the ones that were made on Friday were after ten in the morning, so I'd expect Faye Hemmingway would have taken them. And if so, she'd have surely known about Haverstock-Price."

"Marc's right," interjected Rachel. "Faye maintains that she didn't know he was coming in and that Wall told her the appointment was sorted out that day, before she arrived at the office."

"And what time does she say she arrived at the office on Friday?" Carmichael asked.

"In her statement Faye says she arrived at about eight-forty," replied Rachel.

Carmichael exhaled loudly.

"There is the possibility she could be lying," suggested Lucy. "Maybe she killed Wall and this Haverstock-Price person is just someone she's made up."

"I agree," added Watson. "We only have her word that Wall told her he was meeting this Haverstock-Price character."

Carmichael nodded. "OK, Rachel," he said. "After you've looked at the CCTV, call Faye and confirm when she arrived on Friday morning. Ask her again about what Wall said about this guy Haverstock-Price and then, other than Richard Cox, find out who all the other calls were from on Thursday and Friday. Also check with the pub where she says she met her boyfriend on Friday. Find out what time she arrived."

Rachel looked sideways at Lucy, as she half expected her to again suggest she took that action; but Lucy remained silent and stony-faced.

"Right you are, sir," she said when she was sure Lucy wasn't about to speak.

"Is that everything you've got for us, Marc?" Carmichael enquired.

"Yes, that's everything," Watson replied.

Carmichael nodded. "That's good work from you, too," he added.

Without being asked to contribute, Rachel decided to comment on her progress that morning.

"I've checked for any criminal records of Tim Wall, Cassie Wilson and anyone called Haverstock-Price," she remarked, "and there's nothing for any of them."

"And we found out from Faye that Wall liked to have a drink of whiskey at the end of the day, when he'd completed a big case," Carmichael added. "So, as he was having a drink of that expensive fifteen-year-old Gelston when he was killed, the question has to be, had he just cracked a case?"

"But Faye wasn't aware of him having solved anything on Friday," Rachel added. "And you'd expect he'd have told her if he had."

"Maybe he just fancied a drink on Friday," Watson suggested. "Just because he has a whiskey when he's cracked a case doesn't mean that's the only time he has a whiskey."

Rachel nodded in agreement. "That's true," she conceded.

The room fell silent for a few seconds until Lucy spoke up.

"So, what about Wall's case files?" she asked. "Any potential suspects in them?"

Carmichael shrugged his shoulders. "That's going to be my focus this afternoon," he replied. "From what Faye told us, Wall's main source of income seems to have been from HMRC cases, so I'm going to speak to them first. And according to Faye Hemmingway, he was close to solving a free-of-charge job he was doing, finding the daughter of a lady called Poulter; so, I'll go and see Mrs Poulter, too."

"Maybe that's the case that warranted the whiskey," Lucy added.

"Maybe," replied Carmichael, who paused for a few seconds before continuing. "Then, this evening, I'm off to Mount Rush Park racetrack," he added.

"Why?" enquired Lucy, her brow furrowed, emphasising her bewilderment.

Carmichael smiled. "It would appear that our Mr Wall liked a flutter on the gee-gees and he's there most Monday evenings, so I thought I might have a poke around and see if that's got any bearing on his murder."

It was clear from the look on the faces of both Watson and Lucy that they weren't totally convinced about the value of their boss going to the racetrack.

Although he noticed their perplexed expressions, Carmichael didn't care a jot what they thought about the matter; he knew that gambling and crime were common bedfellows, so he was certainly going to pursue that line of enquiry.

"I've checked and the first race starts at about ten-past five," he remarked. "I reckon I'll be able to conclude my activity there by about six-thirty and, with any luck, be back here by seven-fifteen at the latest. So, let's start our final briefing for today at seven-thirty."

Carmichael's team all nodded in unity, although not with any great enthusiasm.

"Great," continued Carmichael with a smile. "Let's get on with it."

With the team briefing now over, Carmichael headed off in the direction of his office to call HMRC in Newcastle-upon-Tyne.

Chapter 15

Carmichael was so engrossed in the printouts of Wall's case notes that Faye Hemmingway had given him and Rachel earlier in the day, he didn't notice Lucy enter his office.

It was only when he heard the door close that he looked up and saw Lucy's slight frame, then the solemn expression on her face.

"Can we speak?" Lucy asked, although from the way she asked it was clear that she was going to speak however Carmichael chose to answer the question.

"Of course," replied Carmichael. "What is it you want to talk about?"

As he was talking, Lucy had walked halfway from the door to Carmichael's desk, but stopped there.

"I know my return here to Kirkwood is probably tricky for you," she remarked, "but I want you to know that it wasn't my idea. Calum feels he needs to be based within his parliamentary constituency, so I had three choices. I could stay where I was and hardly see him at all, I could leave the force completely or come back here. I chose to come back here."

"I did wonder why you'd decided to return," Carmichael replied.

"Well now you know," replied Lucy. "I thought it was the best option of the three."

"Right," said Carmichael, rather awkwardly. "I'm pleased you told me."

Lucy forced a smile and then half turned to walk away. However, before she had taken even one step, she turned back to face Carmichael, her expression now altogether more relaxed.

"I'll get on with trawling through Wall's red book," she said more cheerily.

"Yes," replied Carmichael. "And I'll get on with my calls."

Carmichael watched as Lucy walked towards the door, and without looking back, made her exit.

As soon as she was out of his office, Carmichael exhaled loudly before taking a deep breath and turning his attention back to the printouts on his desk.

* * *

As Rachel and Watson sat together, the six large screens concurrently showing images of Friday evening from the cameras closest to Timothy Wall's office, Rachel suddenly turned her head to face her colleague.

"Has there always been some friction between those two?" she enquired.

Watson continued to look forward.

"You picked up on that, too," he replied. "They both did seem a bit tetchy today, didn't they? That's not uncommon for the boss, but it's not like Lucy."

"Did they have a falling out when she left last time?" Lucy asked.

Watson shook his head. "Not that I'm aware of," he replied. "But her departure from Carmichael's team was quite sudden. Then, not long afterwards, she got transferred. I always thought it was so she could further her career, as she's always been ambitious, but maybe they did fall out.

It would certainly explain why just about everyone she knew at the station was invited to her wedding, other than Carmichael."

Rachel had not been aware of that. Not being at Kirkwood when Lucy was there before, she'd not been invited either, but Rachel had expected Carmichael and Penny would have made the invitation list.

"Well, I only hope the atmosphere thaws a little in the coming days," Rachel added, "as the last thing we need is there to be tension in the team."

Watson smiled. "It may actually be your doing," he suggested.

"What do you mean?" replied Rachel, her eyes now off the screens and focused in bewilderment on Watson.

"Well, when Lucy was here before, she was the only woman in the team," he explained, "all doe-eyed, hanging on the great detective's last words. Now she's back, her position as the boss's favourite girl's been usurped by you, his new little prodigy."

"Rubbish," exclaimed Rachel.

"It's true," continued Watson, all smiles. "He can't have two favourite girls can he. That would be —"

Rachel interrupted before Watson could think of the right word. "I should have known I'd not get any sense out of you."

Watson laughed out loud. "Don't be so dismissive," he continued, "I may be way off the mark; but just think about it. And if I'm right it will be interesting to see which of you the boss decides he wants to favour now you're both on the scene; you, his latest office darling or Lucy, his ex."

Rachel stared forward, saying nothing but regretting ever having brought up the subject with her colleague.

"It's a pity Carmichael doesn't have a little red book, too," continued Watson, almost hysterical. "We'd then be able to compare your scores."

Rachel, now seething, continued to keep her eyes fixed on the footage playing on the screens in front of her.

"Sod off, Marc," she said irately, through gritted teeth.

Chapter 16

Carmichael leaned back in his chair as he waited for someone at HMRC Newcastle to pick up the phone. It must have rung for nearly thirty seconds before the computerised voice greeted him then instructed him to key in the extension number of the person he wanted to talk to, if he knew it. Carmichael keyed in extension 2257.

"Turnbull," came the voice down the line, which pleasantly surprised Carmichael, who had fully expected to be put straight through to her answer machine rather than speak immediately to the person he wanted.

"Good afternoon," Carmichael announced, "this is Inspector Carmichael from Central Lancashire Police; are you free to talk?"

* * *

Although Nikki Scruton, or rather Nikki McQuade as she was now called, had been made aware of Timothy Wall's death by her father, who'd messaged her as soon as he'd been told, she was still clearly distressed by the news when Lucy got through to her in San Francisco.

"I can't believe he's dead," she said sobbing down the phone.

Lucy didn't want to agitate Nikki any more than she had to, so adopted a soft tone and spoke slowly.

"I'm so sorry, Mrs McQuade," she said. "I'll really try not to keep you too long, but I was hoping you could help me."

"How?" replied Nikki. "I haven't seen Tim in years."

"I just wanted to try and get a better understanding of the sort of man he was and understand why you split up," continued Lucy.

"He was a funny, charming and kind man," replied Nikki, "I loved him dearly, and it broke my heart when we split up. But I know it would have never worked as Tim wasn't able to stay loyal to any one woman. It took me a while to realise that, and even though at the time I was prepared to put up with how he was, in the end it was for the best and I'm now with someone who I love, who loves me, and I know will remain faithful."

"I see," replied Lucy, although she couldn't for the life of her understand how any woman would choose to spend more than ten minutes with a man that wasn't totally faithful. "And was Tim popular?"

Nikki, still sniffing as if she was desperately trying to stifle more tears, paused for a few seconds.

"With women, certainly," she replied. "Especially if they were younger than him and blonde. That sounds a bit shallow I suppose, but that's how he was. He was popular with blokes as well, but I suspect there are a few husbands and partners of some of his relationships that may not be so keen on him."

"Some fathers, too," Lucy added.

"Yes," Nikki agreed, "but not mine. My father really liked Tim."

"So, was there anyone in particular who disliked him?" Lucy asked.

Nikki again took a few seconds before answering. "We're going back years, but there was one person who really hated Tim, mind you it was mutual," continued Nikki.

"Who was that?" Lucy enquired.

"I can't recall his proper name, but he had a weird nickname," replied Nikki. "It was Badger."

"But you can't remember his real name?" Lucy asked.

"I think it was something quite normal like Smith or Jones," replied Nikki, "but I can't remember."

"And why did they dislike each other so much?" Lucy asked.

"I've no idea," replied Nikki, "but knowing Tim, I'd suspect at the bottom of it all was a woman he had been seeing or trying to see."

"And where did Badger live?" Lucy asked.

"I don't know," replied Nikki, "but they'd met when they both played rugby together at Kirkwood Rugby Club. So, he must have been quite local."

It was Lucy's turn to take stock for a few seconds.

"You've been really helpful," Lucy said. "If you do remember anything more about Badger, or anything else that might help us, I'd appreciate it if you called me."

"Absolutely," Nikki replied. "If I think I can help you find whoever killed poor Tim I'll not hesitate to call you."

When the call ended, Lucy cupped her hands behind her head and took a deep breath, before writing Badger in bold letters on her note pad.

* * *

"So you see, there's nobody Tim was investigating who I'd have thought even remotely likely to do him harm," said Ms Turnbull after going through each of the outstanding HMRC cases that Tim Wall was currently working on. "And they were all just surveillance cases, so he probably never got anywhere near any of them; he'd have been many yards away behind a camera. I really can't believe any of our cases will be anything to do with his murder."

Having spent twenty minutes on the phone listening to the details of the three HMRC cases that Wall was working on, Carmichael tended to agree with her.

"What about past cases?" he enquired.

Ms Turnbull paused for a few seconds as she considered Carmichael's question.

"The only one that comes to mind is the Baybutt case from last summer," Ms Turnbull replied. "But we had to close that because of insufficient evidence."

"Can you talk me through the case, please?" Carmichael asked.

For the next fifteen minutes, Carmichael listened intently to Ms Turnbull, as she outlined HMRC's suspicions about the tax returns from the Lancashire-based chain of bookmakers and the efforts they, with Tim Wall's help, had gone to in order to gather enough evidence to make a formal prosecution.

"But you dropped the case in the end?" Carmichael asked as all the details had been divulged by Ms Turnbull.

"It's not been dropped," she replied, "but we don't yet have enough to formally take action against Trevor and Simon Baybutt. Tim was taken off the case, but it still remains open."

Carmichael again took a few seconds to reflect on what he had heard.

"And when were you next due to discuss the current cases with Mr Wall?" Carmichael enquired.

"Tomorrow, as it happens," Ms Turnbull replied. "He was due to come up here for a meeting first thing in the morning."

"You've been very helpful," Carmichael responded. "I'm really sorry to be the one to give you the bad news about Timothy Wall."

"It's tragic," added Ms Turnbull, as they ended their call. "Truly tragic."

Chapter 17

Agnes Poulter lived in a small, detached bungalow on the outskirts of Kirkwood.

Having parked level with her garden gate, Carmichael made his way along the narrow gravel path to Mrs Poulter's front door and rang the bell.

To his astonishment, the person who opened the door was Cassie Wilson.

"Ms Wilson," Carmichael announced with surprise. "I hadn't expected to see you here."

Cassie Wilson smiled broadly.

"I come every Monday to help Agnes with her shopping," she replied. "We used to go to the supermarket together but for the last few months Agnes hasn't been up to it, so I come in the morning to check what she needs, then go and get it for her. I was just putting it all away. You can help me if you'd like."

As she finished her sentence, Cassie opened the door wide and ushered Carmichael inside.

"That's right," Carmichael remarked, as he remembered what Faye had told him. "Mrs Poulter is a friend of your mother, isn't she?"

Cassie nodded. "They are good friends," she replied, "they go back over sixty years from when they were at school together."

"And did you recommended Tim Wall to her to help find her daughter?" Carmichael continued, once he was safely across the threshold and in Agnes Poulter's hallway.

"I introduced them, yes," replied Cassie. "Is that why you're here?"

Carmichael nodded. "I want to talk with her about the work Tim was doing for her and find out how he was getting on."

Turning her head away from Carmichael, Cassie bellowed down the hallway.

"Agnes, it's the police. They want to talk with you about Tim and Debra."

"Is that her daughter's name?" Carmichael enquired.

"Yes," replied Cassie, but now in a hushed voice. "They never got on and Debra did a bunk years ago."

"Did you know Debra?" Carmichael enquired.

"Yes, but not well," replied Cassie with a shrug of her shoulders. "She was a few years older than me and a bit of a wild child. I was a boring, shy swot, so we'd nothing in common at all. In fact, I suspect she never even noticed me."

Carmichael smiled. "And does Agnes know Tim is dead?" he enquired.

"Yes, I told her this morning," replied Cassie, rolling her eyes skyward. "She's very upset. Like every woman who ever met him, she adored Tim."

Carmichael smiled again. "He did seem to have that effect on a lot of people, didn't he?"

Cassie led Carmichael down the hallway to a door at the end, which she opened and walked inside. At the same time, with a sharp jerk of her head, she beckoned Carmichael to follow her.

"This is Inspector Carmichael," Cassie said loudly, her gaze fixed on the small, dark eyes of the crinkly, frail old lady sat quietly in a large, red chair. "He wants to talk to you about Debra and Tim Wall."

"Has he found her?" Agnes enquired; her attention focused on Cassie with a desperate look of hope in her eyes.

"No, Agnes," replied Cassie. "He wants to ask you about how Tim was getting on tracking her down."

Cassie's reply was obviously a disappointment to Agnes, whose head slumped down, her eyes now focused on the floor rather than her visitor.

"Why don't you sit there, Inspector," Cassie suggested, pointing to another armchair a few feet away from Agnes. "I'll just finish putting her shopping away. You'll have to speak up though, as she's really hard of hearing."

Carmichael did as he was told; and Cassie, with another of her engaging smiles directed towards Carmichael, left the room closing the door shut behind her.

* * *

Lucy had considered calling Carmichael to check whether he would agree to her temporarily taking a break from contacting the women in Wall's red book but decided against it. She was convinced that tracking down Badger was the right direction of travel for her, and after closing the red book and putting it to the side of her desk, started to type in Kirkwood Rugby Club on her keyboard, to try and locate a contact name to start her search.

* * *

"When did you last have any contact with Tim Wall?" Carmichael asked, his voice loud and his words delivered with unnaturally long spaces between them.

"I'm deaf, not stupid," replied Agnes Poulter abruptly. "I

71

can understand what you're saying, you just have to speak up. I know most of me isn't working that well, but my mind is as sharp as when I was in my twenties."

"I'm sure it is," Carmichael replied with a wry smile.

As he made himself as comfortable as he could, on what was a very uncomfortable chair, Carmichael could see the old woman start to take some notice of him, her dark eyes suddenly scrutinising him as if she was about to pass judgement.

"I talked with him on Thursday," Agnes replied, "at about four o'clock."

"And what did he say?" Carmichael enquired.

"He said he'd located a man who said he knew where Debra was," replied Agnes. "He didn't say who, but he was confident the man was genuine and that he was going to try and meet up with him."

"Did he say when they were going to meet or how he'd come across this man?" Carmichael asked.

The old lady shook her head. "He didn't say, but then again I didn't ask," she replied. "I should have, shouldn't I?"

Carmichael smiled. "Did he say anything more about this man that you can remember?" he continued.

Agnes shook her head. "Only that he was sure the man was telling him the truth."

At that point, Cassie Wilson re-entered the room.

"I should have asked Tim more questions, Cassie," Agnes said as she saw her walking towards her. "What a stupid old woman I am. If I'd have asked, the police could have found him. Now we may never find him, and I may never see Debra again."

As she spoke Agnes's eyes started to fill with tears and within a few seconds she began to cry uncontrollably.

Cassie looked across at Carmichael and rolled her eyes upwards again.

"You better go," she said.

Carmichael nodded.

"Thank you for your help, Mrs Poulter," Carmichael remarked before getting to his feet and making a hasty exit.

Chapter 18

"Any joy, Rachel?" Watson enquired as the two officers scrutinised the CCTV footage from around Wall's office on that Friday evening.

"Nothing obvious," replied Rachel, who was still unhappy with her colleague. "Apart from seeing Faye at three minutes past five, walking down the road on the opposite side of the street from Wall's office and then a few minutes later entering The Lamb public house, I've not seen anything. How about you?"

"Not much," replied Watson. "There was a guy sat in the front window of Maria's Café across the road from Wall's office, who does look a bit suspicious. He's there from four forty-two to five thirty-five. He then leaves the café, goes across the road and off camera, but then about four minutes later he appears again, but this time marching away, really quickly. I've tried to follow his movements, but I can't pick him up after he turns down Station Road."

"Do you think that might be our man Haverstock-Price?" Rachel enquired eagerly.

"Could be," replied Watson. "Let me roll back the footage and you take a look."

Rachel paused the screens she was watching and stared intently at Watson's main screen as he wound back the tape to five thirty-five and pressed play.

Once out of Agnes Poulter's bungalow, Carmichael checked his watch; it was twenty-past four.

He considered whether he should call his three officers to find out how they were doing but decided against it. He was due to see them in just over three hours, he thought, and as he wanted to get over to Mount Rush Park before the racing started, he opted not to make any calls that could delay him.

They would call him if they'd made a breakthrough, he figured.

* * *

"He does look really suspicious," Rachel remarked as she and Watson looked at the footage for the third time. "That could well be Haverstock-Price. The timing and the speed at which he is trying to get away from the area would tie in with him being our killer."

Watson nodded. "But he's only off the camera for four minutes. Do you think that's long enough for him to enter Wall's office, kill him and then get out?"

Rachel nodded. "There would be no time for small talk, I grant you, but I'd say so."

Watson froze the screen and then enlarged the image of the man they had been observing.

"How old would you say he is?" he asked Rachel.

"I'd say he's in his thirties," she replied. "And I'd guess he's around six foot tall."

Watson looked up at the clock then sent the image to the printer.

"I'll tell you what, Rachel," he said, "if you can check out who that Sara-Jane woman is, who was messaging Wall, for me, I'll get over and talk with the staff at Maria's Café. With a bit of luck someone might know who our man is, and even if not, he may have paid them by card."

Rachel nodded. "That's fine," she replied. "Are you going to tell Carmichael?"

"Can you do that?" Watson asked as he quickly rose from his seat. "I want to get over as quick as I can."

"No worries," responded Rachel. "I'll call him now."

* * *

Carmichael was almost at Mount Rush Park when the call came through from Rachel.

"How's it going?" he enquired impatiently.

"That's why I'm calling," Rachel remarked. "We've found an image on the footage that we think may be Haverstock-Price."

"Really," replied Carmichael. "Why do you think it's him?"

Rachel then proceeded to tell him, in some detail, about what they had seen and how Watson was now travelling hot-foot to Maria's Café to find out if they could help him identify the man.

"Thanks, that sounds promising," Carmichael said, once he'd heard everything Rachel had to say. "So, what are you doing?"

"I'm going to check the calls into the office before Wall died," she replied, "and I'm going to also pick up on Wall's messages with Sara-Jane that you'd asked Marc to do."

"And Faye's alibi, too," added Carmichael, "don't forget that."

"I've already done that," Rachel replied. "The CCTV footage corroborates her story. She leaves the office at just after five as she said and walks to The Lamb. Apart from a short section of her journey, the CCTV captures it all."

"Good," remarked Carmichael. "And do you know how Lucy is getting on?"

"I've no idea," Rachel replied. "I haven't seen or heard from her since the briefing earlier."

"OK," replied Carmichael. "I'll see you at seven-thirty."

In his customary style, Carmichael abruptly ended the call.

Chapter 19

After being passed on by three people at the rugby club, Lucy was eventually put in touch with a man called Peter Machin, a seasoned club member who was there when the man called Badger was a player.

"Good God!" he exclaimed when she mentioned his name. "I haven't thought of Badger in years."

"But you remember him?" continued Lucy, who was excited to, at last, have found someone who knew the man.

"Absolutely," said Machin. "He was a great player here and a character, too. Such a shame about him."

"What do you mean?" Lucy enquired, her heart having sank instantly the word shame had come from the person at the end of the line.

"That he was taken so soon," replied Machin, as if he expected Lucy would have already known.

"When did he die?" Lucy enquired.

Machin thought for a few seconds before replying.

"Must be almost ten years ago now," he said rather vaguely. "The car crash was in the local papers so you could check the exact date with them, but I'd say about ten years ago."

With the thought that she had just wasted nearly two hours on a wild goose chase trying to find Badger, which no doubt Carmichael would have something to say about, Lucy decided to end the call straight away.

"I see," she said meekly. "Well thank you for your time, Mr Machin. I'm sorry to have troubled you."

"No trouble at all," Machin replied. "If I can help you any more please feel free to call again."

Lucy ended the call and put her mobile down on her desk.

"Damn," she said out loud before pulling Wall's red book back towards her.

* * *

Carmichael was not a big horse-racing fan and gambling was totally alien to him. Since a child, like many other people, he had always put a small bet on the Grand National, something he still did, but outside of that he'd never even consider placing a bet on horse. So, the sight of dozens of people clambering to place bets, thrusting wads of notes into the bookies' hands in exchange for a small paper receipt seemed crazy to him. But that was the vision that confronted him when he entered the betting ring looking for Faye's friend, Caitlin, at the champagne and oyster bar.

As he approached the bar, he saw three women serving, and to humour himself tried to guess which one would be Caitlin.

He ruled out the tallest of the three, as she appeared to be in her late thirties, too old to be Faye's friend, he guessed. Of the two remaining ladies he decided upon the one that looked more like Faye: slim, with a youthful-looking face and a friendly smile.

Confident that he'd successfully identified Caitlin he strode up to the young woman and held up his identity card.

"I'm looking for Caitlin," he said, sure that she would confirm it was she.

"Oh right," replied the young woman, who then proceeded to point in the direction of the first woman that Carmichael had eliminated. "That's Caitlin."

Caitlin, who had overheard the conversation, walked over to Carmichael with a slightly concerned look on her face.

"You want to talk with me?" she asked nervously.

"You're not in any trouble," Carmichael reassured her. "I would just like a quick word."

Caitlin wiped her hand on a towel and walked around to join Carmichael on the customer side of the bar.

"What is it you want to talk about?" she asked.

"Why don't we sit down," Carmichael suggested, looking over at one of the bar's vacant small tables.

"OK," replied Caitlin, "but I hope this will be quick. Mr Maloney won't be best pleased if I leave the bar for too long."

Carmichael nodded. "It will take just a few moments," he assured her.

Having sat down at the table, Carmichael took out a photograph of Timothy Wall and passed it over to Caitlin.

"I understand from Faye Hemmingway that you told her Timothy Wall, her boss, is a frequent visitor here," he said.

Caitlin nodded. "Most Mondays," she replied. "Why, what's he done?"

"I'm afraid he's died," Carmichael told her. "I'm heading up the investigation to find out the facts about his death."

Caitlin put her hand to her mouth. "Poor Faye," she said. "She'll be devastated. She loved working for Tim."

"She's bearing up well," Carmichael said trying to reassure her, "but she did tell us about his interest in gambling and told us that you'd told her about him coming here and putting on bets. Is that right?"

Caitlin nodded. "I'm not sure how much he was gambling," she replied, "but I've seen him up at the bookies and there was quite a lot of money changing hands."

Carmichael smiled. "Was he with any particular bookie or did he bet with several?" he enquired.

Caitlin took a few seconds to answer.

"He definitely placed some bets with Fat Malc from Baybutt's," she replied. "He could have been with others too, but I couldn't be certain. Baybutt's are right opposite the champagne bar so he was easy to spot, but I guess he'd use others too, as they check for the best odds don't they."

"Who do?" Carmichael enquired.

"Punters," replied Caitlin. "They walk up and down to try and get the best odds for the horse they want to bet on."

"Of course," replied Carmichael.

"You mentioned Fat Malc," Carmichael remarked. "Who's he?"

Caitlin nodded in the direction of Baybutt's pitch, a matter of ten yards away.

"He's the large guy over there," she replied. "He's forever trying to chat up Rose at the bar, dirty old sod. He's old enough to be her dad and she's not interested, but it doesn't stop him."

"I see," replied Carmichael.

"I'm going to have to go," Caitlin said, as she spied Mr Maloney striding purposefully in the direction of the bar.

"Just one last question," Carmichael said, as the young woman stood up. "When did you last see Tim Wall here?"

"It was last Monday," Caitlin replied without any hesitation. "I don't know how much he bet, but he won a load of cash from Baybutt's after one race. I saw Fat Malc hand it over, there must have been hundreds."

Caitlin started to walk back towards the bar, then turned back to face Carmichael and smiled.

"And you should have seen the look on Fat Malc's face," she shouted over. "He was really miserable."

Carmichael continued to watch as Caitlin walked back to the bar, went behind the counter, and resumed serving customers with her two colleagues.

Chapter 20

Watson reached Maria's Café at four fifty-five and pushed hard on the rustic-looking front door. As it opened there came a tinkling sound from a bell attached to the top of the door, typical of old shops and in keeping with the ambiance of the tiny small-town café.

Except for two elderly ladies enjoying a coffee and cake and engrossed in conversation at a window seat, the café was empty.

"Good afternoon," said Watson when he caught the eye of the only waitress who appeared to be on duty. "I'm Sergeant Watson from Mid-Lancashire police, may I have a word, please?"

"Of course," replied the waitress who walked the short distance to where Watson was standing.

"I was wondering whether you remember seeing this man in here on Friday?" Watson asked. "We know he was in here for some time, around five o'clock."

The waitress studied the photo carefully before nodding.

"Yes, he had two soya lattes and an Eccles cake," she replied. "Good-looking man, didn't leave a tip though."

"And had you seen him before?" Watson asked.

The waitress shook her head. "No," she replied, "I'm certain he hadn't been here before."

The way the waitress answered suggested to Watson that she had rather taken a shine to him.

"Did he talk much?" Watson asked.

The waitress shook her head. "No," she replied. "He was the handsome, silent type. He just ordered his coffee, then after about twenty minutes ordered another and a cake and then asked for the bill, paid and left."

"And did he pay by cash or card?" Watson enquired.

* * *

Baybutt's pitch at Mount Rush Park was the first one the public came to when they got to the grassy area in front of the main stand. When Carmichael arrived, there were only a couple of punters in front of him hastily placing their bets before the first race started.

Carmichael patiently waited a few yards away until the race was off, as he knew then the pitch would be free from punters either placing bets or collecting their winnings.

He strode up to the man whom Caitlin had pointed out as Fat Malc; an imposing figure who looked even bigger standing on his large metal box.

"Book's closed on this race, mate," Fat Malc announced gruffly.

Carmichael smiled and held up his identity card.

"Inspector Carmichael," he said. "I'd like to ask you a few questions."

Fat Malc at first looked suspicious but forced a smile.

"What can I help you with, Inspector?" he enquired, while at the same time thrusting the wad of notes he had in his hand into the large black bag in front of him.

"I'm investigating the death of a man called Timothy Wall," Carmichael said. "I understand he was a frequent punter here at Mount Rush Park."

Fat Malc shook his head gently from side to side.

"That name doesn't mean anything to me," he replied.

Carmichael took out a photo and handed it to Fat Malc.

"This is Timothy Wall," he said. "Ring any bells?"

Fat Malc looked intently at the photo, then passed it to his female colleague.

"Don't recognise this bloke, Mary, do you?" he said to her.

She, too, looked at the photo, then without speaking, shook her head and handed it back to Fat Malc.

"Sorry, can't help you, Inspector," Fat Malc remarked, handing the picture of Tim Wall back to Carmichael. "He may well have been a punter, but we get hundreds each meeting and apart from a few regulars, particularly the lippy ones, I don't get that friendly with them."

Carmichael nodded. "And is it you and Mary here every Monday evening?" he enquired.

"Mostly," replied Fat Malc. "Occasionally it's someone else, but usually me and Mary."

"What about Trevor and Simon?" Carmichael asked. "They own the company, I understand."

"Trevor sometimes," replied Fat Malc, "but never Simon. He's marketing and finance. He doesn't get involved in the sharp end."

Carmichael took out two of his cards and handed one each to Fat Malc and Mary.

"If either of you do suddenly remember something, please don't hesitate to call me," he said with a smile. "And be sure to tell Trevor and Simon about our little chat. I've not met either of them yet but I'm sure I'll make their acquaintance sooner or later."

Fat Malc took the card, pushed it into his pocket and smiled back at Carmichael.

"Fancy a bet on the second race?" he asked, a brash grin now etched across his face. "How about Search Party? That's an apt one for a copper. It's seven to two at the moment, but for you, I'll give you five to one."

Carmichael glared back at Fat Malc, before turning on his heels and quickly walking away.

Chapter 21

It was bang on seven-thirty when Carmichael entered the debriefing room. Watson, Lucy and Rachel were already in there waiting for the session to begin.

Carmichael smiled to himself when he saw that someone had already written the headings 'Facts', 'Unknowns', and 'Suspects' on the whiteboard in anticipation of the lists they would be compiling in the next hour or so.

"Why don't you go first, Lucy?" Carmichael suggested.

Lucy sat upright in her chair and opened her notebook.

"I've now spoke with Dr Scruton's daughter, Nikki, who's still obsessed with Tim Wall as far as I could make out," she announced. "She confirmed that her father also got on well with Wall and with her living in San Francisco, I think we can rule her out."

Carmichael smiled and nodded.

"She did mention a man that Wall didn't get on with from back when they were dating," added Lucy, "but when I checked him out I found that he died about ten years ago, in a car crash, so he's clearly not our murderer either."

"What was his name?" Carmichael asked.

"He was a guy Wall used to play rugby with who they called Badger," Lucy replied. "I didn't find out his real name."

"And why were they enemies?" continued Carmichael.

Lucy shook her head. "Nikki didn't know why," she replied.

Carmichael shrugged his shoulders. "What else did you find out?" he added.

Lucy fidgeted uneasily in her seat before answering.

"In addition to Nikki, I've now managed to track down and talk with Wall's last five girlfriends," she said.

"Is that including Kelly Underwood and Heather Jones, who you'd already talked to this morning?" Carmichael enquired; his question delivered in a way that made it clear to Lucy that if she said yes, he wouldn't be overly impressed.

Lucy could feel herself getting warm.

"I've spoken with Nikki, Kelly, Heather and three other ex-girlfriends," she said. The best way she felt she could respond without saying yes. Carmichael's facial expression indicated his displeasure.

"So how far back does that take you?" he asked.

"Just over five years," replied Lucy.

"And did any of those ladies offer any information that might be pertinent to the case?" Carmichael asked, his tone now quite assertive.

Lucy shook her head. "They all seemed to think the sun shone out of his proverbial," she replied. "To be honest apart from Heather Jones, all the other ex-girlfriends I've spoken with adored him and still do now. It's like something from the *Stepford Wives*."

Carmichael sighed. "So, apart from Heather Jones and this man Badger, whose name we don't know, and is dead, you've not found anyone who is in the slightest way our potential killer?"

"That's the truth of it," replied Lucy.

"There's still Cassie Wilson," interjected Watson. "She's not a fan of his and she's not got a strong alibi for the time Wall was killed."

"True," replied Carmichael, "but I don't see her wanting to kill him just because of his red book. I guess we need to put her down on our suspects list, but I'm not sure she's a strong candidate for our murderer."

As he finished speaking, Carmichael picked up the blue pen and wrote the names of Heather Jones and Cassie Wilson under the heading 'Suspects'.

"Do we know where Heather Jones was when Wall was killed?" Carmichael asked.

Lucy hastily checked her notes.

"She maintains she was doing her weekly shop at her local supermarket on the other side of Kirkwood between five and six," Lucy replied. "I'll check their CCTV to make sure she's telling us the truth."

"And after that?" Carmichael asked.

"After that she says she was at home alone all evening," replied Lucy.

Carmichael nodded pensively before turning his attention to Rachel and Watson.

"How about you two?" he enquired.

Rachel exchanged a quick glance at Watson before answering.

"We've a positive lead on the man calling himself Haverstock-Price, but I'll let Marc update you both on him," she said. "As for me, the CCTV has confirmed that Faye left the office when she said and that she went straight to The Lamb public house. So, her alibi's been validated. I also checked all the incoming calls to the office on Friday and on Thursday, and when you take out a couple of calls from HMRC and the ten incoming calls from Faye's boyfriend, Richard Cox, then there's nothing much left."

"So, what calls are left?" Carmichael asked, clearly not totally satisfied with Rachel's answer.

Rachel looked at her notes before continuing. "One on

Thursday was from a company cold-calling about providing sandwiches at lunchtime, which lasted seventy-two seconds," she replied. "Another was on Friday from a Miriam Thompson who called to enquire whether they would do surveillance on her daughter's boyfriend who she suspected of having multiple affairs. That call lasted a minute and, according to Mrs Thompson, was declined by Faye as she was told they don't do relationship cases. And the last one was a personal call to Wall from a bloke called Peter Grundy, who wanted to know whether Tim Wall was going to be attending the next Rotary Club meeting, which is on Wednesday night."

"And was he planning on attending?" Carmichael asked.

"According to Mr Grundy, he was," replied Rachel.

"And that's everything, is it?" Carmichael enquired.

Rachel nodded. "For the office phone on Thursday and Friday, yes."

Carmichael looked frustrated.

"In the morning I need you to talk with Faye again, Rachel," he said. "She's either lying to us or has misheard what Wall told her; as if nobody called the office or his mobile, Wall couldn't have arranged to meet a new client as she says."

"Unless he took the call on his home phone," suggested Lucy.

Carmichael nodded. "That's possible I suppose," he reluctantly concurred, "but I can't see a prospective client having his private home number."

Carmichael looked across at Rachel.

"Check the incoming calls to his home phone too, Rachel," he instructed her.

"Will do," Rachel dutifully replied.

"Is that everything from you?" Carmichael said.

"It's everything I have so far from the CCTV and on the other actions you gave me," Rachel replied, "but with Marc having to go out, I checked into the messages from Sara-Jane on Wall's mobile."

As she spoke, Rachel's expression changed to one of elation, indicating she had something important to tell them.

"Well," continued Rachel, "I managed to trace Sara-Jane's full name and address through her service provider and it's a name that's come up already. One that Faye Hemmingway gave us."

"Who?" enquired Carmichael.

"It's Ms Turnbull from the HMRC in Newcastle," replied Rachel with a broad smile. "It looks like she was more than just a client of Timothy Wall's."

"Really," remarked Carmichael, who was genuinely astounded. "I only spoke with her a few hours ago and although she seemed shocked by his death, she didn't say they were seeing each other, or seem that upset."

Rachel nodded. "I'm not surprised," she replied. "I found her on Facebook, and it looks like she's already in a relationship up there in Newcastle with a man called Brian. From the photos she's put up, he looks a fair bit older than her and doesn't appear to have a Facebook account himself. It also looks like he may be a doctor or do something medical."

As she spoke, Rachel projected her laptop onto the large white screen to the side of the room, which showed Sara-Jane Turnbull's Facebook home page.

"Can you turn off the lights, please, Marc?" Carmichael asked Watson.

With the lights off, Carmichael looked closely at the beaming face of Sara-Jane Turnbull dominating the screen, with an equally smiley face (presumably that of Brian) cheek-to-cheek with her on some windswept coast.

"Blonde and in her late thirties or early forties," remarked Watson. "I'd say she's just Tim Wall's type."

"Do we add her to our suspects list?" Rachel enquired.

"Absolutely," Carmichael replied. "She didn't tell me about any relationship with Tim Wall, but if they were having an affair and Brian found out, then maybe he'd want to do Wall some harm. I think we add them both."

Delighted by what he'd just said, Rachel sprang to her feet and added both names to the suspects list.

"Get yourself up to Newcastle in the morning," Carmichael instructed Rachel. "Interview Sara-Jane and find out from her the full name of her boyfriend. Then interview him, too. I want to know where they both were on Friday evening and why she never mentioned anything about her relationship with Wall when I talked to her earlier."

"Why don't I go with her?" Lucy suggested. "I'm from Newcastle and I think this might be a job for two people."

Carmichael considered the idea for a few seconds before responding.

"Good idea," he replied, "but before you go home tonight, speak with the desk sergeant and get someone to check out Heather Jones' alibi. And Rachel, you talk to him as well about someone checking Wall's home phone for any conversation with Haverstock-Price."

"What about talking with Faye again?" Rachel added.

"Don't worry, I'll do that," replied Carmichael.

"Do you want my update?" Watson enquired.

"I'm all ears, Marc," Carmichael replied.

"As Rachel said, I went into the town earlier to Maria's Café, which is across from Wall's office," Watson remarked. "We saw a man on the CCTV that we think might be Haverstock-Price. He was at the window seat of the café on Friday evening from about four-forty to just after five-thirty. He then came out of the café, went across the road and about four minutes later he came back across the road walking really quickly, but we lost track of him after that."

"Interesting," said Lucy.

"I've spoken to the waitress at the café who served him," Watson continued. "She remembers him, but couldn't tell me much about him as she says it's the first time she'd seen him in there."

"So, no luck in getting a name?" said Rachel.

"Well, actually I have," added Watson with a broad grin. "He paid by card, which belongs to a man called Pierce Armitage. I've contacted his card company for his details; they've promised to get back to me in the morning."

"What about trying to track him down on social media?" Rachel suggested. "With a name like that, there can't be that many?"

Watson shook his head. "About as many as there are Haverstock-Prices," he replied, "zero!"

"Great work though, Marc," Carmichael remarked. "This guy has to be our prime suspect so far, so your job tomorrow is to track Armitage down."

"Will do, sir," Watson replied.

Carmichael wrote 'Pierce Armitage' at the top of the suspects list.

"That just leaves my update," he added.

Chapter 22

It was twenty-past nine by the time Carmichael brought the team briefing to an end. Having quickly updated his three colleagues on his telephone discussion with Sara-Jane Turnbull and his discussions with Agnes Poulter, Caitlin and Fat Malc, he and the team had spent the last twenty minutes of the meeting making notes on the whiteboard.

With their duties for the next day clear and each having a printout from the whiteboard, Carmichael let the team head off home.

As he sat alone in the incident room, his mood was largely one of disappointment. The team had made some progress, Carmichael could not deny it, but not as much as he would have liked, one day into the investigation. On a positive note however, Pierce Armitage, who Watson had identified from the footage in the café, did sound as though he might well be the man calling himself Haverstock-Price: and the fact that Sara-Jane Turnbull was having a clandestine relationship with Wall was also an important avenue for them to pursue.

Nevertheless, with very few facts known to them and crucial questions still unanswered, Carmichael knew they were still far from discovering the truth.

Although it had been a long day already, Carmichael decided to stay put for a while longer and quietly run through the points the team had recorded during the debrief. He rested the A4 printout on the desk in front of him and went through their meagre output line by line.

Facts:

1. Timothy Wall was killed between 5pm and 10pm on Friday 31st July.
2. He died as a result of a single blow to the back of his head.
3. Faye Hemmingway had left the office at 5.03pm and had gone directly to The Lamb public house; a journey that took her 4 minutes.
4. Wall was a ladies' man, who liked to give scores to his ex-girlfriends.
5. Fingerprints were found at the scene that can't be accounted for.

Unknowns:

1. Who murdered Timothy Wall?
2. Why was Wall killed?
3. Whose fingerprints were on the door into Wall's office?
4. Is his death linked to a previous relationship?
5. Is his death linked to an existing or historical case?
6. Is Pierce Armitage the man who called himself Haverstock-Price?

Suspects:

1. Pierce Armitage
2. Heather Jones
3. Cassie Wilson
4. Sara-Jane Turnbull
5. Brian (Sara's partner)

94

Carmichael could not help feeling they were missing something significant. Having found out that Wall was a frequent race-goer, his antenna had automatically been set to alert. In his experience, big gamblers often had enemies and following his meeting with Fat Malc, Carmichael's gut feeling about the Baybutts being involved in some way had been strengthened. But he didn't know to what extent they were involved.

Then there was Wall's red book. This creepy, meticulous record of his girlfriends seemed so bizarre and unsettling, Carmichael found it difficult to believe its existence hadn't offended more women than just Cassie. And with Wall keeping it for so many years, surely other people would have come across it. But even if they had, would that awareness prove relevant to the case?

Finally, there was Wall himself. Carmichael still couldn't work out what sort of man he was. He was clearly a man who could charm people; his engaging, sociable, and friendly manner often enduring long after relationships had waned. And he was more than capable of demonstrating kindness; his willingness to help Agnes Poulter find her daughter for free and his active involvement with the Rotary Club which, as far as Carmichael was aware, was an organisation focused mainly on supporting good causes, were both evidence of a kind-hearted man. But, in addition to the red book, there was also evidence of a less attractive, almost sinister side to Timothy Wall. The solitary gambler, the philanderer and maybe a secret heavy drinker, too.

None the wiser, Carmichael folded up the printout, put it in his jacket pocket and got up from his chair. Whoever or whatever Timothy Wall was, Carmichael wasn't going to uncover it by remaining at his desk.

Tired and mentally drained from the day's exertions he decided to head off home.

* * *

It was ten-thirty when Carmichael walked up the steps of his house in Moulton Bank and put his key in the lock of his front door, precisely the time a small pane of glass was broken on Tim Wall's back door at Aughton Place.

Penny didn't hear her husband come in, just as nobody noticed the furtive, darkly clad figure as it released the latch and entered Wall's kitchen.

"Oh, you're back," Penny observed as her husband entered the lounge and kissed her on the cheek. "You look worn out."

"I am," confessed Carmichael. "It's been a really long day."

Chapter 23

Tuesday 4ᵗʰ August

With her husband looking so exhausted when he'd arrived home the night before, Penny had decided not to ask him too much about his day and had deliberately not mentioned Lucy. However, if the truth was known, she was desperate to know how that first day back had gone and wasn't going to allow him to get away that morning until she knew more. To make sure he didn't escape to work without having a chance to speak with him, Penny made sure she was down in the kitchen when Carmichael came out of the shower.

"What's the plan for you and the team today?" she asked as she poured her husband a coffee.

"Marc's trying to locate a potential suspect who he spotted on CCTV lurking around the dead man's office at around the time he died, and Lucy and Rachel have gone up to Newcastle," Carmichael replied. "And as for me, I'm going to talk with a few potential suspects."

"What are Lucy and Rachel doing up in Newcastle?" Penny enquired.

Carmichael quickly grabbed a slice of toast that had popped up out of the toaster and started to spread butter over it.

"I've sent them to talk with a woman from HMRC," he replied. "It's where Tim Wall got most of his business from. I spoke with her on the phone yesterday, but it's now emerged that she may have been the latest in a long line of Wall's female friends."

"That will be nice for them both," replied Penny, "a three-or four-hour journey together will give them time to get acquainted, as I guess they didn't know each other before yesterday."

Carmichael hadn't given that much thought, but now his wife had mentioned it, he wasn't sure whether he liked that idea too much.

"No, they didn't," he replied as he put a thick layer of marmalade on his toast.

"And how was Lucy's first day back?" Penny asked, trying to sound as casual as she could.

"Fine, I think," replied Carmichael, as nonchalantly as he could. "I wasn't with her much, but she seemed OK."

"Will be weird for Marc," added Penny, "being the only male in the team under you."

Carmichael laughed. "He'll survive I'm sure," he replied taking a large bite of toast.

As soon as his teeth had sunk into the toast, his mobile rang.

Attempting to swallow in double-quick time, Carmichael put the receiver to his ear.

"Carmichael," he said gruffly, his mouth still full of a mixture of toast, butter and marmalade.

"What," he then said loudly, followed closely by, "I'll be there in thirty-five minutes."

Carmichael threw the bitten slice of toast back on his plate.

"What's happened?" Penny enquired as soon as the call had ended.

"There's been a break-in at Wall's house," Carmichael replied as he gave her a quick, sticky peck on the cheek and headed for the door. "I'll see you later."

Penny hadn't time to ask anything else, as within a matter of seconds, her husband was out the front door and rushing down the steps to his car.

"Have a nice day, dear," she said out loud to the empty kitchen, before wiping her face where it had just been kissed and despondently plonking herself down at the table.

* * *

"So, how are you enjoying being back at Kirkwood?" Rachel asked as she and Lucy sped north up the M6.

"As I told Marc yesterday, so far so good," replied Lucy. "What about you? Do you like it in Carmichael's team?"

"Yeah, I do," Rachel replied. "Occasionally Marc can be a pain in the rear end, but overall, it's good."

Lucy laughed. "And what about the boss?" she asked. "What do you think of Carmichael?"

Rachel wasn't yet sure about Lucy; certainly not sure enough to say anything she might later regret, so she decided to play it safe.

"We get on fine," she replied. "He's been a good boss so far for me."

Lucy nodded. "He's a good detective, that's for sure," she remarked.

"You obviously rate him otherwise you wouldn't have come back," Rachel added, trying hard to get Lucy to open up and give her a little insight into the dynamic between the two of them. But she was to be disappointed.

"I suppose I must," was all Lucy would say before changing the subject, which Rachel saw as hardly the greatest endorsement Lucy could have given Carmichael.

* * *

"Good God," exclaimed Carmichael as he entered Tim Wall's house.

PC Dyer, who had met Carmichael at the door, nodded. "Whoever did this was clearly either hell-bent on turning this place upside down, or desperate to find something," he remarked.

"Or both," replied Carmichael.

He wandered around the house for the next ten minutes, tiptoeing over books and papers that the trespasser had flung wantonly on the floor. It was when Carmichael returned downstairs to the kitchen, where the intruder had gained entry, that a couple of thoughts suddenly came to him.

If the person who killed Wall was also linked to this frenzied act of destruction, why did they wait three days to do this to Wall's house? Why didn't they break into Wall's house on Friday when Wall was murdered?

Before he had had a chance to answer his own questions, one of the forensic team, who was paying painstaking attention to the door and the small, broken glass pane raised his head.

"There's blood on this glass," he remarked with a sense of jubilation in his voice.

Carmichael smiled broadly.

"Really," he remarked, realising that this may be the breakthrough he had been waiting for.

Chapter 24

DS Watson looked intently at the email attachment he had received that morning from Pierce Armitage's credit card company.

"Banks Rise House, Mossy Lea, Near Millom, Cumbria. LA18 5BZ," he said out loud, when he saw the address. "Got you."

Thrilled by this discovery and pleased in the knowledge that the address was no more than two hours away by car, Watson then looked at the other details on the report they had sent him. It had everything Watson wanted to see, including a telephone number for Armitage and a breakdown of his transactions from 4th July to 3rd August.

Watson couldn't help smiling when he found the transaction at Maria's Café for £8.49 on Friday 31st July and next to it another transaction of £52.78 for fuel at Hobsons Garage in Kirkwood; a garage Watson knew well and that had an excellent CCTV monitoring system.

Better still were two more transactions made on 1st and 3rd August; one at what looked like a pub or restaurant called the Farmers in Ulverston, the other at a Tesco supermarket in Millom.

This proved that, at least up until the day before, Pierce Armitage was back in South Cumbria.

Excited and convinced this was a major breakthrough, he called Carmichael.

* * *

Carmichael was still in Wall's house when he received the call.

"I've got an address and a contact number for Pierce Armitage," Watson announced with glee. "He lives in South Cumbria and according to the activity on his card, he was definitely here on Friday. On Saturday and yesterday he was back in the South Cumbria area."

Carmichael considered whether he should or shouldn't put a dampener on Watson's obvious enthusiasm: but decided he had to.

"That's great news," he replied, "but if he was in Cumbria last night it might suggest he's not our man."

"Why's that?" asked Watson, his mood starting to become less optimistic.

"Well, I'm at Wall's house," replied Carmichael, "and last night it was broken into and ransacked. It looks like the intruder was looking for something. And if that intruder is the same man that killed Wall, he couldn't have also been in Cumbria."

Watson looked again at the credit card statement, which didn't give a time.

"I'll check with the credit card company what time he made the payment yesterday," Watson said. "If it was in the afternoon, he could still have come down to Kirkwood, broken into Wall's and driven back."

Carmichael couldn't fault his sergeant's logic, and certainly didn't want to sound too pessimistic.

"That's true," he replied. "Check that out, if you can."

"So, what about Armitage?" Watson continued. "Shall I drive up and interview him?"

"I'd call Cumbria police and get them to detain him while you get yourself up there," replied Carmichael. "He's out of our jurisdiction, so best let them do that."

"Sound like a good plan to me," Watson replied.

"And call me when you've spoken with him," Carmichael added. "Based upon what he says we can decide whether we let him go or charge him and bring him down here."

"Will do, sir," replied Watson, albeit to nobody as Carmichael had already hung up.

* * *

Carmichael put his mobile in his pocket and shouted across at the SOCO, who he had spoken to earlier. "When do you reckon you'll be finished here?" he asked.

The SOCO looked up at him and smiled. "I think we've a good few more hours still to go," he replied.

"Well when you're through, I'd appreciate a quick heads-up on your initial findings," continued Carmichael.

"No problem, sir," he replied, before turning his attention back to the blood on the broken windowpane.

Chapter 25

Lucy's car arrived at the HMRC office at five minutes past ten. The 160-mile journey (which included a brief stop for a coffee at a small farm shop Lucy knew on the A66 called Mainsgill) had taken them approximately three-and-a-half hours. A time that Lucy assured Rachel was good going.

"Forget what they tell you in Yorkshire," Lucy announced with a broad smile and in an accent that to Rachel seemed even more Geordie than normal, "this is actually God's country."

Rachel smiled. "It's the first time I've been to Newcastle," she replied. "It does seem a busy little city."

"It's not so little," Lucy exclaimed in a tone that suggested she was offended by Rachel's observation. "It's the biggest city in the North East by far."

Feeling suitably rebuked, Rachel simply smiled back in Lucy's direction. She wasn't sure if Lucy was expecting her to respond but had no intention of offering either an apology or even more clarification on what she considered a factual and innocuous comment.

"As the senior officer, I'll lead the interview," Lucy remarked firmly. "Feel free to butt in if you think I've missed something but let me take the lead."

"OK," replied Rachel, again with a smile, but this time one that was more obviously forced.

Watson's zeal to prove Pierce Armitage was their killer was enriched as soon as the officer at Millom Police Station answered his call.

"So, what's Pierce been up to now?" DS Patterson replied, which suggested the man Watson wanted to talk to was well known to the local constabulary. This initial opinion, however, was somewhat dented when the officer on the other end of the line took a deep intake of breath on hearing the nature of the case being investigated.

"He's a bit of a rogue is our Pierce," remarked Patterson, "but mainly small-time frauds, handling stolen goods and stuff like that. He's no history of violence and I'd have thought murder's way out of his league."

"It may well not be him," replied Watson, "but he was definitely acting suspiciously at the scene of the crime at about the time the murder took place, so it's crucial we talk with him."

"No worries," replied the Cumbrian officer. "I know where he'll be, so we'll haul him in."

Watson looked at his watch. "I should be with you at about lunchtime," he added.

"He'll be here waiting for you," replied DS Patterson, in a way that suggested he wasn't expecting Pierce Armitage to be particularly hard to find or difficult to apprehend. "I'll see you then."

***

Sara-Jane Turnbull was clearly shocked when, clutching on to a large green folder, she walked into the small meeting room to meet her two visitors from Mid-Lancashire police.

"I'm a bit surprised to see you here," was her opening

remark. "Did Inspector Carmichael not tell you we talked on the phone yesterday afternoon?"

"It was him that sent us," replied Lucy, bluntly.

This clearly only served to make Sara-Jane even more anxious. She rested her folder on the desk and sat down opposite the two police officers.

"So, how else can I help you?" she asked.

Lucy smiled, but kept her eyes focused on the woman who looked far less happy and relaxed than in the pictures on her Facebook page they had all looked over at the debriefing the evening before.

"We want to go through the cases Mr Wall was looking into for you," Lucy continued, "but first I'd like to talk with you about your relationship with Mr Wall, outside work."

Sara-Jane looked stunned by the question but tried hard to retain her composure. "There was no relationship," she replied. "We got to know each other quite well over the last five years, but there was no relationship as you call it."

Lucy smirked, before passing over printouts of some of the text messages the two had exchanged over the past few days.

"I'd suggest these say otherwise," continued Lucy, her laser-like stare remaining directed at the now visibly quivering woman before them.

Sara-Jane carefully read the text messages then placed the printout back on the desk.

"It was a fling," she remarked, clearly trying to play it down. "Nothing serious, nothing heavy, just a fling."

"And how long had this fling been going on?" Lucy enquired.

Sara-Jane shrugged her shoulders. "I don't know," she replied dismissively. "Six months, maybe slightly more."

"And what exactly did this fling entail?" Lucy asked.

For the first time in the interview, Sara-Jane appeared to be more at ease.

"We'd go out occasionally in the evenings when he came up here," she replied.

"Just go out?" Lucy said pointedly.

"Do I have to spell it out?" replied Sara-Jane. "I'd sometimes stay over with him in his hotel room, but not always."

"Roughly how many times?" continued Lucy, who wasn't about to let Sara-Jane off the hook.

"I'd say three or four times in total," Sara-Jane replied.

"And presumably nobody here knew about your relationship?" Lucy continued.

"Of course not," replied Sara-Jane curtly.

"And what about Brian?" interjected Rachel. "Your boyfriend."

Sara-Jane looked shocked that the officers knew she was in a relationship.

"No," she replied, "neither mine nor Tim's partner knew."

"Tim's partner?" Lucy enquired.

"Cassie," replied Sara-Jane, "the current love of his life. That's her name isn't it?"

After a brief pause Lucy continued. "So, why didn't you mention this relationship to Inspector Carmichael yesterday?"

Sara-Jane shrugged her shoulders. "Firstly, he never asked," she replied, "but as it meant nothing to either of us, I didn't see it was of any relevance."

Lucy shook her head. "I think the relevance is something that we should be the judge of, don't you?"

Sara-Jane leant back in her chair. "Look," she said as calmly as she could, "I'm sorry I didn't mention it, but I honestly thought it was irrelevant. And of course, it is not something I'd like people here, or Brian to know about. Does this have to go any further than here?"

"I'm making you no promises," replied Lucy, "but as long

as you are totally transparent with us from here onwards, I'll try not to embarrass you unnecessarily."

Lucy's response seemed to put Sara-Jane at ease.

"I suppose I can't ask much more from you," she remarked. "So, what else do you want to know?"

Lucy shot a brief glance sideways towards Rachel, with a look that appeared to say '*that's how it's done*'.

Chapter 26

Carmichael leaned on his black BMW outside Tim Wall's terraced house. He had three people he wanted to talk to but wasn't sure which to do first.

As Wall's office was just around the corner and Faye Hemmingway was almost certainly going to be there, he decided to see her.

As he strolled down Aughton Place towards the high street, he couldn't help asking himself the same questions over and over again. Firstly, why would someone want to break into Wall's house and secondly, and more intriguingly, why would they wait for three days after Wall's murder before making their forced entry?

By the time he had reached the staircase to Wall's Detective Agency, Carmichael was, sadly, still none the wiser.

As he had anticipated, Faye Hemmingway was sat at her desk, but she was not alone. What Carmichael hadn't expected to see was her boyfriend, Richard Cox, perched next to Faye on her desk.

"Morning," Carmichael announced cheerily as he entered the office. "I was wondering whether I may have another word with you, Faye?"

Richard Cox, who seemed to realise that the Inspector would probably want to talk with Faye alone, nodded at Carmichael, gave Faye a lengthy kiss on her lips and stood up.

"I should be getting back to work," he remarked with a smile on his face.

Carmichael smiled back across at him. "And where is work, Mr Cox?" he enquired.

"I work at Mullion and Thorpe, the estate agents in Moulton Bank," Cox replied.

'I know them well," Carmichael remarked. "We bought our house from them when we moved here. The guy's name we dealt with was Adrian Hope."

Richard Cox grimaced and raised his eyebrows. "That's my manager," he replied. "Actually, I shouldn't slag him off as he's been brilliant with me over the last couple of days, really flexible and understanding."

Carmichael smiled again. "That's good," he said.

"But he won't be as understanding if I don't do the two valuations that have been booked this morning," added Richard Cox.

"I'll see you tonight," Faye told him as her boyfriend headed for the door.

Cox smiled back at her then turned to face Carmichael. "Bye, Inspector," he said before rushing away.

"I'm not sure what I'd have done without Richard," remarked Faye as the sound of his footsteps descending the stairs stopped and they heard the door at the bottom close.

"Have you been dating long?" Carmichael asked.

"About three or four months," replied Faye. "He moved branches from Mullion and Thorpe's branch in Bolton in March and we met about a couple of weeks after that, so about four months."

Carmichael smiled again.

"Anyway, I imagine you didn't come to talk to me about Richard," Faye added. "How can I help you?"

"There are a few things I'd like to talk with you about," Carmichael replied.

"What are they?" Faye asked.

"Firstly, can you remember exactly what Tim Wall said to you when he mentioned his meeting with Haverstock-Price?" Carmichael enquired.

Faye thought for a few seconds before responding.

"He only mentioned it as I was leaving, and then it was only in passing," Faye replied. "He told me to leave his office door open as he had a new client coming in about twenty minutes. He said that if I left the door open, he'd stand a better chance of hearing him arrive. I was a bit confused about that as there was nobody in the appointment book for him that evening. He then said that a man called Haverstock-Price had called him that morning and that they had agreed to meet at twenty-past five to talk about a new case."

"And are you sure the name was Haverstock-Price?" Carmichael enquired.

"Absolutely sure," Faye replied. "I remember thinking, what an unusual name and saying so to Richard at The Lamb."

Carmichael nodded. "I'd also like to ask you about old case files. Would Tim have kept any at home?"

Faye laughed. "He could have I suppose, but I doubt it," she replied. "He was very particular about his house; well, you must have seen just how orderly it is. He wouldn't have old files in there."

"What about soft copies on a memory stick?" Carmichael asked.

"Maybe in the safe," replied Faye, "but not out in the open, if I know Tim."

"Safe," exclaimed Carmichael. "I wasn't aware he had a safe?"

"Oh yes," Faye replied. "It's a floor safe under the red armchair in the lounge."

Carmichael's face must have given away his surprise at hearing that there was a safe.

"Did you not know?" Faye continued. "There's a note with the combination on it under Tim's desk pad." Faye then smiled broadly. "His memory was awful, he wrote it down there so he wouldn't lose it."

Carmichael lifted the pad, revealing the six numbers, 300392.

"Have you a piece of paper?" he then asked Faye. "I want to write these numbers down."

After scribbling down the numbers and placing the paper in his pocket, Carmichael smiled back at Faye. "There's just one other thing," he remarked. "Were you aware of any new woman in Tim's life?"

Faye shook her head. "I'd an idea that Cassie was probably no longer in the picture," she replied, "but he'd never actually told me that, and he'd certainly not mentioned anyone new."

"And what about his relationship with Sara-Jane Turnbull at HMRC?" Carmichael asked.

Faye looked puzzled and shook her head. "I've never met Ms Turnbull," she replied. "Tim always went up there when they had to meet, but I don't think he was in a relationship with her."

Carmichael smiled. "It was just a thought."

Faye suddenly put her hand to her mouth, as if she had just thought of something. "Actually, now you mention it, it was Ms Turnbull who had given Tim that expensive bottle of whiskey," she announced. "It was at Christmas, a thank-you gift from HMRC, I'd thought."

"Had he only just opened it then?" Carmichael enquired. "As the bottle we found was almost full."

Faye shook her head. "No, he opened it before we broke up for New Year," she replied.

"Really," replied Carmichael. "Well she or someone else must have bought him another, as the one we found yesterday was definitely almost full."

Faye shrugged her shoulders. "She must have," she replied, "as I can't see Tim spending his own money on an expensive whiskey. He'd have thought that was far too frivolous."

Carmichael laughed. "A man after my own heart in that respect then," he replied with a broad smile.

Chapter 27

Lucy showed no intention of letting up on Sara-Jane Turnbull. For twenty minutes she pummelled the poor woman with question after question about her relationship with Tim Wall and her movements on the evening Wall was killed, until eventually Sara-Jane started to get annoyed.

"Look, I am happy to help you in any way I can to find out who killed Tim," she said at last, "but to be honest, your aggressive manner is unacceptable. Unless this stops now, I'm going to refuse to answer any more questions."

Out of the corner of her eye, Rachel could see Lucy about to carry on, so decided to intervene.

"Nobody's accusing you of anything, Ms Turnbull," she said calmly. "DS Martin and I just need your help. Why don't we have a quick break, get a coffee and then resume our discussions in say ten minutes? How does that sound?"

Sara-Jane forced a grateful smile in Rachel's direction, got up and headed out of the room as quickly as she could.

As soon as she had gone, Lucy turned her head to face Rachel, her lips tight together and her eyes glaring at her.

"Don't ever undermine me like that again," she said angrily. "I'm the senior officer so that was my call."

Rachel did not want to get into a row with Lucy, but there was no way she was going to roll over.

"You may be senior to me, but Carmichael asked me to

come here and talk with Sara-Jane," she said forcefully. "So far I've hardly been able to get a word in edgeways. You've done your bad cop act and it's worked to an extent, but from now on I think what Sara-Jane would best respond to is a more sympathetic and less aggressive form of questioning."

"And I suppose you think you're best placed to do that, do you?" Lucy snapped back at her.

"I don't see anyone else in the room able to do that, do you?" replied Rachel firmly.

It was at that point that Rachel's mobile rang.

"It's Carmichael," she said before putting the mobile to her ear.

Incandescent with rage, Lucy stood up and headed for the door. "Looks like Carmichael's blue-eyed girl's just been saved by the bell," she remarked, caustically, before leaving the room and slamming the door shut.

* * *

On his short walk back to Wall's house, Carmichael had been mulling over Faye's comment about the whiskey that Wall had kept in his desk drawer.

He also wanted to find out how Lucy and Rachel were doing, so thought now was probably a good time to call them.

It was as he'd leant against his car once more outside Wall's house that he put in the call to Rachel.

"How are you and Lucy getting on?" he asked. A question he had meant to refer to the interview with Sara-Jane Turnbull, but in the circumstances was one that Rachel felt was either ironic or uncannily perceptive.

"We've just called a break," Rachel replied, "but we've made quite a bit of progress."

"Good," replied Carmichael. "Anything specific you think I should know?"

115

"Initially Sara-Jane denied that she was seeing Wall," Rachel replied, "but when we showed her the messages on Wall's mobile, she admitted they'd seen each other about three or four times over the last six months. She described it as nothing serious, nothing heavy, just a fling."

"And do you believe her?" Carmichael asked.

Rachel thought for a few seconds.

"Yes, I do," she replied.

"And what about Lucy?" continued Carmichael. "What does she think?"

Rachel wasn't sure what to say at first but tried her best to answer the question.

"Lucy's just popped out," she replied. "We've literally just stopped with Sara-Jane, so we haven't discussed it yet."

Carmichael sensed that all was not well but decided not to push Rachel on it.

"What about her movements on Friday evening?" he asked.

As he finished asking the question, Lucy reappeared in the room holding two plastic beakers of water.

"Lucy's back now," remarked Rachel. "Do you want to speak with her?"

"Yes, put her on," he replied.

Rachel took one of the plastic beakers from Lucy and then passed her the mobile.

Lucy put it to her ear. "Morning boss," she said.

"I understand that you two are making some headway," he remarked. "Has Sara-Jane told you what she was doing on Friday evening, yet?"

Lucy sighed. "She says that she was at home alone in Gosforth. She ordered a takeaway curry at about seven-thirty, which was delivered at about eight and then in the morning, she drove Brian down to Manchester to catch a plane to Vancouver. He's a senior consultant at the hospital here and is now away in Canada for a week."

Carmichael thought for a few seconds before responding.

"Rachel tells me that Sara-Jane has also been playing down the relationship as just a fling," he remarked. "Do you believe her?"

"I'm not sure," Lucy replied. "She may be telling the truth, but until we verify her alibi, I'm keeping an open mind."

"OK," replied Carmichael. "And is all well with you two?"

Lucy shot a glance at Rachel, who she feared may have been bad mouthing her when she was out of the office.

"Can we talk about that next time we're together?" she replied, evasively.

"Fine," replied Carmichael, who was now feeling very uneasy about what might be going on in Newcastle. "One thing I need you both to do though is ask Sara-Jane about the whiskey she bought for Wall at Christmas," he remarked. "Also, ask her if she'd bought him another bottle recently."

"OK," replied Lucy, slightly bemused by the instruction. "Will do."

In his customary style, Carmichael ended the call abruptly.

Once she realised Carmichael had gone, Lucy calmly handed back the phone to Rachel.

"Let's call her back in again," she said. "And as you're so keen, you can lead from here on in."

Rachel forced a smile, put her phone on the desk in front of her and headed off to find Sara-Jane Turnbull.

Chapter 28

When Carmichael moved the red armchair, he was relieved to see that Tim Wall's floor safe appeared to be locked and intact.

Removing the paper from his pocket, Carmichael put in the six-digit combination and pulled open the door.

To his surprise there were only three items inside: Wall's passport, a brown envelope with the word 'Will' written on the outside and a larger, white, sealed unmarked envelope.

Carmichael put on a pair of blue plastic gloves before extracting all three items and laying them out side-by-side on the low wooden coffee table just a few feet away from him.

The passport was current and had another four years left on it, with stamps inside from immigration in Toronto, three US cities, Hong Kong and Singapore.

"A bit of a traveller," mumbled Carmichael to himself. He then turned his attention to the white envelope.

Carmichael cautiously peeled open the seal. Carefully he extracted the contents; a dozen or so photographs and a series of copied extracts from a ledger of some sort, all handwritten in a distinctive script.

Carmichael looked briefly at the photos. At first he thought they may be risqué shots Wall must have taken of one of his lady friends, but dismissed that thought almost immediately as the photos looked quite recent and the naked young woman looked far too young to have been one of Wall's recent ex-girlfriends. Having looked at each one for a few seconds he placed them on top of the passport.

Carmichael then took a detailed look at the copies from the ledger. It was impossible to work out exactly what it was or who it belonged to, but it seemed to be a record of large sums of money against a series of names. Although there was nothing to link the document with the bookmaker he'd been talking to the night before, Carmichael couldn't help thinking this was something to do with Baybutt and Sons.

Having carefully placed the documents with the passport and photos, Carmichael then picked up the envelope marked 'Will' in blue ink. This envelope was already open, which allowed Carmichael to slide out the document without tampering with the seal, as he had with the other envelope.

The first thing that struck him was that the will was recent, it had been signed and witnessed just nine months earlier. As he started to read it, his mobile vibrated to tell him he had received a text message; it was from Lucy:

'STILL TALKING WITH SARA-JANE. MENTIONED THE WHISKEY. SHE CONFIRMED SHE'D BOUGHT WALL THE GELSTON'S MALT LAST CHRISTMAS, SHE SAYS HE TOLD HER HE'D FINISHED IT LAST WEEK, SO SHE'S BOUGHT HIM ANOTHER BOTTLE ONLINE WHICH ARRIVED ON SATURDAY AND SHE WAS GOING TO GIVE IT TO HIM TONIGHT, AS HE WAS DUE TO BE STAYING OVER. WE'LL CALL YOU WHEN WE'RE ON OUR WAY HOME. LUCY'

After reading the message, Carmichael put the mobile back in his pocket and started to study Wall's will.

* * *

Watson had just driven past Lancaster services on the M6 when he received a call from DS Patterson at Millom Police Station.

"Just thought I'd let you know that we've got Pierce Armitage in our interview room."

"That was quick," replied Watson.

Patterson laughed. "We don't hang around here," he replied.

Watson looked at his satnav. "It says I'll be with you in about an hour," he replied.

"Just thought I'd also let you know that ever since I told him an officer was coming up from Lancashire, he's been very jumpy," Patterson added, "which is unusual for Pierce. He's even asked for a solicitor to be present when you talk with him, even though he knows he's not been arrested or even under caution. Something else I can't remember him doing before."

"Sounds like he's got something to hide," remarked Watson.

"Aye," replied Patterson, "that's what I reckon, too."

"OK," added Watson. "Thanks for the heads-up. I'll see you in about an hour."

Chapter 29

The other two people Carmichael had earmarked to speak to that morning had been the Baybutt brothers, Trevor and Simon. However, it was a quarter to twelve by the time he finally managed to arrive at the office of Baybutt and Sons, a small first-floor set of rooms above the company's oldest high street bookmaker's shop in the centre of Kirkwood.

There didn't seem anything flashy about the premises, but it didn't give the impression it was just eking out a living either which, according to Ms Turnbull, the company's annual tax returns had been suggesting for years.

Armed with several questions that needed answering, Carmichael made his way up the stairs and into Baybutt and Sons' reception area.

He was greeted by a warm, broad smile from the pretty young woman, with long blonde hair, sat behind the desk. Carmichael recognised her immediately.

"Morning, sir," she said cheerily. "Can I help you?"

Carmichael smiled back and showed the receptionist his identity card.

"I'd like to talk with either Trevor or Simon Baybutt, please?" replied Carmichael.

"Simon Baybutt's out," she told him, "but Trevor might be free. I'll see."

After another engaging smile, the receptionist got up out

of her chair. Brushing past Carmichael, she walked towards a dark oak door at the far end of the room, her strong but not unpleasant perfume filling his nostrils.

She was only inside the office for a matter of thirty seconds when the door opened and with yet another friendly smile, she announced that Mr Baybutt was free to see him.

Carmichael entered Trevor Baybutt's office to find its occupant almost at the door to greet him.

A large right hand with thick stubby fingers was thrust in his direction.

"How can I help you, Inspector?" Trevor Baybutt enquired, as the two men enthusiastically shook hands.

"I'm investigating a couple of incidents and I was wondering if you could help me," replied Carmichael.

Baybutt gestured towards a couple of small settees in the corner of the room to his left. "Of course," he remarked. "Why don't we sit down?"

Carmichael smiled and walked over to the sofas.

"Did Shelley offer you a coffee?" Baybutt enquired.

"No," replied Carmichael, "but coffee would be nice."

Baybutt popped his head around the door and shouted across at the receptionist.

"Can you do us a couple of coffees please, sweetie?" he asked. "And bring some of those nice biscuits that we save for special occasions."

Baybutt then shut the door and joined Carmichael on the adjoining settee.

"I don't know whether he told you," Carmichael said, "but I spoke with one of your colleagues at Mount Rush Park races yesterday evening."

"That would be Fat Malc," replied Baybutt. "Malcolm Marsden. He's not due in until one, so I haven't spoken to him yet today."

Carmichael didn't buy that. He was as sure as he could

be that Fat Malc would have called him as soon as he had the chance last night, but decided he'd play along with Trevor.

"It was about a punter called Timothy Wall," continued Carmichael. "I wanted to find out whether Fat Malc remembered ever seeing him at the races."

"And did he?" Baybutt asked.

"He said not," replied Carmichael, "which is weird as we've a witness who is adamant they saw Wall on a few occasions at the Baybutt pitch. And they say some considerable sums of money were being handed over."

"Hopefully, those considerable sums were all coming our way," remarked Baybutt cockily.

Carmichael ignored Baybutt's comment and handed him a copy of Timothy Wall's photograph. "This is Mr Wall," he said. "Do you recognise him?"

Baybutt looked at the photo for a few seconds before handing it back.

"I'm afraid not," he replied.

"He was a private detective from here in Kirkwood," Carmichael said. "However, unfortunately he was found dead on Sunday."

"Sorry to hear that," remarked Baybutt, just as the door opened and Shelley arrived carrying a tray of coffee and biscuits.

"Just lay them down there for me please, love," Baybutt said.

Shelley carefully navigated her way across the office and set the tray down gently on the table.

"I'm going to pop out for half an hour or so to get some lunch. Is that OK?" Shelley asked.

"That's fine, sweetie," Baybutt replied.

Then, after another of her broad smiles in Carmichael's direction, Shelley made a hasty retreat from the room.

Carmichael extracted one sugar cube from the small silver

sugar bowl and dropped it in his coffee. He then proceeded to slowly stir the coffee, as if he were determined to ensure every grain of sugar was dissolved before he took a sip.

"She's a friendly young lady," Carmichael remarked. "Do I detect a family likeness?"

Baybutt looked surprised but pleased by the remark. "Very observant of you, Inspector," he replied. "Shelley's Simon's girl. She's working here over the summer. She's at Plymouth University doing a degree in Criminal Law."

"A bright girl, then," added Carmichael.

"Yes," continued Baybutt. "And a lovely girl, too."

"Talking about your brother, do you think he might have known Timothy Wall?" Carmichael enquired.

Baybutt shrugged his shoulders. "He might," he replied, "but not as a punter as Simon never gets involved in that side of the business; he's finances and marketing."

"And he's not in at the moment, I understand," continued Carmichael.

"No," replied Baybutt. "He'll be back later; he's with our marketing agency discussing plans for some in-branch promotions in September."

Carmichael took another sip of coffee. "Do you have his mobile number?" he enquired. "As I'd like to speak to him, too."

Baybutt grabbed a piece of paper from his desk, quickly wrote down a number and handed it to Carmichael. "Here you go," he remarked with a smile.

Carmichael looked at the numbers on the piece of paper. "That's a very unusual script," he remarked. "You don't see many people with such neat and unique handwriting."

Baybutt smiled. "That's down to Dad," he replied. "He set up this business and made a fair amount of money. Not bad for a lad who could hardly read or write. He did, however, want us both to have a better start than him, so Simon and I both went to private schools. Simon then went on to Durham University and is very highly qualified in finance and law. I was never as smart as him, well, not as academic I should say. So just a few O levels for me, I'm afraid, but nice handwriting." Baybutt then laughed loudly.

Carmichael didn't believe half of what Baybutt had told him so far and with the handwriting on the scrap of paper he'd just been given matching exactly the hand that wrote the notes Wall had copies of in his safe, Carmichael felt ready to push Baybutt further.

He slid across the desk the notes he'd extracted from Wall's safe.

"Are these copies of some of your ledgers?" he asked calmly.

Baybutt looked at them before handing them back to Carmichael.

"The writing does look like mine," he replied, "but these weren't written by me."

"I'm not sure you're being honest with me, Mr Baybutt," Carmichael said in a firm but controlled voice. "I think you did know Timothy Wall and I think you do know what these are."

Rather than being angry or in any way rattled by what Carmichael had suggested, Baybutt remained relaxed; he even managed a forced smile.

"Then charge me with something," he said.

Carmichael glared back at the brash bookmaker, before smiling himself and putting the notes back in his pocket.

"And if you're not going to charge me, I'd appreciate it if you'd leave," Baybutt continued. "I've got things to do and there's nothing more I want to say to you."

Carmichael remained in his seat.

"Can you tell me where you were last night and on Friday evening?" he asked calmly.

Trevor Baybutt laughed. "You don't honestly think I murdered this bloke, do you?" he replied.

"I don't recall saying he'd been murdered," announced Carmichael.

Baybutt stared angrily back at Carmichael.

"If you could just answer my question?" Carmichael responded.

"At home with my wife, Sarah, on both evenings," he snapped back.

Carmichael smiled, rose to his feet and started to walk towards the door.

"Be assured you've not seen the last of me," he remarked as his right hand rested on the door handle, "and next time I come, I may well be back to arrest you."

As soon as Carmichael had left, a door to the right of Baybutt's desk opened and Fat Malc walked into the room.

"He knows something, boss," he remarked.

Trevor Baybutt turned to face his sidekick. "He knows nothing," he replied confidently, "otherwise he'd have arrested me. He's just fishing."

Chapter 30

Although he had not had a huge amount of joy during his interview with Trevor Baybutt, Carmichael left the offices of Baybutt and Sons with a spring in his step and a wry grin on his face.

He was now certain that the copies of the ledger from Wall's safe belonged to Trevor Baybutt, the handwriting had confirmed that; and he'd identified the young woman in the less than tasteful photos Wall had also furtively squirrelled away under lock and key.

He was just trying to imagine where Shelley would go for a quick lunch, when he spotted her, over the road in the window of Starbucks.

Carmichael smiled broadly, checked for cars, then made his way across the road to join her.

* * *

Much to Lucy's frustration, Rachel's more compassionate approach to questioning Sara-Jane Turnbull had paid huge dividends.

In just over an hour from when they'd reconvened their interview, the senior case manager at HMRC Newcastle had willingly provided her visitors with details of all the cases Wall was engaged in for HMRC, in far more detail than she'd given Carmichael the day before on the phone. She'd also told Rachel exactly when she and Wall had started a romantic relationship (which was much earlier than she'd alluded to Lucy), precisely how many times they'd met (which turned out to be on six occasions), the hotel they'd spent the night at (always the same, The Premier Inn in the city centre), the address and telephone number of the Indian takeaway where she'd bought her food on Friday evening and a dated receipt for the Irish whiskey she'd purchased online for Wall.

Although Sara-Jane had pleaded with them on more than one occasion not to tell her partner, Brian, about her fling with Wall, she nevertheless willingly supplied Rachel and Lucy with his work contact number, details of his flights to and from Vancouver and the hotel where he was staying. It was only when Rachel asked for Brian's mobile number that Sara-Jane became more uncooperative.

"If you call him, he'll suspect something," Sara-Jane implored. "Can't you check all this without him knowing?"

Out of the corner of her eye, Rachel could see Lucy about to intervene.

"I can assure you," Rachel said quickly, "if we do call him, we'll not be intending to mention anything about your relationship with Tim Wall. As DS Martin told you earlier, we can't make you any guarantee that we won't contact him, but we're not here to deliberately damage your relationship, so I can promise you that we won't tell him about your fling with Wall unless it becomes critical to our investigations. That's the best I can offer you."

Although she still looked extremely worried, Sara-Jane switched on her phone and reluctantly recited the eleven digits that made up her boyfriend's mobile telephone number.

Rachel couldn't resist shooting a wily smirk in Lucy's direction as she wrote down the numbers.

"You've never confirmed Brian's full name for us," Rachel added. "What is it?"

"It's Dr Brian Shaw," Sara-Jane replied despairingly.

* * *

Shelley Baybutt did not see Carmichael until he'd sat down across the small table from her. With her head down and her earphones in, she had been busily tapping away on her mobile which she held tightly just a few inches above the table in front of her.

"Can I join you for a moment, please, Shelley?" Carmichael enquired with a friendly smile.

It took Shelley a couple of seconds to realise who it was, but when she did, she forced a smile and said, "Yes, of course."

Seeing Carmichael didn't have a drink or anything to eat, Shelley knew immediately he wasn't there for lunch.

"Can we have a quick chat, please?" Carmichael asked.

"What about?" Shelley enquired nervously.

"It's about a man called Timothy Wall," Carmichael replied. "And before you say you don't know him, let me tell you that unfortunately he was murdered on Friday evening; and, in the course of our investigations, certain items have come into my possession which involve you."

The colour instantly drained from Shelley's face.

"What items?" she enquired anxiously.

Carmichael looked directly into the young woman's eyes.

"Some photographs," he replied calmly. "Quite explicit photographs."

Chapter 31

Watson arrived at Millom Police Station at twelve-fifteen. He was later than he'd expected due to a traffic jam on the A590 near a small village called High Newton, which annoyed him. DS Patterson, however, who met him at reception, didn't seem to care a jot that he'd not arrived at noon as he'd said he would.

"Would you like a coffee before you talk with him?" he enquired.

Watson shook his head. "No, let's just get on with it."

Patterson nodded and smiled. "In that case, follow me," he said before opening the door behind the reception and heading off down the corridor.

"His brief is with him, Jennifer Braithwaite," Patterson said as they walked down the corridor. "She's a local lass from Ulverston, but don't let that fool you. She's as sharp as a knife, so be careful how you tread with her."

Watson smiled. "Thanks for the heads-up," he replied, although he doubted he'd have too much trouble with some young, fresh-faced yokel.

Patterson entered the small interview room with Watson close behind, and they took their seats opposite Armitage and Braithwaite.

Watson smiled. "Good afternoon, Mr Armitage," he began. "My name's DS Watson, I'm with the Mid-Lancashire police force. Thanks for agreeing to come in today."

Before he had a chance to say anything more, Armitage's brief leaned forward and started to speak.

"As you say, my client has agreed to come here of his own volition," she said. "He is more than willing to help you, as much as he can, but that is based upon the understanding that he can leave at any time and that he is under no obligation to answer any question he does not wish to."

"All absolutely correct," replied Watson, condescendingly, "but I'm confident that none of my questions will be too taxing for him."

* * *

Horrified that Wall had kept copies of the photographs and worse still that Carmichael had seen them, Shelley sat speechless, her glazed eyes staring straight forward at a point well beyond where Carmichael was sitting.

"He told me that the copies he gave me were everything," she muttered. "What a lying sod."

Carmichael cleared his throat and deliberately adopted a soft, calm tone.

"Look, I'm not that interested in the photos," he assured her, "but I am interested in how it was they came into Timothy Wall's possession and what, if anything, they have to do with his death and a subsequent break-in at his house, last night."

Still reeling from the bombshell Carmichael had just dropped, Shelley took a deep breath and started to tell her story.

* * *

Watson made himself comfortable before starting his questioning.

"Mr Armitage," he began, "can you tell me why you were in Kirkwood on Friday evening?"

Pierce Armitage's mouth turned up at the sides and he gently shook his head.

"Where?" he replied, suggesting he had never heard of the place.

Watson smiled. "Nobody's accusing you of anything, Mr Armitage," he said calmly, "but we have proof that you were there, so I just want you to tell me what business you had in a town almost a hundred miles away."

Armitage turned his head in the direction of his brief, who took that as an instruction to intervene.

"My client is neither confirming nor denying his whereabouts on Friday," she remarked. "Which is his right."

Watson smiled again.

"Well, let me make it easier for you, Mr Armitage," he said, again in a calm, controlled voice. "We have CCTV footage that shows, quite clearly, you were in Kirkwood on Friday, and what's more, your credit card statement confirms that, too."

As he spoke, Watson pushed across the table images taken from the CCTV footage, with the date and times clearly visible, and also a copy of his credit card statement showing the entries for the bill at Maria's Café and from Hobson's petrol station where he'd bought fuel.

As Armitage studied the items, a few small beads of sweat appeared on his brow and Watson noticed him start to fidget in his chair. After about thirty seconds Armitage pushed the items back across the table towards Watson with one hand, while simultaneously swiftly wiping the sweat from his head with the back of the other. He was quite clearly flustered but was trying hard to mask his anxiety.

"So, I must have been there then," he replied, with a shrug of his shoulders, "what of it?"

Watson continued to remain relaxed, deliberately keeping his words and tone measured and calm.

"As I said before, I'm not here to accuse you of anything," he assured him, "however, I need to verify why you were there and if you saw anything that might help us with our enquiry."

"OK, I was there," Armitage replied. "But I didn't see anything."

Armitage then leaned back in his chair, glanced over at his brief and shook his head.

Stony-faced, Ms Braithwaite stared directly at Watson, then Patterson before announcing that her client would be making no more comments and that they would both like to leave.

* * *

Carmichael was still in Starbucks when he received the call from Watson. He had just finished talking with Shelley Baybutt and was watching her forlorn figure crossing over the road towards her father and uncle's office, when he saw Watson's name come up on the screen of his mobile phone.

"Marc," he said as he took the call, "how's it going with Pierce Armitage?"

Chapter 32

Once Watson had updated him on his interview with Pierce Armitage, Carmichael saw no option other than for Armitage to be detained and brought down to Kirkwood Police Station, so they could both talk with him.

Delighted with the decision, Watson rushed off to tell Armitage and his brief what had been decided, and to sort out the logistics of getting their suspect down to Kirkwood Police Station as quickly as practically possible.

Carmichael toyed with the idea of getting himself a coffee, but finally decided that it probably made more sense to head back to the station, where he could spend a bit of time quietly mulling over the developments so far that day.

* * *

Despite having had a highly successful couple of hours with Sara-Jane Turnbull, Rachel hadn't enjoyed the day at all. She had never thought for one second that she and Lucy would automatically hit it off. In fact, from the moment she'd been told about Lucy coming back she'd been nervous and slightly wary about another female joining the team. However, Rachel had expected their newly returned team member to be, at the very least, professional and civil; neither trait having been much in evidence yet, as far as Rachel was concerned.

Lucy hadn't enjoyed the day either. There was no doubting that Rachel was a very bright and capable officer, but Lucy couldn't warm to her. In Lucy's eyes Rachel was far too cock-sure of herself for a lowly DC and had been thoroughly disrespectful to her as the senior officer. Although Lucy felt she should talk with Carmichael about Rachel when they got back to the station, she wasn't sure about that being the correct way forward; especially as she thought there was more than a fair chance that Rachel's lack of respect for her may well have been born from knowing she was now Carmichael's blue-eyed girl, as Watson had suggested. And, although Lucy had not appreciated Watson reminding her, it was true enough; she had once felt that she was Carmichael's prodigy, a status that had always allowed her to take a few liberties.

It was, therefore, unsurprising that the two detectives hadn't talked at all about finding somewhere to go for lunch once the interview was over and instead had requested the use of a private room from where they could each carry out the various tasks they'd divided between them, before heading back to Lancashire.

They remained in that small room until one thirty-five, when they agreed they'd each achieved what they needed to do and headed out of the office towards Lucy's car and the long journey home.

* * *

Carmichael went straight to the canteen when he arrived at the station. Then with coffee in one hand and an only moderately appetising ham salad roll in the other, he headed over to the incident room.

Having made himself comfortable at one of the desks facing the whiteboard, Carmichael started to relook at the three lists he and the team had documented the evening before. From the feedback he'd had so far from Lucy and Rachel in Newcastle and from his conversation with Watson, Carmichael was able to make a few adjustments to their lists. However, as a result of what he had uncovered that day, there was a great deal more he wanted to add, too.

He'd almost finished making the changes when his mobile rang. It was Rachel.

"I take it you're on your way home," Carmichael observed, from the background noise coming from the other end of the line.

"Yes," replied Rachel, before putting the call on speaker. "We should be back at the station at around five."

"So, what have you discovered up there?" Carmichael asked.

"Well, first of all we've just spoken with PC Twamley, who's checked out Heather Jones's alibi for Friday and got the activity report on Tim Wall's landline at home."

"What did she say?" Carmichael enquired.

"Heather Jones was in the supermarket on Friday, as she claimed," interjected Lucy. "According to PC Twamley she was there, clear as day, on the CCTV until well after six."

"And there were no incoming or outgoing calls on Tim Wall's landline on either Wednesday, Thursday or Friday," added Rachel.

"OK," replied Carmichael, "I'll leave Heather Jones on the list of suspects, but I think she's a long shot. What about Sara-Jane Turnbull and her boyfriend?"

"I've checked and Sara-Jane did order a takeaway curry at about seven-thirty on Friday evening which was delivered at about eight," replied Rachel.

"And on Saturday morning she did drive Brian down to Manchester to catch a plane to Vancouver. His flight left at eleven-thirty, he checked in at nine forty-five and the airline confirmed that he boarded."

"He could still have killed Wall on Friday night though," suggested Carmichael. "Have you spoken to him yet about his movements on Friday evening?"

Lucy smiled broadly, as she'd already made that point to Rachel, so was pleased Carmichael had the same view.

"Not yet," Rachel replied. "It's still only six in the morning there, at the moment."

"So, we take Sara-Jane off the list but leave Brian whatever his name is for now," said Carmichael.

"It's Dr Brian Shaw," interjected Lucy. "And yes, I agree, we should leave him on the list for now."

"Did you find out anything else?" Carmichael enquired.

"We know that the relationship between Sara-Jane and Wall has been going on since before Christmas, and that they'd met on six occasions, always at The Premier Inn in Newcastle city centre," replied Rachel.

"We also know that Sara-Jane did buy more of that Irish whiskey for Wall," added Lucy. "I checked and she ordered and paid for it online last Monday and she received it on Saturday."

"That's more evidence that she's not our killer," Carmichael suggested. "You'd not order him an expensive bottle of whiskey on Monday if you planned to kill him on Friday."

"I agree," replied Lucy.

"Anything more on the cases Wall was working on?" Carmichael asked.

"We've got chapter and verse on all his active cases," Lucy remarked, "but there's nothing that immediately stands out as being linked with his murder."

"That's what I thought yesterday when I spoke with her on the phone," replied Carmichael.

"There is the Baybutt case though," Rachel added. "Although that was never successfully resolved by Wall, Sara-

Jane reckoned that he'd initially told her he was confident that he was going to get enough on them to allow HMRC to take legal action, but within a few days had suggested that he'd been overly optimistic and that he'd actually drawn a blank."

"Yes," remarked Carmichael. "I've spoken with one of the brothers there, Trevor Baybutt, and although he denies he knew Wall, I know he did."

"How come?" Rachel asked.

"Well, I discovered that Wall has a safe at home and inside it I found copies of ledgers, which I think were written by Trevor Baybutt. They record large sums of money against several different names. Baybutt denies having written them, but his handwriting is really distinctive and even I can see it's a clear match. Also, I've had an interesting discussion with the receptionist at their office, a young woman called Shelley, who also, as it happens, is Simon Baybutt's daughter. She was horrified when I told her I'd found some very risqué photos of her, in Wall's safe."

"What a creep," exclaimed Lucy.

Carmichael quickly intervened. "In fairness to him," he added, "Shelley told me that he hadn't taken them. She stupidly allowed a boyfriend to take them and of course when they split up, he wouldn't give them back."

"So, where does Wall fit into all this?" Rachel enquired.

"Well, according to Shelley," replied Carmichael, "she became acquainted with Wall when he came to see her father at the office. She didn't seem to know why he'd been there, but she remembered him being charming and, as she still had his business card in her desk, she called him and asked him to help her, which he duly did, successfully retrieving the photos from this old boyfriend and giving them back to her. He didn't charge her either. However, it now seems like he kept a set of copies for himself."

"Wall still sounds like a creep to me," Lucy remarked.

Carmichael laughed. "He certainly appears to have been a bit of a dodgy chancer," he concurred, "but also, at times he's clearly quite kind and benevolent with his services."

"So, are the Baybutt brothers and this ex-boyfriend going on our suspects list?" Rachel asked.

"Absolutely," replied Carmichael. "Trevor and Simon Baybutt are now on there, as is Trevor's henchman Malcolm Marsden, better known as Fat Malc. I've also added Shelley's ex-boyfriend, Marcus Rigby."

"Sounds like you've been busy today, sir," Rachel remarked.

"Yes," replied Carmichael. "The other things I need to tell you about are that last night Wall's house was broken into," continued Carmichael. "It was completely ransacked. We don't know if anything was taken, but it was left in a right old mess."

"Did the intruder leave any clues to who he was?" Rachel enquired.

"There was some blood on a broken pane of glass, which the SOCO team are on to," replied Carmichael, "but other than that nothing, as far as I'm aware, although they still haven't sent me their report."

"Do you think the break-in's linked to Wall's murder?" Lucy asked.

"I suspect so," replied Carmichael, "but I've been wracking my brains trying to find a logical reason why the break-in happened three days after the murder. It doesn't make sense to me."

There was a slight pause before Carmichael spoke again.

"The final thing I need to tell you is that I've found Wall's will," he said. "It was also in the safe."

"Really," exclaimed Lucy. "Who are the recipients?"

"A lady called Rene Rothwell, who Faye mentioned as being Wall's assistant before her; she gets half the detective agency with Faye Hemmingway getting the other half," Carmichael replied. "And Cassie Wilson gets everything else."

Rachel and Lucy exchanged a quick look of surprise before Lucy spoke.

"So, are we going to add this Rene Rothwell to our suspects list?" she asked.

"No," replied Carmichael, "but clearly we'll need to talk with her."

"So, who do you think is our main suspect?" Rachel enquired.

"That's a very good question," Carmichael replied thoughtfully. "The most likely candidates I think are either one of the Baybutts, or someone working for them. However, with the CCTV evidence we have on him, the guy in Maria's Café, Pierce Armitage, must be up there, too. Marc's been up in Cumbria talking with him this afternoon, but he has not been very helpful, so Marc's now bringing him down here. According to Marc, Armitage has admitted he was in the area at the time Wall was killed, but he's refusing to say why. The issue with him is that he does appear to have a strong alibi that almost certainly rules him out of the break-in at Wall's house, last night."

Keen to get on with updating the whiteboard before Watson arrived with Pierce Armitage, Carmichael quickly brought the call to an end.

"OK, good work, ladies, I'll see you both at about five then," he said, before ending the call, putting the mobile on his desk, and turning his attention once more to his three lists.

Chapter 33

Carmichael knew he had at least two hours alone before DS Watson with his suspect, or DS Martin and DC Dalton, heading south from Newcastle, would arrive back at Kirkwood Station.

He intended to use the time to finish updating the three key lists, call Simon Baybutt and, most importantly of all, to think.

He decided to do his thinking first.

* * *

Once again DS Patterson astounded Watson by the speed with which he was able to get things done.

No sooner had Watson told him that he'd been ordered to bring Pierce Armitage back down to Kirkwood, Patterson had sprung into action and sorted out firstly, the approval from his boss, the Chief Inspector of South Cumbria; then, within a matter of minutes, advised Watson that a prison van was on its way from Barrow-in-Furness to take his prisoner down to Lancashire.

With the prospect of being back at Kirkwood Police Station at about four and then Armitage arriving before five, Watson felt jubilant as he clambered into his car for the drive back home.

* * *

The frosty atmosphere in Lucy Martin's car was palpable during over half an hour of total silence. Since they left Newcastle, the only break in the quiet hostility between the pair was their five-minute call to Carmichael; a call that had been suggested by Lucy, politely enough, but was preceded and followed by zero conversation whatsoever.

* * *

Totally unaware of either Watson's glee or the smouldering animosity in Lucy's car, Carmichael leaned back in his chair and tried to collect his thoughts about the case.

Although they had made reasonable progress and they had many strong lines of enquiry to pursue, Carmichael still felt they were missing something obvious.

Due to the fact he had been caught on camera and was apparently being so awkward in the interview with Watson, it seemed inconceivable that Pierce Armitage wasn't in some way involved. Also, all the evidence Carmichael had personally gathered surrounding Baybutt and Sons suggested there was probably at least one person at the bookies, possibly more, who were implicated in Wall's death.

Carmichael knew they still had a long way to go before they were going to get to the heart of this case.

There were lots of little things that were muddying his mind, small questions that he still couldn't answer, which collectively meant he was worried.

The new, full whiskey bottle in the desk, the fact they couldn't find any trace of the man calling himself Haverstock-Price contacting Wall, the break-in at Wall's house happening three days after the murder, all didn't stack up. And then, of course, there was the red book.

Despite Lucy so far drawing a total blank, Carmichael was convinced at least part of this conundrum was going to be resolved by something that was in Wall's red book.

For almost forty minutes Carmichael remained in his seat, his head a whirl with theory after theory; sadly, none of which seemed to hold water once he challenged them in any depth.

Frustrated, he decided to give up hypothesising and focus the remaining time left before the others arrived on updating the lists and calling Simon Baybutt. To allow his head to clear itself a little, Carmichael decided to make the call to Simon Baybutt next.

Chapter 34

Simon Baybutt was at his desk when he received the call from Carmichael.

"Good afternoon, Mr Baybutt, my name's Inspector Carmichael," he said in a friendly tone. "Are you free to answer a few questions I have regarding a man called Timothy Wall? I assume your brother has mentioned that we talked about him this morning."

"Yes, he did mention it," replied Simon Baybutt, "and yes, I am free."

"I'd just like to know if you'd ever come across Timothy Wall, either socially or in his official capacity as a private detective?"

There was a long pause before Simon Baybutt replied.

"I knew Wall through the Rotary Club," he replied. "We're both members."

Carmichael had fully expected Simon Baybutt to adopt the same stance as his brother and Fat Malc had, and deny any knowledge of Wall, so Simon's response threw him totally for a few seconds.

"How well did you know him?" Carmichael asked.

"He wasn't a friend, by any means," replied Baybutt, "but I've known him for about ten years."

"What about professionally?" Carmichael enquired.

Simon Baybutt laughed. "God, no," he replied, "I've never needed a private investigator."

Carmichael considered how to phrase the next question, which he wanted to pose without dropping Shelley in it with her dad.

"I've been informed by a reliable source that Timothy Wall did visit your offices on at least one occasion," Carmichael continued, "and my understanding was that he came to meet with you."

Carmichael was sure he heard a swift intake of breath from the man on the other end of the phone, before he received an answer.

"Oh, yes," Simon Baybutt replied, his voice stuttering a little as he spoke. "It was Rotary Club business, a fundraiser that he wanted to talk to me about. I can't quite recall what the event was, we do so many you see, but yes, now you mention it he did come to the office. But only on that one occasion."

Carmichael was convinced that, like his brother, Simon was being far from honest, but decided not to press him too hard.

"And what was your impression of Timothy Wall?" Carmichael asked.

Again, Baybutt took a few seconds before replying.

"A bit of a chancer," said Baybutt. "Outwardly very sociable and charming, but I didn't trust him. He was also renowned as a womaniser, too, but I suspect you've discovered that already. All in all, I didn't like him much, but I wouldn't have wanted any harm to come to him."

"Do you know anyone else who would?" Carmichael asked.

Baybutt laughed again.

"Half the husbands in Kirkwood, I'd expect," he replied glibly, "and probably most of his ex-partners, too. Of which there were many, Inspector."

Carmichael couldn't help thinking that Baybutt's remarks might possibly be founded on some personal experience.

"Finally," Carmichael said, again in a cool, calm manner, "can you tell me what you were doing on Friday evening and then again last night, please?"

"Last night I was in all night," Baybutt replied, "and on Friday…" Baybutt paused for a few seconds as if he were trying to remember. "Yes, I was in on Friday evening, too."

"Can anybody vouch for this?" Carmichael asked. "Your wife maybe?"

Baybutt laughed loudly. "My wife and I separated over ten years ago, Inspector. She was the female equivalent of Timothy Wall and is now living in a godforsaken hamlet down in Devon with her boring optician partner, presumably enjoying clandestine trysts with all and sundry in sleepy Noss Mayo."

"I see," Carmichael replied. "So, there's nobody who can corroborate that you were at home on Friday and last night?"

"Not on Friday," replied Baybutt. "Shelley, my daughter, was out with her friends, but she was with me at home last night."

Carmichael felt he had got as much as he could from the call so decided to end their discussion. "You've been really helpful," he said. "Thanks for your time."

"Not at all," replied Baybutt before the line went dead.

Chapter 35

Carmichael had just finished modifying the facts, unknowns and suspects lists when Watson entered the incident room. "Afternoon, sir," he said chirpily before studying the updated board.

"Yes, take a look at the revised board and then I'll fill you in on any changes you don't understand," Carmichael told him. "And while you're doing that, I'm going to grab myself a coffee. Do you want one?"

Watson smiled. "Yes please," he replied, "two sugars in mine."

Carmichael departed leaving Watson alone to study the thirty-three entries on the whiteboard.

Facts:

1. Timothy Wall was killed between 5pm and 10pm on Friday 31st July.
2. He died as a result of a single blow to the back of his head.
3. Faye Hemmingway had left the office at 5.03pm and had gone directly to The Lamb public house; a journey that took her 4 minutes.
4. Wall was a ladies' man, who liked to give scores to his ex-girlfriends.

147

5. Fingerprints were found at the scene that can't be accounted for.
6. Wall's house was broken into on Monday evening.
7. Traces of blood were found on the broken pane of glass.
8. Wall had compromising photos of Shelley Baybutt in his safe.
9. Shelley says that Wall had helped her get the photos from an ex-boyfriend, Marcus Rigby, but did not know Wall still had copies himself.
10. Wall had a copy of pages from a handwritten ledger in his safe.
11. Wall had told Agnes Poulter and Faye Hemmingway about having a strong lead in his hunt for Mrs Poulter's daughter, Debra.
12. Both Trevor Baybutt and Fat Malc deny knowing Wall.
13. Wall left his business to Rene Rothwell and Faye Hemmingway, and everything else to Cassie Wilson.

Unknowns:
1. Who murdered Timothy Wall?
2. Why was Wall killed?
3. Whose fingerprints were on the door into Wall's office?
4. Is his death linked to a previous relationship?
5. Is his death linked to an existing or historical case?
6. Is Pierce Armitage the man who called himself Haverstock-Price?
7. What was the true relationship between Wall and Baybutt and Sons?
8. Who broke into Wall's house?
9. Why was Wall's house broken into?

10. Why did the break-in happen three days after Wall's murder?
11. Are the break-in and Wall's murder linked?
12. Who was the lead that Wall had found in the Poulter case?

Suspects:

1. Pierce Armitage
2. Heather Jones
3. Cassie Wilson
4. Dr Brian Shaw
5. Trevor Baybutt
6. Simon Baybutt
7. Malcolm Marsden (Fat Malc)
8. Marcus Rigby

"Looks like you've had a productive day, sir," Watson observed when Carmichael returned to the incident room.

Carmichael smiled. "Yes, there have been quite a few developments while you three have been away."

* * *

Rachel had deliberately held back on phoning Dr Brian Shaw until they stopped for a break. This was partly because she wanted the reception to be as clear as possible, but mainly so that she could make the call without Lucy listening in.

It wasn't until they arrived at Tebay services, just over an hour away from Kirkwood, that Lucy finally decided she needed a break.

"I'll join you in a minute," Rachel remarked when the car pulled up. "I'll just give Brian Shaw a call in Vancouver."

Lucy nodded, opened her door then handed Rachel

the keys. "Lock the car will you when you've finished. I'll be having a coffee."

Without bothering to wait for a reply, Lucy jumped out of the car, firmly shut the door and strode away.

"Stroppy cow," Rachel announced out loud, but to herself, as she watched her new colleague disappear behind a parked white Transit van.

Then with the scrap of paper Sara-Jane Turnbull had given her perched on her knee, Rachel started to dial Brian Shaw's number.

* * *

"So, tell me about Pierce Armitage?" Carmichael enquired, once he had appraised Watson of his eventful day so far.

"Not much to say, really," replied Watson vaguely. "He's in his early thirties and according to DS Patterson, he's got a string of petty offences to his name, but nothing too serious."

"So, we'll have his fingerprints on file," Carmichael observed.

"I expect so," replied Watson.

"Then compare them again with the prints SOCO found at Wall's office," Carmichael added. "I know we did a general check, which drew a blank, but get someone to check Armitage's again."

"Will do, sir," replied Watson.

"What else can you tell me about him?" Carmichael asked.

"Not that much, really," replied Watson rather hazily. "He wasn't at all cooperative, but by the way he and his brief behaved I'm convinced he's our man."

"Brief!" exclaimed Carmichael. "But I thought you hadn't charged him when you talked with him. Why did he have a brief?"

Watson shrugged his shoulders. "No idea," he replied, "but she was with him throughout and she's coming down here, too."

"Really," remarked Carmichael, who then took a few seconds to consider what he had just been told.

"Clearly, either your Mr Armitage is a wealthy guy," Carmichael remarked, "or there's something serious he's worried about."

Chapter 36

Lucy was halfway through her coffee when Rachel arrived at her table. "I got you a latte," she remarked. "I didn't put any sugar in."

"Thanks," replied Rachel who sat down and raised the cup to her lips.

"Did you manage to talk with Dr Shaw?" Lucy enquired.

Rachel placed the cup back on the table and nodded.

"Yes," she replied. "He was a bit shocked by my call and it took a few seconds before he believed that I was a police officer, but he was very helpful."

"So, what did he say?" Lucy enquired.

"His story was exactly in line with what Sara-Jane told us," replied Rachel. "He was alone on Friday evening then Sara-Jane drove him to Manchester airport on Saturday morning to catch his flight."

"So, he has no alibi for Friday evening when Wall was killed," Lucy remarked.

"He may have," replied Rachel. "He reckons they'd had a busy afternoon and he'd worked right up until seven-thirty before getting home. His hospital is in the city centre of Newcastle, so if what he's saying is true, there's no way he could have been in Kirkwood during the window forensics gave us. I'll double check with his hospital, but I think he can probably come off our suspects list."

Lucy took a large swig of her coffee, then rested the cup back on the table.

"Did you manage to avoid telling him why you needed to check his movements?" she asked.

Rachel raised her eyebrows. "I think I got away with it," she replied. "I didn't tell him anything about the case other than we were calling a number of people to eliminate them from our enquiries. I'm not sure he was that comfortable with my explanation, but he didn't ask any difficult questions."

"Well done," remarked Lucy, "that's a result then."

Rachel smiled. "Yes, I didn't want to have to drop Sara-Jane in it," she replied. "However, it does mean that we've probably had a wasted day."

Lucy nodded. "It looks like it," she replied.

As both officers continued to sip their drinks, Lucy suddenly cleared her throat.

"I'm sorry if I came across as a bit overbearing when we were with Sara-Jane," she said. "I was just keen to make sure we got it done properly. You know, my first case back and all that."

Rachel's initial impulse was to come back at Lucy with a reply to emphasise just how pissed off she was feeling; however, she didn't like the frosty relationship between them, and certainly didn't want it to escalate, so elected to accept Lucy's olive branch.

"No worries," she replied as nonchalantly as she could, "I get worse from Marc."

Lucy laughed. "You and me both," she replied. "At least he's consistent in that respect."

Lucy then drained her cup and stood up. "Come on," she said, "let's see what Boy Wonder and Carmichael have been up to."

With half the contents still in her cup, Rachel quickly put the white plastic lid on her drink before following Lucy, who was already halfway to the exit.

The van from South Cumbria arrived at Kirkwood Police Station at ten to five and by quarter past five, Pierce Armitage and his brief were sat opposite Carmichael and Watson in interview room 1, the customary introductions having been completed and the tape recording.

"I understand from Sergeant Watson that you have confirmed that you were in Kirkwood last Friday evening," Carmichael stated. "Is that correct?"

Armitage looked sideways to his brief before answering.

"Yes, I was," he replied.

"Why was that?" Carmichael enquired.

Armitage shrugged his shoulders. "I just was," he replied.

"Do you often travel down to Kirkwood from where you live in Cumbria?" Carmichael added.

"I travel all over," Armitage responded offhandedly.

Carmichael paused for a few seconds before asking his next question.

"What is it you do for a living, Mr Armitage?" he asked.

Again, Armitage shrugged his shoulders.

"This and that," he replied ambiguously.

"So, were you in Kirkwood on business?" Carmichael asked.

"No," replied Armitage.

"Why were you here?" Carmichael asked for a second time.

"As I said before," replied Armitage, "I just was."

Carmichael leaned back in his chair and paused again for a few seconds before continuing.

"Mr Armitage," he said slowly, "this is a murder investigation, and I would appreciate it if you would answer my questions with a little more detail, as I think you might know something that could help us ascertain why the poor victim of this crime was killed and who is responsible for his death."

"That's not what this is about," Armitage replied angrily. "You're just trying to get me to say something wrong so you can fit me up. You coppers are all the same. But I'm not falling for it. I've done nothing wrong and I'm not going to give you any ammunition for you to twist and throw back at me."

On finishing his sentence Armitage folded his arms, looked at his brief and sat back in his chair.

Carmichael gathered his papers together as if he were about to bring the interview to a halt.

"You've had a long day, Mr Armitage," he said calmly, "and you obviously need time to reflect on what we're asking you, and probably more time to talk with your solicitor. Why don't we break for a few hours while you decide what you are going to say and then get back together and resume the interview later, or even tomorrow morning."

"You intend to keep my client in overnight?" enquired Ms Braithwaite, her tone indicating she was not happy with the idea.

"If Mr Armitage continues to be as uncooperative as he's been so far, then absolutely, we will," replied Carmichael. "It's entirely up to him."

Carmichael then smiled at the solicitor, stood up and walked out of the room.

"Interview terminated at five thirty-one," Watson uttered for the tape, before he, too, got up and made his exit.

Chapter 37

"What do you make of him?" Watson asked as he tried to keep up with Carmichael, who was marching rapidly down the corridor.

"His silence doesn't prove he's guilty," Carmichael replied, "but he's certainly hiding something. I'm still confused as to why he felt he needed a brief as soon as he was brought in by the guys in Cumbria, and even more baffled by the fact that she's followed him down here."

"Well, I think he's our man," remarked Watson.

Carmichael suddenly stopped walking.

"He may well be, Marc," Carmichael replied, "but at present, we've nowhere near enough to charge him. Let's see if he's more talkative after he's had an hour or two to chat with his brief and stew a little more about his predicament. And while he's doing that, get as much background as you can on him. I want to know where he's from, where he lives and what he does for a living, if anything. I'm sure the DS you met up in Cumbria can help you with that. Also do we have his mobile?"

Watson nodded. "Yes, it was on him when he was taken in," he replied. "It's in the bag with all his other personal possessions."

"Check his call activity in the last week," continued Carmichael, "and also see if there's any GPS tracing that will tell us whether or not he was down here again last night when Wall's house was broken into. His credit card activity may suggest he was up in Cumbria but see if you can get that double-checked against his mobile."

"Will do," replied Watson.

* * *

Lucy and Rachel had arrived back and were already looking at the revised lists on the whiteboard when Carmichael and Watson entered the incident room.

"Evening, ladies. Did you have a nice day trip to Newcastle?" remarked Watson sarcastically.

"Delightful," replied Lucy sullenly.

"Looks like you've both been busy though," piped up Rachel, who had just about finished reading over the points on the whiteboard.

Carmichael looked at his watch.

"Marc, why don't you get the ball rolling with those background checks on Armitage," he remarked. "I'm sure Rachel can help you. Then let's reconvene in about an hour for a debrief and agree our action plan for tomorrow."

Watson and Rachel both nodded.

"What about me?" Lucy enquired.

"Why don't you get back onto Wall's red book," he replied. "See if you can track down a few more of his ex-girlfriends."

Without waiting for a reply, Carmichael headed off towards his office, oblivious to the disapproving look Lucy was giving him.

* * *

Carmichael was on the phone to forensics when Lucy entered his office.

He saw her but carried on with his conversation.

"So, no match for either the prints at Wall's office or the blood found on the broken glass at Wall's house," he remarked despondently.

He then remained silent as the technician confirmed that they had nothing more concrete to share before sighing deeply and ending the call.

"Lucy," he then said with a forced smile. "What's up?"

By the expression on her face, it was obvious that Lucy was not happy.

She sat down on the other side of the table.

"I'm not convinced my time is best spent going over Wall's red book," she said. "With all the other leads we have and all the avenues we still need to explore, would it not be better if that was put lower down the list of priorities or given to someone junior to follow up?"

Part of him admired Lucy for challenging his specific directive, but Carmichael was not about to let Lucy dictate what role she played in the investigation. He wasn't used to dealing with dissent and didn't appreciate it one bit.

"I disagree," Carmichael replied firmly. "As you know, most murders are carried out by someone known to the victim, so why would we not look closely at Wall's ex-partners as a matter of priority? Marc may well be right, and we may already have our murderer downstairs in custody, but it's by no means cut and dry. So, while he and Rachel are doing some spadework on Pierce Armitage, it's important that we still look at other avenues. And, in my opinion, the women in Wall's book and their husbands, boyfriends, relatives and close friends are all potential suspects."

"You're the boss," Lucy responded testily, "but I want to register that I'm not convinced it's the best use of my time, at the moment."

Carmichael glared back at her.

"Your view's been noted," he replied firmly, "but I'd still like you to follow through my instruction."

Lucy stood up and went to walk away.

"Don't go yet," Carmichael said. "What was the other issue you wanted to talk to me about?"

Lucy turned back to face him. "Oh, it was nothing," she said.

"Did I sense a degree of friction between you and Rachel when we spoke on the phone, earlier today?" Carmichael enquired.

"No," replied Lucy, "we're fine."

Carmichael didn't believe her for one second but decided to let it go.

"She's a good officer," he remarked. "In fact, she reminds me a lot of you when I first arrived here."

Lucy forced a smile. "I'll be getting on with things then, sir," she said before turning and slowly walking away.

"Let's just hope you treat her better than you did me," Lucy muttered to herself as she exited; not that Carmichael heard her.

Once Lucy was out of the office, Carmichael puffed out his cheeks. He didn't like disharmony within the team but feared, with Lucy's return, that he may well have a problem; and one that he may have to address in the not-so-distant future.

Chapter 38

It was six-forty when the debrief started.

Carmichael pointed up at the whiteboard and his three lists.

"Is there anything up there that anyone needs some clarity on before we start to look at things in more detail?" he enquired.

"Can you just give us a quick update on the break-in last night at Wall's house?" Rachel asked.

Carmichael nodded. "We've no exact fix on what time the break-in occurred," he said. "And there's no way of knowing whether anything was taken. However, whoever did it ransacked the place and, in the process of breaking in, they cut themselves on a small glass pane in the door."

"Have forensics been able to match anyone on the DNA database with the blood sample?" Lucy enquired.

Carmichael shook his head. "Unfortunately, neither the blood sample at Wall's house nor the prints they found at Wall's office match with anyone we know."

"And those prints at Wall's office aren't Pierce Armitage's either," Watson added. "I got them checked with the records we had for Armitage from a previous incident he was involved in. They're definitely not his."

"Any thoughts on who it may have been and what they were looking for?" Rachel asked.

Carmichael shook his head. "Not really," he replied, vaguely but honestly. "My guess is that whoever it was, they were looking for Wall's safe," he replied. "But they didn't find it."

"So, you think they were looking for the ledgers?" Lucy asked.

"I don't know," Carmichael replied. "It could have been the ledgers, but equally it could be the photos of Shelley Baybutt or Wall's will."

"Or maybe they were after Wall's red book," suggested Watson, with a wry smug smile in Lucy's direction.

Carmichael was keen to get the discussion back on track, so quickly moved the conversation on.

"OK," he pronounced, "is there anything up here that needs to be removed or changed?" he asked. "And does anyone want to add anything?"

Watson spoke first. "I think we need to add under facts that Pierce Armitage admits to being near Wall's office at the time he died."

Carmichael nodded. "Agreed," he confirmed before adding the note as number fourteen on the facts list.

"We can remove Brian Shaw from the suspects list," added Rachel. "I've called the hospital and they confirmed he didn't leave on Friday until early evening. The person I spoke to, Dr Shipley, a close colleague of his, didn't know the exact time but says it was certainly after him and he left at seven."

"Do you agree, Lucy?" Carmichael enquired.

"Yes," Lucy replied. "There's no way he could have got from central Newcastle to Kirkwood before ten. I think Rachel's right."

Carmichael nodded and wiped Dr Brian Shaw off the suspects list.

"You should also take Heather Jones off, too," Lucy added. "If PC Twamley is right, she's probably not the killer."

161

"What time did Twamley say she'd got Heather Jones on CCTV at the supermarket?" Carmichael asked.

"She said it was after six," replied Lucy.

"Which still gives her four hours to get home, drop off the shopping and then go across town and kill Wall," pointed out Carmichael. "Unlikely, I know, but she needs to stay on our list as it is possible, she could have done it."

"I guess so," conceded Lucy.

Carmichael thought for a few seconds before moving on.

"I know you've only had a short while, Lucy," he said, "but any joy with tracking down any more of Wall's exes?"

Lucy shook her head. "I think one of them, a lady called Patricia Ward who he dated seven years ago, may well still be living in the area," Lucy remarked. "I've not got a telephone number for her, but I think I've found her on LinkedIn. I've sent her a contact request, so hopefully should be able to talk with her tomorrow."

Carmichael did not use LinkedIn, so didn't fully understand how it worked, but decided not to show his ignorance by asking any further questions. He was just happy that Lucy had made some progress since they'd exchanged words earlier.

"Did you two manage to find out more about Pierce Armitage?" Carmichael asked, his question aimed at Watson and Rachel.

"I've contacted his network provider and asked if they can send over a report on the most recent locations they have for Armitage's phone," Rachel remarked. "They've promised it should be available sometime in the morning."

"And I spoke just now with DS Patterson," added Watson. "He informs me that Armitage is originally from Workington, further north up the coast but still in Cumbria. He has been in the Millom area for about four years and has been picked up dozens of times by them for minor offences,

162

the most serious being on suspicion of handling stolen goods, though they did not have enough in the end to press charges. He's not particularly violent, although he was once arrested on a breach of the peace charge, but again, that charge was dropped."

"And what does he do to earn a living, other than crime?" Carmichael enquired.

Watson laughed. "According to Patterson, he's done a few things but never seems to last too long at anything. The latest venture, he reckons, is running a mobile sandwich delivery service to some business workers in the Millom area. Patterson says he's been doing that for about six months and for once, Armitage actually seems to be making a go of it."

"Really," exclaimed Rachel. "What's it called?"

Watson shrugged his shoulders. "I've no idea," he replied.

Rachel suddenly grabbed hold of a couple of A4 sheets of paper on her desk and started to look closely at them and the notes she had made when she was talking to Pierce Armitage's network provider.

"Bingo!" Rachel exclaimed with a huge smile on her face. "I've found the connection."

"What's that?" Carmichael asked eagerly.

"Remember I told you that one of the calls into Wall's office on Thursday was from a sandwich company, who said they were touting for new business?" Rachel said excitedly. "Well, their number is the same as Pierce Armitage's. It must have been him I talked to when I followed it up, yesterday."

"When was it he called Wall?" Carmichael asked.

Rachel checked the date and times on the report to make sure she got it right.

"Three twenty-four on Thursday last week," Rachel replied.

"Great work, Rachel," Carmichael remarked, a huge smile now etched across his face.

"I bet that's when he introduced himself as Haverstock-Price," added Watson.

"And it's probably when they set up the meeting for Friday evening."

"It could well be," replied Carmichael pensively. "Let's take a short break and go and ask him."

Chapter 39

Lucy and Rachel sat together behind the two-way mirror as Carmichael and Watson started to question Pierce Armitage in interview room 1.

Again, Armitage's brief, Jennifer Braithwaite, sat upright next to her client, seemingly ready to intervene when she felt she needed to.

"Mr Armitage," Carmichael began, his voice calm and words measured. "Having had more time to consider your situation and to talk with your legal representative, are you now prepared to be more open about your visit to Kirkwood on Friday evening?"

Pierce Armitage remained still and silent, which prompted his brief to open her notebook and eyes fixed, start to read out a prepared statement.

"My client is no longer prepared to answer questions from Mid-Lancashire police in connection with his presence in Kirkwood on Friday 31st of August. He has willingly confirmed that he was in Kirkwood, but his rationale for being there is a private matter, totally unconnected with the death of Timothy Wall, who my client has never met. Based upon his experience with the Cumbrian police force, who have detained but not charged Mr Armitage on two separate occasions, my client no longer trusts the police and is of the opinion that anything he says may be distorted to wholly and unfairly implicate him in this serious incident.

With no evidence being forthcoming from the Mid-Lancashire police to associate Mr Armitage with the crimes being investigated, and with there being no formal charge having been made against my client, we respectively request that he is released immediately."

On delivering her statement, Ms Braithwaite closed her book and glared directly at Carmichael.

"I trust you will now let my client go and return home to Cumbria," she added firmly.

Carmichael smiled. "Are you sure you didn't know Timothy Wall?" he asked calmly, his eyes focused directly on Armitage rather than his brief.

Armitage said nothing.

"You see," continued Carmichael, "we've checked your mobile phone activity with your network provider and it's telling us that you put a call in to Timothy Wall's office at three twenty-four last Thursday afternoon."

Carmichael paused and at the same time pushed over the activity report for Armitage's mobile, with the call in question highlighted for Armitage and his brief to locate.

"How do you explain that, Pierce?" Carmichael enquired.

Carmichael found it gratifying to see the man across the table begin to look decidedly uneasy. Although Armitage didn't speak, he started fidgeting in his chair and shot an anxious look towards Ms Braithwaite, as if he was pleading for some help.

As Ms Braithwaite studied the report, Carmichael spoke again.

"Another thing I'd like you to clarify for me," he continued, "is when DC Dalton, from my team, called your number yesterday, as she did with all the numbers on the activity report we obtained from Mr Wall's phone provider, she informs me you told her that you'd called Wall's office to see if there was any chance of you supplying lunchtime sandwiches. Do you remember that call with DC Dalton?"

Once more Armitage remained silent.

"Seems a long way to come each day to sell a few sandwiches," interjected Watson. "It's a three-to-four-hour round trip. Surely, it doesn't make economic sense to try and deliver sandwiches in Kirkwood when you live in Millom."

Jennifer Braithwaite cleared her throat.

"As he has said in his statement," she announced, albeit not as convincingly as she sounded just a few minutes earlier, "my client is unwilling to answer any more questions and we demand that he is released immediately."

Carmichael smiled and collected up his papers.

"I'm afraid that's not going to happen," he replied, firmly. "As you know, we have twenty-four hours before we are obliged to release your client. And due to his reluctance to answer some very basic questions coupled with strong evidence which links your client to Mr Wall, I will be keeping him here until twenty-four hours has elapsed. We'll then decide whether he'll be formally charged with the murder of Timothy Wall."

Carmichael stood up and with Watson close behind, headed for the door.

Chapter 40

As the team gathered back in the incident room, Lucy looked over at Watson and nodded.

"I think you may well have our killer down there," she remarked.

"I'm sure of it," Watson replied.

"Maybe," observed Carmichael, his response more cautious, "but remember, we've no forensic evidence that Armitage has ever been in Wall's office and we've no idea what his motive would be. And, as for the break-in last night at Wall's house, there's not only no obvious motive and no forensic evidence linking Armitage, but also, at the moment, with his credit card bill saying he paid for a meal in a pub in Ulverston, we've got fairly strong evidence he was not there. Unfortunately, despite what I inferred to him and his brief in there, I think we're far from having enough to convince the powers that be that we can charge him."

"Hopefully, that may change if we get some tracking information on his mobile in the morning," Rachel added optimistically.

"Yes, that has to be your top priority in the morning, Rachel," Carmichael remarked. "We need that before his twenty-four hours are up."

Rachel nodded. "Understood," she replied.

Carmichael then turned and glanced at the whiteboard.

"Let's agree the other priority actions for tomorrow," he said.

Carmichael paused for a few seconds before continuing. "The first thing we need to do is to check a few of the alibis we've had so far," he continued. "I'd also like you to do that, Rachel. Talk with Trevor Baybutt's wife and find out if he is telling the truth about being at home on Friday and last night. Also, talk to Trevor's henchman, Fat Malc. Find out what his movements were on Friday and find out what time he left the racetrack last night and where he went afterwards. Then talk with Shelley Baybutt. Find out from her if she was at home with her dad last night, like he told me."

"Will do, sir," Rachel dutifully replied.

"Lucy," Carmichael said, "I don't want you to stop tracking down and speaking to Wall's exes from his red book. That must remain your focus. However, the first thing I need you to do tomorrow is to track down Marcus Rigby, Shelley's ex-boyfriend. Get his version of what happened with those photographs he took of her. I want to know chapter and verse not only on why, how and when they were taken, but also on how Wall went about extracting them from him and, as he's also a suspect, find out what he was doing on Friday evening and last night."

"Will do, sir," Lucy replied, who looked relieved she had some, albeit slight, respite from ploughing through Wall's red book.

"Also, check if he's got any previous on file," continued Carmichael.

Lucy nodded.

"As for you and me, Marc," added Carmichael, "we obviously need to keep our attention on Pierce Armitage for now, but I also want us to talk with the three beneficiaries of Wall's will. I'd like to know if they knew they were in line to inherit something."

"Do you want to interview them together or shall we split up?" Watson asked.

"Why don't you talk with Faye first thing and I'll try and track down Rene Rothwell," Carmichael suggested. "Then let's get back here to continue our discussions with Armitage."

"What about Cassie Wilson?" Watson asked. "After all, she would appear to be the person who gains the most from Wall's will."

Carmichael thought for a few seconds.

"Why don't you call her and ask her to come into the station," Carmichael replied. "I want to have another good chat with her, as her name keeps popping up all the time, and being his last major girlfriend, she has to be a serious candidate for our murderer."

It was clear from the expression on Watson's face that he wasn't so sure, but he didn't argue the point with Carmichael; mainly because he didn't want the meeting to go on much longer, his thoughts having moved to getting off home as soon as possible.

"See if she can come in sometime late morning," Carmichael continued. "Eleven-thirtyish would be good. We should have made a decision about whether we are going to charge or release Armitage by then."

Carmichael looked up at the clock then down at his team for a few seconds.

"I think that's enough for today," he said with a smile. "Well done everyone. I think we've made some good progress. Let's see if we can get this case wrapped up quickly."

As his team filed out of the room, Carmichael printed off a copy of the updated lists so he could study them again once he'd got home.

Chapter 41

It was just after nine when Carmichael arrived home and entered his kitchen.

"You're earlier than I expected," remarked Penny, before planting a huge kiss on his lips. "How was your day?"

Delighted that his wife's foul mood from the weekend seemed to have vanished as quickly as it had arrived, Carmichael put his arms around her and kissed her again.

"Pretty good," he replied. "We've got a lot to do, but we've made good progress in the last couple of days."

"You can tell me all about it while I sort out dinner," Penny added.

"Where are the others?" Carmichael asked, the others being their children and any of their children's friends that may also be in the house.

"Natalie's in her room and the other two are out," replied Penny.

Carmichael wasn't quite sure what his wife was rustling up for dinner, but there was clearly something in the oven and it smelled good. He walked a few paces to the worktop where he'd left a half full bottle of pinotage the night before and poured himself a large glass.

"Sorry, do you want some?" he enquired after he'd put the stopper back in the bottle and taken a large sip from his glass.

Penny shook her head. "No, I'm fine," she replied.

* * *

"Tell me about your case then," Penny asked after they had finished eating.

Strictly speaking, Carmichael wasn't supposed to discuss his cases at home, but he'd always done so with Penny, ever since they'd been together. Over time he'd come to rely on her as his sounding board, frequently making observations that were not only astute and pertinent to the case, but also from a perspective neither he nor his team had offered so far. The golden rule, however, which he'd followed meticulously over the years, was never to discuss his cases when the children were about.

Carmichael smiled and poured the last dregs from the wine bottle into his glass.

"Well, as I said before, we're making headway," he replied confidently. "We have a man from Cumbria in custody who initially said he wasn't in Kirkwood on Friday, but after being informed that we have CCTV footage of him and a credit card receipt for a café he was in, across the road from the murdered man's office, he's now admitted he was there but won't tell us why. He also said that he'd never met the dead man, but we know a call was made from his mobile to the dead man's office the day before the murder."

"That all sounds pretty compelling," remarked Penny, who was listening intently.

"It is, but unfortunately we've no forensic evidence to prove our man was in the dead man's office," continued Carmichael, "and there's nothing we can find that links our man from Cumbria to a break-in that happened at the dead man's house last night."

Penny tried to take in everything her husband was telling her.

"And you are sure the two incidents are linked?" she enquired.

172

Carmichael shook his head. "No," he replied, "but it's a massive coincidence for the man to be murdered, then three days later his house is broken into and ransacked."

Penny shrugged her shoulders as if to suggest she didn't totally agree.

"Do you have any other suspects?"

Carmichael took a swig of his wine.

"Loads," he replied. "We've a couple of ex-girlfriends of the dead man who could have done it, there's an ex-boyfriend of a young woman who allowed him to take some less than desirable photos of her, which the dead man gallantly retrieved, there are a couple of brothers who own a few betting shops and there's a heavy that works at the bookies, too."

Penny nodded. "So, what's the plan?" she enquired.

"Well, tomorrow I've got Rachel checking alibis and the rest of us looking at other potential avenues," he replied.

"What avenues?" Penny asked.

"Lucy is looking into more ex-girlfriends, and Marc and I are going to talk with the three people who benefit from Wall's will," replied Carmichael.

"And how is Lucy settling in?"

Carmichael shrugged his shoulders. "OK," he replied, but without much conviction.

"You don't sound so positive," Penny added.

"No, she's OK," Carmichael said for the second time, "but I don't think she and Rachel have hit it off. They were in Newcastle together for most of the day and I sense they didn't gel that well. I asked Lucy about it and she said they were fine, but I'm not convinced."

"And what does Rachel say?" Penny asked.

"I've not asked her," replied Carmichael.

"Well, if I had to choose between the two, I know who I'd pick," Penny remarked.

Carmichael knew that Penny really liked Rachel, so it was obvious who she was talking about.

"It's probably nothing," he said. "Anyway, they'll have to sort it out between them. I'm not their relationship councillor."

Penny laughed. "You may have many talents, darling," she said, "but relationship guru you ain't."

As Carmichael pondered over what his wife had just said, Penny kissed him on the forehead.

"I'm going to bed," she announced. "Try not to be up too late."

Carmichael smiled, nodded gently and watched as his wife left the room and disappeared into the hallway. Then, once he was alone, he extracted his copy of the three lists they'd updated that evening and placed them on the table in front of him.

It would be another two hours before he eventually went to bed.

Chapter 42

Wednesday 5th August

Carmichael had often seen the signposts to the tiny hamlet of Newton Hool, as he headed north on the A59, but had never visited.

He hadn't given much thought to the sort of house Rene Rothwell would be living in but had certainly not expected the satnav to guide him to a large, impressive-looking converted barn at the end of a long gravel drive.

Carmichael clambered out of his car and crunched across the driveway up to the large, panelled wooden door.

It took only a few seconds from him banging on the door with the large lion-head door knocker to it opening, revealing the tiny frame of a woman in her early seventies smiling broadly.

"Can I help you?" enquired the woman.

* * *

By contrast, Marcus Rigby lived on the third floor of a tired-looking apartment block on the rougher side of Kirkwood.

Lucy Martin had to ring his door bell twice, rap countless times on the door and eventually announce who she was through the letter box before a dishevelled-looking woman in an oversized, threadbare onesie opened the door; a less than glamorous sight matched only by her unwelcoming expression.

"What the hell do you want?" the woman enquired gruffly in a broad Mancunian accent.

"I need to talk to Marcus Rigby," replied Lucy, holding up her identity card. "Is he in?"

The woman didn't reply but stepped back, opened the door wide and shouted down the corridor. "It's the police, Marcus," she yelled. "Get your lazy arse out of bed."

Lucy gingerly stepped into the hallway, not fully knowing what sort of creature was about to emerge from one of the closed doors along the corridor and wishing she had taken someone with her for this interview. Her concerns, however, were soon to evaporate when a fully dressed, smart-looking young man appeared from one of them.

"I've been up for a few hours, Mother," he replied dismissively, "I'm working on my thesis."

The young man, who Lucy took to be Marcus Rigby, strode confidently down the hallway and smiled. "How can I help you?" he enquired politely.

* * *

Having already spoken with Sarah Baybutt on the phone, a conversation in which Trevor Baybutt's wife had, predictably, corroborated his claim that he had been at home with her on Friday evening and again on Monday evening, Rachel checked her inbox to see if the tracking report on Pierce Armitage's movements had arrived from his network provider. It hadn't. Keen to get over to Baybutt's to talk with Shelley and with Fat Malc, Rachel scribbled a Post-it note and stuck it firmly in the middle of Watson's computer screen. It was a short note asking him to look out for the activity report while she was out.

Rachel chuckled to herself as she pressed the note hard on his screen. She knew full well that her colleague would be miffed to be delegated a task by her, given he spent most of the time trying to offload his work in the other direction.

Having ensured the note was secure and could not be missed by the intended recipient, Rachel left the incident room and made her way down to the station's reception area. As she got to the main entrance, Rachel stepped back to allow Jennifer Braithwaite to come in.

Pierce Armitage's brief had no idea who the smiley young officer holding the door for her was and didn't return the smile, choosing instead to march up to the desk, introduce herself to the officer on duty and ask to be taken to see Pierce Armitage.

Conscious that Carmichael had given her a lot to get through, Rachel rushed out of the station and headed for her car.

* * *

Carmichael instantly warmed to Rene Rothwell, who despite her advancing age looked extremely healthy and, as he almost immediately discovered, had a mind as sharp as a thirty-year-old.

"I'd like to know more about Tim Wall," Carmichael said as he sat forward on the large black leather settee. "You must have got to know him well."

Rene took a sip of her tea then smiled.

"Yes, I did," she replied with a glint in her eye, "and I loved him dearly. He was a lovely, lovely man. I'm so sad to hear he's been killed."

Carmichael nodded. "How long did you work for him?" he enquired.

"Over fifteen years," Rene replied. "I started with him

not that long after he started the detective agency and stayed until I retired about three years ago. I could have retired much earlier, but I enjoyed it so much I stayed on."

"That was when Faye took over," Carmichael added.

Rene nodded. "And she's a lovely girl, too. They became a great team. I was pleased about that."

"And were you aware of the details of his will?" Carmichael enquired.

"No," replied Rene, "I didn't even know he had made a will."

"Well, you appear to inherit half the detective agency, with Faye owning the other half."

Rene Rothwell looked genuinely shocked.

"I didn't know about that," she replied with a small smile. "How thoughtful of him."

Carmichael had been watching the old lady's face as he told her about the will and was in no doubt she was genuinely surprised by the news of her inheritance. He smiled back at her.

"He does appear to be quite an unusual man to fathom," Carmichael remarked. "How would you describe him?"

Rene smiled again. "Very complex," she replied. "On the one hand he was forever happy and smiling, always full of energy and the life and soul of the party. He was exceedingly kind, too. He'd often take on cases for people and not charge them."

"Faye mentioned that," Carmichael remarked. "Had he always done it?"

"Yes," replied Rene, "right from the outset. He was very generous in that respect. He did lots for charity through the Rotary Club and I know for a fact that he also gave hundreds of pounds each year to various charities."

"How do you know about that?" Carmichael asked.

Rene smiled. "Because I used to do his annual tax returns

for him, so I made him keep a list of everything he'd given so I could include it on his tax return."

Carmichael smiled. "Generous but not stupid, then," he remarked.

"Oh, certainly not stupid," replied Rene. "Anything but stupid."

"So, would you describe Tim as being basically a good, honest man?" Carmichael asked.

Rene smiled but also shook her head.

"Honest, yes, good, most of the time, but as I said before he wasn't straightforward," she replied. "There was much more to Tim than the outwardly friendly, life and soul of the party image he projected."

"What do you mean?" Carmichael enquired.

"I think it stemmed from him being basically very insecure," replied Rene. "He craved attention and wanted so much to be liked. I'm not a psychologist, so I don't know why, but he was desperate to be adored, I think."

As she spoke, Rene's expression changed to one of nostalgic reflection.

"Well, he had many, many girlfriends as far as I can see," added Carmichael, "and most seem to have been smitten with him. So, he seems to have achieved the adoration he craved."

"I'm not so sure," replied Rene with a slight shake of her head.

"What makes you say that?" Carmichael asked.

Rene considered the question carefully, as if she were keen to pick her words carefully.

"I genuinely don't think I've ever met anyone who could get himself so many lovely women so easily," Rene remarked. "He'd fall head over heels in love with each and every one of them but then lose interest. Over the years there were literally dozens of really nice girls he had dated, and each time I thought this might be the one, but no sooner did I think that the relationship was serious than he'd drop them and start seeing another girl. Sometimes, I'm afraid to say, he would start seeing the new one before he'd finished with the previous one, which is something I didn't like."

Rene took another sip of her tea.

"He was never cruel or unkind to them though," she added. "He adored them all initially and was always the perfect gentleman. At first, he would do everything he could to make them feel special. He was just not…"

"Not the committing type," Carmichael said, as Rene appeared to be struggling to find the right words.

Rene nodded. "Yes," she remarked, "that is certainly true of Tim."

"I understand he liked his drink," Carmichael added, "and was keen on the horses."

Rene recoiled slightly and shook her head.

"He liked good wines and he adored Irish whiskey," she replied, "but I'd not call him a drinker. And as for horses, I am fairly sure you've got that wrong, Inspector. He wasn't even that bothered about picking a horse for the Grand National. No, as far as I am aware, he wasn't a betting man at all."

Carmichael considered what he had just been told for a few seconds before continuing.

"There was a red stone paperweight in Tim's office," he remarked. "Was that there when you worked for him?"

Rene smiled. "Yes," she replied instantly. "He brought it back from a weekend break he had many years ago with…"

Rene stopped. It was clear that she couldn't remember who Tim had taken on that particular break. It was also evident in her eyes that she realised the stone may well be the murder weapon.

"Is that what he was killed with?" she asked, her expression suggesting she didn't want to be told it was.

"It's possible," replied Carmichael vaguely, "but we aren't sure."

"So, his murder wasn't premeditated then," remarked Rene astutely, clearly taking Carmichael's hazy response as being yes rather than maybe. "As if poor Tim's death was planned, surely the killer would have brought a weapon rather than use something that was already in the office."

Carmichael nodded gently and smiled but decided not to make any comment about Rene's shrewd deduction.

"When did you last see or speak with Tim?" Carmichael asked.

Rene paused for a moment before answering.

"I hadn't seen him for months," she replied, "but he called me every few weeks to see how I was doing. Had done ever since I retired."

"So, when was the last call you had with him?" Carmichael asked.

Rene thought for a few more seconds.

"It was the Friday before last, I think."

"And did he seem OK?" Carmichael asked.

"He was absolutely fine," Rene replied.

"I know it's been a while since you worked closely with him," continued Carmichael, "but do you know anyone who might have wanted to harm Tim?"

Rene shook her head. "Not that I can think of."

"No enemies he'd made that you can remember?" Carmichael added.

Rene shook her head again, but then suddenly stopped, as if she had recalled something.

"There was a man who Timothy had a massive falling out with many, many years ago," Rene said, "but he's dead now."

"Who was that?" Carmichael asked.

Rene's face screwed up as she tried to dig deep into her memory.

181

"It was so long ago," she said, "I don't remember."

"But they were at loggerheads?" Carmichael confirmed.

Rene nodded. "Yes, they really hated each other, as I recall," she replied.

"And do you know why?" Carmichael asked.

"It was over a woman, of course," Rene said.

"Of course," Carmichael remarked with a wry smile.

"I wish I could remember their names," Rene said, clearly frustrated by her inability to bring the details to mind. "I believe they were all at school together, so they went back years. I think her name was Harriet, and he had a strange nickname."

"It wasn't Badger, by any chance?" Carmichael asked.

Rene's eyes opened wide. "Yes, Badger Stockley," she said triumphantly. "And his wife was Harriet. I remember now, she was Harriet Price before they married."

It was now Carmichael's turn to be wide-eyed.

"And do you know what happened with Harriet?" Carmichael asked once he had managed to take in what he'd just heard.

"No idea," replied Rene.

Chapter 43

Marcus Rigby didn't seem fazed at all by a female officer quizzing him about the steamy photographs he'd taken of Shelley Baybutt. From the moment he'd suggested that he and Lucy go through to the lounge, he appeared completely calm and relaxed about everything.

"So, let me just recap," Lucy said. "You say that you met Shelley at Baybutt and Sons where you had been working for Trevor."

"That's right," replied Marcus. "I was a junior there for a couple of years, working part-time and during breaks from college. Just doing odd jobs and helping out in the office."

"And you dated Shelley for about a year," Lucy continued.

Marcus nodded. "Ten months," he replied.

"And the photos were taken after you'd been together about six months," Lucy added.

Marcus nodded. "As I've told you, the photos were just innocent pictures that Shelley was happy for me to take," Marcus insisted. "They were just for my own personal use and I didn't share them with anyone. I never posted them on social media, I never had any intention of doing so and, to be honest, as far as I was concerned, they were mine to keep even after we broke up."

"But Shelley didn't share that view," Lucy added.

"No," replied Marcus, "she demanded I gave them back. I

think she was scared I would share them. I told her I wouldn't and that they were a gift from her. I didn't see what right she had to demand them back. She was fine about me having them for months before we broke up."

"And you say that Friday evening you were out with mates in town until about two in the morning?" Lucy said. "And on Monday you were here all evening until midnight when your mum came back from a night out at bingo."

"That's right," Marcus replied. "On Friday we did a few pubs in town then went on to the Marquis Night Club until about two. I then walked home."

Lucy nodded. "I'll check this out, so I hope you're not lying to me, Marcus."

"It's the truth, you can check all you like," Marcus replied confidently.

Lucy looked sternly back at the self-assured-looking lad a few feet from her. "Now tell me how the photos came into Timothy Wall's possession?" she asked.

For the first time Marcus started to look anxious.

"I was on my way home from work when Wall stopped me," Marcus replied. "I had no idea who he was, and he didn't introduce himself at first, but he was threatening right from the start. He said if I didn't hand over all the copies and destroy anything I had electronically he'd tell Fat Malc and Trevor Baybutt and they'd make sure I regretted it."

"And you believed him?" Lucy asked.

"Too right, I did," Marcus replied. "He wasn't messing about. And I know how much Trevor loves Shelley. If he knew about them, I'm sure he'd have got Fat Malc to work me over."

"So, you did what Wall asked?" Lucy continued.

Marcus nodded. "Yeah, I did," he replied. "I met him the next day and gave him the copies I had. I didn't have them electronically so there was nothing to destroy, but I knew he wouldn't believe me, so I told him that I deleted them and that I also had no more printed copies, which I don't."

"And that was that was it?" Lucy asked.

Marcus looked a little sheepish and started fidgeting in his chair.

"Not quite," he replied.

Chapter 44

Marc Watson had not needed to leave Kirkwood Police Station that morning.

Having called in to see Faye Hemmingway on his way to work, to find out whether she had known about her legacy in Timothy Wall's will, which she maintained she hadn't, Watson then headed straight to the office to start ploughing through his other actions.

When he saw Rachel's Post-it note on his computer screen, and realised his actions now included chasing up the tracking report from Pierce Armitage's mobile network provider, his reaction was almost exactly as Rachel had anticipated. In short, Watson did not appreciate being given his additional task in the slightest.

* * *

Rachel had hoped to find both Shelley Baybutt and Malcolm Marsden (AKA Fat Malc) at Baybutt and Sons' office but was disappointed to learn from Shelley that he had already left to go to White City greyhound track for an afternoon meeting.

Resigned to the fact that she'd have to return to talk with him later in the day, Rachel decided she'd try and justify being there by having a long chat with Shelley, to see if she could not only provide corroboration of her father's alibi, but also maybe a bit more insight into the workings at Baybutt and Sons which may help the enquiry.

Shelley, however, was not in a talkative mood. The welcoming, smiley young woman that Carmichael had met the day before had been transformed into a very guarded, anxious and suspicious interviewee.

Shelley was at pains to confirm her father's claim that he had been alone at home on Friday evening and with Shelley all evening on Monday. Her support was so emphatic, and expressed so strenuously, that Rachel was certain Shelley had been told exactly what to say. However, beyond verifying her dad's alibi, Rachel couldn't get much more out of the young woman, so decided not to prolong the futile one-way discussion and made her exit.

* * *

Carmichael called Lucy from his motionless car just as soon as he was out of Rene Rothwell's house. Coincidently, it was at about the same time as Lucy clambered into her car following her discussion with Marcus Rigby.

"That guy, Badger, you mentioned the other day," Carmichael said forcefully, "did you ever find out any more about him?"

"No," replied Lucy, frustrated that Carmichael was again harping on about him. "He died years ago."

"That may be the case," replied Carmichael, "but I've just found out his surname. Do you know what it was?"

Lucy immediately sensed the conversation was not going in a positive direction.

"No, what was it?" she asked hesitantly.

"His surname was Stockley," announced Carmichael. "I don't know his first name, but I know his wife was called Harriet Stockley, her maiden name being Price."

At the mention of the name Price, Lucy's throat went dry and she could feel herself starting to get warm.

"And you think she might be something to do with the guy, Haverstock-Price?" Lucy remarked. "Price is a fairly common name so it might just be a coincidence."

Carmichael took a deep breath before answering.

"I'm told that this guy, Badger, his wife and Wall had all been friends at school," Carmichael said as placidly as he could. "Then Badger and Wall fell out big time, and it was something to do with a woman. So, I wouldn't be at all surprised to find that he's either dated Harriet before she married Badger Stockley or, knowing Wall's track record, it may well have been after she was married. Maybe he was even dating her before and after she married Badger."

By the time Carmichael had finished sharing his theory, his voice was no longer calm, which made Lucy even more anxious.

"And if so, she will be in his red book," added Lucy.

"Exactly," replied Carmichael.

"I'm just on my way back now," Lucy said sheepishly, "I'll get on to it right away."

Frustrated and angry, Carmichael ended the call and started his engine. It was only when he had gone a few hundred yards that he realised he'd not asked Lucy how she had got on with Marcus Rigby. Lucy realised sooner but wasn't about to call him back. Her sole objective was now to return to the office and check the entries in Wall's red book before Carmichael arrived.

Chapter 45

Watson realised that Lucy was stressed out as soon as she entered the incident room. With a face looking like thunder, but without uttering a word or even acknowledging that Watson was there, Lucy grabbed the red book and started to turn the pages rapidly.

"Bugger it!" she exclaimed loudly as she stopped at a page with a picture of a smiling, attractive young woman, blonde of course, which had been taken some twenty years previously.

Lucy then turned over a few more pages before stopping again.

"Oh Christ!" she uttered even more despondently. "He's going to kill me."

* * *

It took Carmichael a further twenty minutes to arrive at Kirkwood Police Station, by which time Rachel had also arrived back. Having been handed Pierce Armitage's GPS activity report by a less than amused Watson, Rachel had studied it carefully. It confirmed that Armitage had not ventured out of Cumbria between Friday evening and when he had been detained the morning before.

"There's no way Armitage did the break-in," she advised

Carmichael, holding up the report as soon as her boss entered the incident room.

Carmichael took the report from her hand and checked it for himself.

"But he's still our most likely suspect for Wall's murder," he replied. "Mind you, unless he starts talking this morning, I'm not sure we can hold him much longer. We've certainly not enough to charge him."

Carmichael puffed out his cheeks and looked up at the clock.

"I thought Lucy would be back by now," he remarked.

Watson looked up from his computer screen. "She was in earlier," he replied, "but only for a few minutes. She grabbed Wall's red book and dashed off."

Watson decided not to elaborate on Lucy acting as if she was stressed out or repeat anything she had said.

"Really," replied Carmichael, his tone suggesting he was not pleased.

"I met with Sarah Baybutt and then Shelley Baybutt," interjected Rachel. "As you'd expect, they backed up what Trevor and Simon told you about their movements on Friday and Monday evenings."

"What about Fat Malc?" Carmichael asked. "What did he have to say?"

"He was out at White City greyhound stadium until later on," Rachel replied. "So, I'll have to go back to Baybutt's this afternoon."

"Right," remarked Carmichael.

"But I've looked online at the time of the last race at Mount Rush Park on Monday evening," Rachel continued. "It started at eight twenty-five, so he'd easily have been away by nine."

"So, he's certainly a candidate for the break-in," Carmichael observed.

Rachel nodded. "Definitely," she replied.

"What about you, Marc?" Carmichael asked. "Did you speak with Faye Hemmingway?"

"Yes," replied Watson. "She said she didn't know Wall had left half the business to her."

"And do you believe her?" Carmichael continued.

Watson nodded. "I'm sure she was telling me the truth. She seemed really shocked," he replied.

"Any joy finding out more on Pierce Armitage?" Carmichael added.

"Looks like he's from a decent family up in Workington," Watson replied. "I spoke with one of his old teachers at the school up there who said he was a clever lad, who just got in with the wrong crowd. Although he has not been convicted of anything, since he was about sixteen it looks like he's been on the fringes of a lot of petty stuff."

Carmichael nodded slowly. "So, not a profile that suggests he's violent?"

Watson shook his head. "No," he conceded.

"Well, I suppose it's about time we talked with him again," Carmichael announced. "I assume his brief is still here?"

As Watson shrugged his shoulders, Rachel nodded vigorously.

"She arrived earlier," Rachel remarked. "I saw her as I was leaving to go to see the Baybutts."

Carmichael frowned. "I don't get that," he announced. "Why is she here? He is just a normal young man, presumably not that wealthy. He's hardly Mr Big in the South Cumbria criminal fraternity. What on earth justifies her being with him for twenty-four hours and who's paying for her?"

"Maybe it just demonstrates that he's actually guilty," suggested Watson.

"Or maybe they're in a relationship," added Rachel.

For a few seconds Carmichael considered what his two

officers had just suggested. He didn't think much of either theory but on balance, favoured Rachel's explanation.

"Let's go and talk with them again, Marc," he said, "and while we're in there, Rachel, why you don't try and find out as much as you can about Ms Braithwaite."

Rachel nodded. "Will do, sir," she replied.

Chapter 46

After finding the entry for Harriet Stockley in Timothy Wall's red book then, worse still, six years earlier finding another entry for her, this time as Harriet Price, Lucy had decided to remove herself sharpish from the incident room. There was no way she wanted to be there when Carmichael arrived. She figured it prudent to ensure that the next time she saw her boss she had the full low-down on Harriet and was able to either confirm categorically that Harriet was innocent of any part in Wall's death or have strong evidence to make her a prime suspect. Lucy knew anything else would leave her open to Carmichael's wrath, which she was naturally desperate to avoid.

So, without acknowledging the fact that Watson was even in the room, Lucy had grabbed the red book and scurried away to make her enquiries about Harriet, well away from the rest of the team.

Once safely out of harm's way, Lucy had decided to call Norfolk George. The owner and lead reporter of the local newspaper was always a mine of information on local issues, so she figured if anyone was going to be able to point her in the right direction, it was him.

* * *

Carmichael and Watson sat in the same seats in interview room 1 as they had the day before, as did Pierce Armitage and his brief, Jennifer Braithwaite.

"I trust you had a good night," began Carmichael with a smile. "And, having had a chance to sleep on things, I hope you're now prepared and willing to answer the questions Sergeant Watson and I put to you yesterday."

It was clear, within a split-second, that Armitage still had absolutely no desire to talk. Leaning back in his chair with his arms folded, he simply turned his head to his left and looked towards his brief, her prompt to deliver what was almost certainly another well-rehearsed statement.

"As stated by my client yesterday, my client is no longer prepared to answer questions from Mid-Lancashire police in connection with his presence in Kirkwood on Friday 31st August. He has willingly confirmed that he was in Kirkwood, but his rationale for being there is a private matter, totally unconnected with the death of Timothy Wall, who my client has never met. My client does confirm that he had spoken to Mr Wall by phone on an unconnected private matter, which he does not wish to discuss as it has no relevance to Mr Wall's murder. With no evidence being forthcoming from the Mid-Lancashire police to associate Mr Armitage with the crimes being investigated, and with there being no formal charge having been made against my client, we, once again, respectively request that he is released immediately."

On delivering her latest statement, Ms Braithwaite gave Carmichael a look of triumphant defiance.

Inside Carmichael was seething but tried hard to avoid letting it show. Everyone in the room knew he didn't have nearly enough evidence to charge Armitage with Timothy Wall's murder, but Carmichael wasn't about to concede just yet.

He looked up at the clock on the wall; it was four minutes past eleven.

"By my reckoning we still have over half an hour before we have to decide whether to charge your client or not," Carmichael announced as calmly as he could. "So, let me ask you a few more questions."

Armitage let out a huge sigh and kept his lips shut tight and arms folded firmly across his chest. Even Ms Braithwaite, who up until then had appeared ice-cold calm, let out a sigh suggesting she, too, was getting frustrated.

"Tell me about that call?" Carmichael asked. "Surely if it is as unconnected with Mr Wall's death as you are claiming, you have no reason not to explain what it was about?"

Armitage didn't answer; he stared directly at Carmichael, but his lips remained shut.

"OK," continued Carmichael. "Does the name Haverstock-Price mean anything to you?"

Almost instinctively, Armitage shrugged his shoulders before replying, "Not a thing." It was clear by the stern look Ms Braithwaite shot in his direction that she wasn't pleased he'd broken his silence. However, Armitage didn't notice and continued. "Who the hell's Haverstock-Price?"

Delighted he'd finally managed to get some words out of Armitage's mouth, Carmichael continued, "It's the name we believe the killer gave Timothy Wall before he murdered him."

Armitage glanced quickly at his brief, who shook her head.

"No comment," Armitage said.

"We think Haverstock-Price may be you," continued Carmichael, "but it may well be someone else. Someone that you may have seen or heard when you went to see Timothy Wall. So, why don't you just tell us what happened on Friday evening?"

For a couple of seconds, Carmichael thought Armitage was about to talk more freely, but his hopes were fleeting, as after another severe look from Ms Braithwaite, Pierce

Armitage, arms still folded, simply stared back at Carmichael and Watson, his expression one of insolence.

Carmichael waited a moment before speaking.

"OK, you're free to go," he said. "Sergeant Watson will escort you both off the premises."

Armitage looked relieved. Clearly being held for almost twenty-four hours had been a strain for him.

"But I want to make it very clear, Mr Armitage, you are still very much a murder suspect," Carmichael said firmly, "and at the very least you can expect to hear from us again about your unwillingness to help and potentially concealing evidence from us, so please don't think this is the last you will be seeing of DS Watson and I."

Carmichael then collected his papers and left Watson alone to chaperone Armitage and Ms Braithwaite out of Kirkwood Police Station.

* * *

Within five minutes, both suspect and solicitor were in the reception area making a swift exit out of the building.

As Watson watched Armitage and Braithwaite scurry away, he was joined by Cassie Wilson, who had been in reception having just arrived for her meeting with him and Carmichael.

"Are they suspects?" she enquired, her curiosity seeming more than just a casual interest. "Were they involved in Tim's death?"

Watson turned to face her. "I obviously can't say," he replied. "Why do you ask?"

"Oh, no reason," Cassie replied quickly. "I'm just being nosey."

Watson smiled before gesturing towards the swing doors that led to the interview rooms.

"Thanks for coming in," he remarked with a smile. "It's this way."

Cassie smiled back. "After you," she said.

As Watson headed over towards the doors, he didn't notice Cassie take another long look out towards Armitage and his brief who were walking briskly towards Ms Braithwaite's car.

Chapter 47

Just as Lucy had expected, Norfolk George remembered Badger Stockley and his tragic death. Within minutes of taking the call, George was able to give her a rough summary of when, where and what had taken place, with a promise to root out more specific details from his archives by the time Lucy got to his office.

Pleased to have made some early progress, Lucy headed off to meet the eternally well-informed newspaper proprietor.

* * *

"How did it go with Armitage?" Rachel enquired once her boss returned to the incident room.

Despondently, Carmichael shook his head.

"We had to let him go," he replied. "To be honest I'm not sure he's our man, but he knows something. His unwillingness to cooperate makes him seem suspicious, but I don't think he's our killer."

Rachel gave a small shrug of her shoulders.

"I've still more work to do on Jennifer Braithwaite's background," she remarked, "but I can tell you that she's thirty-six and she graduated in law from the Open University four years ago."

"So, she was a mature student," observed Carmichael.

"Yes," replied Rachel. "I'm not sure yet what she did before or where she was born, but I'm working on it."

"From her accent she's not a Cumbrian," Carmichael remarked. "Even a southerner like me can spot that."

Rachel smiled. "I'll keep digging."

"Good work," Carmichael added as he started to walk over to his office.

As he reached his door, he turned back to face Rachel.

"What about an address for her?" he enquired.

Rachel looked through her notes.

"She works for a law firm in Ulverston called Hackett and Palmer," Lucy replied. "And according to the electoral role her home address is Banks Rise House, Mossy Lea, Near Millom."

Carmichael's eyes widened. "Isn't that where Marc said Armitage lives?"

Rachel shrugged her shoulders. "I don't know," she replied.

She had only just finished talking when Watson came into the incident room.

"What's Armitage's home address, Marc?" he eagerly enquired.

Watson walked over to his desk and rustled through his papers.

"Banks Rise House, Mossy Lea, Near Millom, Cumbria," he read out.

Carmichael smiled. "So, that explains why our Ms Braithwaite put herself out for him. They are either housemates, or your theory may not have been so farfetched, Rachel. They may well be something more."

Rachel smiled. She had never thought her suggestion was anything but the most likely scenario, but she said nothing.

"And I've got something else that's interesting," Watson added. "I've just put Cassie Wilson in interview room one, but when she was in the reception area, she saw Armitage as he was leaving and asked if he was a suspect. Of course, I didn't tell her, but when I asked why she wanted to know, she said she was just being nosey. That may be all it was, but I got a feeling that she might know him."

Carmichael considered what Watson had just told him for a few seconds.

"Well, once we've talked with her again about Wall's death and her inheritance, we can ask her," he said with a wry smile as he started to stride purposefully towards the corridor.

Watson quickly dropped his papers back on his desk, looked across at Rachel, rolled his eyes upwards then shot off after Carmichael who was already bounding quickly away towards interview room 1.

Chapter 48

"Thanks ever so much for coming in this morning," Carmichael remarked as he and Watson took their seats in the interview room; the exact same seats they'd occupied during their earlier interview with Pierce Armitage.

Cassie Wilson smiled. "That's no problem," she replied. "I've no more sessions booked in until later today."

"What exactly is it you do?" Carmichael enquired. "I gather you have a blog to do with health and wellbeing. I imagine that covers quite a lot of ground?"

Cassie seemed thrilled to be asked about her work.

"I do have a blog and I also run a small company that focuses on providing bespoke strategies for our clients to help them improve their overall wellbeing," Cassie replied. "As the plans are tailored to the individual, they will differ dependent upon a whole range of factors, but essentially I concentrate on five key areas: nutrition, exercise, sleep, managing stress and the client's social life."

"And you're busy?" Carmichael asked.

"Unbelievably so," Cassie replied with a broad smile, "which I really like."

"It must pay well," Watson added. "We saw that nice car you have when we came to your house on Sunday."

For a split-second Cassie looked puzzled, but she quickly smiled again and chuckled.

"You mean the Tesla," she remarked. "That's not mine, I just borrowed it from a friend for a few days to try out. I'm thinking about buying a new car, as my old thing is starting to get tired and I fancy an eco-friendlier one, so they kindly loaned me theirs for a few days."

"And what did you think?" Carmichael asked.

Cassie shrugged her shoulders. "It's probably a bit too expensive for me," she replied.

Carmichael laughed. "They are expensive aren't they," he concurred.

"Your colleague said you needed to talk to me about Tim's will," Cassie remarked, her question aimed at Carmichael, but a brief movement of her eyes towards Watson indicated who she meant by 'colleague'.

"Yes," replied Carmichael. "Are you aware of what Mr Wall put in his will?"

Cassie shook her head. "To be honest, I didn't know he'd made one," she replied.

"Well, he did," continued Carmichael, "and you are one of his beneficiaries."

"Really," Cassie replied. "That was very thoughtful of him. Well, it is as long as it's not his awful red book he's left me."

Carmichael smiled. "It's much more than that," he continued. "Other than the private detective business, he's left you everything."

"What?" exclaimed Cassie. "His house and everything?"

Carmichael nodded. "I don't know what it's all worth, but I'd say it's a considerable sum."

Cassie looked dumbfounded.

"I can't believe that," she said slowly, her face drained of colour and her expression one of utter astonishment.

* * *

Lucy hadn't seen Norfolk George since she'd returned to Kirkwood, so the first thing she did when she entered his small, cluttered office was give him a warm embrace.

"Welcome back," George said in his broad East Anglian accent. "So, you couldn't keep away."

Lucy grinned. "I won't lie to you George," she replied, "this wasn't the plan, but with Calum now the local MP we need to be based in the area, so it made no sense me working somewhere else, especially as I've lived here before and have lots of friends here still."

"And of course," added George, who was grinning from ear to ear, "you again get to work for the great Carmichael."

"Yes," Lucy replied, trying hard to maintain a straight face, "another big plus."

* * *

For a few seconds Carmichael was concerned that Cassie might faint, so he instructed Watson to get her some water, which, with shaking hands, Cassie duly gulped down.

"But surely now we aren't together, that part of his will isn't valid anymore," Cassie remarked.

Carmichael shook his head. "No, unless there's a more recent will which doesn't mention you, or you have had anything to do with his murder, it is valid. Whether you were or weren't in a relationship with him anymore, doesn't matter."

Observing Cassie's stunned reaction to the news of her windfall, Carmichael found it hard to believe the shock she was displaying was anything other than genuine. That being so, the theory they'd had about her being Wall's killer with the motive being personal gain, now seemed highly unlikely to him. But, of course, not totally out of the question. During his time in the force, Carmichael had met many suspects who'd feigned surprise or plausibly protested their innocence, only to have it proven later that they were just good actors; so he wasn't about to leap to any premature conclusions.

"What happens now?" Cassie enquired.

"Well, the coroner will have to make a judgement first," Carmichael explained, "and as we are still investigating the murder that might not happen straight away. But once that's all concluded, whoever is responsible for probate and administering Mr Wall's estate will no doubt be in touch with you to talk about your legacy."

"Right," said Cassie. "So, I do nothing."

Carmichael nodded and smiled. "That's correct," he replied.

* * *

"Well, this is what I have for you on the Stockleys," announced Norfolk George as he pointed over to a long table with three separate newspaper articles laid out neatly, side by side.

Lucy smiled. "So, what have we here?" she enquired.

"I've found three articles that mention your couple," continued Norfolk George. "The first one is Badger Stockley with Timothy Wall in an old Kirkwood Cricket Club photograph."

Lucy picked up the cutting, which was thirty-three years old, showing a tall, strikingly athletic-looking young man with long, wavy dark hair, smiling and holding a cricket bat over his head, next to another slightly shorter young man, with an equally broad smile, holding out a cricket ball in his right hand. The caption beneath the photograph read… '*local duo Justin Stockley and Timothy Wall help Kirkwood to semi-final victory*'.

Lucy carefully read the short article, which exalted Justin 'Badger' Stockley for his 155-not-out innings and Tim Wall's seven wickets for just eighty-nine runs; exploits that had enabled Kirkwood Cricket Club to gain victory in the semi-final of the Sefton Cup against Congleton Cricket Club.

"They look like close buddies there," Lucy remarked.

She then picked up a second cutting; this time just a picture of Justin Stockley on his wedding day, again smiling broadly with a radiant-looking, blonde bride. The short caption below read simply… *Justin Stockley and Harriet Stockley (née Price)*.

Lucy looked closely at the date on top of the picture, which was dated six years after the first article.

Placing the wedding photograph down onto the table, Lucy then picked up the third cutting; a more detailed and decidedly less jovial article which related to a tragic car accident twelve years before.

She took her time reading the piece that had been penned by Norfolk George at the time, before looking over at the author.

"Can I borrow these?" Lucy asked.

Norfolk George nodded. "Certainly," he replied, "but I'd like them back when you've finished with them."

Chapter 49

Having finished her drink of water, Watson had been instructed to fetch Cassie Wilson a cup of tea, which she held tightly in her hand.

"When we spoke on Friday," Carmichael remarked, "you described Tim as a really nice guy. In fact, I think you called him lovely."

Cassie nodded. "He was," she replied.

"However, you also said he was crazy and annoying as hell at times," Carmichael added.

Cassie allowed herself a fleeting smile. "He was that, too," she said, before taking a sip of tea.

"You also told us that you were alone at home on Friday 31st," Carmichael continued.

"That's also correct," Cassie replied.

"What about on Monday evening?" Carmichael enquired.

Cassie considered the question for a few seconds. "I was home by myself again on Monday," she replied. "Why do you ask?"

Carmichael's initial thought was to avoid giving Cassie a direct answer to her question but decided there was no reason why he shouldn't be more forthcoming.

"Tim's house was broken into on Monday evening," Carmichael replied, "so we need to confirm what everyone close to him was doing that evening."

"Well, it wasn't me," replied Cassie firmly. "I've no reason to break into the house. And if I did want to gain entry, I'd just use the key."

"You still have a key to Tim's house?" Carmichael asked.

"Yes," replied Cassie. "I kept meaning to give it him back, but I never seemed to get around to it."

"Do you have the key on you?" Carmichael asked.

Cassie took her key ring from her jacket pocket and picked out the Yale key.

"It's this one," she said. "Do you want it?"

"No, that won't be necessary. As you've inherited the house, you'll be needing that key," Carmichael replied.

Cassie nodded and put the keys back in her pocket.

"And tell me again, why did the relationship with Tim end?" Carmichael asked.

Frown lines suddenly appeared on Cassie's forehead, suggesting she was starting to become a little concerned by some of Carmichael's questioning.

"I ended it, because it had run its course," Cassie replied firmly. "I once had very strong feelings for Tim, but when I found out he was seeing another woman, I just couldn't trust him anymore. Once the trust had gone it was never going to work. As I told you on Sunday, I value my independence, and my self-respect means everything to me, so I ended it."

"I see," remarked Carmichael.

"I've moved on and don't regret that decision in the slightest," continued Cassie. "But I am very sad that Tim was murdered. For all his faults and foibles, we were close once and he didn't deserve that."

Carmichael paused for a few seconds while Cassie took another sip of tea.

"And are you seeing anyone else?" Carmichael enquired.

Cassie shook her head. "No," she replied with a wry smile. "I'm not ready for another relationship; not just yet."

Carmichael smiled back as if to reassure her that he was close to finishing the meeting.

"Just a couple of last questions," he added. "Do you know, or can you ever recall Tim mentioning a man called Armitage?"

Cassie slowly shook her head as she tried to check her memory bank.

"No," she replied, but with some doubt in her voice, "not that I'm aware of. I can't recall ever meeting anyone with that name, and I can't recall Tim ever mentioning anyone of that name, either. Why do you ask?"

Carmichael shrugged his shoulders. "It's just a name that's come up during the enquiry."

Cassie smiled as if she accepted Carmichael's imprecise explanation.

"What about Haverstock-Price?" Carmichael added.

Again, Cassie shook her head, but this time more assuredly.

"I'd have definitely remembered that one if Tim had mentioned it," she remarked. "I'm certain I don't know anyone with that name."

Carmichael smiled again and stood up.

"Thanks for your time," he said, holding out his hand to shake hers.

Cassie Wilson smiled back, shook hands with Carmichael, then Watson, before heading towards the door.

"I'll see you out," remarked Watson, who within a few seconds had got out of his chair, rushed over to the door and opened it widely so that Cassie Wilson could exit the room.

Chapter 50

"How are you getting on?" Carmichael asked Rachel as he burst through the doors of the incident room.

Rachel frowned and shook her head. "I've not managed to find out anything more on Jennifer Braithwaite," she replied.

Carmichael walked across the room and looked out of the window, where he saw Cassie Wilson cycling out of the station car park and down the road.

"How did you get on?" Rachel enquired.

Carmichael considered the question for a few seconds.

"I'm pretty certain she didn't know about the inheritance," he replied, "and she had a key to Wall's house, so I don't see her being our burglar."

"So, do we scrub her off our list?" Rachel asked.

Carmichael shook his head. "No, she stays," he replied assuredly. "She has no alibi for Friday evening, so she needs to remain on the list even though I'm sure she didn't kill him."

"What about Armitage?" Rachel continued. "Did she say she knew him?"

Carmichael turned back to face his colleague. "No," he replied. "She maintains she doesn't know anyone by the name of either Armitage or Haverstock-Price."

As Carmichael finished talking, the door of the incident room opened again and in walked Lucy and Watson.

"I was wondering where you'd got to," remarked Carmichael, his cynical comment aimed at Lucy.

"I've been following up on Badger and his wife," she replied. "As you asked me."

"And what have you uncovered?" Carmichael enquired.

"With the help of Wall's red book and some old newspaper cuttings supplied by Norfolk George, quite a lot," she replied with a triumphant grin on her face. "I can tell you that Badger's real name was Justin Stockley. That he and Wall both played for Kirkwood Cricket Club and I have a cutting relating to Justin Stockley's marriage to Harriet Price."

As she spoke, Lucy placed two of the newspaper articles on the desk in front of Carmichael.

As Watson, Rachel and Carmichael all looked at the picture of Badger on his wedding day and the article that mentioned Badger and Wall's heroic achievements on the cricket field, Lucy inserted Post-it notes on the two entries of Harriet in Wall's red book and placed the book with the third article on another desk.

"I can also confirm that Wall did have a relationship with Harriet," continued Lucy. "In fact, he dated her twice. Once when she was Harriet Price, around thirty years ago and then again six years later when she was Harriet Stockley."

Carmichael moved over and looked at the two entries in the red book, then turned his attention to the other newspaper article that Lucy had borrowed from Norfolk George. "What's this?" he enquired, picking up the last news cutting.

"It's a piece Norfolk George printed twelve years ago," replied Lucy. "It's probably best you read it as it describes what happened to Badger and explains quite clearly why Harriet won't have anything to do with Wall's murder."

Carmichael looked deep into Lucy's eyes as she spoke. Although her face remained calm and motionless, he sensed what Lucy was really saying was *I told you so.*

Carmichael sat down and started reading.

It took him a good couple of minutes before he stopped looking at the article, during which time his three colleagues waited in silence.

Once he'd finished, he passed the cutting to Watson and Rachel, who both examined it intently.

"So, she died in the car crash too," Carmichael remarked.

Lucy nodded vigorously. "I'm sorry to say that's true," she replied. "And to be honest, I'm still of the opinion that following up on the women in Wall's red book is going to prove to be a waste of time."

As she spoke both Watson and Rachel stopped reading and, anticipating fireworks, nervously waited to hear Carmichael's response.

Carmichael took a deep breath before replying.

"You're absolutely right about Harriet not being the killer," he remarked, "but I don't agree with you about Wall's red book. Have you read the article properly?"

Lucy bristled at the insinuation that she hadn't been as thorough as she could have been.

"Several times," she replied, her voice raised and indignant.

"Then I suggest you read it again," Carmichael added. "It may be nothing, but it states that Harriet had a sister."

"Yes, an accountant called Mary," replied Lucy. "So, what?"

"It says a turf accountant," Carmichael remarked firmly. "Didn't that ring any bells with you?"

Lucy looked puzzled. "I don't know what you're suggesting," she said.

"Do you know what a turf accountant is?" Carmichael asked.

Lucy shook her head. "Some sort of specialist accountant I suspect," she replied vaguely.

Carmichael shook his head. "It's a bookmaker," he replied. "Like Baybutt and Sons."

Lucy's earlier triumphant look had now totally evaporated. In its place was the appearance of someone feeling decidedly uncomfortable.

"And, as it happens, there is a lady who works at Baybutt's called Mary," Carmichael continued. "I met her at the races on Monday night. Now if she turns out to be Harriet's sister, do you think it's worth following up?"

Lucy nodded slowly. "I guess so," she replied sheepishly.

Carmichael looked at his watch.

"It's been a busy morning so why don't we all take a quick thirty-minute break," he said, "but I need you all back here in half an hour so we can review where we are and decide our next steps."

Chapter 51

Watson made sure he arrived back in the incident room well before the half an hour was up. There was no way he was going to be late and risk recreating the tense atmosphere that had existed earlier.

He figured Lucy and Rachel must have had the same idea, as when he entered the room, he found that both were already there, albeit sat a fair distance apart. He took his seat next to Lucy.

"Are you OK?" Watson quietly asked Lucy.

Lucy smiled and nodded. "I'm fine," she replied.

Carmichael suddenly came through the door and immediately started talking.

"Let's go through our suspects first," he suggested, pointing at the names on the whiteboard.

His three officers duly looked up at the seven names they'd listed previously.

Suspects:

1. Pierce Armitage
2. Heather Jones
3. Cassie Wilson
4. Trevor Baybutt
5. Simon Baybutt
6. Malcolm Marsden (Fat Malc)
7. Marcus Rigby

"I think Cassie Wilson and Heather Jones are both really long shots," suggested Watson. "We should keep them up there, but I don't think either of them is our killer."

"I'd agree with that," added Rachel.

"I'd add Marcus Rigby to our list of long shots," interjected Lucy. "I met him this morning and having taken those photos of Shelley, he's no angel, but he's actually a nice enough lad and an unlikely murderer in my view."

"Did he tell you anything else?" Carmichael enquired.

"As it happens, he did," replied Lucy. "He was adamant that he never did nor intended to do anything with the photos other than look at them himself. He argues that Shelley was willing for him to take them and as far as he was concerned, they were his property, even after he and Shelley split up."

"An interesting argument," observed Rachel sarcastically.

"I know," continued Lucy, "but in fairness there's absolutely no evidence he did or intended to do anything with them."

"So, what happened with him and Wall?" Carmichael asked.

"That's where it gets interesting," Lucy remarked. "According to Marcus, Wall approached him and threatened to tell Trevor about the photos if he didn't hand them over to Wall. At the time, Marcus was working at Baybutt's and was terrified that if Trevor or Simon knew, they'd get Fat Malc to work him over."

"So, he gave them to Wall," interjected Rachel.

"Yes," continued Lucy, "but that's not all. Wall also said that he wanted Marcus to do something else for him before he was off the hook."

"What was that?" Carmichael asked.

Lucy smiled. "This is the exciting part," she added. "Wall said that to wipe the slate clean, he wanted Marcus to let him into the office one Sunday when there was nobody about. Wall knew that Marcus had a set of keys."

"And did he?" Carmichael asked.

Lucy nodded. "Yes, according to Marcus, he let Wall in and allowed him to snoop in both Trevor's and Simon's offices. Marcus also said Wall photocopied something from Trevor's office although he maintains he doesn't know what."

"The ledger," remarked Carmichael. "So, that's where he got it from."

After a slight pause, Carmichael continued. "Anything else from Marcus?" he asked.

Lucy shook her head.

"What about his movements on Friday evening and Monday night?" Carmichael enquired.

"He says that on Friday evening he was out with mates in town until about two in the morning," Lucy replied. "And on Monday he was at home alone all evening until midnight when his mum came back from bingo, which his mum confirmed before I left."

Carmichael nodded. "You'll need to get someone to check his alibi for Friday evening," he said, "but I'm happy to treat him like Heather Jones and Cassie Wilson, as possible but long shots."

"What about Armitage?" Lucy asked. "Is he still our prime suspect?"

Carmichael shook his head. "He's definitely involved in something and might well be our killer," he replied. "But we've nothing we can pin on him. Although I can't say I like him, I'm not convinced he's our murderer."

"What about Rene Rothwell and Faye Hemmingway?" Rachel asked. "They both inherit the business so maybe they were involved."

"It can't be Faye," Watson replied. "We know she went to The Lamb on Friday evening, we have it on CCTV. And I'm sure she knew nothing about her legacy."

"I'd rule Rene Rothwell out, too," added Carmichael.

"She didn't know about Wall's will either and to be frank, at her age I suspect being part owner of the business will be more of a hassle than anything else. No, as far as I'm concerned, she's not in the frame."

"Which just leaves the three gentlemen from Baybutt and Sons," Watson stated.

"Exactly," replied Carmichael.

"Well, Trevor's wife has confirmed his alibi," Rachel remarked, "and Shelley backed up Simon's story, but I haven't spoken yet to Fat Malc."

Carmichael thought for a few seconds.

"Maybe it's time we brought them all in and gave them a bit of a grilling," he suggested, "and if Mary Price does turn out to be the Mary that works at Baybutts, we could bring her in as well."

"Sounds like a plan," said Watson. "When should we do that?"

Carmichael smiled. "I think now is as good a time as any," he replied. "You and Lucy get over to the greyhound stadium and bring in Fat Malc and Mary. Take a few uniformed guys with you in case he cuts up rough."

"Will do, sir," replied Watson as Lucy nodded her support.

"That leaves you and me, Rachel, to bring in the brothers Baybutt," added Carmichael with a wide grin. "I suspect they'll not put up a fight, but we should also take a couple of uniformed guys, just in case."

Rachel smiled back at the boss. "Sounds good to me," she replied.

Chapter 52

As soon as Faye Hemmingway had been told by Watson about her legacy from the will, she sprang into action.

By ten o'clock she was at the office busily moving her stuff from the reception area into Tim Wall's office, placing all his personal stuff in two sturdy cardboard boxes she'd bought from the post office on her way in, which she left in the far corner of the room.

Once she'd finished installing herself in her new office, Faye made a list of people she needed to call then leaned back on what was now her high-backed leather chair. With her hands clasped behind her head, the new empress of all she surveyed smiled broadly.

* * *

"How are you feeling now?" Watson asked Lucy as the two of them headed over to White City greyhound stadium in Lucy's car. "If it's any consolation, I didn't know what a turf accountant was, and I bet Rachel didn't either."

Lucy forced a smile. "I'm fine, Marc," she replied, "just annoyed with myself for not checking."

Watson laughed. "Don't let it get to you," he remarked glibly. "He just loves it when he's right and you're wrong, but in fairness to Carmichael, he doesn't usually dwell on stuff like that. He'll have forgotten about it in a few hours."

Lucy's sceptical glance over at Watson suggested she didn't agree.

"I think the thing that annoys me most is that I just cannot see our killer being in any way linked with that damn red book," she continued. "We all know it will be someone from Baybutt's or more likely either Armitage, Faye Hemmingway or Cassie Wilson. Why Carmichael's so obsessed with that book is beyond me."

Watson nodded gently. "And I guess what makes it even more irritating for you is that it's you he's asked to plough through it rather than…"

Watson paused for a few seconds before continuing… "well, Rachel."

Lucy took a deep intake of air through her nose and put her foot down harder on the accelerator.

"It's got nothing to do with Rachel," she announced firmly. "Anyway, we've not established that this Mary at Baybutt's is Harriet Stockley's sister."

Watson raised his eyebrows. "Don't hold your breath on that, Lucy. I think we both know she will be," he replied.

* * *

The journey from Kirkwood Police Station to Baybutt and Sons was less than two miles, so no more than five minutes in the car. However, it was the first time Carmichael had been alone with Rachel since she'd arrived back from Newcastle and he was keen to find out how things had been between her and Lucy.

"How are you getting on with Sergeant Martin?" he asked as they headed out of the police station car park.

"Yes, OK," replied Rachel, who didn't want to say

anything that was either untrue or that she might regret in future.

"She's a capable officer," continued Carmichael.

"So I believe," replied Rachel, deliberately keeping her answers short.

"I'm pleased you're getting on fine with her," Carmichael added. "It's always better when there isn't any friction within the team."

Rachel nodded. "I fully agree with you there, sir," she replied.

"But if there are issues," Carmichael continued, "I'd hope you'd talk with me before they got out of hand."

"Thanks, sir," replied Rachel, "I will."

Rachel's unwillingness to be forthcoming about Lucy merely confirmed Carmichael's worst fears. It was clear she wasn't going to open up and tell him how she really felt, so he reluctantly decided to change the subject.

"When we arrive let's keep the brothers apart," he announced. "It'll help us when we're questioning them if they haven't had time to discuss things on the way back to the station."

Rachel nodded. "Understood, sir," she replied, her response sounding more like her normal self, eager and positive.

* * *

Trevor Baybutt was at Shelley's desk, both of them looking at something on her computer screen, when Carmichael, Rachel Dalton and the two uniformed officers walked in.

"What do you guys want now?" Trevor said, his voice slightly raised and full of frustration.

"We need to take you and Simon down to the station," Carmichael replied. "Is he in his office?"

Trevor stood up straight. "He's out," he replied.

Carmichael moved his head slightly towards Simon Baybutt's office door, to indicate to the two uniformed officers that he wanted them to check.

"If you don't believe me by all means take a look yourselves," Trevor remarked sarcastically.

The two policemen entered the office, then within a few seconds emerged back through the open door: the first one shaking his head.

"It will just have to be you that accompanies us," Carmichael said, his eyes firmly on Trevor.

Baybutt puffed out his cheeks. "This is police harassment," he remarked loudly.

The two uniformed officers walked over and stood next to Trevor, who despite being a well-built man, was at least six inches smaller and over twenty years older than the two burley policemen.

"Contact your dad and tell him what's going on," Trevor told Shelley. "And get on the phone to that expensive solicitor of ours and get him to come over to the police station."

Shelley, who looked terrified by what was going on in front of her, nodded.

"And when you do talk with your dad," interjected Carmichael, "tell him we want him to come down to the station as well, as we've a few questions we want to ask him."

"Call Fat Malc, too," added Trevor as he was ushered towards the door.

Shelley remained motionless and silent as the four police officers exited the office, her uncle in tow.

* * *

Midweek greyhound races ended at two-fifteen at White City, so when Lucy, Watson and the two uniformed officers arrived at the stadium, the crowds were already filing out.

Being a small track with only five bookmakers' pitches, it took them no time at all to locate Fat Malc, who was on his mobile and had virtually finished taking down his small stand.

"Malcolm Marsden?" Lucy enquired.

Fat Malc stood up straight, looked Lucy up and down, then turned his head away from them.

"Yes, they're here now," Fat Malc whispered down the phone. "I'll have to go."

"Malcolm Marsden," Lucy said again, this time holding her identity card up so he could see who she was.

"Yes," he replied, "I'm Malcolm Marsden."

"Are you alone?" Watson asked.

Fat Malc frowned and nodded. "Yes," he replied as if it was a stupid question. "Who else were you expecting?"

"I just thought Mary Price might be with you?" Watson asked, deliberately adding Price to see how Fat Malc responded.

Fat Malc shook his head. "Daytime dog racing is just a one-man job," he replied. "It's Mary's day off. You'll probably find her at home or, knowing Mary, on some massive bike ride somewhere."

"It's you we really wanted to talk to," Lucy remarked. "We'd like you to accompany us back to the station."

"Are you arresting me?" Fat Malc replied, aggressively.

Lucy shook her head. "We hadn't planned on it," she remarked, "but if you don't come voluntarily, we can."

Despite being a big bloke, Fat Malc didn't put up a struggle. Having the bookmaker's stand and the morning's takings to carry, and with it being four against one, he decided to go quietly.

Chapter 53

Faye Hemmingway's busy morning continued. Having spoken first to Agnes Poulter to advise her that from now on the search for her missing daughter would be chargeable, she then spoke with Rene Rothwell, a call that lasted for over thirty minutes. Her third call was to Sara-Jane Turnbull at HMRC Newcastle; another lengthy conversation, during which Faye reassured the agency's best customer that the attention Ms Turnbull would receive from her would be as great, if not greater, than she'd experienced when Tim was in charge; a claim which Sara-Jane knew was impossible for Faye to deliver upon in full.

Having made these three calls, Faye then tried Richard's mobile again. She'd already left him two messages, but as yet he'd not responded. This time, however, he picked up.

"Hi babe," Faye said, her voice shrill and relieved to have got through. "Did you get my other messages?"

"Sorry, no," replied Richard, who sounded frazzled. "I've been snowed under this morning. I've had three viewings to go to and have done two valuations. I've not had a minute."

"Well, there's some good news," continued Faye excitedly, her words coming out in rapid fire. "Tim's left me half the business in his will. I've just spoken to his previous assistant, Rene, who inherits the other half, and she says she doesn't want to be involved in the day-to-day work here, so you're talking to the new MD. Isn't that brilliant news?"

With Trevor Baybutt safely installed in interview room 1 waiting for his brief, Carmichael and Rachel headed back up to the incident room.

"Do you still want me to carry on digging into Jennifer Braithwaite's background?" Rachel asked.

Carmichael paused for a few seconds. "Yes," he replied. "I'd also like you to try and locate Simon Baybutt and, once you find him, get him to come into the station."

"Will do," replied Rachel.

"But when Trevor's brief arrives, I want you in there with me when I talk to him," added Carmichael.

Rachel smiled and headed over to her desk. She loved it when she worked closely with Carmichael, as although he could be demanding at times, occasionally moody and often extremely hard to please, he was the best inspector by far at Kirkwood, and as good a mentor as she could hope to have.

** ** **

It was a further ten minutes before Lucy and Watson entered the incident room.

"We've got Fat Malc downstairs," Watson remarked, "but Mary Price wasn't at the track today."

"You're sure she's Harriet's sister then, are you?" Carmichael asked, slightly smug that his assumption appeared to be proven right.

Lucy nodded. "Yes," she replied. "Fat Malc confirmed it earlier."

Carmichael thought for a few seconds.

"I need one of you to interview Fat Malc with me and the other one to locate Mary and talk with her about her sister and Wall," he said.

Neither Lucy nor Watson replied.

"I also want to know why she told me she didn't know Wall," continued Carmichael. "If her sister dated him twice, I'm sure Mary would have recognised Wall when he was placing bets at her pitch every Monday evening. I want to know why she didn't admit that to us."

For a couple of seconds there was silence.

"I'm happy to do that, if you'd like," volunteered Watson.

"OK, Marc," Carmichael replied. "Track her down and get as much as you can out of her."

Lucy and Watson made brief eye contact, during which Lucy mouthed 'thank you', which Watson responded to with a faint smile.

Carmichael then turned his attention towards Rachel, who was studiously looking at her computer screen.

"Did you locate Simon Baybutt?" he enquired.

Rachel shook her head. "It's the next thing on my list," she replied.

Carmichael nodded slowly before looking back over at Watson.

"We also only picked up one of our suspects, Marc," he confessed. "Simon Baybutt was out somewhere. So, in addition to your search for Mary, can you locate Simon as well and get him to come in here, please?"

Rachel couldn't help smiling. It wasn't often Carmichael took a task away from her and offloaded it to Watson. And she knew he'd now be regretting being so chivalrous and volunteering in such an uncharacteristic fashion.

"How do you want to play these interviews?" Lucy asked.

"I'll lead both," replied Carmichael. "With you for Fat Malc and with you, Rachel, for Trevor Baybutt. I think it's important we all know what each of them is saying, so whichever of you isn't in the interview needs to watch and listen to what's being said, through the one-way glass."

By the way the two officers nodded positively, it was clear they were happy with Carmichael's plan.

"Has Fat Malc asked for a brief?" Carmichael enquired.

Lucy shook her head. "No," she replied.

"Great," continued Carmichael, "we can start with him."

Chapter 54

Carmichael and Lucy sat inches apart from each other facing Fat Malc; the closest they'd been since their trip to Winston Salem several years earlier.

"Mr Marsden," Carmichael said calmly, "the first thing I need to do is to ask you where you were last Friday evening between five and ten o'clock."

Fat Malc leaned back in his chair, folded his arms and looked up towards the ceiling. As he did, his sleeve moved up his arm to reveal a nasty-looking long gash, which looked recent.

"How did you do that?" Lucy enquired, nodding towards the wound.

"Oh, it was a scratch I got working on my car over the weekend," Fat Malc replied.

Lucy looked across at Carmichael to make sure he'd also recognised its significance.

Carmichael nodded gently so Lucy was aware he understood.

"It looks a bad one," Carmichael added. "Did you need stitches?"

Fat Malc frowned, shook his head, unfolded his arms and pulled down his shirt so the injury was covered again.

"No need," he remarked. "It looks worse than it is."

Carmichael smiled. "Anyway, where were you on Friday evening?" he asked again.

"I was playing poker with some mates," Fat Malc replied. "Just a fun game you understand, no gambling involved."

Carmichael sniggered. "Heaven forbid," he replied sarcastically.

"And where was this game?" Lucy added.

"At my house," replied Fat Malc.

"And who was there with you?" Carmichael asked.

"Just three mates," responded Fat Malc again, trying his best not to say too much.

"And do these mates have names?" Lucy asked.

Fat Malc screwed up his face. "Why do you want to know?" he enquired.

"Because, Mr Marsden," replied Carmichael, "on Friday evening Timothy Wall, a man you told me you didn't know, was murdered. And, if you want to know the truth, I don't believe you didn't know him. What's more, I'm also very suspicious about this card game you claim was taking place when he was killed."

"Well, that's your problem," responded Fat Malc. "If you think I've done something wrong then charge me."

Carmichael smiled. "That's a distinct possibility, Mr Marsden," he replied calmly.

The two men eyed each other across the table before Carmichael spoke again.

"What about on Monday evening after the races?"

"What about it?" Fat Malc replied curtly.

"What did you do?" Carmichael continued.

Fat Malc shrugged his shoulders. "I dropped Mary off home and then went straight to my house and went to bed."

"For the benefit of the tape that's Mary Price you're talking about," Carmichael added.

"Yes," responded Fat Malc, his answer spat out with as much frustration as one short word could possibly muster.

"What time would that be?" Lucy enquired.

"No idea," replied Fat Malc.

"Eight, nine, ten, eleven," continued Lucy. "You must have a rough idea what time you got home."

Fat Malc shrugged his shoulders again. "I don't know, about ten or maybe ten-thirty," he replied.

"You haven't asked us why we want to know," remarked Carmichael.

Fat Malc shrugged his shoulders for a third time. "Am I supposed to be bothered?" he replied brazenly.

"Well, let me tell you," Carmichael continued. "On Monday evening someone broke into Timothy Wall's house. They were looking for something and made a real mess. We think the person who did that is also likely to be the person who murdered Wall on Friday. And do you know what, I think that person was you."

Fat Malc laughed. "That's nonsense and you know it," he shouted.

"There's one easy way we can prove it," Carmichael added. "We can take a DNA sample from you. From that we'll know whether we're right to make you our prime suspect. Are you happy to do a test?"

For the first time during the interview, Fat Malc looked rattled. He rubbed his hand over his lips then shuffled nervously in his seat.

"Why do you need my DNA?" he asked.

Carmichael smiled. "Because whoever broke into Timothy Wall's house carelessly left some blood on a broken pane of glass in the kitchen door. They cut themselves —"

"In a similar way to how you've cut yourself, Mr Marsden," interjected Lucy.

Fat Malc pushed himself back into his chair.

"I think I'd like a solicitor," he remarked.

Carmichael and Lucy exchanged a brief look of satisfaction before turning their heads back to face Fat Malc.

"No problem at all," Carmichael replied. "We'll get that sorted right away."

"Interview suspended at three twenty-two," Lucy said for the benefit of the recording, before she and Carmichael rose and left the room to join Rachel behind the one-way mirror in the room next door.

Chapter 55

"He's rattled," remarked Rachel as Carmichael and Lucy entered the viewing area.

"He's more than rattled," replied Carmichael, looking through the glass at a sweating Fat Malc as he fidgeted in his chair. "I'm confident he's our man for the break-in."

"I agree," added Lucy eagerly. "I was convinced he was as soon as I saw that cut on his arm."

"I'm not so sure about him being Wall's murderer, though," Carmichael added. "But let's focus our attention on the break-in for now and see where that takes us."

"What if he doesn't agree to a DNA test?" Rachel enquired.

"Then we charge him, and we can take his DNA without his permission," replied Carmichael with a broad grin.

"So, he's stuffed either way," added Lucy with a wry smile.

* * *

Watson fully expected Simon Baybutt's mobile to ring a few times and then get diverted to his voicemail; so, it was a pleasant surprise to him when he was connected after just two rings.

"Simon Baybutt," the bookmaker said in a cheerful tone.

"Good afternoon, Mr Baybutt," began Watson. "I'm from Mid-Lancashire police. Inspector Carmichael has asked me to call you. He wants you to come down to the station."

"When?" Baybutt asked.

"Now please, sir," replied Watson.

"What for?" enquired Baybutt, whose mood was now anything but jovial.

Watson didn't want to go into too much detail on the phone but equally wanted to make sure Simon Baybutt knew it was important.

"Your brother and Malcolm Marsden are already here helping us with our enquiries," Watson advised him, "and we'd like you here, too."

Despite a few attempts, Shelley hadn't managed to get through to her dad, as Trevor had asked her to, so the news of his brother and Fat Malc being at the police station came as a big shock to Simon.

"I'll be forty minutes," announced Baybutt before ending the call abruptly and placing his mobile on the pristine white passenger seat of his gleaming white Tesla Model S.

* * *

Carmichael and his two female officers were still in the viewing area when Trevor Baybutt's lawyer entered interview room 1.

"I might have guessed," Carmichael said as he saw it was the familiar figure of Arthur Brewster, a solicitor well known to him. "He's got to be guilty if he employs that man as his brief."

Lucy smiled. "I'll go and organise some legal representation for Fat Malc," she said as she headed for the door.

"How long do we give them together?" Rachel asked as she and Carmichael watched Trevor Baybutt and Brewster shake hands and start their meeting.

"As long as they like," replied Carmichael flippantly. "He's got a lot of explaining to do, as Fat Malc wouldn't have carried out the break-in unless either Trevor or Simon Baybutt told him to. Anyway, I want to interview Fat Malc a bit more before we start with him."

Rachel nodded before she and her boss vacated the viewing area and headed back up to the incident room.

* * *

Watson was just about to head off when Carmichael and Rachel arrived.

"I've spoken with Simon Baybutt," he said, "and if he's true to his word, he should be here in about thirty minutes."

"What about Mary Price?" Carmichael enquired.

"I'm on my way there now," replied Watson. "She lives in Cranley Gardens, that new housing estate just around the corner, so hopefully I won't be long."

Carmichael looked at his watch. "Actually, I'll join you," he said. "It will be at least an hour before Fat Malc's brief gets here and they have a chance to chat, so I think I've plenty of time."

"What do you want Lucy and I to do?" Rachel asked as Carmichael headed towards the door.

"You sort Simon Baybutt when he arrives," replied Carmichael. "Put him in interview room 3 and if he wants a brief sort that out for him, although I'd expect he'll be using Arthur Brewster, like his brother."

"What about Lucy?" Rachel asked.

"Tell her I want her to keep working through that red book," Carmichael replied as he disappeared out the door.

"Thanks a million for that, boss," muttered Rachel, knowing full well that Lucy wasn't going to be best pleased when she heard what Carmichael wanted her to do; and she'd be even more annoyed to be given the message by a lowly DC.

Chapter 56

Cranley Gardens Estate, where Mary Price lived, was still referred to as the new estate by the locals in the area, even though it had been built for well over ten years.

It was made up of about 150 small houses, which were predominantly built in or around a series of compact cul-de-sacs, uninspiringly named after British trees and shrubs. The address Watson had for Mary was 6, The Oaks.

After abandoning their car on the tiny turning circle, half on the road and half on the pavement, Carmichael and Watson strode up the narrow drive to Mary Price's front door.

However, before they'd had a chance to ring the bell, Mary appeared from behind them on an expensive-looking bicycle, clad from head to toe in gaudy yellow and green Lycra and sporting a distinctive red helmet with a small black camera fitted on the top, facing forward.

"Can I help you?" she asked before realising that one of her visitors was the police inspector that had been at Mount Rush Park on Monday evening.

"Hello again," replied Carmichael. "May we have a few minutes of your time?"

* * *

Still parked in his white car Simon restlessly looked at his wristwatch, which merely indicated that only two minutes had lapsed since the last time he'd checked.

Suddenly, the passenger door opened, and Cassie Wilson climbed in.

"Did you get it sorted?" Simon asked.

"Oh, yes," replied Cassie with a wry smile, "it's sorted."

Simon started up his engine, checked over his left shoulder for traffic, then swung the car out across the road and headed off down the high street.

"I'm going to have to get back here after I've dropped you off at home," he remarked as the car picked up speed.

"Why's that?" Cassie asked, her expression one of disappointment.

"I've been summoned to the police station," Simon replied. "It would appear that Trevor and Fat Malc have been taken down there and they want me, too."

"Is this still about Tim?" Cassie asked.

"I'd expect so," replied Simon. "God knows why they want me."

Cassie ran her hand through her blonde hair. "You were telling me the truth when you said you weren't involved in Tim's death, weren't you?" she enquired.

Simon looked across at her. "I was with you when he was killed," he replied.

"Not until eight o'clock," remarked Cassie. "He could have been killed already by then."

Simon laughed. "Well, thanks for the vote of confidence, Cassie," he said. "At least I'm an improvement on your last boyfriend. I don't have a pervy scrapbook where I score your performance out of ten."

Cassie bitterly regretted ever telling Simon about Tim's red book. From the moment the words had sprung from her lips, two months earlier, she knew it was a mistake. The expression on his face when she'd told him and the constant references to Tim's red book had started to become more than a little tiresome for her.

"I wish you'd just shut up about that bloody book," she snapped back at him.

As she spoke, Simon noticed graze marks and some traces of blood on the knuckles of Cassie's right hand.

"What's that?" he asked.

Cassie ran the palm of her left hand over the scuffed fingers.

"Oh, nothing," she said dismissively. "I caught my hand on a metal cabinet when I was with Faye."

"I believe you," Simon said, "and you need to believe me when I tell you that I didn't have anything to do with Tim Wall's death."

Cassie's face remained stern. "But what about your brother and that maniac Malcolm?" she asked.

Simon frowned and shook his head before turning his face forward and concentrating fully on the road ahead.

"He says not," Simon remarked, "but I can't deny that what Trevor says and what Trevor does, don't always marry up."

Chapter 57

"You're kidding me," Lucy said despairingly. "What the hell is it with him and that damn book."

Rachel shrugged her shoulders. "I'm just telling you what he told me," she replied.

"And what task has he assigned to you?" enquired Lucy, her slightly raised voice suggesting she expected it to be far more interesting.

"He just told me to sort out Simon Baybutt into interview room three when he arrives and, if he asks, to get him some legal representation," Rachel replied.

By the disparaging look on Lucy's face, Rachel could see she wasn't happy.

"Why don't we swap?" suggested Rachel. "I'll go through Wall's red book and you sort out Simon Baybutt when he arrives."

Lucy took a second to consider Rachel's proposal before replying.

"Sounds good to me," she remarked with a wry smile. "A fresh pair of eyes might be what it needs. Thanks Rachel."

Rachel smiled back and picked up Wall's red book. "Where have you got up to?" she asked.

* * *

If Carmichael had been invited to describe in detail someone who was least likely to be a keen cyclist, he'd have selected Mary Price. With short legs and a pear-shaped physique, she was hardly Laura Kenny, but Mary was living proof that appearances can be deceiving, as although she clearly didn't look the part, she was in fact a fanatical and formidable cyclist. As a long-standing member of the Kirkwood Dynamo, Mary would regularly cycle over fifty miles at a time, and on occasions, if the weather was good, over one hundred miles in a day.

Still clad in her Lycra cycling gear, Mary sat facing Carmichael and Watson, whom she'd ushered through into her tiny lounge.

"So, how can I help you?" she enquired.

Carmichael leaned forward and looked directly into Mary's eyes.

"I am aware that on Monday, when I asked if you knew Timothy Wall, you weren't honest with me," he said. "We know that he did go most Monday evenings to Baybutt's pitch at Mount Rush Park. I also happen to know that he had been known to you for around thirty years, having dated your sister on not one but two occasions; when she was single and then again after her marriage to Justin Stockley."

It was clear from her body language and her inability to maintain eye contact with either Carmichael or Watson, that Mary was feeling uncomfortable.

"I did know Tim Wall," she said in a quiet voice. "He did go out with Harriet, and he had started to come to the pitch on Monday evenings."

Carmichael maintained his serious face, but deliberately kept his voice calm and relaxed.

"Why don't you tell us about his relationship with Harriet," he suggested.

Mary looked up into Carmichael's eyes.

"It was so long ago," she replied, "I don't remember too much. Harriet was ten years older than me, so I was just a kid at primary school when Harriet and Tim were going out together."

"And did she like him?" Carmichael asked.

"Oh, yes," replied Mary. "Mum and Dad as well as Harri."

"And you?" interjected Watson. "Did you like Tim?"

Mary nodded. "I adored him," she replied without hesitation. "He was like a big brother to me."

"So why did they split up?" Carmichael asked.

"I don't know," Mary answered. "He just stopped calling. I guess it must have run its course."

"But your sister did start seeing him again," continued Carmichael, "about six years later when she was married to Justin Stockley."

"I don't know anything about that," Mary replied. "If she did, then she didn't make it common knowledge. But if she was seeing him, she'd have been careful not to let Badger find out, as he could be quite nasty when he wanted to be."

"What do you mean by nasty?" Watson asked. "Was he violent?"

Mary considered the question carefully before shaking her head. "No," she replied, "I don't think he ever hit Harri, but he could be very moody and heartless, when he wanted to be."

"And I understand your brother-in-law and Tim didn't get on," Carmichael added. "Why was that?"

Mary shook her head. "I think they were mates at one time," she replied. "They both played rugby and cricket together for the local team here."

"But that friendship turned sour," Carmichael stated. "Why was that?"

"I don't know the details," Mary replied, "but I'd imagine it was to do with Harri, or maybe another girl. They were both fond of the ladies, so I'm sure there will have been some rivalry, but I honestly don't know."

Carmichael nodded, as if to indicate he wasn't going to probe her anymore about the acrimony between Badger and Wall.

"It must have been a terrible shock when they were both killed so tragically?" he suggested.

Mary nodded. "It was awful," she said in a hushed voice. "It broke my mum and dad's hearts. They both passed away within two years of Harri dying. I've always felt that it was because they were so broken-hearted."

"Did Harriet and Justin have any children?" Carmichael asked.

Again, Mary shook her head. "I know they tried," she replied, "but they found out they weren't able to have kids, which was a massive disappointment to them both. To my mum and dad, too."

"I can imagine," Carmichael remarked sympathetically.

"In the years after Harriet dated Tim, did you see much of him?" Watson enquired.

"Not really," Mary replied. "I occasionally saw him about town, always with a new girl; but not to talk to. In fact, I'm convinced he didn't recognise me when he came onto the pitch at Mount Rush Park. Well, if he did, he never let on that he knew who I was."

"Tell me about those visits?" Carmichael asked. "When roughly did they start?"

Mary thought for a few seconds.

"About two or three months ago," she replied. "When the evening races started."

"But before that he hadn't been to the pitch?" Carmichael enquired.

Mary gently shook her head. "No," she replied.

"And what sort of bets did he place?" Carmichael asked.

Mary looked uneasy. "I didn't get involved," she replied offhandedly. "Fat Malc handles all the bets, I just key them into the computer."

"But surely, you know what sort of bets he made and how successful he was?" Carmichael remarked.

Mary shrugged her shoulders. "I think he won mostly," she replied. "But you'd have to ask Fat Malc about the details."

Carmichael was sure Mary knew more than she was saying, but decided they'd probably got about as much from her as they were going to get.

"You've been really helpful," he said with a smile. "Call me though if you remember anything more. Do you still have my card that I gave you on Monday?"

Mary seemed thankful it was over.

"I have," she said with a relieved, nervous-looking smile on her face.

* * *

As they clambered into Carmichael's car, Watson looked back at Mary Price's house. Behind the curtain he could see she was watching them intently; well, she was until she saw him look back at her, at which point her head vanished behind the curtain.

"What did you make of that, sir?" he enquired.

Carmichael raised an eyebrow.

"I reckon there's much more she could have told us about her sister and about Wall's Monday evening visits to Baybutt's pitch," he said. "But we got enough from her to be able to ask Fat Malc and the Baybutt brothers some really awkward questions. She knows more, for sure, but she's not our killer and I'm confident she didn't break into Wall's house, so let's concentrate our efforts on Fat Malc and the two main men at Baybutt's."

As his car disappeared down the road, Mary Price fiddled with Carmichael's business card, which she'd taken from her coat pocket. She felt guilty about not being as forthcoming with them as she ought to have been, but her sense of loyalty had got the better of her.

Chapter 58

Richard Cox strode confidently down the high street with a broad smile on his face.

"Afternoon," he said sociably to a young couple who were looking through the window of Jessop's, the jewellers.

"Afternoon," they replied, before turning their gaze once again towards the sparkling rings and expensive watches.

Bounding up the stairs, two at a time, Richard discovered the office door slightly ajar.

The young couple hadn't moved from their position at Jessop's window when no more than a minute after they had been greeted by Richard so warmly, they heard his loud unnerving cry emanating from the detective agency on the first floor next door. This was quickly followed by the sound of someone flying down the stairs and then the distraught figure of Richard Cox running out onto the high street.

His face pale and with sweat pouring from his forehead, Cox started dialling 999 and shouting, "Help me. Please help me," at the top of his voice.

Within seconds he was through to the emergency services and the young couple and a small crowd of onlookers had gathered around him.

"Police and ambulance," he shouted down the phone. "My girlfriend's been attacked. I think she's dead."

* * *

It took just a matter of minutes for Carmichael and Watson to arrive back at Kirkwood Police Station.

"Right," Carmichael said, "let's see if Fat Malc's going to be a bit more cooperative."

As he and Watson clambered out, a white car sped past them and pulled into a parking space between them and the station entrance.

"Isn't that the car we saw outside Cassie Wilson's house the other night?" Watson remarked.

Carmichael nodded. "Could be," he replied. "There can't be too many Tesla model S cars around here."

As they reached the white Tesla, Simon Baybutt climbed out and started walking towards the station entrance.

Carmichael couldn't be sure the person in front of them was Simon Baybutt, having only spoken to him on the phone, but there was a distinct family resemblance between the man, and Trevor and Shelley Baybutt.

"Simon Baybutt," Carmichael shouted.

The man stopped and turned. "Yes, I'm Simon Baybutt," he replied.

Carmichael smiled and walked up within a few feet of the now stationary bookmaker.

"Thanks for coming in," Carmichael remarked with a smile and his right hand outstretched. "I'm Inspector Carmichael and this is my colleague, Sergeant Watson."

"I hope this isn't going to take too long," replied Baybutt, as he gingerly shook Carmichael's hand. "I had plans for this afternoon."

"It shouldn't take long at all," Carmichael assured him with a confident smile. "Sergeant Watson will sort us out with a room, and I'll be with you shortly."

As he spoke, Carmichael glanced across at Watson.

"Interview room three, please, Marc," he said, before smiling again at Simon Baybutt and ushering him towards the door with a theatrical wave of his right arm.

* * *

Carmichael was still in reception when Lucy and Rachel burst through the double doors.

"There's been another incident at Wall's office," announced Lucy breathlessly.

"What?" replied Carmichael.

"It sounds like someone has attacked Faye Hemmingway," she continued.

"We'll take my car," Carmichael said. "You can fill me in on the way."

As the three officers dashed across the car park, Carmichael suddenly remembered about Watson.

"Call Marc," he instructed Rachel. "Let him know where we're going and tell him to make sure neither Fat Malc nor either of the Baybutt brothers leave until I'm back."

"Will do, sir," replied Rachel, who clambered into the back of Carmichael's black BMW, leaving the front passenger seat vacant for Lucy.

Chapter 59

When Carmichael, Lucy and Rachel arrived at Wall's Detective Agency, there were already two police cars at the scene and an ambulance.

The uniformed guys had cordoned off the area around the entrance and one officer had posted himself by the door.

Recognising Carmichael and his team, the officer at the door lifted the cordon to allow them to duck under and head up the stairs.

As they reached the top of the stairs, they saw Richard Cox looking as white as a sheet and sitting silently, a female uniformed officer crouching by him, her hand on his arm.

Carmichael didn't linger to talk or even acknowledge Cox or the PC; he headed straight into Wall's office, where another uniformed officer was stationed.

"How is she?" he asked the ambulance crew who were bending over the lifeless-looking figure of Faye Hemmingway on the office floor, an oxygen mask over her nose and mouth.

One of the ambulance crew looked up at him.

"Not good," she replied. "She's alive, but only just."

As she finished speaking, her colleague shouted, "She's stopped breathing," and started performing CPR.

Carmichael signalled to Lucy and Rachel that they should leave the office, which both officers did without hesitation.

Once back in the reception area, Carmichael took them to one side with their backs to Richard Cox.

"Go downstairs and get statements from anyone that saw anything," he instructed. "And while you're both doing that I'll talk with the boyfriend."

Carmichael waited for Lucy and Rachel to vacate the room before he walked slowly over to Richard Cox.

"Can you tell me what happened?" he asked.

Richard Cox remained motionless and maintained his eerily zombie-like stare at the floor by Carmichael's feet.

"I don't know," he mumbled. "She was just like that when I arrived."

"How long ago was that?" Carmichael enquired.

"I'm not sure," Cox replied. "Twenty minutes ago, maybe a bit less."

Carmichael could see that Faye's boyfriend was still in shock, so decided not to prolong the conversation for now.

"Will she live?" Cox enquired, his head turning up to look at Carmichael.

"I don't know," Carmichael replied sensitively, "but I'm sure the medical team are doing all they can."

As he finished talking, Rachel appeared at the door.

"Can I have a word, sir?" she enquired.

Carmichael smiled down at Richard Cox and walked over to where Rachel was standing.

"We've got a couple of interesting statements that I think you need to hear," she said.

"What have you got?" Carmichael asked.

"Lucy talked with a couple who said they saw Richard Cox go into the office then a minute later, come out saying that his girlfriend had been attacked," Rachel said, her voice hushed so as not to be heard by Cox. "I've also spoken to a couple who have been in Maria's Café across the road. They reckon that before they went into the coffee shop, they saw a blonde woman, slightly built, aged late thirties or maybe forty, come out of Wall's doorway and climb into a very smart-looking, white sporty car, driven by a man in his fifties."

"When was that?" Carmichael asked.

"She says it was about forty minutes before Richard came out shouting about the attack," replied Rachel.

"Did anyone see anybody else enter or leave the office?" Carmichael asked.

"The couple in the café didn't," replied Rachel, "but they say they weren't seated near the window, so they didn't have a view of the office entrance while they were having their coffees."

Carmichael nodded. "I think I know who the couple in the white car might have been."

Rachel looked over at Richard Cox. "Was he able to tell you anything?" she asked.

Carmichael shook his head. "He's still in shock," he replied. "We'll have to interview him properly later."

* * *

PC Dyer appeared from behind the incident room door. "Just to let you know, the Baybutts' solicitor is asking when you plan to start interviewing his clients."

Watson looked up from his computer screen and shrugged his shoulders.

"Tell him he'll have to wait until we're ready," he replied.

PC Dyer smiled. "Will do," he said.

"What about Malcolm Marsden?" continued Watson. "Is his solicitor here?"

PC Dyer nodded. "Yes," he replied. "They still seem to be in deep discussions, but he's here. It's Mr Fairfax."

Watson nodded. "He doesn't get Brewster like the Baybutt brothers," he remarked. "Obviously, the staff don't get the same quality brief as the bosses."

* * *

After twenty minutes of constant attention from the ambulance crew and a paramedic who turned up a few minutes after Carmichael had arrived, the medical team felt able to move Faye Hemmingway down the stairs and into the ambulance.

Richard Cox, who seemed to have regained some of his colour and appeared to be more able to cope with the trauma he'd witnessed, hovered by the ambulance door.

"Can I go with her?" he asked one of the ambulance staff.

"Is it OK if he comes with us?" she in turn asked Carmichael.

Carmichael still hadn't got a proper statement from Richard but wasn't about to stop him from going with Faye to the hospital, given how serious her injuries looked.

"Yes, Richard, you can go," he replied, "but I need you to give us a statement, so I'll be sending one of my officers with you."

As he finished speaking, he looked across at Rachel who nodded. "I'll go with them," she said.

Carmichael handed Rachel his car keys. "You and Richard go in my car," he said. "They won't want two people in the back of the ambulance with Faye."

"I'll keep you up to speed," said Rachel as she grabbed the keys out of Carmichael's hand.

Carmichael and Lucy watched as the ambulance headed away, followed by Rachel and Richard Cox in Carmichael's car.

"So, what's the plan for us?" Lucy enquired.

"You finish off taking statements," replied Carmichael. "I'm going to have a look around in the office, get a quick update from the SOCO team and then give Marc a call."

"To pick you up?" asked Lucy with a smile.

Carmichael shook his head. "No, I want Marc to pick up Cassie Wilson."

Chapter 60

"We've only got five interview rooms, sir," remarked Watson. "So, once I pick up Cassie Wilson, we'll only have one free, and if she wants a duty solicitor, we may struggle to get one."

Carmichael smiled to himself as Watson's points regarding the congestion he was causing in the interview area at the police station were certainly valid.

"I'm hoping we won't need to arrest anyone else today," Carmichael replied, while at the same time bending down to retrieve the only bit of paper that lay in the wastepaper bin in the room where Faye had been attacked.

"Mind you, I can't promise anything," he then added as he opened the scrunched-up paper and read the three names Faye had scribbled on it.

"I'll get on to it straight away," Watson remarked.

"I'll see you back at the office in about thirty minutes," continued Carmichael as he first smoothed, then laid out the paper onto what had once been Tim Wall's desk and studied the three names Faye had written down.

1. Agnes Poulter
2. Rene Rothwell
3. HMRC – Sara-Jane Turnbull

* * *

Although they followed directly behind the ambulance, by the time Rachel had parked at the hospital, the medical team had already rushed Faye into the critical care unit; an area the nurse in charge wouldn't allow Richard or Rachel to enter.

"Why don't we get a coffee," Rachel suggested to Faye's still extremely anxious boyfriend.

Richard nodded. "Good idea," he replied.

Rachel smiled and placed a comforting hand on Richard's arm.

"You wait here," she said. "I'll fetch them."

Leaving Richard sitting alone on a chair outside the critical care unit, Rachel wandered down the corridor towards a bank of coffee machines about twenty metres away.

* * *

The three scenes of crime officers were still busily looking for evidence when Carmichael left Wall's office to walk the short journey back to Kirkwood Police Station.

Although he was keen to resume his interview with Fat Malc and start to question the Baybutt brothers, there was one fact that Carmichael could be absolutely sure of; neither Fat Malc nor Trevor Baybutt could have attacked Faye Hemmingway as both were inside Kirkwood Police Station when the assault happened.

But as for Simon Baybutt and Cassie Wilson, they were a completely different matter.

* * *

"Here you go," remarked Rachel as she handed Richard the hot, plastic coffee cup. "I didn't put any sugar in it."

Richard took the cup from Rachel's hand and smiled up at her. "Thanks," he replied. "I'm fine without it."

Rachel sat down close to Richard and took a small sip from her cup.

"So, what exactly happened?" she asked.

Richard turned his head to face her.

"I was really busy today," he replied. "Adrian, my boss, wanted me to accompany several people on viewings and I had to do a few valuations, too," he explained. "So, I only got to talk with Faye well after lunch, not that I had a lunch break."

Rachel nodded, encouraging him to keep talking.

"She was really excited," he continued. "She'd been told that Tim had left half the detective agency to her and she was at the office sorting out stuff. She even suggested I quit my job with Mullion and Thorpe and work with her."

"What time did you speak with her?" Rachel asked.

Richard took out his mobile and checked.

"It was twelve minutes past two," he replied, at the same time showing Rachel the screen on his mobile, which had Faye as an incoming call at 14:12.

"And are you tempted to work with her?" Rachel enquired.

Richard nodded. "As it happens, I am," he replied. "Although I'm an estate agent now, I did a criminology degree at Lincoln University, so it does appeal to me. Ironic really, isn't it, that I should end up with a girl who works in a detective agency."

Rachel smiled. "Yes, life can be a bit strange like that."

"Anyway," continued Richard, "I had one more client to see when I spoke with Faye, so I said I'd come over as soon as I'd finished, which I did."

"And what time did you arrive at the agency?" Rachel asked.

"About three-thirty," Richard replied.

"And you found her on the floor?" Rachel added.

"Yes," replied Richard. "I thought she was dead."

"So, what did you do then?" Rachel asked.

"I didn't know what to do," he replied. "I shook her gently, then when there was no response, I just ran out of the office to get help and I also phoned nine nine nine. I hope my panicking hasn't made things worse for her."

Rachel smiled and put a reassuring hand on his arm.

"I'm certain it didn't," she replied. "It sounds like you did exactly the right thing."

Chapter 61

When Carmichael arrived at Kirkwood Police Station, the first thing he did was to ask the front desk whether Watson had arrived back.

"Not as far as I know," replied the desk sergeant, with a slight shake of his head, "but Mr Brewster's been asking when you're going to speak to him and his client. He's walked over here at least three times. He's not happy at all."

Carmichael grinned. He liked Arthur Brewster and, even though the brief was bordering on crooked himself and was forever defending the most notorious criminals in the area, Carmichael always relished sparring with him. He also enjoyed agitating the burly solicitor, which he tried to do as frequently as he possibly could.

"When he next comes down, tell him Trevor Baybutt is second on my list," Carmichael remarked, his smile now even broader than before. "That should annoy him even more." Carmichael didn't wait to get a reply or observe whether his remark had brought a reaction to the desk sergeant's face. He simply strode confidently through the double doors and down towards the suite of interview rooms.

* * *

After almost thirty minutes waiting outside the critical care unit, one of the senior nurses emerged.

"Are you relatives?" she enquired.

Both Rachel and Richard shook their heads.

"I'm her boyfriend," announced Richard.

"And I'm from the police," added Rachel. "I'm part of the team trying to investigate her attack."

The nurse smiled. "She's now quite heavily sedated," she told them. "I don't expect she'll be coming round for a good few hours at least."

"Will she be OK though?" Richard asked, his voice shaking as if he feared the answer might be bad news.

"You'd have to ask the consultant," the nurse replied with a faint smile, "but she's stable."

"Did she say anything?" Rachel enquired.

The nurse nodded. "She did, but she's very confused so it may not mean anything," she replied.

"What did she say?" Rachel asked.

"As I say, she wasn't making much sense," replied the nurse, "but I'm sure she said 'why did she hit me'."

"Faye definitely said 'she'?" Rachel asked, keen to make sure the nurse was sure.

"It was definitely 'she'," replied the nurse with a positive nod of her head. "But she wasn't totally with it, she also kept saying something about whiskey, so it's probably just nonsense."

Whether it was semi-conscious gobbledygook or not, Rachel thought Carmichael needed to know about it.

"Will you be alright here on your own for a few minutes?" she asked Richard.

Richard Cox nodded. "Sure," he replied, not bothering to enquire why Rachel was about to leave him.

Rachel smiled. "I won't be long," she told him.

Richard watched as Rachel walked hurriedly down the corridor and finally out of sight.

* * *

Carmichael stood in the viewing area adjacent to the interview rooms and watched the three detainees in their respective rooms as they each waited to be spoken to.

Simon Baybutt, who'd been there the shortest time, seemed the most relaxed, followed by Fat Malc, who had clearly finished talking with Mr Fairfax as the two, although sitting together, were both silent, seemingly just killing time.

Trevor Baybutt, on the other hand, looked extremely agitated. He and Brewster were still in deep conversation, and while Brewster remained in his chair, Trevor Baybutt constantly got up and paced around restlessly, waving his arms as if he wasn't happy with the way the conversation was going with his brief.

This lively performance would go on for a few minutes before he'd sit down again, but only for a few seconds before once again jumping to his feet and engaging in an animated and on the face of it, one-way conversation.

Carmichael smiled. In truth he was desperate to get in there with each one of them but wanted to make sure at least one of his three officers was with him before he started his interrogations. Anyway, he thought, a long period of reflection might do them all some good.

He was just about to vacate the viewing area and head up to the incident room when Rachel's call came through.

"How's Faye Hemmingway?" Carmichael asked as soon as he answered the call.

"She's in critical care, but the nurse says she's stable," replied Rachel.

"And has she been conscious at any point?" Carmichael enquired.

"That's why I'm calling," Rachel replied enthusiastically. "The nurse also told us that Faye did come round for a short while and mumbled a few things. Apparently, she said 'why did she hit me?' and kept saying something about whiskey."

Carmichael listened intently.

"It may just be complete nonsense," Rachel added, "but I thought you'd like to know."

"Was it definitely 'she' that the nurse heard her saying?" Carmichael asked. A point that Rachel was pleased to hear her boss make, as it mirrored her own question to the nurse.

"I asked that too," replied Rachel. "And the nurse was adamant that it was 'she' that Faye said."

Carmichael felt a sudden rush of adrenalin. "Thanks for telling me," he remarked.

Pleased that Carmichael had appreciated this new information, Rachel proceeded to update her boss on her conversation with Richard Cox.

"I've also managed to talk with Richard Cox about what happened," she added.

"What did he say?" Carmichael asked.

"He talked with her on the phone at fourteen twelve," Rachel said. "He says Faye was really excited as she'd just learned that Wall had left half the detective agency to her. He says she told him she was in the office sorting out stuff and suggested he should quit his job with Mullion and Thorpe and work with her."

"She wasn't letting any grass grow under her feet, then," remarked Carmichael.

"That's what I thought, too," replied Rachel.

"What else did he tell you?" Carmichael asked.

"Richard says he had another client to see but told Faye he'd come over as soon as that appointment had ended, which he did."

"And what time was that?" Carmichael enquired.

"About three-thirty," Rachel replied, "which ties in roughly with when he was seen entering, then quickly exiting, the office."

"And she said nothing to him when he found her," Carmichael added.

"No," replied Rachel. "When he went into the office, she was on the floor unconscious. He said he thought she was dead."

Carmichael paused for a few seconds. "Is Cox still with you?" he asked.

"Yes," Rachel replied. "We've been waiting together outside the critical care unit. Do you want me to remain here?"

"I think so," replied Carmichael. "If Faye comes round, I'd like you there to talk with her. Also, although it now seems highly unlikely it was Richard who attacked Faye, given Faye's ramblings and the fact that he was only in there for a minute or so, we still need to consider him as a suspect; so, keep an eye on him."

"Understood," replied Rachel. "I'll let you know if Faye gains consciousness."

"Good work, Rachel," Carmichael remarked, before abruptly ending the call.

Chapter 62

When Carmichael arrived back in the incident room Lucy was already there, looking through the statements she'd taken.

"Any new developments?" he asked her.

"Nothing of any significance," replied Lucy. "Just those eyewitness accounts of the woman coming out and getting into the white car and of Richard Cox going into, then coming out of, the office."

"What about SOCO, anything more been identified by them?" he asked.

"Not so far," replied Lucy.

Carmichael nodded. "Well, we've got four people to interrogate this afternoon, so we may as well get started."

Lucy rubbed her hands and smiled. "Who's first?" she asked.

"Fat Malc," replied Carmichael, without a moment's hesitation.

* * *

Fat Malc and his brief looked surprised, but relieved, when Carmichael and Lucy entered the interview room.

"So sorry to have left you so long," Carmichael remarked as he and Lucy sat themselves down, "but hopefully, Mr

Marsden, you've now had ample time to reconsider what we talked about earlier."

Fat Malc looked momentarily towards his brief, Mr Fairfax, before answering.

"I'll hold my hands up to the break-in," he said, "but I took nothing, and I had nothing to do with Wall's murder."

Carmichael looked briefly at Lucy before turning back to face Fat Malc.

"Do you know, Mr Marsden," he replied, "I believe you."

Fat Malc looked flabbergasted by Carmichael's admission. "So, will I be charged?"

Carmichael laughed. "Too right you will," he replied, "but I'd like to know why you broke in."

Fat Malc shook his head gently. "It's a private matter," he replied. "But it's nothing to do with his murder, that's all I'm saying."

Carmichael frowned. "What's so important that you can't tell us?" he asked. "If you come clean it will certainly help you in court, so why don't you?"

Fat Malc shook his head again. "I'm sorry, Inspector," he replied, "as I say, I'll admit that I broke in, but that's all you're getting."

Carmichael leaned back in his chair.

"Do you know," he said, "I think one of the Baybutt brothers told you to break in and do you know what else I think?"

Fat Malc rolled his eyes. "No, but I'm sure you're going to tell me," he replied.

Carmichael smiled. "I think it's to do with stuff that was in Wall's safe. Which we've found. Isn't that right Malcolm?"

Fat Malc folded his arms and pressed tight his lips.

Carmichael allowed a few seconds to pass before he spoke again.

"We'll need a full statement from you," Carmichael said, as he got to his feet, "then you'll be formally charged, and we'll take it from there. I have to say, you're making a big mistake in not telling us everything. In my view, a good prosecution brief will find it easy to suggest to the court that you're shielding whoever did kill Timothy Wall. And, if he convinces a jury of that, then it's a whole different ball game for you, Malcolm."

Fat Malc looked back, impervious to Carmichael's veiled threat.

"I'll leave you with DS Martin," Carmichael continued. "She'll organise the statement with you, then get you charged and processed so Mr Fairfax can get on with his day. And while you're doing that, I'll have a chat with your two bosses."

Carmichael smiled broadly and made his exit from interview room 2.

* * *

Carmichael was delighted to find Watson was in the incident room when he got back.

"Did you pick up Cassie Wilson OK?" he enquired.

Watson nodded. "She's very unhappy and quite edgy," he replied. "What's more, she has a nasty looking set of scratches on the knuckles of her right hand. Like she has hit something, or someone, with a fist."

Carmichael smiled. "Really," he remarked. "Did she say how she did it?"

Watson shook his head. "I didn't let on I'd noticed," he replied. "I also didn't tell her anything other than we needed to talk with her urgently, that it was important and that I'd arrest her if she didn't come voluntarily. I thought you'd like to be the first one to interrogate her properly."

Carmichael smiled broadly. "Good tactic, Marc, but she's going to have to wait a wee while, as I want us to talk with Trevor Baybutt next."

"Sounds fine to me," replied Watson.

Carmichael turned on his heels and headed back out of the door.

"On the way down, I'll update you on our interview just now, with Fat Malc," he said, as Watson tried desperately to catch up. "In short, he's held his hands up to the break-in…" began Carmichael as the two officers made their way down towards interview room 1.

Chapter 63

It was exactly five-thirty when Carmichael and Watson entered interview room 1.

Trevor Baybutt and his immaculately dressed solicitor, Arthur Brewster, were both seated when the two officers took their seats. Brewster looked relaxed and as unruffled as ever, while Baybutt appeared just as edgy and annoyed as he was when Carmichael observed him earlier, through the one-way mirror.

"We've been here almost three hours," snapped Baybutt. "I've got a business to run, you know."

Carmichael smiled. "This shouldn't take too long," he calmly replied.

"Well, let's get on with it," continued Baybutt aggressively.

Carmichael smiled again. "The first thing I want you to be aware of is that I know you weren't telling the truth when we last talked, Mr Baybutt," he began. "At that meeting you told me you'd never heard of Timothy Wall. I now have evidence that was a lie. I also need to inform you that your employee, Malcolm Marsden, has now made a full and unequivocal statement to myself and one of my colleagues, which has been recorded. He's put his hands up to committing the break-in at Timothy Wall's house on Monday evening. So, before we start, I want to make you totally aware that if you, in any way, give any more false evidence, you will be prosecuted for perverting the course of justice. And as Mr Brewster will confirm, that's a serious charge in a murder enquiry such as this."

As he finished, Carmichael looked across at Brewster who remained calm and silent.

"Let me first ask you whether you knew Timothy Wall?" Carmichael asked.

Baybutt leaned back and folded his arms against his chest. "Yes, I did," he conceded.

"And how well did you know him?" continued Carmichael.

"Not well," replied Baybutt. "My brother knew him through the Rotary Club, and he came to the office to see me once."

"Why was that?" Carmichael asked.

Baybutt leaned forward. "To blackmail me," he replied, his eyes looking directly into Carmichael's.

"About the copy of the ledger he stole from your office?" Carmichael asked.

Trevor Baybutt laughed. "No," he replied curtly, "he tried that, but I told him where to get off. There was no way he could prove that was written by me, just as you can't. And even if it was, which it isn't, then what of it? Which is what I told him in no uncertain terms."

"But it gives details of large amounts of money in it," Carmichael added. "Surely if HMRC were to see it, it may cause you some problems with them."

Baybutt laughed again and shook his head. "It's a nonstarter," he replied confidently. "Just names and numbers, they mean nothing."

Carmichael inwardly knew what Baybutt was saying was right. The photocopied ledger, while it was certainly written in Baybutt's hand, on its own wouldn't be enough to prove any wrongdoing on Baybutt's part, and Carmichael expected Tim Wall probably realised that, too.

"So, what was he trying to blackmail you about?" Carmichael asked.

"A private matter," replied Baybutt. "Nothing that's connected with his murder."

"It's got to be the photos in that case," suggested Carmichael, in a tone of surprise.

Baybutt thought for a few seconds before nodding. "Yes, the photos," he confirmed. "The ones Shelley foolishly allowed that little pervert, Marcus Rigby, to take."

Carmichael frowned. "But why was he trying to blackmail you?" he asked. "I get that he wouldn't blackmail Shelley, as she's probably not got much money, but surely it's your brother, Simon, he should have been blackmailing?"

Baybutt leaned back in his chair again, looked across at Watson and slowly shook his head.

"Your guvnor's a bit thick, isn't he?" he remarked with a smug smirk on his face. Then he turned his gaze back to Carmichael.

"I was paying him not to show them to Simon," Baybutt replied. "Simon doesn't know they exist. Apart from Rigby, Shelley, me and Wall nobody else knew about them. And that's how I wanted it to stay."

"What about Fat Malc?" Watson asked. "He must have known."

Baybutt shook his head. "He knew about the payments, as he made them each week for me," confirmed Baybutt, "but he had no idea why he was paying the money."

"But you had him break into Wall's house on Monday evening," continued Watson.

Baybutt shook his head. "I told him that evening," he replied, "after you spoke with him at the racecourse. I realised then you didn't have the photos, so I wanted to get them before anyone else saw them. It was then I told Fat Malc about them."

"So, you admit ordering Fat Malc to commit the break-in?" Carmichael confirmed.

Baybutt nodded. "I admit it, but not the murder. Neither me, Simon nor Fat Malc were involved in that. That was someone else. Probably some other mug he was blackmailing."

Carmichael paused for a few seconds before asking his next question.

"Tell me how much you paid Timothy Wall and how you made those payments?" he enquired.

Baybutt fidgeted in his chair.

"The deal was he'd be paid two hundred and fifty pounds each week until the flat racing season ended," he replied. "Then I'd get the photos back and it was done."

Carmichael's brow furrowed as he absorbed what he'd just heard.

"That seems a peculiar arrangement," he said. "Why did you agree to that?"

Baybutt shrugged his shoulders. "Contrary to what you might think, it's not easy to hide large sums of money anymore through the books," Baybutt replied. "So, when he asked for five grand, I told him he'd have to take it in small chunks, and we did it on race nights every Monday."

"So, how did that work?" Carmichael asked.

"It's quite easy," continued Baybutt. "When Wall came to the pitch he'd bet on a horse and we'd give him odds of four to one. He'd get a ticket saying he'd put fifty quid on it. He wouldn't give Fat Malc any money, but the system would say he paid fifty quid. Then during the race, Fat Malc would send Mary, or whoever was with him, to get a drink or a sandwich and while they were away, would mark Wall's ticket number as a winning number, whatever the actual outcome. After the race, Wall would then come back with the ticket and we'd pay him two hundred and fifty quid."

"And it all goes through the books," observed Carmichael.

Baybutt nodded.

"Sounds very elaborate," Watson remarked.

"It's actually very simple in practice," replied Baybutt, his response suggesting it wasn't the only time he'd carried out this scam.

"And Simon knew nothing about it?" Carmichael remarked.

"He knew about me paying Wall," Baybutt replied, "but he didn't know why. He doesn't like to know details. And he still has no idea about the photos, so I'd appreciate it if that stays in this room."

"I understand," Carmichael said, "but I'm afraid I can't give you any guarantees."

Baybutt leaned forward. "He worships that girl," he said. "And ever since his wife buggered off to Devon, Shelley's become his world. If he knew she'd posed for those sorts of photos it would crush him. So, do me a favour and keep this from him."

For the first time since he'd met Trevor Baybutt, Carmichael recognised a side of the bookmaker other than the outwardly tough persona he was keen to portray.

"I'll do my best," Carmichael replied with a slight nod of his head, "but I'm making no promises."

Carmichael turned to Watson. "I'll leave you to take a new statement from Mr Baybutt, Sergeant Watson," he said. "Then charge him with being involved with the break-in."

"So, I assume you're not pursuing my client on any other matter, other than the break-in?" Brewster remarked.

Carmichael smiled. "I can't promise that either," he replied, before getting to his feet. "We'll be keeping him and Fat Malc in the station for now, while I decide how we're going to proceed from here."

Neither Trevor Baybutt nor Brewster said anything more, which suggested to Carmichael that they were both probably relieved that Trevor was, so far, only being charged with being involved in the break-in.

Carmichael walked slowly towards the exit. With one hand on the door handle, he turned back to face Baybutt and Brewster.

"One last question," he said calmly. "Who told you about Wall being murdered?"

Baybutt shrugged his shoulders. "I don't remember," he replied, his words lacking any great plausibility.

"I'd lay money on it being your brother, Simon," replied Carmichael. "On Sunday evening, to be precise. What odds would you give me on that, Trevor?"

Carmichael stared deep into Trevor's eyes for a few seconds before turning away and leaving the room.

Chapter 64

Rachel Dalton and Richard Cox had remained outside the critical care unit for ninety minutes, occasionally making small talk but mostly just sitting next to each other, in silence.

Rachel was about to take a short stroll down the corridor to stretch her legs when the doors of the unit opened abruptly and out walked the nurse they'd spoken to earlier, with a younger woman dressed in green overalls and matching soft footwear.

"I'm Dr Borchini," the woman in the green overalls said in a strong Italian accent. "I take it you're waiting for news about Ms Hemmingway?"

"I'm her boyfriend," replied Richard, who stood up as he spoke.

"Well, the good news is that she is stable and appears to be doing reasonably well," replied the doctor authoritatively, "but I very much doubt whether she'll be conscious much, if at all, for the next five or six hours. She was complaining of a very severe headache, so we've sedated her and she's on a monitor."

"Will she recover?" Richard asked.

The doctor nodded gently as she considered how to answer. "She's sustained a really nasty blow to her head, and she has some bruising around her neck. It looks like someone hit her hard and then tried to choke her. All in all, your girlfriend appears to have been on the wrong end of a vicious attack and she's quite lucky to survive."

"But the prognosis is good?" Rachel asked.

"She'll be very closely monitored through the night," replied the doctor, her accent strong but her grasp of the English language impeccable. "Then I'll assess her again in the morning. However, she doesn't appear to be in any imminent danger and, miraculously, the scans we've done so far suggest only superficial damage, which is good news. But until she gains full consciousness it's really impossible to be certain. Put it this way, we haven't found anything on the scans that suggests any permanent damage to the brain, but we still need to keep a close eye on her."

"So, can I see her?" Richard asked.

Dr Borchini shook her head. "I'm afraid not," she replied.

Richard was noticeably dismayed by the doctor's response.

"My advice to you is to go home, have a good night's rest, then come back in the morning," continued the doctor with an encouraging smile.

Rachel put her hand on Richard Cox's arm. "I'll give you a lift home," she said.

Richard nodded. "OK," he muttered before slowly heading away down the corridor.

Rachel remained behind with the doctor for a few moments.

"I'm DC Dalton," she said. "Did Faye mention anything about her attack when she came around?"

Dr Borchini smiled. "To be honest, she was mainly complaining about her headache, but she also mumbled something about whiskey and she also said 'why did she hit me' a couple of times," the doctor replied. "But she wasn't fully conscious, and patients can say some strange things when they are concussed."

Rachel smiled and nodded. "Thank you, Doctor," she replied, before walking quickly down the corridor to catch up with Richard.

* * *

When Carmichael arrived at the incident room, Lucy still wasn't back from taking Fat Malc's statement and processing him with the custody team.

He walked across to the whiteboard, fully aware that it now required a major update. He grabbed the coloured pens and started to write.

It was a further fifteen minutes before Lucy appeared, by which time Carmichael had virtually rewritten the three lists.

"Have you sorted him out?" he asked.

Lucy smiled and nodded. "Yes, his statement's all done, and he's been charged," she replied. "He's currently in a cell, asking when he can go home. I told him he'd have to wait as I didn't know what you wanted to do with him."

Carmichael nodded. "I'm pretty sure Fat Malc didn't kill Wall," he replied. "And I'm as certain as I can be that whoever did kill Wall also attacked Faye Hemmingway this afternoon."

"When he and Trevor Baybutt were nicely tucked up here," added Lucy, realising where Carmichael was heading.

"Exactly," continued Carmichael. "But, before we let him go, I'd like Fat Malc's card school alibi to be checked out. Can you do that?"

Lucy nodded. "No problem," she replied. "I've got the names and mobile numbers of the other guys he says were there, so I'll call them now."

Carmichael glanced up at the clock.

"No, let's interview Cassie Wilson first," he remarked. "You can check Fat Malc's alibi when we're finished. He'll just have to wait in the cells until we're ready to let him go, like his boss."

Lucy smiled. "Sounds fine to me," she replied, before following Carmichael out of the incident room and back down towards their next encounter, this time in interview room 4.

Chapter 65

Carmichael and Lucy were just about to enter the interview room when a call came through on Carmichael's mobile. It was from Rachel.

"You go in and set up the recording paraphernalia," Carmichael instructed Lucy. "I just want to get this update from Rachel."

Lucy nodded, entered the interview room and shut the door behind her.

"What's been happening at the hospital?" Carmichael enquired.

* * *

Cassie Wilson looked a little surprised when an officer she'd not met before entered the room.

"I'm DS Martin," Lucy announced with a warm smile, as she switched on the recording equipment. "Inspector Carmichael will be with us shortly."

* * *

Carmichael listened intently as Rachel outlined what Dr Borchini had told her.

"So, let me get this straight," Carmichael reiterated. "The nurse and then the doctor both maintain Faye said 'she'?"

"Absolutely," replied Rachel. "And both mentioned that Faye said 'whiskey', too."

Carmichael paused for a few seconds before continuing.

"Lucy and I are just about to interview Cassie Wilson now," he remarked. "Let's see what she has to say about it."

"I've just dropped off Richard Cox at his house," added Rachel. "It's not that far from the station, so I'll be back in about ten minutes. Is there anything you want me to do?"

"I've just updated the three lists on the whiteboard," Carmichael replied. "Take a look at them and see if there's anything more that should be added. Once Marc emerges from taking Trevor Baybutt's statement, get him to look at it as well."

"Will do," replied Rachel, although her words were wasted, as Carmichael had already ended the call.

* * *

Cassie Wilson looked apprehensive when Carmichael started the interview. Sat alone, without any representation, the previously confident woman he'd first met on Sunday evening didn't appear so self-assured. In fact, she now looked more like someone who needed to visit a wellbeing expert rather than being one herself.

"I suspect you know why you are here?" Carmichael said in a measured, calm voice.

With a guilt-ridden, crestfallen expression on her face, Cassie nodded. "It was wrong, I know," she replied, "but she just infuriated me. Barely ten minutes in charge of the agency and she's already reversing all the good things Tim had been doing."

"Do you resent her being given half the business in Tim's will?" Lucy asked.

"No," replied Cassie sharply. "She can have it with my blessing, but I wasn't having her making Agnes so worried. Not in her condition."

"What do you mean?" Carmichael enquired.

Cassie adjusted her posture, then took a deep breath.

"She phoned Agnes this morning to tell her that from now on she'd be charged for any work the agency did to find Debra," replied Cassie. "Poor Agnes called to tell me what she'd said. She's very ill now and was obviously distraught."

"So, you went to see Faye to —" continued Carmichael.

"To have it out with her," interrupted Cassie indignantly. "Absolutely I did."

"And what happened when you arrived at the office?" Carmichael asked.

"She just laughed," replied Cassie. "She said that Tim had been soft and that from now on there wasn't going to be any work done for free."

"I see," remarked Carmichael. "So, what happened then?"

Cassie went quiet.

"Is that when you hit her?" Lucy asked. "Is that when you bruised your knuckles?"

As she spoke, Lucy pointed at Cassie's right hand.

Cassie remained silent.

"Cassie," remarked Carmichael softly, "is that when you attacked Faye?"

"I didn't attack her," replied Cassie robustly. "It was more of a slap."

Carmichael frowned. "To cause those bruises I'd say it was more than just a slap," he remarked. "And Faye's now in critical care."

Cassie's eyes opened wide, as did her mouth.

"In hospital," she exclaimed. "There's no way that little slap I gave her would cause her to be hospitalised. She's trying it on."

Carmichael shook his head. "You need to realise, Cassie," he said sternly, "what you did constitutes a serious offence, and you will certainly be charged. In fact, this is so serious I think you need to get some legal representation before we continue with this interview."

Cassie looked gobsmacked and terrified.

"Do you want me to organise that for you?" Lucy asked.

Cassie nodded slowly. "Yes, please," she replied, her head clearly spinning.

Chapter 66

When Carmichael and Lucy returned to the incident room, Rachel and Watson were both stood at the whiteboard, making their final adjustments to Carmichael's three lists.

"How are you getting on?" Carmichael enquired.

"I think we're about there," replied Watson.

Carmichael took a few seconds to read through the lists.

"After our conversation with Cassie Wilson, I think we can now add a few more points," he said, grabbing the pens from Rachel.

Lucy, Rachel and Watson all looked on as Carmichael documented his additions.

"Anyone have any anything more to add?" he asked when he was finished.

The silence suggested the team were happy with the lists and prompted Carmichael to print them off.

"Here you go," he remarked, handing out a copy to each of his three officers.

As they looked over the details, Carmichael clapped his hands together.

"Right, Rachel," he said, "you're with me interviewing Simon Baybutt. Marc and Lucy, while we're doing that can you please check out Fat Malc's and Marcus Rigby's alibis for Friday evening."

Lucy looked somewhat perplexed. "I'll need to sort out

Cassie Wilson's legal representation first," she remarked abruptly.

Rachel looked sideways at Lucy before moving her eyes to focus on Carmichael. There was no way she'd ever have the gall to answer him back so insolently. She waited to see how he'd react.

Carmichael nodded. "Of course," he replied without appearing to be in the slightest bit put out, "but make sure Marc has the details of who Rigby and Fat Malc maintain they were both with when Wall was murdered."

He then turned to face Watson before again looking back at Lucy, a broad grin on his face. "You never know, Lucy, he may have got that all sorted before you've finished getting Cassie her brief," he said sarcastically.

Lucy looked across at Watson and shrugged her shoulders. "Chance would be a fine thing," she muttered despairingly.

"I am still in the room," announced Watson; a remark which amused Carmichael and Rachel, but not Lucy, who retained her sullen expression.

* * *

"Well, we meet again," announced Carmichael jovially as he bounded into interview room 3, Rachel Dalton a few steps behind him.

Arthur Brewster, the recipient of Carmichael's greeting, remained seated and didn't reply.

"These Baybutts must be a good little earner for you today," he continued, with a broad grin on his face. "Who said crime doesn't pay."

The tiny smirk on Brewster's face indicated that he'd found Carmichael's comment amusing, but he stayed silent.

With Carmichael and Rachel now seated, Carmichael looked directly at Simon Baybutt. "To save a great deal of time, Mr Baybutt," he said, "I want to first clarify that you're not under arrest. However, there have been a number of serious crimes committed in the last four or five days and unless you can satisfy me that you aren't involved, you may well be charged and kept in the cells for at least tonight."

On hearing he might be detained, Simon Baybutt looked across at Brewster before turning back to face Carmichael.

"Just hang on a minute," he said. "I've not done anything."

"Then you've nothing to worry about," replied Carmichael, the smile still on his face. "And presumably, as you haven't done anything wrong, you'll give full and honest answers to the questions I'm about to ask you."

"Of course," replied Baybutt, as if it were a given.

"Before I start," continued Carmichael, "it's only fair I advise you that, as Mr Brewster can testify, I've already interviewed your brother this afternoon. And, in addition to Trevor, I've spoken to Malcolm Marsden and to Cassie Wilson."

Carmichael stared intently at Baybutt when he mentioned Cassie to try and gauge what reaction he'd get, but learned very little.

"I'd like you to tell me again, Mr Baybutt, where you were on Friday, the 31st?" Carmichael asked. "I'd also like you to tell me where you were on Sunday evening, too? That's the second."

Simon Baybutt took a few seconds to consider how he should respond.

"I was with Cassie," he replied meekly. "On both evenings."

"For the purposes of the recording, Mr Baybutt, can you confirm that you are talking about Cassie Wilson?" Carmichael remarked.

"Yes, Cassie Wilson," replied Baybutt, this time his words were delivered in a much clearer voice.

"So, when Sergeant Watson and I arrived at Cassie Wilson's house to talk with her, late on Sunday evening, you were somewhere in the house?" continued Carmichael.

Baybutt nodded. "Yes," he replied sheepishly, "I was upstairs."

"So, why didn't you make yourself known to us?" Carmichael asked. "And more importantly, why, up until now, have you and Cassie both told us you were alone on Friday?"

"We've been trying to keep our relationship private," replied Baybutt. "Until now, we've not told anyone."

"Why?" enquired Rachel. "You're both single. What's the issue?"

"It's Shelley," replied Baybutt ruefully. "When her mum left us, she took it very badly and she's been really difficult with any women I've dated ever since. I care a lot about Cassie and I just wanted to pick my moment to tell Shelley about her."

"Well, I'd say that moment has come," remarked Carmichael crassly.

Simon Baybutt nodded. "I know," he replied. "It's the first thing I'm going to do when I get home."

"What about the money your brother was paying to Wall?" Carmichael asked. "You must have known about that?"

Simon Baybutt looked across at Brewster, who gave him a tiny nod, as if to advise it alright to answer.

"I told Trevor that those ledger copies Wall had were meaningless, but he still went ahead and paid up," Baybutt replied. "I don't know how much as I didn't want to get involved."

Carmichael looked across at Brewster, who looked slightly uncomfortable. He'd clearly not told Simon the real reason why his brother had been paying Wall, a dilemma that clearly put the brief in an awkward situation.

"And the break-in at Wall's house on Monday," continued Carmichael. "What did you know about that?"

"Nothing," replied Baybutt without hesitation. "I know nothing about any break-in."

Carmichael sighed and leaned back in his chair.

"Well, it was Fat Malc who broke into Wall's house," Carmichael advised him. "And it was on the instructions of your brother."

Baybutt shook his head. "That's news to me," he replied.

"They've both confessed to it," interjected Rachel, "so we know it's true."

Baybutt just shrugged his shoulders. "As I say, it's news to me."

Carmichael suddenly leaned forward. "Tell me about your afternoon?" he asked, deliberately being vague. "What have you done today since midday?"

Baybutt fidgeted in his chair as if he were starting to feel uncomfortable.

"I was at the office until just after lunch," Baybutt replied. "Then I went to see Cassie."

"And where did you meet her?" Carmichael added.

"I met her at her house, and we came into town," continued Baybutt.

"And what time did you arrive in town?" Carmichael asked.

"It would have been about two when I got to Cassie's house," he replied vaguely, "and we must have arrived in town about twenty minutes later. We'd only been here about five minutes before your colleague rang and asked me to come into the station."

Carmichael maintained eye contact with Baybutt the whole time he was talking.

"So, tell me about the visit you and Cassie made to Wall's Detective Agency this afternoon?" Carmichael enquired. "Why did you do that?"

Baybutt's anxiety was now unmistakeable. He loosely

folded his arms in front of him, then released them and placed his hands on top of each other on the desk, before finally resting the palms of his hands on his thighs.

"I assume Cassie has told you all about that," he replied. "I'm sure there's nothing I can add."

Carmichael frowned. "I'd like to know from you what happened at Wall's office today, Mr Baybutt?" he stated firmly. "Why it was you both went there and what happened when you were there?"

Baybutt looked across at Arthur Brewster, who gently shook his head.

"I'm not sure I want to answer any more of your questions, Inspector," remarked Baybutt, his voice trembling. "I've nothing more to say."

In complete contrast to the man across the table, Carmichael remained calm and composed; he even managed to produce another smile.

"Cassie has told us she hit Faye," he remarked. "I just want to hear from you what you witnessed."

Baybutt didn't even try to hide his uneasiness anymore. Wiping his now sweaty palms on his thighs, he looked a very worried man.

"That's not true," Baybutt replied angrily. "Cassie wouldn't hit anyone. She just gave her a piece of her mind."

Carmichael shook his head. "That's not what she's told us," he stated firmly. "She's admitted striking Faye Hemmingway, and the grazing on her knuckles tends to suggest it wasn't a gentle slap."

"I didn't go in," Baybutt muttered, his eyes no longer wanting to make any contact with Carmichael's. "I just dropped Cassie outside the door and waited for her in the car to come out. She was only in there about ten minutes."

"Have you ever been in Wall's office?" Carmichael added.

"No," replied Baybutt with a firm shake of his head, "never."

"In that case, would you mind allowing us to take your fingerprints?" Carmichael asked. "We found a set which we believe to be those of the murderer of Timothy Wall. Having yours should enable us to eliminate you."

"You are under no obligation to do this," Brewster advised his client.

"I've nothing to hide," Baybutt announced confidently. "If that's all it takes to prove to you that I'm not your killer, I'm happy to oblige."

"Thank you, Mr Baybutt," responded Carmichael with a quick glance across at Rachel, to let her know that she was picking that action up.

Rachel got what he was saying and nodded to show she not only acknowledged what he wanted but would sort it out.

Although pleased to have got Baybutt's approval to give them his fingerprints, Carmichael desperately wanted to get back on track and find out what part Baybutt had played in the afternoon's assault.

"The abrasions on her knuckles," he continued. "Did you see them when she came out?"

"It was nothing," Baybutt remarked. "Cassie caught her hand on a metal cabinet when she was talking with Faye."

"Is that what she told you?" Carmichael asked.

Baybutt raised the palms of his hands upwards and shook his head.

"Her job is to give advice on managing stress," he replied angrily. "She's the last person in the world that would be violent towards anyone. She just wouldn't do that."

"But that's exactly what she did," said Rachel.

"And Faye Hemmingway's now at the hospital in critical care," added Carmichael.

Baybutt's expression immediately changed to one of total horror. He sat back in his chair and folded his arms tightly across his chest.

"There's no way Cassie would do that," he shouted angrily. "You've got that completely wrong."

Chapter 67

"What do you think?" Rachel asked as soon as they were out of the interview room. "Do you think he's telling the truth?"

Carmichael nodded. "I do," he replied. "And I think he was genuinely shocked when we told him how serious it is with Faye. He's not stupid, he probably knew Cassie hit her, but I don't think he knew the extent of the assault."

"Do we let him go then?" Rachel asked.

Carmichael thought for a few seconds before answering.

"Go back in and get a statement from him, then take his prints," responded Carmichael. "If they match, we charge him, but if not then let him go."

Rachel smiled. "Will do, sir," she replied before turning on her heels and re-entering interview room 3.

* * *

Rather than go back up to the incident room, Carmichael opted to pay a visit to the station canteen to get a coffee and to give himself some time to think long and hard about where they were with the investigation.

Upon entering the small, sterile white room, Carmichael was relieved to find it almost empty; just two of the station's traffic PCs in the corner, having a late dinner.

Carmichael selected a black coffee from the large coffee machine and situated himself as far away from the two PCs as he could. Then, after a tiny sip of the scolding hot drink, he pulled out the printout of the three lists and rested the papers on the table in front of him.

He read then re-read the lists. Repeatedly he studied the lists; and with every read-through, he'd ruthlessly strike out at least one of the entries based upon how important he viewed it in finding the killer of Timothy Wall.

By the time his coffee cup was empty, fifteen minutes later, the lists had been whittled down to just twenty-four entries.

Carmichael looked at them once more.

Facts:

1. Timothy Wall was killed between 5pm and 10pm on Friday 31st July.
2. He died as a result of a single blow to the back of his head.
3. ~~Faye Hemmingway had left the office at 5.03pm and had gone directly to The Lamb public house; a journey that took her 4 minutes.~~
4. ~~Wall was a ladies' man, who liked to give scores to his ex-girlfriends.~~
5. Fingerprints were found at the scene that can't be accounted for.
6. ~~Wall's house was broken into on Monday evening by Malcolm Marsden looking for the photos of Shelley Baybutt.~~
7. ~~The break-in was ordered by Trevor Baybutt.~~
8. Wall had been blackmailing Trevor Baybutt with the compromising photos of Shelley Baybutt.
9. ~~Shelley says that Wall had helped her get the photos from an ex-boyfriend, Marcus Rigby, but did not know Wall still had copies himself.~~

10. ~~Wall also had a copy of pages from a handwritten ledger in his safe.~~

11. Wall had told Agnes Poulter and Faye Hemmingway about having a strong lead in his hunt for Mrs Poulter's daughter, Debra.

12. ~~Both Trevor Baybutt and Fat Malc lied about knowing Wall.~~

13. Wall left his business to Rene Rothwell and Faye Hemmingway, and everything else to Cassie Wilson.

14. Pierce Armitage has admitted being close to Wall's office at the time Wall died.

15. Jenny Braithwaite is living at the same address as Pierce Armitage.

16. Faye Hemmingway was attacked by Cassie Wilson this afternoon.

17. Cassie Wilson was seen leaving the detective agency at approximately 2:35pm, she got into a white car similar to Simon Baybutt's and was driven off.

Unknowns:

1. Who murdered Timothy Wall?

2. Why was Wall killed?

3. Whose fingerprints were on the door into Wall's office?

4. Is his death linked to a previous relationship?

5. Is his death linked to an existing or historical case?

6. Is Pierce Armitage the man who called himself Haverstock-Price?

7. ~~Were the break-in and Wall's murder linked?~~

8. Who was the lead that Wall had found in the Poulter case?

9. Was Faye Hemmingway's attack linked with Tim Wall's murder?

Suspects:

1. Pierce Armitage
2. Heather Jones
3. Cassie Wilson
4. ~~Trevor Baybutt~~
5. Simon Baybutt
6. Malcolm Marsden (Fat Malc)
7. Marcus Rigby

Feeling pleased with himself, Carmichael folded up the printouts and headed back up to the incident room, discarding his plastic cup into the canteen's metal pedal bin on his way out.

Chapter 68

When Carmichael arrived back in the incident room it was eight o'clock, and his two sergeants were behind their respective desks, both sitting in silence and each of them looking bored to tears.

"Has Rachel not come back up yet?" Carmichael asked, as he burst through the incident room door.

Watson looked up from behind his desk, his brow furrowed in bewilderment.

"I thought she was with you, interviewing Simon Baybutt?" he remarked. As he spoke, Watson got to his feet, stretched out his arms as if he was doing some half-hearted warm-up exercise, then ambled across to the window.

"That finished ages ago," replied Carmichael as he found himself a seat. "She was taking his statement, then she was going to take his fingerprints, and unless they match the ones SOCO found at the murder scene, I told her to let him go."

"Well, we haven't seen her," remarked Watson.

"I take it you don't think he's our murderer then?" Lucy suggested.

"I wouldn't rule him out completely," replied Carmichael, "but if his prints don't match the prints we found at Wall's office then we don't have anything on him. Not yet anyway."

"I think we can scrub off Fat Malc from our list of suspects," Lucy added. "I contacted the four names he gave us. They all confirm that they were at his house, playing cards from six until midnight when Wall was killed. He lives about forty minutes away from Wall's office, so for him to have killed Wall and then got home by the time his mates arrived would be almost impossible."

"Same goes for Marcus Rigby," Watson added. "He met his mates at the Kicking Mule, a sports bar on the other side of town, at five-thirty. They remained there playing pool for about three hours before going to a club, where they stayed until the early hours of Saturday morning."

Carmichael put a line through the names of Malcolm Marsden and Marcus Rigby on the suspects list on the whiteboard.

"I guess we'll have to release Fat Malc in that case," Carmichael remarked. "And although his alibi is flimsy, just based upon his wife's say-so, I think we'll have to let Trevor Baybutt go, too."

"If Trevor is involved, I can't see him doing it himself," added Watson. "He'd pay someone to do it, so his alibi is probably worthless anyway."

Carmichael nodded gently. "Good point, Marc," he replied.

"So, that just leaves us with Pierce Armitage, Heather Jones, Cassie Wilson and subject to Rachel checking his prints, Simon Baybutt," Lucy stated.

"Well, it's not Simon Baybutt," interjected Watson, whose attention had been momentarily distracted by something he'd just seen in the car park. "Simon Baybutt's just climbed into that nice-looking Tesla of his, so Rachel can't have found a match for those prints."

"Which just leaves us with Pierce Armitage, Heather Jones and Cassie Wilson," announced Carmichael.

As he spoke, Rachel Dalton entered the incident room.

"What about Simon Baybutt's daughter or maybe Faye's boyfriend, Cox?" Watson suggested. "Maybe it's one of them?"

"I can't see it being Shelley," replied Carmichael. "She'd have no reason to kill Wall. As far as she was aware, he'd given her back all the copies of the photos. She didn't know he kept a set and was blackmailing Trevor. No, I don't see Shelley as a suspect."

"And I don't think it was Richard Cox," added Rachel. "He didn't even know Wall."

"And remember, he was in the pub with Faye on Friday evening," added Lucy. "So, Rachel's right, it can't be him."

Carmichael nodded. "Which just leaves us with those three," he said, pointing at the three names at the top of their suspects list.

"So, what's the plan now?" Rachel asked.

Carmichael exhaled deeply, theatrically puffing out his cheeks as he did so.

"Lucy and I will go down and talk to Cassie Wilson again," he said. "Let's see what Cassie has to say for herself now she's had a chance to think things through and talk with her brief."

Lucy smiled and stood up, ready to go down to the interview rooms.

"And while we do that," continued Carmichael, "you two can release Fat Malc and Trevor Baybutt. It's clear they're almost certainly not our killers, but tell them not to go too far without asking us first. I don't want them to think they're completely off the hook."

Chapter 69

With her brief sat beside her, Cassie Wilson appeared much more composed and self-assured when Carmichael started to interview her for the second time that afternoon.

"Picking up from our conversation earlier," he began, "I'd like to ask you again what happened this afternoon when you met Faye Hemmingway at Wall's Detective Agency?"

"I went to confront Faye about the call she'd made to Agnes Poulter," replied Cassie calmly. "She had called Agnes a few hours before to tell her that the detective agency would now start to charge her for finding her daughter."

"And that incensed you?" Carmichael added.

"Yes," replied Cassie. "Tim had been doing that for free and now that Debra was found, that money-grabbing cow wanted to cash in. It wasn't right and Tim would have been appalled if he'd have known what Faye was proposing."

"So, what happened?" Carmichael asked.

"I arrived and told her it wasn't on, but she just laughed in my face," replied Cassie.

"So, you hit her?" Lucy suggested.

Cassie nodded her head. "We had a row and to my shame, I did strike her."

Carmichael maintained eye contact with Cassie as she spoke.

"How many times did you hit her?" he enquired.

"Just once," replied Cassie without hesitation. "And it was more of a slap really."

"That doesn't tie up with the bruising you have on your knuckles, Cassie," Carmichael remarked. "As DS Martin said to you earlier today, to cause those sorts of bruises you must have given her more than just a slap."

Cassie shook her head vigorously. "No, it was just one slap," she insisted. "The bruises were caused after I hit her as my hand then connected with the corner of her metal filing cabinet."

Carmichael maintained his composure. "Did Faye retaliate in any way?" he asked.

Cassie shook her head. "No," she replied. "She just stood there, holding her face where I'd slapped her and shouting that she was going to report me, which is what I thought she'd done when your sergeant brought me here."

"Cassie," he said firmly. "Faye is now in hospital; she's sustained a severe beating and is unconscious. That couldn't have happened because of one small slap."

"Exactly," replied Cassie. "Someone else must have done that after I left."

"Are you honestly trying to tell us that when you left Faye this afternoon, she was basically OK?" interjected Lucy. "And the nasty-looking damage you've sustained to your hand was due to it hitting a cabinet, after you hit Faye?"

"Yes, that's exactly what I'm saying," insisted Cassie. "I shouldn't have hit her, I know, but when I left her, she was a little shaken but essentially fine."

Carmichael thought for a few seconds before continuing.

"Did you tell Simon Baybutt that you'd hit Faye?" he enquired.

Cassie looked a little shocked that Carmichael had mentioned her boyfriend, and for a few seconds remained silent and motionless, before eventually shaking her head slowly.

"No," she replied. "He asked about my knuckles and I just told him I'd bashed them against the cabinet."

"So, he's no idea that you physically assaulted Faye?" Carmichael sought to confirm.

Cassie shook her head again. "No," she replied sheepishly. "I lied to him."

"You appear to find lying quite easy," Carmichael continued. "You've lied to Simon, you lied to me and DS Martin when we spoke to you earlier today, and I now understand that you also lied to us when we asked you about your movements on Friday, when Tim was murdered. You said you were alone, but Simon now says you were with him."

Cassie looked decidedly uncomfortable but said nothing.

"So," continued Carmichael, "how can we be confident that you're not still lying to us?"

Looking thoroughly crestfallen, Cassie exhaled loudly before replying.

"I am telling you the truth," she implored, with tears starting to flow from her eyes. "I only hit Faye once and she was perfectly fine when I left. Whoever put her in hospital must have come into the office after I left."

Lucy pushed across a box of tissues, so Cassie could wipe her eyes; a gesture Cassie acknowledged with a faint, forced smile.

"I need you to be aware, Cassie," Carmichael said calmly, "that we will be charging you with assault and due to the severity of the injuries to Faye Hemmingway, I will be keeping you here in the cells overnight."

Upon hearing this news, Cassie Wilson's tears flowed even more, and she sobbed uncontrollably into her hands.

Carmichael stood up.

"I'm going to leave you now with DS Martin, who'll charge you, take your fingerprints and ask the custody sergeant to find you a cell for the evening," he said calmly. "I'll talk to you again tomorrow."

Although she must have heard him, Cassie Wilson didn't answer or even look up at Carmichael, she just kept weeping into her hands.

Carmichael made eye contact with her brief, then nodded at Lucy, before heading to the door.

With his hand on the door handle, Carmichael then half turned to look back into the room.

"You mentioned earlier that Mrs Poulter's daughter, Debra, was found," he said with a degree of bewilderment in his voice. "We are aware that Tim told Faye and Mrs Poulter that he'd made a breakthrough, but I wasn't aware that Debra had been found."

Cassie lifted her head up with a look of incredulity on her face.

"But I saw her," she said, her eyes still tearful, "when I arrived here this morning. She was getting into a car with some bloke. It may be over twenty years since I last saw her, but it was certainly Debra. Did your colleagues not tell you she'd been here?"

Carmichael shook his head slowly. "Clearly not," he replied, before quietly slipping out of the room.

Chapter 70

It was nine twenty-five by the time Lucy Martin entered the incident room.

"Cassie Wilson's fingerprints don't match the ones the forensic guys found at Wall's office on Sunday evening," she said, with a disconsolate shake of her head.

Carmichael nodded gently, as if Lucy's update was no more than he'd been expecting.

"But the big news, of course, is that Armitage's brief appears to be Agnes Poulter's long-lost daughter," he announced.

"Which explains why Armitage was hanging around Wall's office last Friday," added Watson.

Carmichael nodded. "It also explains why Ms Braithwaite was always at Armitage's side when we interviewed him."

"So, what's the plan now, sir?" Rachel enquired, the late hour not appearing to have dampened her enthusiasm one iota.

Carmichael smiled. "The immediate plan is to get off home and get some rest," he replied. "It's been a long day for all of us and I reckon tomorrow will be just as demanding."

"What time do you want us in?" Rachel added, her boundless enthusiasm showing no signs of abating.

Carmichael gathered his thoughts for a few seconds before replying.

"I'd like you, Rachel, to get back to the hospital as early as possible," he told her. "Try and get there before Richard Cox arrives and if Faye's conscious, talk to her and find out what happened this afternoon."

Rachel nodded enthusiastically. "Will do," she replied.

Carmichael then turned to face his two sergeants. "I'd like one of you to remain here in Kirkwood and talk to Heather Jones again and to check out her alibi in more detail. I'm pretty sure she's not our killer, but I want to find out once and for all whether she could have killed Wall or not."

"And what about you and the other one of us?" Lucy enquired, clearly wanting to know the other option before committing to anything.

"A five-thirty start, to drive up to Cumbria with me to talk again with Pierce Armitage and Jennifer Braithwaite, or should I say, Debra Poulter," replied Carmichael with a mischievous grin. "I want to arrive before they set off for work."

Lucy glanced across at her colleague, whose expression gave her no doubt at all about what he thought of such an early start. "Looks like I'm with you, sir," she remarked.

Carmichael nodded. "In that case I'll see you in the morning," he replied with a wry smile.

* * *

The drive back from Kirkwood Police Station to his house in Moulton Bank took just thirty-one minutes, forty-five seconds; by no means a record, but one of his quicker journeys home. And, as Carmichael had expected, Penny was still up when, at ten-fifteen, he opened their front door.

"Busy day?" Penny enquired as she planted a warm welcoming kiss on his lips.

Carmichael smiled. "A very busy day," he replied.

296

For the next hour Carmichael furnished Penny with the details of his day and the progress he and the team were making, which Penny listened to with undivided attention.

"It sounds like you may actually have three different people responsible for the three incidents," Penny remarked shrewdly as Carmichael finished his summary of the day's events.

"It's quite possible," Carmichael replied. "We, of course, now know who was responsible for the break-in and why that happened, and hopefully, when I get to Cumbria tomorrow, I'll have a better idea of who killed Wall."

"And, once Faye Hemmingway comes round," Penny added, "you should be able to find out exactly how she came to be in such a state. Do you not think it's that Cassie Wilson woman who attacked her?"

"Everything does point to her," replied Carmichael, "but I'm not totally convinced it was Cassie. Implausible as it seems, I tend to believe she did just give her a slap."

Penny smiled and kissed her husband on the forehead.

"It sounds as though Cassie Wilson's managed to tug at your heart strings," teased Penny.

"Nonsense," replied Carmichael indignantly. "I just think it's highly unlikely she battered Faye. She's not the battering type."

"And what do women who assault other women look like?" enquired Penny.

Carmichael smiled and nodded. "Smart arse," he replied.

Penny snuggled up closer to her husband, smugly pleased with herself.

"And have you come to a conclusion about the sort of man Tim Wall was, yet?" she enquired.

Carmichael shook his head. "No, the jury is still out on that one," he replied. "It's still not sure if he's a saint or a sinner, but I suspect we'll find he was neither."

Penny yawned. "I'm going to bed, are you coming?"

Carmichael shook his head. "I'll be along shortly," he replied.

From experience, Penny knew when her husband said 'shortly' it could mean anything up to two or three hours.

"I'll see you in the morning," she said, before kissing him again and heaving herself up from the comfy sofa.

"Good night," replied Carmichael, as his wife slipped out of the room.

Penny purposely hadn't asked which team member was travelling up to Cumbria with him in the morning, but she was desperate to know. And, to her annoyance, her husband hadn't offered that nugget of information; an intentional omission on his part.

Despite being tired, it took Penny almost an hour to get off to sleep, her mind infuriatingly preoccupied with thoughts of the travelling companion she'd least like her husband to have chosen for his trip up north. However, she'd been asleep for over half an hour before Carmichael eventually joined her in bed.

Chapter 71

Thursday 6ᵗʰ August

Lucy was already waiting at the kerbside when Carmichael's black BMW pulled up outside her house.

"Morning, sir," she said cheerily as she climbed in next to him.

Carmichael smiled. "Morning, Lucy," he replied before speeding off in the direction of the M6.

* * *

"Hello, my dear," the kindly nurse remarked quietly, as Faye Hemmingway slowly opened her eyes.

"Where am I?" Faye asked, her voice croaky and sounding thoroughly confused.

"You're in hospital, my dear," replied the nurse, while at the same time gently stroking Faye's thin arm. "You've been in the wars, but there's nothing to worry about."

Faye's eyes blinked rapidly as they tried to adjust to the light.

"Where's Richard?" she enquired.

The nurse smiled. "It's only five-thirty," she replied with a smile. "He's probably back home in bed. But I'm sure he'll be along shortly."

Faye continued to blink but less so, as she became more aware of her surroundings.

"Can you tell him to come?" she asked.

The nurse nodded. "I'll get someone to phone him," she promised.

Seemingly happy that her boyfriend was being contacted, Faye drifted back off to sleep.

* * *

"With a bit of luck, we should be there by seven-thirty," remarked Carmichael, as his car sped quickly down the slip road onto the M6 at junction 27. "I'm hoping they'll be still at home at that time. If not, we may have to track them down at work."

Lucy maintained her gaze out the front window. "I've got her Ulverston office address," she replied. "I don't have any details of where he works, but I'm sure if we need to, we'll find him easily enough. It's not like it's a busy place, South Cumbria."

Carmichael nodded. "No, I suppose not," he concurred. "Hardly a great metropolis."

* * *

It was six o'clock when Richard Cox received the call from the hospital.

"I'll be there in half an hour," he said to the nurse as he wiped the sleep from his eyes with the back of his right hand.

* * *

"So, how are you enjoying married life?" Carmichael enquired, as he and Lucy sailed past Lancaster services.

Lucy glanced over at him and nodded. "It's all good," she replied. "Calum's really busy with his constituency work and sorting out his office, so to be honest I've not seen a lot of him this week. And the party leadership have been talking with him about him maybe taking on a more important role soon, so he's been discussing that with them. But when I do see him it's good."

Carmichael smiled. "It must be difficult you both having full-on careers," he added.

Lucy forced a smile and nodded. "Yes," she replied. "That's the main reason I came back here. We figured that if I were at a station further away, we'd never see each other."

"Makes sense," remarked Carmichael.

"It's early days but so far it's working out OK," continued Lucy.

"If Calum gets this additional responsibility, will that mean him being in London a fair amount?" Carmichael enquired.

Lucy nodded. "That's likely," she replied.

"And how do you feel about that?" Carmichael asked.

Lucy turned her head ninety degrees so that she was facing her boss.

"Do you mind if we talk about something else," she said almost apologetically. "Please don't take it the wrong way, but I find it a bit awkward talking to you about Calum and me."

"That's fine," remarked Carmichael firmly, his eyes still looking directly ahead. "I'll not ask you again."

It hadn't been Lucy's intention to annoy Carmichael, however, she realised immediately from his curt response that she had, a fact that was categorically underlined by the absence of any further conversation until they arrived at the address in Mossy Lea, on the outskirts of Millom, an hour later.

* * *

Despite arriving at the hospital within thirty minutes of receiving the call from the nurse, Richard Cox had been left waiting in the corridor outside Faye's room for another hour before he was finally allowed to go to her bedside, where he was greeted with a warm smile and loving eyes.

* * *

"I think we're in luck," announced Carmichael as his car stopped at the entrance of Banks Rise House, Pierce Armitage and Jennifer Braithwaite's address. "There are a couple of cars in the drive, so I'm guessing neither has left for work yet."

Chapter 72

The flabbergasted look on Jennifer Braithwaite's face when she opened the front door to find Carmichael, all smiles, with Lucy standing behind him, was almost enough to justify the two-hour trip on its own.

"Good morning, Ms Braithwaite," Carmichael announced loudly. "We were hoping we'd catch you and Mr Armitage before you went to work."

Dressed in a smart floral summer dress, with her make-up already done and her hair neatly brushed, Carmichael guessed that it was probably only a matter of minutes before she'd have left for work, so he was pleased they'd set off so early.

"Can we come in?" Carmichael continued, before Jennifer Braithwaite had managed to say anything.

"It's not very convenient," Ms Braithwaite replied. "I'm due at work."

Carmichael maintained his smile.

"It won't take long," he assured her. "DS Martin and I just want to talk with you and Mr Armitage again about his trip to Kirkwood last Friday. We'd also like to talk to you about Debra Poulter."

Jennifer Braithwaite, fully realising that the game was up, opened the door wide.

"In that case, you'd better come in then," she said with dismay.

***

Rachel never imagined that when she arrived at the hospital, she'd find Faye Hemmingway awake, propped up in bed, with Richard Cox already at her bedside, holding her hand.

She checked her watch again, just to confirm that she wasn't going mad, and it was still barely eight o'clock.

"Goodness," she exclaimed with a warm smile, "you're looking a lot better this morning."

Although clearly still a little tired, Faye looked fully cognisant.

"Thank you," Faye replied in a croaky voice.

Rachel smiled at Richard before pulling up a chair and sitting herself on the opposite side of the bed to Faye's boyfriend.

"So, what exactly happened yesterday?" Rachel enquired.

Faye looked up at Richard for a few seconds before returning her gaze in Rachel's direction.

"I'm not totally sure," she replied vaguely. "It's all a bit of a muddle in my head."

Rachel smiled. "I guess that's to be expected," she said understandingly. "Just try to tell me what you do remember, and we can take it from there."

Faye nodded and tried hard to concentrate.

"I was in the office," Faye began. "I made a lot of calls to people then…"

Faye stopped, as if she wasn't sure what happened next.

"Take your time," Rachel said in a quiet, reassuring tone of voice.

"Then she breezed in," added Faye.

"Who?" Rachel asked.

"Cassie Wilson," replied Faye. "And she was really angry. She shouted a lot."

"What was she shouting about?" Rachel asked. "Can you remember?"

Faye looked befuddled and shook her head.

"Did she hit you?" Rachel asked.

Faye nodded and put her hand to her cheek.

"Yes," she replied. "She slapped me, hard."

"And did she do anything else?" Rachel continued.

Faye looked confused, but eventually shook her head.

"No, just a slap," she replied. "But it hurt."

"So, who was it who attacked you, Faye?" Rachel enquired.

Faye shook her head. "It was a man, I think," she replied ambiguously. "Yes, a big man, with angry eyes and big fists."

"Do you know the man?" Rachel asked. "Had you met him before?"

Faye started to cry. "No," she replied firmly, putting her hands over her ears and bowing her head low so her nose was almost resting on the blanket covering her. "I've never met him before."

"I think you need to stop now," remarked Richard irately, whilst also putting his arm around her. "She's not ready to be questioned."

Rachel nodded. "I'll leave you with her for now and maybe come back in an hour or so when she's calmed down."

"Thank you," responded Richard firmly, although with much less annoyance in his voice.

Rachel lingered for a few more seconds before getting to her feet and leaving the room; just long enough to see Richard tenderly kiss Faye on her forehead.

* * *

Unlike his partner, Pierce Armitage didn't seem anywhere near ready for work. With his hair looking like it still needed a comb and his chin still dotted with yesterday's growth, he'd slumped down next to Jennifer Braithwaite at the large wooden kitchen table facing Carmichael and Lucy.

"It's time you both were honest with us," Carmichael stated in a firm but cordial tone. "You've wasted enough of our time with your evasive behaviour."

Jennifer Braithwaite glanced sideways at Armitage, who clearly didn't look like he was going to take the lead.

"We were being honest with you when we said we hadn't anything to do with Mr Wall's murder," she began. "But I guess we need to give you an explanation of why Pierce was in Kirkwood on Friday."

Carmichael and Lucy remained silent as Jennifer again glanced briefly at her partner, who remained tight-lipped.

"As you've worked out," she began, "I was born Debra Poulter. However, I never really got on with my parents and I decided to run away. I wasn't mistreated or anything like that, we just didn't ever seem to see eye to eye on anything."

Carmichael deliberately chose to stay silent. He figured she was going to tell them most of what they needed to know without any need for prompts from him.

"When I left home, I initially went to London and worked in a bar," Jennifer continued. "Then, after some difficulties, I decided to make a new start. I began calling myself Jennifer, my middle name, and then joined a group of likeminded people in a commune up near Carlisle. It's where Pierce and I met. After a few years, I then changed my name by deed poll to Braithwaite and started to study law at the Open University. I got my degree and for the last few years have been a practising solicitor here in Cumbria. Apart from Pierce, nobody here knows my history."

Carmichael nodded. "So, what has this to do with Pierce's trip to Kirkwood?" he asked.

"I don't know how he found out," continued Jennifer, "but a few weeks ago, Pierce bumped into a guy who used to live in the commune, who told him that a private detective had been there, asking questions about Debra Poulter. He didn't know that Debra Poulter was me, but he told Pierce there was potentially a thousand-pound cash payment for anyone who could help trace me."

"So, Pierce went to Kirkwood to get a cash reward?" Lucy suggested.

Jennifer shook her head. "No," she replied firmly. "Pierce called Wall last Thursday and said he wanted to find out more about the reward."

"I didn't say who I was or what I knew," interjected Armitage. "I just wanted to find out what was going on."

"So, that was the call that was recorded coming from your mobile?" Carmichael confirmed.

Armitage nodded. "Yes," he replied.

"And what did he say?" Lucy asked.

"He told me that if I could put him in touch with Debra, and she agreed to meet up with her mum, I'd get a cash reward of a thousand pounds," he replied.

"And what did you tell him?" Lucy continued.

"I said I'd think about it and call him back," replied Armitage.

"Did Wall know you were coming down on Friday?" Carmichael asked.

Both Jennifer Braithwaite and Pierce Armitage shook their heads.

"No," Jennifer replied. "We only decided on Friday morning that it might be a good idea for one of us to meet Wall, face-to-face. I was tied up in court and anyway, I didn't want Wall to see me, so Pierce said he'd go down and talk with him on his own."

Carmichael nodded. "And what did Wall say when you saw him?" he asked.

Armitage looked across at Jennifer before answering.

"That's just it," he replied sheepishly, "I didn't meet him. I went across to his office at about twenty-past five, but I never went up."

"Why?" Lucy enquired.

Armitage appeared awkward and again glanced at his partner, as if to draw some moral support, before replying.

"Because when I got to the bottom of the stairs, I heard shouting from the office and I…"

Jennifer shook her head gently and sniggered. "He bottled it, Inspector," she remarked bluntly. "He left having not met or talked with Wall. And whoever he heard upstairs was probably your killer."

"You should have told us this earlier," Carmichael remarked, his voice stern and annoyed. "If you'd have been more forthcoming with us sooner, it would have prevented us from wasting time and may have saved someone getting badly hurt."

Jennifer Braithwaite seemed shocked. "Who's been hurt?" she enquired.

"That's none of your business," responded Carmichael abruptly.

It was clear from the look on Jennifer's face that she was full of regret.

"I'm sorry," she replied. "I'm just not sure I want to meet my mum. But we should have come clean with you earlier."

"You'll both be charged with wasting police time," Carmichael announced, his eyes staring directly at Jennifer. "Which isn't going to look that good on you, being a solicitor."

Jennifer Braithwaite nodded again. "I understand," she replied.

Carmichael then turned his gaze on Armitage.

"Do you remember anything about the person you heard arguing with Wall on Friday evening?" he asked.

Armitage shook his head. "It was unquestionably two men's voices I heard, but I can't recall exactly what they were saying," he replied. "They were definitely arguing. I'm sure one of them said the other one should be ashamed of himself and that his behaviour was disgraceful, but other than that, I can't recall anything else that was said. To be honest, I was only at the foot of the stairs for about twenty seconds."

"What about going in and coming out?" continued Carmichael. "When you were in the café across the road, did you see the man enter?"

Armitage shook his head. "That's the weird thing," he replied. "I saw nobody go in, so after the young woman left at about five, I thought he'd be all on his own."

"And afterwards?" Lucy added. "Did you see anyone leave the office after you left?"

Armitage shook his head. "I didn't hang around," he replied. "I just headed off home."

Carmichael stood up, which indicated the meeting was over.

"I don't know what your plans were for today, but I want you both to report to Kirkwood Police Station at some stage," he announced, his expression dour and serious. "And you will be charged with wasting police time."

Neither Ms Braithwaite nor Pierce Armitage appeared pleased by the prospect of a two-hour journey south, but neither offered any form of resistance.

Carmichael then walked over towards the door, followed closely by Lucy.

"One final thing," Carmichael said as he reached the door. "Did you introduce yourself to Wall as Haverstock-Price?"

Armitage pulled a puzzled expression and shook his head.

"You asked me that before," he remarked. "I never mentioned any name to Wall, and I've no idea who Haverstock-Price is."

Carmichael exchanged a quick look with Lucy before turning away again and making his exit out of the house.

Chapter 73

"Do you believe them?" Lucy enquired, as she and Carmichael walked towards his car.

Carmichael shrugged his shoulders and shook his head slowly.

"I'm not sure what I should believe," he replied honestly. "We've been fed so many lies and half-truths by so many people in this case, it's almost impossible to work out what's genuine and what's fake anymore. I'm sure a lot of what they told us just now is true, but maybe not everything. What about you?"

"I'm not sure," Lucy remarked. "Take his claim about not entering the office and hearing an argument upstairs. I find that difficult to swallow. He'd travelled for two hours to see Wall. He'd sat in the café for the best part of another hour, waiting for Wall to be alone. Then, when he hears voices, he just bottles it and runs off back to Cumbria. I don't think that's remotely plausible."

As they reached the car, Carmichael stopped and looked down at Lucy, who was a good six inches shorter than him.

"I agree, that's the part he may be lying about," conceded Carmichael. "But on balance, I think they've at last come clean. Remember, we've no forensic evidence that confirms Armitage ever entered Wall's office, so he may well be telling us the truth."

Lucy's expression suggested she didn't agree with him, but she didn't offer any further counter argument.

"Also," added Carmichael, "I can't think of a motive for them to kill Wall, can you?"

Lucy shook her head. "No, I can't," she begrudgingly acknowledged.

The two officers climbed back into Carmichael's BMW.

"Do you think we could find somewhere to get a coffee, before we head off home?" Lucy asked.

Carmichael looked across at her imploring expression and smiled.

"That's the most sensible thing I've heard so far today," he replied. "And a bacon roll wouldn't go amiss either."

* * *

Knowing that Carmichael and Lucy were likely to still be with Braithwaite and Armitage when she came out of Faye Hemmingway's room, Rachel had also decided to get herself some breakfast before calling her boss.

Sat alone at her table in the hospital café, with her croissant finished and her coffee cup almost empty, Rachel decided to make the call.

"Morning, Rachel," Carmichael said, as he and Lucy arrived outside a small roadside café on the A590, the main road back to the M6 motorway.

"Any progress with Faye?"

"She's awake but still very confused," replied Rachel.

"Has she been able to tell you anything yet?" Carmichael enquired as he put the call onto loudspeaker, his mood now much improved having heard that Faye was conscious.

"I'm going to go back and see her in a minute," replied Rachel. "But she's confirmed Cassie Wilson's account of things. It does seem that Cassie only slapped her once. Faye's very confused still, but she says her attacker was a man who she'd never met before."

"Was she able to give you a description of him?" Lucy asked.

"Unfortunately, not much of one," replied Rachel. "All she could say was that he was a big man, with angry eyes and big fists."

"That could be anyone," Carmichael remarked. "It would even have described me a few minutes ago."

Lucy smiled and Rachel could be heard laughing at the other end of the line.

"She was quite emotional before," Rachel added. "So, I've left them for a while and told her I'd come back and talk to her again once she'd calmed down."

"Them," repeated Carmichael. "Is Richard Cox with her?"

"Yes," replied Rachel. "He was there when I arrived."

Carmichael thought for a few seconds.

"If it wasn't Cassie, who can it be?" Carmichael said, thinking aloud and looking towards Lucy for inspiration.

"What about Armitage?" Lucy suggested. "He's a big chap and we don't know where he went after he left the station with Jennifer Braithwaite. Or Simon Baybutt. We only have his word that he came straight to the office after he dropped off Cassie. He could have doubled back and returned to the detective agency."

"They're both possibilities, I suppose," Carmichael admitted, "but I'm not convinced that either had a motive to attack Faye. To my knowledge, Faye doesn't know either of them."

"Maybe, whoever it was was after something in the office and she was just in the wrong place at the wrong time," suggested Lucy.

"It's possible, I suppose," replied Carmichael, his expression suggesting he wasn't convinced by Lucy's theory.

"Did Faye give any explanation about why she was mumbling about whiskey?" he asked Rachel.

"No," Rachel replied. "She was still very confused, and I didn't get a chance to bring it up. I'll ask her when I go back, but don't you just think when she mentioned it last night, she was probably just rambling?"

"Maybe," replied Carmichael pensively, "but make sure you ask her about it when you talk to her."

"Will do," Rachel confirmed.

Carmichael took another few seconds to think, before speaking again.

"Yes, get yourself back to Faye's bedside," he instructed Rachel. "Try and find out as much as you can about her attacker. And if it's at all possible, get her alone. It's not beyond the realms of possibility that it was Richard Cox who attacked her and she's too scared to tell you while he's there."

Having seen the two together and having spent some time alone with Richard in the last twenty-four hours, Rachel was convinced he wasn't Faye's attacker, but chose not to share her opinion with Carmichael and Lucy, as her view was based purely on her gut feel, something she knew Carmichael wouldn't put any great store behind.

"Will do, sir," she replied again, in a seemingly compliant manner. "And I'll call you if I get anything more concrete from her."

"See you later, Rachel," said Lucy, just a split second before Carmichael ended the call.

"Now for a coffee and that bacon roll," Carmichael announced as he quickly clambered out of the car. "I don't know about you, but I always think clearer when I have a drink to help me along."

313

Chapter 74

Watson's day started much later than that of his three colleagues. Knowing Carmichael was going to be tied up until lunchtime, and also safe in the knowledge that his assignment was the least important of anyone's in the team, so he was unlikely to be contacted by Carmichael, Watson had allowed himself a small lie-in.

When he eventually did leave his house, it was nine-fifteen.

Feeling relaxed and anticipating a stress-free, easy morning, Watson jumped into his car and headed off to meet with Heather Jones.

* * *

From its exterior, the roadside café looked tired and in need of a great deal of love and attention, but to Carmichael's relief, inside it was clean and welcoming.

Having placed their orders, Carmichael took out his amended copy of their three lists and with a black pen, started to put lines through even more of the items. When he'd finished doing that, he then added a few new items.

By the time the waitress arrived at their table and unceremoniously dumped their mugs of coffee and bacon rolls in front of them, Carmichael had finished editing the lists, successfully narrowing the items down to just nine facts, eight unknowns and, after adding Richard Cox, a mere three suspects.

He positioned the lists so that they were at ninety degrees to both him and Lucy, who was sat opposite.

"So, this is what we've got, Lucy," he remarked as Lucy studied the lists carefully, her head cocked at an angle to help her read the items more easily.

Facts:

1. Timothy Wall was killed between 5pm and 10pm on Friday 31st July.
2. He died as a result of a single blow to the back of his head.
3. ~~Faye Hemmingway had left the office at 5.03pm and had gone directly to The Lamb public house; a journey that took her 4 minutes.~~
4. ~~Wall was a ladies' man, who liked to give scores to his ex-girlfriends.~~
5. Fingerprints were found at the scene that can't be accounted for.
6. ~~Wall's house was broken into on Monday evening by Malcolm Marsden looking for the photos of Shelley Baybutt.~~
7. ~~The break-in was ordered by Trevor Baybutt.~~
8. Wall had been blackmailing Trevor Baybutt with the compromising photos of Shelley Baybutt.
9. ~~Shelley says that Wall had helped her get the photos from an ex-boyfriend, Marcus Rigby, but did not know Wall still had copies himself.~~
10. ~~Wall also had a copy of pages from a handwritten ledger in his safe.~~
11. ~~Wall had told Agnes Poulter and Faye Hemmingway about having a strong lead in his hunt for Mrs Poulter's daughter, Debra.~~

12. ~~Both Trevor Baybutt and Fat Malc deny knowing Wall.~~

13. Wall left his business to Rene Rothwell and Faye Hemmingway, and everything else to Cassie Wilson.

14. Pierce Armitage has admitted being close to Wall's office at the time Wall died.

15. Jenny Braithwaite ~~is living at the same address as Pierce Armitage. And she~~ is Debra Poulter, Agnes's daughter.

16. ~~Faye Hemmingway was attacked by Cassie Wilson this afternoon.~~

17. Cassie Wilson was seen leaving the detective agency at approximately 2.35pm, she got into ~~a white car similar to~~ Simon Baybutt's ~~and was driven off.~~ car.

18. Faye Hemmingway was struck by Cassie Wilson but claims to have been attacked later by an unknown man.

Unknowns:

1. Who murdered Timothy Wall?

2. Why was Wall killed?

3. Whose fingerprints were on the door into Wall's office?

4. Is his death linked to a previous relationship?

5. Is his death linked to an existing or historical case?

6. Is Pierce Armitage the man who called himself Haverstock-Price?

7. ~~Were the break-in and Wall's murder linked?~~

8. ~~Who was the lead that Wall had found in the Poulter case?~~

9. Was Faye's attack linked with Tim Wall's murder?

316

10. Is the whiskey Faye mentioned at the hospital relevant in any way?

Suspects:

1. Pierce Armitage
2. ~~Heather Jones~~
3. ~~Cassie Wilson~~
4. ~~Trevor Baybutt~~
5. Simon Baybutt
6. ~~Malcolm Marsden (Fat Malc)~~
7. ~~Marcus Rigby~~
8. Richard Cox

* * *

To her surprise, when Rachel returned to Faye's room the door was open, but Faye was alone.

"Can I come back in?" Rachel asked.

"Of course," replied Faye, with a smile.

"Has Richard gone?" Rachel enquired.

"He's just gone out to call his boss," explained Faye. "I think he's worried he'll get the sack as he's been spending so much time with me over the last few days."

Rachel smiled. "He works at Mullion and Thorpe, doesn't he?" she remarked.

Faye nodded. "Hopefully not for too much longer," she replied. "I want him to come and work with me at the detective agency, I think he'd love it."

Rachel smiled again. "Are you fit enough and ready to talk a bit more about what happened yesterday afternoon?" she asked.

Faye nodded. "I think so," she replied.

* * *

"You've made a huge amount of changes," Lucy observed, the inference being he'd cut the lists back too much.

Carmichael nodded. "I know," he conceded. "And I may have been a bit too ruthless, but I think these are the key points we need to focus on and, most importantly, the three people who are our main suspects." As he spoke, Carmichael pointed to the three remaining names on their suspects list.

Lucy pushed the three lists back across the table in Carmichael's direction, before delivering her opinion.

"With Cassie Wilson and Heather Jones off the list, are you now agreeing that the murderer wasn't someone from Wall's red book?" Lucy asked.

Carmichael smiled but shook his head. "I never said the murderer would be someone mentioned in the book," he replied. "My point has always been that there may well be something in that book that helps us unlock this case."

Satisfied that she'd made her point, despite Carmichael not totally conceding she was right, Lucy decided to let it rest there.

"If we are working on the assumption that the person who attacked Faye also killed Wall, I don't see it being Richard Cox," she remarked. "Richard didn't know him, and we know he was with Faye on Friday evening from just after five, so I think we can rule him out. I also think it's unlikely that Simon Baybutt came back and attacked Faye after he dropped off Cassie, and remember she provided him with an alibi for Friday evening."

Carmichael nodded. "Good points," he acknowledged. "Which, if you're right, just leaves us with Pierce Armitage."

"He's got to be our man," Lucy pronounced firmly.

Carmichael took a last long swig from his coffee mug.

"Unless, of course, I'm wrong and it is someone like Heather Jones, or even someone who's not on the list at all," he remarked.

Chapter 75

Rachel moved one of the chairs in Faye's room as close as she could to her bed.

"Can you remember anything more from yesterday?" she asked.

Faye shook her head.

"Not much," she replied, her facial expression slightly contorted as she tried hard to recall the details of her traumatic episode.

"But you are sure it was a man that attacked you and not Cassie Wilson?" Rachel asked.

"Oh, yes," Faye replied. "It wasn't Cassie. She hit me, but only once and I remember her leaving. She was in a foul mood and I remember her stomping down the wooden stairs as she left."

"The man that attacked you," Rachel continued, "did you hear him coming up the stairs to the office?"

Faye tried hard to remember, her face deep in concentration. Eventually she shook her head. "No," she replied, a hint of surprise in her voice. "He was just there. He hit me hard then put his hands around my throat. I was trying to stop him, but he was too strong."

Faye's attempt to evoke those painful events was clearly upsetting for her, but despite her anguish and with tears now running down her cheeks, she continued to strain her mind to recall as much as she could.

"I can't remember anything more, I must have passed out," she muttered, plainly frustrated and perplexed that she couldn't bring to mind any further details.

"That's fine," Rachel said with a reassuring smile. "You're doing great."

As Rachel finished talking, one of the nurses entered the room.

"I'm afraid you'll have to leave now," she told Rachel. "The specialist is making her rounds and she'll not want any visitors by the bedside. Come back, maybe in a few hours."

Rachel smiled at the nurse and stood up.

"I'll see you later," she remarked, while also giving Faye a small friendly stroke on her hand.

As she headed off towards the door, Rachel suddenly remembered what Carmichael had told her to ask.

"When you were semi-conscious last night, you apparently mentioned something about whiskey," Rachel said. "Does that mean anything to you?"

Faye looked mystified by Rachel's question.

"Nothing whatsoever," she replied. "I don't like whiskey."

Rachel smiled. "It's probably nothing," she added. "I just thought I'd mention it."

As the nurse busily tidied around Faye, and Rachel closed the door behind her, Faye tried once again to recall more details of her attack.

Feeling exhausted and exasperated at her failure to recollect much from the previous afternoon, Faye closed her eyes. It was then she remembered.

* * *

When Watson arrived at Heather Jones's house, he found her in the garden, perched precariously on a stepladder, stretching up to try and lop branches from an overgrown hedge.

Heather Jones didn't see him at first, but as he approached and she caught sight of him, she came down off her tiptoes and narrowed her eyes, squinting as if to try and see if she recognised him.

"Morning," he said in a friendly voice. "I'm DS Watson from Mid-Lancashire police, are you Ms Jones?"

Heather Jones climbed down the four steps and stood waiting for Watson to arrive.

"Yes," she replied, "I'm Heather Jones."

* * *

"We need to release Cassie Wilson," remarked Carmichael as his black BMW sped south down the M6. "Can you call the station and get them to do that, please? There's no need for them to wait until we get back."

Lucy nodded, took out her mobile and pressed the speed dial number for the station.

* * *

Rachel decided to go back down to the hospital coffee bar, which was a far more attractive proposition as a place to kill time than waiting on the hard, plastic seats in the corridor outside Faye's room.

As she arrived at the entrance to the café, Rachel bumped into Richard Cox, who was going back up to see Faye.

"I've been sent away," Rachel remarked. "The specialist is making her rounds so they wanted Faye to be left alone. Do you want to join me for a coffee?"

Richard Cox considered Rachel's offer for a few seconds before shaking his head.

"I've just had one," he replied. "I'll just go up and wait outside Faye's room."

Rachel smiled. "OK," she added. "I'll see you later."

* * *

Watson was pleased to have been asked in for a cup of tea. Having not met Heather Jones before, he'd imagined her to be a middle-aged woman with her best years behind her, so he was delighted when he came across an attractive woman of about his age who had quite clearly taken extremely good care of herself.

"Just one sugar," he said, which was one less than he normally took, but was his stock answer when he wanted to impress.

"I know you've spoken to my colleague," Watson continued, "but I just wanted to talk to you a bit more about your movements on Friday and about your relationship with Tim Wall."

"Well, I guessed you hadn't come here to help me cut the hedge," replied Heather with a smile, as she put one spoonful of sugar in his tea, stirred it enthusiastically and started to carry their drinks over to the kitchen table where Watson was sitting.

"As I told DS Martin and then PC Twamley, I went shopping on Friday evening and then came back here," announced Heather casually. "After my shopping, I was home at about six-thirty. I put the shopping away and made myself some dinner; Keralan curry, one of Jamie Oliver's recipes. Then I watched TV with a bottle of rose for company and went to bed alone, at about eleven."

Watson smiled. "I've never heard of Keralan curry," he remarked. "What's in that?"

Heather Jones smiled. "Mainly chickpeas, cauliflower and pineapple," replied Heather. "It's vegetarian."

Watson nodded. "That's probably why I've never heard of it," he conceded with a smile.

Watson had already read through PC Twamley's notes from when she'd checked Heather Jones's alibi. Twamley had concluded that from Heather's last sighting on CCTV, leaving the supermarket at six-thirteen, the earliest she could have arrived at Wall's office on Friday would have been six-forty. Twamley had arrived at this time based upon the notion that Heather had taken her shopping home first: an assumption Twamley had made as Heather's till receipt showed she'd bought a large number of frozen items which she'd have wanted to get in her freezer as soon as possible.

Although Twamley's calculations still meant that Heather could have killed Wall, Watson couldn't see why a killer would have done their weekly shop before committing murder. Not unless Heather was a cold-blooded, professional assassin, which, having met her, Watson felt sure she wasn't.

"I understand you didn't like Tim Wall?" Watson remarked.

Heather's eyes widened. "I did once," she replied. "In fact, I liked him very much, but he was a charlatan, Sergeant Watson, a big fraud."

Watson nodded as he listened, which prompted Heather to clarify her comment.

"I'm sorry he's been killed," she added. "But it's true to say that in the end, I wasn't Tim's biggest fan."

Watson smiled. "Did Tim have any enemies to your knowledge?" he asked.

"I suspect there were many," replied Heather with a telling look on her face. "But none that I know. Mind you, I'm probably not the best-placed person to ask. I hadn't a clue about his philandering when we were together, although I learnt later that everyone else knew."

"What do you mean?" Watson asked.

Heather shrugged her shoulders and heaved a great sigh.

"My older brother has told me, after Tim and I'd split up I hasten to say, that Tim's reputation with women was almost legendary in the area," she explained. "Something I hadn't a clue about when we were together."

"Did your brother know Tim well?" Watson asked.

Heather shook her head. "No," she replied, "they were at school together, but Pete was a lot younger than Tim, so he knew him, but not well."

"So, what did he tell you?" Watson asked.

"Just that it was well known that Tim and a couple of other boys at the school had a competition about how many girls they could go with," Heather replied. "He says that it was such common knowledge that no girl in their year would go out with any of them in the end."

"Really," remarked Watson.

"And I learned to my cost that Tim continued this adolescent, misogynistic game into adulthood," added Heather.

"And is that how you saw Tim?" Watson asked. "A misogynist?"

Heather considered her answer for a few seconds. "It's all semantics," she replied. "Ladies' man, laddish, sexist, misogynist; when it boils down to it, aren't they pretty much all the same thing?"

In truth Watson had no idea, so chose to move the conversation on.

"Did Pete mention who the others were?" he asked.

Heather thought for a moment. "One was that bloke Badger Stockley, who got killed in a car accident," she replied. "The other was Adam Collier. He runs the family butchers on Kirkwood high street."

"I know it," replied Watson, who occasionally popped in with his wife, Susan, when they were in town.

Heather smiled. "You'd not think Adam Collier was the same age as Tim, would you?" she remarked. An observation that Watson had already thought about himself, given the person he assumed to be the owner of the butcher's shop was an unhealthy-looking, chubby, bald man, who he'd have sworn was in his mid-sixties.

"I may go and have a word with him," Watson remarked before taking a large gulp of his tea.

Chapter 76

"After meeting her, I'm convinced it's not Heather Jones," Watson announced, his voice loud and clear on Carmichael's car speakerphone.

"Why do you say that?" Carmichael asked.

"She's just a really nice woman," Watson continued. "She fell out of love with him big time, but she's no real motive and if she did kill him, the earliest she could have done it was between six-forty and seven."

It was clear from the expression on Lucy's face that she was baffled by Watson's logic.

"But Dr Stock reckons he could have been killed at any time up until ten," Lucy remarked, emphatically.

"I know Stock and his team gave a window up to ten o'clock," continued Watson, "but Wall wouldn't have been hanging around in the office on a Friday evening much after six-thirty. He'd have been away somewhere, probably chasing another one of his blonde women friends. No, I am sure Heather Jones is not our killer."

Lucy rolled her eyes and shook her head in total disbelief at what she was hearing.

"I agree she's a long shot, Marc," she remarked, "but the timings indicate she could have done it. We can't rule her out just because you think she's a nice woman."

Despite totally agreeing with Lucy's logic and fully

accepting that Watson's reasoning was more than a little distorted, Carmichael didn't feel that Heather Jones was a serious contender for being Wall's murderer, a view that he'd come to that morning when he'd crossed her off the suspects list.

So, while he could have driven a coach and horses through Watson's dubious rationale, Carmichael didn't want to spend any time scrutinising his sergeant's conclusion in any depth.

"So, your morning's been wasted?" he remarked.

"Actually, no," Watson replied. "I did find out something that I'm going to follow up on."

"What's that?" Carmichael enquired.

"Well, according to Heather, she found out from her older brother that when he was at school, Tim and a couple of other boys had a competition to see how many girls they could go with," Watson replied. "Her brother told her that it became common knowledge within the school and in the end, no girl in their year group would go out with any of them."

"I'm not surprised," remarked Lucy, her voice filled with indignation.

"Who were the other boys?" Carmichael asked, interested less in what they had done and more in whether it could have any bearing on the case.

"One was that bloke, Badger Stockley," replied Watson. "The other was a man called Adam Collier. He runs a butcher's shop on Kirkwood high street."

"I assume you're on your way to talk with him?" Carmichael enquired.

"Absolutely, sir," replied Watson.

"Find out what he was doing on Friday evening," continued Carmichael. "Call me when you've finished talking to him."

Before Watson could reply, Carmichael abruptly ended the call.

"Do you think this guy, Collier, might be Wall's murderer?" Lucy asked.

Carmichael took his eyes off the road ahead briefly and glanced over to his left.

"No idea," he replied candidly, "but let's face it, he's probably as likely as anyone else we've considered so far."

* * *

After spending only fifty minutes in the hospital coffee bar, Rachel decided to join Richard in the corridor outside Faye's room. From what the nurse had said earlier, Rachel knew she'd probably still have to wait a good while longer before she could return to Faye's bedside, but she felt it better to be outside with Richard when that happened rather than down in the coffee bar.

However, when she arrived back upstairs, the door to Faye's small private room was wide open and to her astonishment, neither Faye nor Richard Cox were anywhere to be seen.

"Where's Faye?" Rachel asked the nurse in the room, who was stripping the sheets from the bed.

The nurse didn't stop what she was doing or even take a second to gaze in Rachel's direction.

"Stupid girl's discharged herself and left with her boyfriend," she replied, her words delivered in a way that suggested she wasn't best pleased.

"What!" exclaimed Rachel, before taking to her heels and heading off down the corridor.

* * *

Adam Collier was a jolly-looking, rotund man. He had a chubby round face with flushed red cheeks.

When Watson introduced himself and told the butcher

that he wanted to ask him a few questions about Tim Wall, he was immediately ushered into the back room, leaving the counter in the hands of Collier's two younger male assistants.

"How can I help?" Collier asked as they sat in the small room behind the main shop.

"I understand that you were once good friends with Timothy Wall and Justin Stockley," Watson replied.

"I was," Collier answered, "but that was years ago. It must be ten years since Badger Stockley was killed, and I heard the other day about Tim being murdered, but to be honest I've probably not spoken to him much in about ten years either."

"But he worked not five minutes away from here," continued Watson. "Did you never bump into him?"

Collier shrugged his shoulders. "I saw him about, but he never came in here and I didn't need a private detective, so we never had the need nor the opportunity to speak."

Although his explanation seemed a little peculiar, Watson saw no need to disbelieve what Collier was telling him.

"But is it true to say that when you three were at school you were close?" Watson reiterated.

Collier nodded. "Thick as thieves," he confirmed with a smile. "From the age of about eleven until we were sixteen, we did everything together."

"And I believe you had a competition at school?" Watson added. "To see who could date the most girls."

Collier rolled his eyes. "I'm ashamed to say we did," he replied with a wry grin on his face. "But that only lasted for a year or so."

Watson smiled. "Until all the girls got wind, I suppose," he remarked.

Collier nodded. "Yes, once they found out, that was just about that really. They wouldn't have anything to do with us. Well, most of them at any rate."

Watson's smile remained on his face. "So, what happened to the friendship? Why did it break down?" he asked.

"In a word, girls," replied Collier. "Well, actually one girl."

Watson's eyes widened. "And who was she?"

"Her name was Harriet Price," replied Collier. "The prettiest, most popular girl in the school by far. She knew it, too, and although I know it wasn't deliberate, she was the main cause of us all drifting apart, and in their case, falling out massively."

"I'm aware that Harriet married Justin Stockley," Watson added. "And I know she dated Tim, but did you go out with her, too?"

Collier nodded. "I dated her first," he replied almost proudly. "Tim stole her from me. Then she took up with Badger, and they married."

Watson nodded. "But I'm led to believe that she went back with Tim after she'd married Badger," Watson added.

Collier shook his head disapprovingly. "She did, I'm sorry to say," he confirmed. "It was at about that time that it all became a big mess."

"Why?" Watson asked, keen to make sure Collier told him more.

"I'd remained good friends with Harriet and she confided in me a little," Collier continued. "So, I knew a bit about what was happening, but not everything."

"So, what do you know?" Watson asked.

Collier looked as though he was unsure whether he should divulge anything more. "I swore to her that I'd not tell anyone," he said uneasily. "But with them all now dead, I guess it doesn't matter anymore."

Watson's eyes widened in anticipation of what he hoped would be a crucial piece of news.

Chapter 77

"She's what!" exclaimed Carmichael as he and Lucy listened to Rachel on the other end of phone. "Why on earth has she done that?"

Having raced down to the hospital entrance and scoured the car park, Rachel had made her way to her car and called Carmichael to put him in the picture.

"I've no idea," Rachel replied despondently. "She did seem a lot better when I saw her this morning, but nowhere near ready to go home."

Carmichael's car had already left the motorway and was heading along the A5209 towards Kirkwood.

"We're not far away now," he said, quickly trying to decide how to proceed. "They'll most likely have gone to one of their houses."

"Hopefully, hers," added Lucy. "As we don't know where he lives."

"We do," Rachel replied. "I dropped him off there, yesterday. He lives on the Cranley Gardens Estate, not far from the office."

"What's the address?" Carmichael enquired.

"It's in a small cul-de-sac called The Oaks," she replied. "Number six."

Carmichael slowly turned his head and made eye contact with Lucy.

"That's Mary Price's address," he exclaimed. "Cox is living in Mary's house."

The significance of what they'd just discovered didn't need to be explained, all three knew instantly what this almost certainly meant.

"What do you want me to do?" Rachel enquired.

"Get hold of Marc," Carmichael replied. "I want both of you to get over to Faye's house. Make sure he's with you before you go in and get a couple of uniformed officers to join you, too. We'll head off over to Mary's house to see if they're there."

* * *

Buoyed by the news he had gleaned from Adam Collier, Watson had just clambered into his car when the call from Rachel came through.

"Where are you, Marc?" she enquired enthusiastically. "Carmichael wants us to get over to Faye's house. She's discharged herself from the hospital and we think she may be there with Richard Cox, who we now think could well be Wall's killer."

"Why do you think that?" Watson asked.

"Because he lives with Mary Price," Rachel replied. "So, there's a clear link between him and the Price family. It's too much of a coincidence, don't you think?"

"That makes sense," replied Watson, "and based upon what I've just been told, I'd say his involvement isn't a possibility; it's a certainty."

* * *

Having ended the call with Rachel, Carmichael switched on his blues and sped, sometimes precariously, down the country lanes towards Kirkwood.

With her left hand gripping tightly onto the strap above the door, Lucy kept taking deep breaths as each hazard was approached and successfully negotiated by her boss.

"Let's give Marc a call," Carmichael suggested, his eyes momentarily looking down at his mobile in its cradle; meaning he wanted Lucy to dial the number.

Releasing her hand from the strap above her door, Lucy found Watson's speed dial number on Carmichael's phone and initiated the call.

"Marc," announced Carmichael loudly as soon as Watson's voice came through the speakers. "Have you spoken with Rachel?"

"Yes," Watson replied. "I'm just a few minutes away from meeting her outside Faye's house."

"Did she update you on Cox living in the same house as Mary Price?" continued Carmichael.

"She did," confirmed Watson. "And what's more, you'll never guess what Adam Collier just told me."

"What's that?" Carmichael asked.

"Harriet and Wall had a child, about thirty years ago, before she married Justin Stockley," announced Watson, with a heavy mixture of enthusiasm and delight in his voice.

Carmichael and Lucy exchanged a shared stunned look.

"How does he know that?" Lucy asked.

"She told him," replied Watson. "She also went out with Collier. In fact, he reckons he dated her before either Wall or Stockley. Anyway, they remained friends and a few years after she had the child and gave it up, she told him."

"She got herself about a bit," remarked Carmichael.

"Unlike Wall," responded Lucy as quick as lightning, the cynicism palpable in her voice.

Carmichael nodded as if to acknowledge being suitably admonished.

"And was the child a boy?" Carmichael asked.

"That's the weird thing," Watson replied. "Collier says she only mentioned it to him once, swore him to secrecy and wouldn't say anything more about the baby. So, he has no idea what sex it was or who Harriet gave the child to."

"Well my money's on the child being Cox," Carmichael proclaimed. "And I'm sure Aunty Mary will be able to fill in the gaps."

"I've just arrived at Faye's house," announced Watson. "Rachel and a couple of uniformed officers are here already, so I'm going to have to go."

"OK, Marc," replied Carmichael. "Call me once you've gained access and let me know if they're there."

"Will do, sir," replied Watson.

Chapter 78

The startled expression on Mary Price's face when she opened the door to Carmichael and Lucy quickly changed to a look of dread when Carmichael asked if her nephew was in.

Mary made no attempt to deny what Carmichael was implying.

"You know then," she simply remarked as she opened the door wide to let the two officers inside.

"He's not here," she eventually replied as Carmichael and Lucy walked through into Mary's small lounge, "I think he's at the hospital with Faye."

"You know Faye, do you?" Lucy asked as she sat herself down on the small sofa, next to Carmichael and opposite Mary.

"Well, I've not met her yet," replied Mary, "but he talks about her a lot."

"It's a shame you never mentioned him to me the other day when I was here," remarked Carmichael firmly. "It would have saved us a lot of time."

"I didn't feel it was relevant," Mary replied, her embarrassed look suggesting she fully understood its importance.

"So, he's Harriet's son," Lucy said, her eyes focused intently on Mary.

Mary nodded. "He's Harriet and Tim's son," she confirmed. "But Tim didn't know about him. Harriet never told Tim about the child."

"What about Justin Stockley?" Carmichael enquired. "Did he know?"

Mary shook her head. "Not when they were first married," she replied. "Harriet did tell him a few years into the marriage. I think it's what pushed them apart."

"How do you mean?" Lucy asked.

"When they learned that they, well he, couldn't have children," continued Mary, "they talked about adoption and I understand Badger was very keen."

"But Harriet wasn't," Carmichael suggested.

"No," replied Mary. "She decided she wanted her own baby back, which was out of the question as once a baby is adopted it is almost impossible to get the child back. And anyway, when Badger found out who the father was, he forbade her from trying to track her son down; and he told her that if he learnt that she'd told Tim, he'd make her life a misery."

"And would he have carried out his threat?" Lucy asked.

"I'm sure he would have," replied Mary. "Badger was a nasty bit of work."

"But did she not tell Tim, when they had an affair?" Carmichael asked.

Mary smiled. "No, she went back with him to see whether it would be possible to maybe jointly try to get the child back," replied Mary. "But within a short time, she realised that Tim was still playing the field, acting like a little boy in a sweet shop wanting a different sweetie on a whim. She quickly and regrettably concluded that Tim wasn't reliable enough to be a responsible father."

"So, she dumped him," remarked Lucy.

"She did," replied Mary. "As rapidly as she could."

"But without him knowing they'd had a child together," added Lucy.

Mary nodded. "As far as I'm aware that's right."

"How did Richard come to be living with you?" Carmichael enquired.

"That's the sad irony," replied Mary. "Although it's very hard, if not impossible, for a birth parent to track down a child they've given up, nowadays it's quite easy for a child, once they are a certain age, to try and find their birth parents."

"And that's what Richard did?" Lucy enquired.

"Yes," replied Mary. "About five years after Harriet had died Richard started to search for his parents and in January, he contacted me to say that he thought we might be related."

"So, before he moved to Kirkwood?" Carmichael asked.

"Yes," replied Mary.

"When did you first meet him?" Lucy asked.

"It was in February," Mary replied. "He came over here and we hit it off straight away. He's such a lovely boy. Kind-hearted and caring, just like his mum."

"And when did he move in with you?" Carmichael asked.

"That was in March," replied Mary. "When he got the job with Mullion and Thorpe in town, I told him not to bother renting as I had room here. So, he's been with me ever since, which is just fantastic."

As she spoke, Mary's eyes shone, and her face lit up.

"An unbelievable coincidence him being transferred here, wasn't it?" remarked Carmichael, remembering what he had been told by Faye.

Mary frowned. "You've got that wrong, Inspector," she replied. "Richard was keen to move to the area where his mum was from and was working in another estate agents, but he wasn't transferred. I know Adrian Hope, we're both in the same cycling club; I asked him if he had any vacancies and as luck would have it, he did, and Richard was interviewed and got the job."

"I see," Carmichael replied, pausing for a few seconds

before continuing his questioning. "What about Tim Wall? Did Richard contact him, to your knowledge?"

Mary shrugged her shoulders. "I don't think so," she replied vaguely. "He said he wasn't intending to, but of course, after he started seeing Faye, he knew he'd have to meet him at some stage."

"Another massive coincidence, him dating the only employee of his father's company," Carmichael remarked, his tone one of total incredulity.

"I know," responded Mary, seemingly oblivious to what he was suggesting.

Carmichael glanced over at Lucy, who, by her expression, clearly shared his astonishment at Mary's apparent naivety regarding Richard Cox's intentions.

"Do you not think Richard may have wanted to come back to be near his father?" suggested Lucy. "And maybe started seeing Faye to get close to him?"

Mary took instant offence at Lucy's insinuation.

"Certainly not," she replied indignantly. "Richard told me he wasn't going to tell either Faye or Tim about being Tim's son. And I believe him."

Carmichael smiled and nodded, his attempt to create some calm and reassure Mary.

"When did you last see Richard?" he enquired.

Mary still looked less than best pleased.

"As he was leaving the house this morning," she replied, "he got a call from the hospital saying Faye had regained consciousness, and he shot out almost immediately. He didn't have any breakfast, not even a slice of toast."

"What time was that?" Lucy asked.

"He left at about six-thirty," replied Mary.

"Going back to when Richard was born," remarked Carmichael, "did Harriet have the child here in Kirkwood?"

Mary shook her head. "As I told you when we first met,

Inspector, I was very young when that all happened, so I'm not sure where Richard was born," she replied. "But it couldn't have been here as people would have known. I can only guess, but I'd expect our mother would have taken her off to somewhere else where they didn't know her, that's the sort of thing they did back then, isn't it?"

Carmichael again exchanged a quick look with Lucy, before rising from the settee. "If Richard comes back here or contacts you, I want you to let me know straight away," he told her. "It's very important you do that."

Mary nodded implying she would, but Carmichael wasn't convinced at all. It was patently obvious to him that Richard Cox had Mary wrapped around his little finger.

"We'll see ourselves out," added Lucy as she also got to her feet and the two officers headed for the door.

Chapter 79

"They're definitely not here," Rachel declared as she and one of the uniformed PCs emerged from behind Faye's small, terraced cottage.

Begrudgingly Watson nodded. "I'll call Carmichael," he replied dejectedly.

* * *

"Is that woman on a different planet to the rest of us?" announced Carmichael as he and Lucy reached his car and looked back at Mary Price's house.

Lucy shook her head slowly. "I reckon Mary knows she's being played by him, but she's too embarrassed to admit it," she said. "I'd not be surprised if she already suspects him of killing Wall, too."

"I tend to agree with you," Carmichael concurred. "But it might not be Cox. Remember we've no proof, and he's got a cast-iron alibi for Friday night. He was with Faye."

"Don't you think it's Cox then, sir?" Lucy asked, a puzzled look on her face.

Carmichael continued to stare back at Mary's house, as he thought how to answer.

"If he did it," he replied, "I don't know how he did it. Even if he didn't have an alibi for Friday evening, there are no sightings of him entering or leaving Wall's office. And as for the attack on Faye yesterday afternoon, if the witnesses are to be believed, he wasn't in there long enough to render her so much harm."

Lucy was still certain it was Cox, but couldn't fault what Carmichael was saying.

"And, of course," Carmichael continued, "Faye's adamant it was some man she'd never met before."

"With big hands," Lucy added derisively.

Carmichael nodded. "Yes, big hands and an angry face," he remarked.

"Maybe they were both in on Wall's death, then he turned on her," suggested Lucy.

Carmichael continued nodding slowly. "Maybe," he replied, although he didn't seem particularly enthusiastic about Lucy's off-the-cuff hypothesis.

It was at that moment that Watson's call came through.

"Tell me something positive, Marc," Carmichael pleaded with his sergeant as he took the call.

"I'm afraid I can't," replied Watson gloomily. "They're not here."

* * *

With no response after several attempts to dial both of their mobiles, Carmichael made the decision to send out details of Richard Cox's car to all officers from the Mid-Lancashire and neighbouring police forces. He also gave instructions that he wanted all the hotels and guest houses in the area checked out, and he ordered for there to be officers stationed outside both Faye's and Mary Price's house. He then ordered his three lieutenants to go back to the station and await further instructions.

Carmichael didn't join them. Instead he made his way

the short distance to Timothy Wall's office, to think. He often took himself back to a crime scene when he was struggling to unlock a case, and the murder of Timothy Wall still had lots of locks that needed opening.

He sat in Wall's large leather chair with his three lists spread out across the desk. As he studied them, his left hand dropped down to the handle of the desk drawer, which he pulled open. Inside lay a variety of items, placed there by Faye the day before.

Carmichael didn't pay much attention to them; he was thinking of the bottle of Gelston's fifteen-year-old Irish whiskey he'd seen there on Sunday evening, when Wall's body was still slumped across the desk. He then pulled out the scrap of paper from under Wall's desk pad, the one on which he'd written his safe combination. He looked at it briefly before sliding it back under the pad.

For almost ten minutes he remained at the desk, practically motionless as he thought.

Then, abruptly, Carmichael discarded two of the lists, folding them up and putting them in his jacket pocket.

"Maybe I've been looking at this the wrong way," he muttered to himself, with just the list of unknowns left open in front of him.

With a sudden rush of adrenalin surging through his veins, Carmichael grabbed his mobile to call his team.

* * *

Lucy arrived back at Kirkwood Police Station on foot, having been abandoned by Carmichael outside Mary Price's house. When she entered the incident room, she immediately heard Carmichael's voice booming through the speakerphone as he gave Watson and Rachel their instructions.

And, five minutes later, with her specific, crystal-clear

instruction from Carmichael to search for Richard Cox's adoption papers, Lucy got down to work.

With his assignment from Carmichael being to investigate Cox's more recent life, Watson glued himself to his computer screen, scouring social media sites to try and find as much information as he could on Faye's boyfriend.

As for Rachel, in both of her colleagues' eyes, she'd drawn the short straw. The mission Carmichael had given her was to find out exactly when Cox had arrived at The Lamb public house on Friday evening; a task that required Rachel to go to another part of the station to study the CCTV images from cameras in the streets around the pub on Friday evening.

* * *

Still sat at Wall's desk, Carmichael once more looked at the list of unknowns.

He took out a pen from his pocket and scratched out one of the items straight away. He then proceeded to write notes against a further six items, his words underlined in capital letters. Finally, he added a new item to the list, point 11, which he underlined in heavy black ink to signify its importance.

Unknowns:

1. Who murdered Timothy Wall? <u>RICHARD COX?</u>
2. Why was Wall killed?
3. Whose fingerprints were on the door into Walls office? <u>COX's?</u>
4. Is his death linked to a previous relationship? <u>YES</u>
5. ~~Is his death linked to an existing or historical case?~~
6. Is Pierce Armitage the man who called himself Haverstock-Price? <u>NO</u>
7. ~~Were the break-in and Wall's murder linked?~~

8. ~~Who was the lead that Wall had found in the Poulter case?~~

9. Was Faye's attack linked with Tim Wall's murder? <u>YES</u>

10. Is the whiskey Faye mentioned at the hospital relevant in any way? <u>YES</u>

11. <u>How could Cox manage to kill Wall when he was in the pub with Faye?</u>

With a self-satisfied expression, Carmichael placed the updated list in his jacket pocket and stood up.

As he was leaving, Carmichael stopped. With its door concealed from view at the end of a short corridor, Carmichael's attention was suddenly drawn to the fire exit, just off the landing. He briskly walked over to it and pressed the release bar firmly. It opened easily, out onto a metal set of stairs that led down to the rear of the building. Carmichael walked through the open door and, without closing it, checked to see if the fire door could be opened from the outside. His examination confirmed what had been mentioned in the forensic report, namely that it couldn't.

With a disappointed look on his face, Carmichael stepped back into the corridor, shut the fire door behind him, walked down the stairs and out into the high street.

Turning left he then headed off towards the office of estate agents Mullion and Thorpe, no more than a few minutes' walk away.

Chapter 80

"Is Adrian Hope available?" Carmichael asked the adolescent-looking young woman who'd greeted him at the reception desk at Mullion and Thorpe.

"Who shall I say wants him?" the young woman asked with her best welcoming, confident smile.

Even after looking closely at her for a few more seconds, Carmichael could not believe she was old enough to be employed.

"Inspector Carmichael," he replied, suddenly realising, by her slightly perturbed expression, that his close scrutiny was unnerving the young woman. "And can you tell him it's urgent."

Carmichael smiled, an attempt to demonstrate that he wasn't either a creepy middle-aged man or a threat to her in any shape or form.

The receptionist returned the smile, but not an open welcoming smile; it was more forced than anything. She then turned ninety degrees to her right and departed into the main office, leaving Carmichael alone.

For some reason, Carmichael had never warmed to Adrian Hope, the estate agent who had accompanied him and Penny when they'd first viewed the house they later bought, in Moulton Bank.

It wasn't that he was in any way aggressive or opinionated, in fact the opposite was true. However, his seemingly inoffensive, friendly manner, in Carmichael's eyes, appeared feeble, obsequious, insincere and in short thoroughly distasteful. 'A modern-day Uriah Heep' was how Carmichael had initially described him to Penny. An opinion he'd not changed much since that first meeting.

"Inspector Carmichael," Hope exclaimed as he arrived in the reception area, his listless right hand held out ready to exchange a lifeless handshake. "How can I help you?"

"I want to talk with you about an employee of yours, Richard Cox," Carmichael replied, observing the social nicety of shaking Hope's hand, which was as limp as he'd remembered.

"Certainly," remarked Hope, who looked slightly perturbed. "Is he in any trouble?"

"No," Carmichael assured the estate agent. "It's just routine."

Hope seemed to accept this succinct yet vague reply.

"So, how can I be of help?" he enquired for a second time.

"I was wondering if you knew where he was?" Carmichael asked.

"He's at the hospital with his girlfriend, Faye," Hope replied, a look of bewilderment on his face. "Did you not know she's been attacked?"

"Yes, of course," replied Carmichael. "It's just that she discharged herself earlier and we believe she left with Richard."

The estate agent shook his head. "Then, I've no idea where he's gone," he replied, a hint of exasperation in his voice.

"You seem a bit annoyed," Carmichael remarked.

Adrian Hope put his hands on his hips.

"To be honest it's starting to become a bit of an irritating habit of his," he replied. "I don't want to sound uncharitable, and I know his girlfriend has had a truly awful few days, but his constant absence is causing havoc with our viewings and valuations."

Carmichael nodded. "I'm sure it is," he replied, although in truth he didn't have any empathy with Hope whatsoever. "Can you tell me how long he's been working for you?"

"He started in March, I think," replied Hope, imprecisely. "He was recommended to me by a friend from Kirkwood Dynamo, that's the cycling club I belong to."

"Mary Price," confirmed Carmichael. "Yes, we know. And is he working out here?"

Hope shrugged his shoulders. "He's a bright young man and is picking things up very quickly," he remarked. "But I don't think his heart is in it. It seems to be Faye first and work a long way back in second place."

Carmichael smiled. "Is it possible to see Richard's desk?"

Adrian Hope looked puzzled. "Are you sure everything is alright with Richard?" he asked.

"Yes," replied Carmichael. "I'm just hoping I can find something on his desk that might help us locate where he is."

Carmichael could see that Hope didn't buy what he was being told, but that didn't bother Carmichael.

"Well, he's not in Newbold at Cherry Farm Cottage, measuring up, as he's supposed to be," remarked Hope caustically, his hands still firmly placed on his hips.

"Richard's desk," Carmichael reminded him.

Adrian Hope put on a forced smile and started to walk slowly towards the door at the back of the reception area.

"It's through here," he said as he pushed it open.

* * *

"How are you getting on, Marc?" Lucy asked.

"I've found his Facebook page," Watson replied, "but it's only been running for three months, so there's not much posted and he only has twelve Facebook friends. How about you?"

Lucy shrugged her shoulders. "Nothing yet," she replied. "The person I spoke to says they have no record of anyone adopted and now called Richard Cox on their files. They have a couple of males called Price, who were taken in from around the time Richard was adopted, but neither are our Richard as their adopted families were called Spencer and Partridge."

With matching despondent expressions, Carmichael's two sergeants both returned to their respective computer screens.

"By the way, did you ask that butcher about his movements on Friday, as Carmichael asked?" Lucy enquired.

Watson looked across at her, his expression suggesting he'd been remiss.

"I totally forgot," he replied honestly. "I'll call him later and ask."

"What are you like," remarked Lucy, with a slow shake of her head. "I'd do it now if I were you in case Carmichael asks you."

Watson nodded. "Good idea," he replied.

Alone in the video room, Rachel had spent thirty minutes simultaneously trying to watch footage from six CCTV cameras, which she started viewing when their times were all set at four-thirty. So far, she'd not seen anyone even resembling Richard Cox on any of them.

* * *

Carmichael delved into Richard Cox's drawers and flicked through his note pad. However, there was nothing that looked as though it offered any value to their investigation.

"Are you looking for anything in particular?" Hope enquired.

348

Carmichael shook his head. "As I said, I'm just trying to see if there's anything here that would lead us to where we might find him."

Carmichael suddenly saw something that he thought might be useful, however, as hard as he tried, he couldn't think of a plausible reason to give Hope for wanting to take it.

"Could I trouble you for a glass of water, please?" Carmichael asked, thinking that a simple distraction was his only option.

"Certainly," replied Hope, who immediately walked away towards the water fountain at the other side of the office.

As soon as Hope's back was turned, Carmichael, as quick as lightning, pulled a plastic evidence bag from his jacket pocket and without touching it himself, bagged then pocketed the orange metal hole punch on Cox's desk.

When Hope returned with the plastic beaker of cold water, Carmichael gulped it down in one go, before smiling.

"I'll not take any more of your time," he announced. "You've been a great help."

Looking surprised, but also relieved that Carmichael was going, Hope led his visitor back into the reception area.

"Thank you, Mr Hope," Carmichael remarked once they arrived at reception. "I'm sorry to have troubled you."

Hope once more held out a limp right hand.

"I'm not sure if this is at all relevant," the estate agent remarked in a whisper as Carmichael took his hand and gave it a firm shake. "But there is something that's a bit unusual about Richard."

"What's that?" replied Carmichael in a hushed voice.

"It's his name," continued Hope, keen to make sure their conversation wasn't heard by the receptionist, who was now positioned back behind the front desk. "He wants to be called Richard Cox," Hope continued, "but when we put him on the payroll, the name we registered him under was Richard

Purnell. It's apparently his real name but he is in the process of changing it to Cox, and wants to be known as Cox, being in a new position and in a new town."

Carmichael frowned. "Why does he want to change his name?" he enquired, his voice no longer hushed.

"Well I did ask him that," continued Hope, again in little more than a whisper, "and he was a bit evasive about it. He just said that he'd had a massive falling out with his father and as a result, didn't want to be known by the same name as him anymore."

Carmichael shrugged his shoulders. "That's very unusual," he remarked, before nodding in Hope's direction, smiling at the young receptionist and making his way back out onto the street.

Chapter 81

Cherry Farm Cottage was an old, sandstone detached cottage set back from the main road in the small village of Newbold, ten miles from Kirkwood and two miles from Moulton Bank.

The fact it was furnished and empty, and Richard had the key, in his eyes made it a perfect place for him and Faye to hunker down, undetected.

With there being a small wood to the right of the property and high, unkempt leylandii growing at the front and to the left, Richard was also confident that his car would not be spotted from the road.

"How are you feeling?" he asked Faye, who'd been slumped on the large sofa, drifting off then abruptly waking herself up, ever since they'd arrived.

"I'm still a little tired," she replied, a considerable understatement given that her head was pounding, and her throat was sore from his attempt to throttle the life out of her the day before.

Richard gently stroked her hair, almost as though she were his pet rather than his partner.

"I'm so sorry," he said, the umpteenth time he'd apologised to her since she'd told him she'd remembered. "I don't know what came over me. You know I love you and I'd never want to harm you."

As he spoke, his face looked full of remorse and compassion, and small tears appeared in his eyes.

Faye smiled, a tired but loving smile, a smile of someone whose utter devotion to the tall, handsome young man prevented her from seeing any malice in him and made her want to believe every word he told her.

"I know," she said with calm reassurance. "You don't have to keep saying sorry."

* * *

Rachel froze the screen and checked the six digits in the bottom right-hand corner that accurately indicated the time. It read 17:35:37, a full half an hour after Faye had arrived at The Lamb public house.

"Got you," she said, her voice quiet but elated, as she immediately knew the significance of what she'd just discovered.

* * *

After leaving the office of Mullion and Thorpe, Carmichael planned on doing a couple of tasks before heading back to the police station. The first was to put a call in to Lucy.

"Any sightings of Richard Cox or Faye Hemmingway yet?" he enquired brusquely, although he knew full well that if there had been, he'd have been told by now.

"No," replied Lucy. "We've heard nothing."

"And how are you getting along?" Carmichael asked.

"So far I've had no luck either," replied Lucy. "I've drawn a blank with male adoptions in the name Price and there's no record at all of anyone adopted and now calling himself Richard Cox."

"Try the name Richard Purnell," Carmichael suggested.

"Adrian Hope, his boss at Mullion and Thorpe, just told me that's his real name. He just goes by the name Cox."

"Why's that?" Lucy asked.

"According to Hope, Richard fell out with his father and no longer wants to be called by the family name. It sounds a bit far-fetched to me, but whatever the reason for him using a different name, the fact is he's really called Purnell."

"I'll tell Marc, too," Lucy added. "It'll probably help him with his social media search."

"How's Rachel doing?" Carmichael asked, a serendipitous question given Rachel had just burst through the doors into the incident room, her face flushed with success.

"Funny you should mention Rachel," Lucy said loudly, while at the same time beckoning her colleague to come over to her. "She's just arrived, looking like she's got some good news."

"Put her on," Carmichael instructed.

Lucy held her phone out to Rachel. "It's the boss," she said.

"I've found Richard Cox on the CCTV footage, going into The Lamb on Friday evening," Rachel announced excitedly. "He didn't enter the pub until five thirty-five, that's almost half an hour after Faye arrived."

"Are you sure it's him?" Carmichael asked, his pulse racing.

"There's no doubt at all," replied Rachel. "It's clear as day."

"Brilliant," continued Carmichael. "I've just got one more thing to do then I'll come back to base. But in the meantime, can you check for CCTV footage from around Wall's office yesterday afternoon. See if you can spot when exactly Cox arrived and how long he was in there before he left."

"Will do," replied Rachel, who handed Lucy back her phone.

Lucy put the mobile to her ear in case Carmichael was still on the line, but as she'd expected, he'd gone.

"Looks like you're the only one to have made any progress," Lucy remarked, the congratulatory smile on her face in total disharmony with the spiteful look in her eyes.

Rachel didn't reply. Instead she smiled back in Lucy's direction; as friendly a smile as she could manufacture, before turning on her heels and leaving the room.

Chapter 82

"I'm just popping out to get us something to eat and drink," Richard informed Faye, his face close to hers as she lay wearily on the sofa. "I won't be long."

Faye forced a smile. "Get plenty of drink and biscuits," she replied. "Orange juice would be nice. And Oreos."

Richard Cox smiled tenderly, stroked Faye's hair, then kissed her gently on the lips. "I'll be ten minutes," he said reassuringly.

Faye closed her eyes and drifted back to sleep, at which point Richard's kindly, loving smile abruptly faded from his face.

* * *

Carmichael placed the box containing six clinking bottles of his favourite wine, a full-bodied, dark red pinotage, on the floor behind his seat in the back of his black BMW. Buoyed by his conversation with Rachel and a thoroughly gainful visit to McMillan's, the upmarket wine merchants down Bank Street, Carmichael switched on his engine, checked his mirror and, with a contented smile on his face, headed off towards Kirkwood Police Station.

* * *

From inside their parked-up patrol car, PC Jamieson and PC Hill were enjoying a bag of chips from the Jolly Friar, Moulton Bank's popular chippy, when PC Hill spotted a familiar-looking car pulling into the car park behind the small parade of shops.

"Isn't that the car we've been asked to look out for?" he said excitedly.

Despite having greasy hands, PC Jamieson checked the licence plate against the message he had on his mobile.

"It bloody is," he replied rather irritated, his mouth still full of chips. "Typical, I was looking forward to these all morning."

Screwing up their half-finished meals in the paper wrapping they'd been served in, then chucking them behind their seats, PC Jamieson kept his eyes fixed firmly on the car while PC Hill called the sighting in.

At first Richard Cox didn't notice the marked police car and having found a suitable empty parking bay, started to reverse his car into the vacant space.

It was only when he was halfway in that he spied the police car, which prompted him to shift the car into first gear and start to pull out again; slowly, to avoid being spotted.

"We've been rumbled," shouted PC Jamieson who, lightning quick, drove at speed to the exit and blocked it with their car.

As PC Hill relayed what they were doing back to the control centre, Cox's door opened and the tall young man shot out of the car and ran, as if his life depended upon it, in the opposite direction to the two still sedentary police officers.

"He's on his toes," exclaimed PC Jamieson, who was out of the car in a flash and in pursuit.

PC Hill, who was much older and far heavier than his colleague, remained seated for a few seconds before he, too, got out of the car and followed on after Cox and PC Jamieson;

much to the annoyance of a couple of shoppers who now found themselves blocked in the car park by the abandoned police car.

* * *

Having arrived back at the station, Carmichael was just entering the incident room when he got the call to say that Cox had been spotted but had escaped on foot.

"Where was he?" he enquired of the desk sergeant who was relaying the message on. "I know it," Carmichael added, when he learned that Cox had been seen and had done a runner from the small parade of shops almost across the road from where he and Penny lived. "Get as many officers as you can down there immediately," he ordered. "If he's on foot he can't get too far."

As soon as they'd got an inkling of what the call was about, Lucy and Watson had stopped what they were doing and were listening intently to Carmichael, in the hope of trying to work out exactly what was happening despite only being able to hear one side of the conversation.

"I take it that was about Cox?" Lucy asked as soon as Carmichael had finished the call.

"Yes," replied Carmichael, the exasperation in his voice unmistakeable. "Jamieson and Hill spotted him in Moulton Bank, but they let him get away on foot."

"Was Faye Hemmingway with him?" Lucy asked.

"They didn't mention her," replied Carmichael.

"Hopefully, she's been left somewhere and hasn't come to any harm," added Lucy.

Carmichael nodded but looked concerned.

"I wonder what he's doing there?" Watson asked. "It's miles away from the hospital or where either of them lives."

Carmichael thought for a few seconds.

"That's a good point, Marc," he replied. "Why on earth would he go out that way?"

"Shall we get over there, too?" Lucy added.

Carmichael didn't answer, he was still mulling over what Watson had said.

"Shouldn't we get over to Moulton Bank?" Lucy asked again.

Carmichael looked across at her and nodded. "Yes," he replied. "You both get over there now. I'll grab Rachel and we'll follow you."

By the look on Lucy's face he could see that she was puzzled by his answer.

Carmichael pulled out the evidence bag from his pocket which contained the hole punch he'd borrowed from Richard Cox's desk. "I need to get the fingerprints checked on this and I also need to make a quick call," he explained, not that his explanation had any success in removing the look of bewilderment on Lucy's face as she and Watson left the incident room.

Carmichael shook his head slowly. He'd seen Lucy's expression and wasn't impressed, but he wasn't going to dwell on it. He had things to do; the most important was to call Adrian Hope.

Chapter 83

Gasping for air, and with his shoes and trouser bottoms covered in mud from his journey across the farmers' fields, Richard Cox eventually arrived back at Cherry Farm Cottage. It was mid-afternoon and he was tired and hungry.

With one final check to see if he'd been followed, he took the keys from his pocket, opened the front door and quickly went inside.

Still panting, Richard made his way into the lounge, where he found Faye just as he'd left her an hour earlier, curled up in a ball and fast asleep on the sofa.

Relieved that he'd managed to elude his pursuers, but annoyed that he'd been seen, Richard slumped down into an armchair, looked up at the ceiling and tried to work out what he should do now.

* * *

"Any joy with the CCTV from yesterday?" Carmichael asked Rachel, as they rushed across the police station car park.

"It took me a while to locate all the footage," she replied, "so I've only just started to look. But nothing so far."

"You drive," instructed Carmichael, throwing his keys over to her, "I want to call Marc and Lucy on the way."

It was a bad throw, but Rachel's reactions were quick, and she managed to catch the keys before they hit the floor.

"No problem," she replied with a smile. "So, we're heading over to Moulton Bank?"

"No," replied Carmichael as they arrived at his car. "We're heading for Newbold, a house called Cherry Farm Cottage. I've got the post code."

* * *

With the previous owner of the cottage, a single man called Townend, having died suddenly, Richard Cox knew that the chances of them being disturbed were extremely low. However, he also knew that it was almost two months since Mr Townend had passed away, so the chances of him finding anything to eat was close to zero. He rummaged through the dead man's cupboards and all that he could find were a few teabags in a jar, a half empty bag of self-raising flour, a packet of gravy granules and a tin of peaches.

Grabbing the tin of peaches, Cox started opening the drawers in the kitchen to see if he could find a can opener.

* * *

Rachel liked driving Carmichael's car and had high hopes of getting something similar for herself once she made sergeant. However, she didn't enjoy being behind the wheel so much when Carmichael was in the car with her. She knew how much he loved his car, which made her feel especially anxious, particularly when she needed to drive at speed.

"Can you hear that rattling sound?" Rachel asked as soon as Carmichael had finished talking on his mobile with Watson.

"What rattling?" Carmichael replied, before listening for a few seconds.

"There it goes," Rachel shouted when the car took a minor right-hand bend.

"That's just my wine," Carmichael replied with a snigger. "I bought it earlier, it's in the foot well behind your seat."

"I see," Rachel replied.

She was curious as to why Carmichael had been buying wine during work time in the midst of such an important case, but she didn't feel confident enough to ask, so changed the subject.

"How do you know he'll be at this house?" she asked as they sped down the winding country lane, blue lights flashing.

"It was something Hope said when I was with him earlier," replied Carmichael. "He told me he wasn't happy about Cox not being able to measure up at this house in Newbold. And with it being just five minutes away from where Cox was spotted, it occurred to me that he'd have the keys and might be there."

Rachel nodded. "You might make a good detective yet," she remarked cheekily.

* * *

When Watson and Lucy arrived at the house, the road was already blocked by a couple of marked police cars, albeit well out of sight of the windows at the front of the house, and PCs Hill and Jamieson were positioned behind the large leylandii.

"Any movement from inside?" Watson asked as he and Lucy walked over to the PCs.

"No," replied PC Hill.

"Anyone round the back?" Lucy asked.

PC Hill nodded. "PC Dyer and PC Richardson," he replied.

"I'll go and join them," remarked Lucy. "Then we've equal numbers front and back."

"Good idea," Watson added as his colleague dashed away in the direction of the woods to the side of the house.

* * *

Relieved that he'd managed to find a can opener, Richard Cox opened the peaches and returned to the lounge, can in one hand and two forks in the other.

He placed the forks on the small table in the middle of the lounge floor and was just about to shake Faye to wake her, when through the window he saw the head of a man quickly move so it was out of sight behind the leylandii.

Although it all happened in a flash, Richard Cox was in no doubt that there were police out the front. Suddenly consumed with fear, he abandoned the peaches to the table and headed for the back door.

He turned the key that had been left in the keyhole and shot out of the door and into the garden. Within seconds he arrived at the low sandstone wall that divided the back garden from the cow field behind and, without stopping, he vaulted over the wall. He'd just recently returned that way, but in his panicky state, he'd forgotten the drop was at least three feet lower on the other side, so when he landed, he stumbled forward onto his knees.

He didn't see Lucy and the two uniformed officers, crouching behind the wall just yards away from where he landed, until it was too late.

In an instant Lucy had jumped on his back and within a few seconds PC Dyer and PC Richardson had joined her. A minute later Richard Cox was being dragged to his feet, his hands cuffed behind his back.

Chapter 84

By the time Carmichael and Rachel arrived at Cherry Farm Cottage it was all over. Cox was being bundled into the police car and Watson and Lucy were already in the front room gently trying to rouse Faye from her slumbers.

"Great work, you two," exclaimed Carmichael as he entered the room.

"It was Wonder Woman here," replied Watson with a massive smile on his face. "According to PC Dyer, she was on him in a flash, like an NFL line-backer," he continued.

Although Rachel was quite knowledgeable about American football, her older brothers having been big fans, neither Carmichael nor Lucy knew what a line-backer was, but they got his drift.

"In that case, well done, Lucy," Carmichael remarked, a broad smile on his face.

Still very tired and clearly disorientated, Faye opened her eyes and started to look around.

At first, she seemed quite calm, but once she realised her boyfriend wasn't there and she was surrounded by less familiar faces, her manner changed completely.

"Where's Richard?" she asked frantically.

"He's safe," Lucy reassured her, but her words didn't seem to make any difference.

"It wasn't him," Faye said, her voice shrill and anxious. "It was a stranger. I told you that already."

Watson leaned over and whispered into Rachel's ear. "Me thinks the lady doth protest too much," he said.

Although she was marginally impressed that her colleague had obviously not only read *Hamlet*, but was able to recite the quote almost correctly, Rachel had no intention of showing even the slightest sign of approval to Watson. Her first and only thought was to try and comfort Faye, who was visibly distressed.

Kneeling next to Faye, Rachel put a gentle hand on her arm.

"Hi Faye, it's Rachel," she said, her voice soft and soothing. "Richard's safe, you're safe and nobody's saying he did anything to you. Just try and rest."

Rachel's presence seemed to do the trick as Faye appeared to relax as soon as she heard Rachel's voice.

"I'm so tired," she said, before closing her eyes once more and drifting off.

"We need to get her some medical attention," Rachel remarked, looking back up at Carmichael.

"There's an ambulance on its way already," replied Watson, who'd made the call as soon as he and Lucy had entered the lounge and seen Faye looking so frail.

"I'm not sure there's the need for all four of us to stay here," Carmichael remarked. "Lucy, Marc and I will head back to Kirkwood, but you wait here, Rachel, and when the ambulance arrives, go with her to the hospital. This time tell them she's not to be discharged unless it's on medical advice. I don't know what they were thinking this morning, even I can see she's nowhere near recovered from the attack yesterday."

Rachel nodded. "Will do, sir," she replied.

* * *

Carmichael was roughly mid-way between Newbold and Kirkwood when he received a call from one of Dr Stock's team.

"There's a match between the prints on that hole punch and the prints we found on the door frame at the crime scene, on Friday," was the clear message from the caller.

"Thank you for letting me know," replied Carmichael, who, once the call had ended, took one hand off the wheel, punched the air and shouted, "Result!"

Chapter 85

The first thing that confronted Carmichael when he entered Kirkwood Police Station was the sight of Jennifer Braithwaite and Pierce Armitage standing at the main reception desk, doubtless there to provide the updated statement he'd insisted upon that morning. Fortunately for him they had their backs to the station doorway, so they didn't see him arrive. They didn't see the jubilant smirk on his face either, as he slipped quickly through the double doors and scuttled away down the corridor.

* * *

Despite feeling frail, Faye Hemingway was able to get into the back of the ambulance without too much help from the ambulance crew. With Rachel sat opposite and with one of the crew paying close attention to the drowsy patient, the ambulance pulled out of the gateway of Cherry Farm Cottage and headed off back towards the hospital.

* * *

"Reception have just rung, and Armitage and Braithwaite are downstairs, sir," Lucy remarked as Carmichael entered the incident room.

"Really," replied Carmichael, making out he didn't know. "Can you sort out their new statements, please."

"What about Cox?" added Lucy indignantly. "I'd like to be in on that interview."

Carmichael could see in her eyes that she was desperate to be in on the interrogation but, given the run-around they'd been given up to now, he wanted to ensure the statements they got from Armitage and Braithwaite were complete and this time, totally factual. Also, despite feeling confident he had enough already to nail their suspect with the murder, he wanted to find out as much as he could about the man who now called himself Richard Cox.

"I'll do this initial interview with Marc," replied Carmichael firmly. "You sort those two out downstairs, then get on to checking out as much as you can about Richard Purnell's adoption. If that is his real name."

It was evident from her expression that Lucy wasn't best pleased, but she didn't say anything more. Instead she rose sharply from her chair and stormed out of the incident room.

"She doesn't seem happy," remarked Watson dryly.

"I don't care how she feels," replied Carmichael firmly, "I'm heading up this team and I decide who does what."

"Absolutely, sir," added Watson, who could see that Carmichael wasn't best pleased with Lucy and had no desire to incur the boss's wrath as well.

"Anyway, I haven't the time or the inclination to discuss DS Martin's attitude," Carmichael continued. "Let's keep our focus on the interview with Richard Cox, 'cos let's face it, with what we've got on him, he's got quite a lot of explaining to do."

As he spoke, Carmichael was already making strides towards the door.

Watson nodded vigorously and started following Carmichael out of the incident room. However, his progress was stopped abruptly in its tracks when his boss unexpectedly came to a sudden halt and spun around to face him.

"Bring down the report you got of the incoming calls to Wall's office," he instructed Watson.

Watson nodded and went back to his desk to retrieve the report.

* * *

Rachel Dalton positioned herself directly outside the cubical while Faye was being looked over by the admissions team. Having been given the slip once already that day there was no way Rachel was going to be caught out a second time.

Sitting alone on a green plastic chair, Rachel took out her mobile and, while she waited, sent a text message to Matt, her boyfriend, to see if he fancied coming round to her apartment that evening.

A broad smile lit up her face as he enthusiastically accepted her offer.

* * *

The atmosphere in the small meeting room adjacent to the reception area in Kirkwood Police Station was anything but cordial. With neither Lucy, nor the two people from Cumbria she was taking statements from, wanting to be in that room, there had been a complete absence of any small talk. And with all their expressions conveying a mutual sense of outrage and irritation, the mood was certainly one of getting things done as quickly as possible and bringing proceedings to a rapid close.

In total contrast, Carmichael entered interview room 1 in a buoyant frame of mind.

Certain that Richard Cox was the killer of Timothy Wall and, being as confident as he could be that his prisoner was also Faye's attacker, irrespective of her continual denials, Carmichael was relishing the chance to grill him and bring the case to a swift and satisfactory conclusion.

Chapter 86

Richard Cox looked as nervous as anyone Carmichael had questioned for some time when the interview started. With his duty solicitor, Mr Fairfax, at his side, Cox's trembling right hand picked up the plastic cup of water he'd been given. He took a large gulp.

"Richard," Carmichael started, "we now have strong evidence that you killed Timothy Wall last Friday and it was you that viciously attacked Faye yesterday afternoon. What do you have to say to that?"

Cox took a deep breath then shook his head. "You've no proof," he replied, "because it wasn't me. I was with Faye last Friday and Faye's already told you it wasn't me that attacked her yesterday."

Carmichael hadn't expected Cox to confess, so this response was in no way a surprise to him.

"OK," continued Carmichael slowly. "Let's take it step by step."

Despite his firm denials, Carmichael could see in Cox's eyes that he was worried.

"First of all," Carmichael continued, "what is your real name, Richard? Is it Cox, is it Purnell or is it something else?"

It was clear from his expression that Cox hadn't expected that question. He looked nervously over at his brief.

"I go by the name Cox," he replied.

"So, what about the name Purnell?" Carmichael enquired. "Adrian Hope tells me that according to HMRC, that's what you're called."

"I've told you," responded Cox, "I go by the name Cox."

Carmichael remained calm. "And I understand you were adopted," he continued.

Cox shrugged his shoulders but said nothing.

"OK," remarked Carmichael. "Tell me about your adoptive parents. Where are they now?"

Again, Cox refused to answer.

Unperturbed, Carmichael ploughed on.

"What about Mary Price?" he enquired. "She tells us that she's your aunty. Is that true?"

Cox leaned back in his chair and folded his arms, but again remained silent.

"She says you told her that you are her sister Harriet's child and she also says that Timothy Wall was your father. Is she correct?" Carmichael asked.

Cox sat perfectly still with arms still folded but said nothing.

"What about Wall," Carmichael continued. "Did you make an appointment to see him on Friday evening, calling yourself Haverstock-Price?"

Cox gently shook his head from side to side but maintained his silence.

"Tell me about your relationship with Faye," Carmichael asked. "When did you meet her?"

Cox took another sip of water. His hand still trembled as he lifted the plastic cup, but the shakes were not as pronounced as earlier.

Carmichael smiled and turned his head to the right to face Watson.

"I don't think Mr Cox, or rather, Mr Purnell, is that keen to cooperate," he remarked loudly. "Maybe we should tell him what we have on him so he and Mr Fairfax here can have a think and maybe be a little more forthcoming."

"Sounds a very sensible idea, sir," replied Watson.

Carmichael turned back to Cox, his face stern and his blue, laser-sharp eyes aimed directly at the man across the table.

"I believe you called Timothy Wall at the office on Friday morning," began Carmichael, placing the telephone activity statement in front of him but with the details facing Cox so he could read them.

"One of the first things we spotted, when we checked the statement, was that you appear to be making lots of calls to the office," Carmichael announced, pointing at the various calls recorded against Cox's mobile. "You can't leave her alone can you, Richard. It must be love."

Despite pausing for a few seconds to give Cox an opportunity to react, Carmichael received no response.

"It's this first call that I'm interested in," Carmichael continued. "It's from your mobile, it came in at eight-twenty and it lasted two minutes."

Again, Carmichael paused but again, Cox declined to speak.

"I think this call was made before Faye arrived at the office," remarked Carmichael. "I think you would have known that, when you called, and you did that deliberately as you wanted to speak with Wall, not Faye."

Once more Carmichael paused and once more Cox remained silent.

"I think it was during this call you arranged the appointment at five-twenty that evening, calling yourself Haverstock-Price," continued Carmichael with a broad smile. "How am I doing so far?"

Cox leaned back in his chair and gave a tiny shrug of his shoulders.

"You also arranged to meet Faye at The Lamb, at five that evening," Carmichael added. "But we have CCTV evidence that clearly shows you arrived a good half an hour after Faye."

Knowing full well that Cox wasn't going to comment, Carmichael continued. "I think in that half an hour you entered Timothy Wall's office, probably using the fire escape you'd unlocked earlier and propped open. You then confronted Wall and an argument ensued. And I think it got ugly, so much so that it resulted in you picking up Wall's stone paperweight off his desk and hitting him on the back of the head. A blow so hard that it killed him. Isn't that what happened, Richard?"

Cox maintained his silence; however, his brief did interject.

"What evidence do you have that my client killed Mr Wall?" he enquired. "Everything you've said so far is just speculation."

Carmichael glanced over at Mr Fairfax and smiled.

"A good question," he replied. "Let me tell you what I have. Firstly, we have the record of the call between your client and Mr Wall on Friday morning before Faye arrived. Then we have a fingerprint on the door into Mr Wall's office that matches exactly fingerprints we found on a hole punch that I borrowed earlier today, from Richard's desk at Mullion and Thorpe. An exact match."

After re-emphasising the strength of the match, Carmichael glanced over at Cox, who was looking decidedly uncomfortable. "Added to that, we have CCTV footage showing your client arriving at The Lamb public house at seventeen thirty-five and thirty-seven seconds on Friday. And there's also the Irish whiskey."

"Irish whiskey?" Fairfax repeated, his voice quizzical.

Carmichael smiled. "Not just any Irish whiskey, Mr Fairfax, a very special and rare bottle," announced Carmichael. "A Gelston's fifteen-year-old Irish whiskey. It's a whiskey that Wall liked. He'd had a bottle in his bottom drawer since

Christmas and took a glass on special occasions, like when he'd cracked a case. Well, this bottle ran out a few weeks ago. We know this as he told the lady friend who'd bought it for him. However, when we discovered Wall's body, a brand new, recently opened bottle was in his drawer. In fact, he'd had just one glass from it."

"I don't see what this has to do with my client," remarked Fairfax.

Carmichael looked first at Fairfax then at Cox.

"You may not," replied Carmichael, "but I think your client does."

Fairfax glanced briefly at Cox and from the expression on his face, it was clear that Carmichael was right.

"Let me explain," Carmichael said, the elation in his voice now almost uncontainable. "At about a hundred pounds a bottle, a Gelston's fifteen-year-old Irish whiskey is an exceedingly rare bottle of whiskey. You don't find it in your usual outlets. To purchase a bottle, you must either go online or buy via a very specialised wine merchant. And it just so happens there is one such wine merchant in Kirkwood; it's called McMillan's, down Bank Street not five minutes' walk from Timothy Wall's office."

Cox was clearly not enjoying hearing what Carmichael had to say. His face had reddened, and small beads of sweat were starting to gather on his brow.

"I had a terrific conversation with a man called Mr Dod, the manager there, this afternoon, a nice man with a great memory. He informed me that late afternoon last Friday, a gentleman whose description matches your client exactly, bought a bottle of Gelston's fifteen-year-old Irish whiskey from him and paid with a credit card. The name on that card was Richard Purnell."

As he spoke, Carmichael took a copy of the credit card payment receipt that Mr Dod had given him earlier that

374

afternoon and placed it on the desk in front of Fairfax and Cox.

"Do you think that's enough evidence, Mr Fairfax?" Carmichael asked triumphantly.

Looking genuinely concerned, Fairfax glanced across at his client, before turning his head back to face Carmichael.

"I'd like some time with my client," he requested.

Carmichael smiled, stood up and gathered his papers.

"Take as long as you like, Mr Fairfax," he replied. "Your client's not going anywhere and we're in no rush to get home tonight, either."

Carmichael then exited the room with Watson a few paces behind him.

Chapter 87

By the time she'd finished taking new statements from Jennifer Braithwaite and Pierce Armitage, and the pair had left the station, it was five o'clock; and Lucy was still seething.

Her mood wasn't helped when, after just ten minutes back at her desk starting to search for anything relating to the adoption of Richard Purnell, the peace and quiet was shattered by the cheery banter of Carmichael and Watson as they made their way up the corridor and through the incident room doors.

"He's our man, Lucy," announced Watson jubilantly. "Absolutely no doubt about it. Richard Cox, or whatever his real name is, is our murderer. The boss had him on the ropes down there."

Although inwardly he was thrilled with Watson's unconstrained praise, Carmichael wanted them all to keep their feet on the ground, so deliberately remained in control of his emotions and consciously didn't join Watson in appearing to celebrate either too enthusiastically or too prematurely.

"We've still a few more unanswered questions," he remarked calmly. "The first one being about his real identity. Any progress with that, Lucy?"

"Not so far," she replied, "but I've only just got back up here after taking Jennifer Braithwaite's and Pierce Armitage's statements."

"How did that go?" Carmichael enquired.

"Absolutely fine," replied Lucy. "Their statements are on your desk, but I think it's all there, and this time it's believable."

Carmichael nodded. "Great," he remarked, "I'll have a look at them now."

"How long do you want to leave Cox before we go down again?" Watson asked.

Carmichael looked up at the clock to check the time.

"I'll leave them to it until six-thirty," he replied. "That should give them long enough to consider their position. And it will provide us three with plenty of time to see if we can find out more about Richard."

Upon hearing the word, *us*, Lucy looked up from her screen.

"If you brief Marc on what you're looking into, maybe he can help you," Carmichael remarked, his comment aimed at Lucy. "I'll have a look at those statements, then I want to talk with Rachel and see what's going on with Faye Hemmingway at the hospital, but I'll put my shoulder to the wheel, too, once I've done that."

Recognising that he was at least trying, Lucy directed as friendly a smile as her mood would allow in Carmichael's direction. Not that it was of any use, as her boss had already turned and was halfway towards his office at the far end of the incident room, so he saw nothing of Lucy's half-hearted gesture of appreciation.

* * *

Rachel stood up as soon as the curtains opened, and Faye emerged from the small cubical; awake, but lying flat on the bed. With a burly porter providing the power and steering, Faye's bed glided slowly towards the main corridor.

"She's going up to Charlotte Ward on the second floor,"

proclaimed the nurse who accompanied the patient, making sure the drip bag attached to Faye's left arm through a cannula remained in place.

"Am I able to join you?" Rachel enquired.

The nurse nodded. "I see no reason why not," she replied.

Faye smiled up at Rachel as she swept past where she'd been sitting, the porter doing a great job in negotiating his way around the various obstacles along the narrow passageway.

They'd not quite arrived at the lift when Rachel's mobile started to ring. Although she initially thought to just ignore the incoming call, Rachel did relent and take a quick peek at the name on her screen.

"I'll follow you up in a few minutes, Faye," she announced when she saw it was Carmichael. "I just need to take this call."

Although Faye didn't answer, Rachel stopped walking, leaving the small procession to advance without her.

"How's it going?" Carmichael asked.

"She's just out of the admissions area and is going up to the ward," replied Rachel.

"And what are they saying?" Carmichael continued.

"Nothing yet," Rachel replied.

"OK," continued Carmichael. "If you do get to talk to her let me know what she says."

"Will do, sir," Rachel replied. "How did it go with Richard?"

"It's still on-going," Carmichael remarked. "He refused to answer any questions, so we've taken a break. I'm going to interview him again at six-thirty."

"I see," replied Rachel.

"Anyway, I'll let you get on," continued Carmichael. "As I say, let me know if she tells you anything and don't let her out of your sight. I don't want us to lose her again."

"Understood, sir," replied Rachel as she watched the lift door close at the far end of the corridor, and the patient and her carers, ironically, disappear completely from view.

Chapter 88

After ending the call with Rachel, Carmichael again looked at the statements from Jennifer Braithwaite and Pierce Armitage. He'd read them once already but was keen to make sure he didn't miss anything.

As Lucy had said, this time what they'd written made sense and, at last, appeared to be a plausible account of events as they'd probably happened.

What they were now saying certainly didn't excuse their desire to hide the truth from Carmichael and his team before, but at least now they'd provided a logical explanation of why they'd not been honest in the initial interviews.

Carmichael was particularly drawn to a paragraph in Armitage's statement where he reiterated in writing something that he'd told him and Lucy that morning, namely that he'd heard raised voices when he was at the bottom of the stairs to Wall's office.

Although, annoyingly, Armitage went on to reiterate that he didn't see the person arguing with Wall, on the plus side, despite only being able to remember a little of what was said, Carmichael was pleased and reassured that what Armitage could remember, and what he'd put in the statement, was very helpful; specifically that he heard one of them telling the other that he should be ashamed of himself and that his behaviour was disgraceful. This alleged rebuke was totally in keeping with the picture Carmichael had built in his head of that meeting; and explicitly of Wall being informed by Cox, the young man he'd only just met, that he was, in fact, his son. Carmichael concluded that what Armitage heard was almost certainly Wall being admonished by Cox, presumably for not embracing him as his son with open arms.

He couldn't say for sure, but Carmichael imagined that Cox probably had expected a far more welcoming reaction, especially as he'd just given his father a very expensive bottle of Irish whiskey as a present.

Carmichael found himself wondering how he'd react if someone, out of the blue, introduced himself to him as his son. A predicament that he found impossible to imagine fully, but one that did send a few shivers through him. He decided he wasn't sure how he'd react if it were to happen to him, but Carmichael was fairly certain he'd do as Wall had probably done and not accept it as fact until he had indisputable scientific proof to back up the claim. Maybe that's what Wall had asked, he mused. And maybe that's why Cox reacted so badly and, in a rage, had killed his father.

With that thought still ringing in his head, Carmichael left the statements on his desk and headed out back into the main incident room to join Lucy and Watson.

* * *

Rachel had no problems finding Charlotte Ward and fortunately, no issues in locating Faye's bed.

"How are you feeling now?" Rachel asked her as she pulled up a chair close to Faye's side.

"Where's Richard?" Faye responded, her expression suggesting she was more worried about her boyfriend than she was about herself.

"He's fine," replied Rachel. "He's in Kirkwood helping Inspector Carmichael."

"It wasn't him," exclaimed Faye loudly. "It was someone else."

"No one's suggesting it was him," Rachel lied, "but we'd like to know more about what happened, just as soon as you feel able to tell us."

Faye stared back at Rachel. "So, it's clear it wasn't him that attacked me, and he was with me in The Lamb when Tim was killed. So, whoever did these awful things, it wasn't Richard."

Rachel put a comforting hand on Faye's arm.

"Don't get yourself in a state about it," she said in as reassuring a tone as she could muster. "Just try and get some rest."

Chapter 89

For thirty-five minutes, Carmichael, Lucy and Watson scoured their computer screens, trying desperately to find as much as they could about Richard Purnell and his adoption almost thirty years earlier.

As the clock reached six twenty-five, Carmichael looked across at his two colleagues.

"How are you getting along?" he enquired.

"Nothing yet," replied Lucy. "I've tried to get through on the phone to Barnardo's, but when I spoke to them, they were just about to go home for the evening, so they said they'd check their records in the morning. And I've tried the government adoption services, but they are saying without knowing the area of the country where he was adopted, it might be hard to find his records."

"I've had a bit more luck," Watson remarked. "I found eight Richard Purnells on Facebook, but none have been active for the last couple of years and some not for eight or nine years. There are also four people with that name on LinkedIn, and one does seem to be a match, although I'm not totally sure."

"Is there not a photograph you can check?" Lucy asked.

Watson shook his head. "There is, but whoever this is has just put up a photo of themselves as a young child, so it's not possible to say whether it's our Richard or not."

"What does the profile tell us on that one?" Carmichael asked.

"It says he went to school in Bakewell in Derbyshire," replied Watson. "Then worked for the local government office in Bakewell. He was there three years in their IT department. He then moved on to work at a company, still in Bakewell, called Thomas Mallings, who seem to make or sell industrial heaters and air control systems. But that's where it stops and there's been no updates on his page for the last three years."

"Well, if that is our Richard Purnell then at least we have Bakewell as a possible place of birth for you, Lucy," remarked Carmichael optimistically. "That's a tiny place so it shouldn't be too difficult to locate him if that's where he was born."

Lucy nodded in agreement. "How did you get on?" she asked, her question directed back at her boss.

Carmichael shook his head. "He's not got a criminal record on our system, either as Richard Purnell or Richard Cox," Carmichael replied. "So, I'm afraid I can't contribute much either on Richard's past."

"Shall we have another go at Cox now?" Watson asked.

Carmichael nodded. "I think so," he replied, "but this time why don't you join me, Lucy. You never know, he might be more forthcoming with a new face across the desk."

Lucy's delighted expression indicated that she approved.

"No worries for me," remarked Watson nonchalantly. "I'll grab a coffee and watch you perform your magic through the one-way mirror."

Carmichael smiled, shook his head and made off in the direction of the interview rooms, musing about the extreme contrast between Watson's response to being left out of the interview and the petulant, childlike one he'd encountered from Lucy earlier that evening.

Chapter 90

Richard Cox and his brief, Mr Fairfax, sat stony-faced across the small table opposite Carmichael and Lucy.

"Have you had a chance to talk?" Carmichael enquired.

"We have," replied Mr Fairfax, "and my client has decided not to answer any more of your questions."

Carmichael looked over at Lucy, then at Mr Fairfax before theatrically giving a pronounced shrug of his shoulders and aiming his response directly at Richard Cox.

"I find your position very strange," Carmichael announced. "Having been provided with the substantial evidence we have against you, I can't understand why you don't want to put your side of the story on record?"

Richard, who looked much less nervous than he had during the last interview, remained expressionless. "No comment," he replied.

Carmichael shook his head gently. "As you know, we believe you called Timothy Wall at the office on Friday morning to arrange an appointment, introducing yourself as Haverstock-Price, a fictitious name which appears to be made up from a mix of your mother's maiden and married names."

Richard smiled, almost as if he were pleased his amusing ruse had been spotted and acknowledged by Carmichael.

"Why did you do that?" Lucy asked.

"No comment," replied Richard.

"You arranged with Faye to meet her at The Lamb, at

five," continued Carmichael. "I think you did that in order to get her out of the office. It was a meeting that you didn't make until over half an hour later. And we know you bought a bottle of Gelston's fifteen-year-old Irish whiskey from Mr Dod at McMillan's, just before you met with Mr Wall."

Richard Cox maintained his deadpan expression. "No comment," he replied again.

"Why don't you want to answer these allegations?" Carmichael enquired, pausing to allow Richard an opportunity to respond.

Richard, however, remained resolute in his silent stance.

Carmichael shook his head once more, before turning his head to face Lucy.

"Don't you think it's all rather strange, DS Martin?" he enquired.

"I do, sir," replied Lucy. "I also think it's funny that Mr Cox hasn't once asked about his girlfriend. If he loved her so much, you'd think he'd be keen to know how she was doing."

"Good point, DS Martin," remarked Carmichael. "Maybe he's secretly hoping she doesn't pull through; 'cos let's face it, when she does, I'm sure she'll have a lot to say about her assault."

Richard Cox shook his head gently. "No comment," he remarked again.

"Well, the good news is that she's doing fine," continued Lucy. "In fact, one of our colleagues is talking with her right now."

Cox didn't flinch. "No comment," he said again with no emotion in his voice whatsoever.

"Well, I don't see any point in wasting our time anymore, DS Martin," announced Carmichael, who quickly rose to his feet. "Let's formally charge Mr Cox and he can go back to his cell."

Lucy also got up. "Will do, sir," she replied.

Carrying all his papers, Carmichael made his way over to the door and put his hand on the handle. However, before he made his exit, he turned back to face Cox.

"I understand you're originally from Bakewell in Derbyshire," Carmichael announced.

For the first time in the interview, Cox looked surprised.

Seeing the expression on his face, Carmichael grinned broadly.

"Maybe we can talk a little about that tomorrow," he remarked. "Have a comfortable evening and I'll see you in the morning."

With the smile still on his face, Carmichael turned away and left the interview room.

* * *

Rachel remained by Faye's bedside until Faye had drifted off to sleep, which was her prompt to call Carmichael.

The call came through just as Carmichael and Watson arrived back at the incident room.

"She's still insisting it wasn't Richard who attacked her," Rachel announced.

"It's as if she's got Stockholm syndrome," replied Carmichael, expecting Rachel to enquire what that was, but she didn't.

"Possibly," she replied, "although I think Stockholm syndrome is more to do with a strategy for survival, isn't it?"

Carmichael didn't know, so said nothing.

"I'd say it's more simplistic than that," continued Rachel. "I think Faye's just madly in love with him."

"You might be right," replied Carmichael, knowing when he'd been outsmarted. "So, what's she doing now?"

"She's asleep," Rachel informed him. "Do you want me to stay here?"

Carmichael looked up at the clock, which told him it was now five past seven.

"No," he replied. "I'll sort out someone to sit with her overnight. When they arrive, you get yourself home and I'll see you in the morning."

Rachel was relieved to hear Carmichael's words, as that meant she stood a good chance of being able to get home and have a shower before Matt arrived at eight-thirty.

"How's it going there?" she asked.

"Lover boy's still saying nothing," Carmichael replied, sarcastically, "so Lucy's now formally charging him with Wall's murder."

"Do you think we have enough evidence already then?" Rachel asked.

"I'm sure we do, for the murder," Carmichael replied with confidence. "I'll talk with him again in the morning, hopefully he'll be more forthcoming then, although that's probably a pipe dream. But it wouldn't half help if Faye started telling us the truth about him attacking her. That's your mission in the morning. She seems to have a bit of a bond with you, so I'm hoping you can talk some sense into her."

"I'll try," Rachel replied, just before her boss abruptly ended the call.

Rachel took the phone from her ear and exhaled deeply, before smiling and shaking her head.

Of all Carmichael's little foibles, and there were many, Rachel found his penchant for suddenly ending calls without any notice one of the most annoying. But then again, he was the boss and was by far the best detective in the station, so, despite it taking her by surprise whenever it happened and infuriating the hell out of her every time he did it, Rachel knew he'd never change his ways, and she would just have to deal with it.

Chapter 91

It was seven-thirty by the time Lucy joined Carmichael in the incident room.

"That's him all charged and banged up in his cell," she announced.

"Good," replied Carmichael. "Thanks for doing that, and well done on your quick thinking when he jumped over that wall."

"It was easy," Lucy replied. "If he hadn't stumbled, he may have got away."

Carmichael shrugged his shoulders. "But he didn't, and you apprehended him, so well done."

"Where are the others?" Lucy asked.

"They've both finished for the day," replied Carmichael, "and I suggest you do the same."

After having such an early start, Lucy felt bushed, so she wasn't about to argue. She grabbed her bag and jacket.

"Good night," Lucy said, a small smile appearing on her face as she spoke.

"Good night," replied Carmichael, who'd already started flicking through his notes and was seemingly thinking about something else.

As Lucy reached the door, Carmichael looked up and shouted across at her.

"There was one thing," he said, his voice still warm and friendly.

Lucy turned to face her boss. "What's that?" she enquired.

"I know you like to be in the thick of things and I know you enjoy being involved in formal interviews," Carmichael remarked, "but there are times when you need to roll your sleeves up and do some of the grunt work."

Having just been praised for apprehending Cox, Lucy wasn't expecting to be admonished, and was completely taken by surprise. Instantly incensed at what she was hearing and astounded at the timing of his remarks, Lucy glared back at her boss, who clearly had more to say.

"So, when I ask you to do stuff like contacting the women in Wall's red book," continued Carmichael, "or doing research into Cox's adoption, I expect you to get on with it without questioning my motives."

Lucy was fuming but remained silent.

"There's no doubt that you're more than competent in interviews," added Carmichael, "but there's more to this job than just interrogating suspects."

Lucy could feel her blood pressure rising, but it was late, she was tired and most annoyingly she knew there was some truth in what Carmichael was saying.

She took a deep breath and forced a couple of nods of her head, as if to show she'd taken onboard his criticism.

"I hear you, sir," she replied. "You won't have to tell me again."

Pleased that his mild rebuke had been received and understood, without any unnecessary drama, Carmichael smiled across at Lucy.

"Anyway, get yourself home and have a nice evening," he said.

Lucy couldn't bring herself to smile back. "Thanks," she

replied, before turning her back on him and heading out of the door and away down the corridor.

* * *

Carmichael spent a further hour alone in the incident room going over the evidence and looking through the numerous statements they'd assembled over the last four days. Despite feeling satisfied they'd successfully established who'd killed Tim Wall and who it was that had broken into his house, Carmichael still had a few nagging questions that required answering; the main one being how Richard Cox, who must have had such high hopes of being accepted warmly by his father and who had spent a considerable amount of money on that expensive bottle of whiskey, could have ended up killing the very man he wanted to bond with. Also, why did he feel he needed to gain entry via the emergency exit, as Carmichael was sure he had. Then there was the assault on Faye. Although Carmichael was certain Cox was responsible for that, too, he couldn't prove it, and Faye Hemmingway's determination to exonerate her boyfriend was making that task so much harder.

Carmichael eventually arrived home at five-past nine, tired and hungry, but satisfied with the team's accomplishments that day. His mood was buoyed considerably by having six new bottles of pinotage, purchased that afternoon from his new friend, Mr Dod, in the back of his car. One of which he was planning to open as soon as he got indoors.

Chapter 92

Friday 7th August

It was another warm summer morning. According to the weatherman on Carmichael's car radio, it was going to be the thirty-seventh day in a row without any rain on the West Lancashire plain, some sort of record for that part of world. Carmichael wasn't complaining, he loved sunny weather, normally a rarity in Lancashire and one of the things he missed the most about not living in the south.

As his car motored sedately along the narrow, quiet country roads towards Kirkwood, Carmichael felt at ease; probably for the first time in many weeks. After all, he'd virtually cracked the case and despite his concerns about Lucy's return, the last four days hadn't gone too badly. It certainly wasn't the same as it had been when Cooper was the third member of his team, and he still wasn't totally sure that Lucy and Rachel were getting along that well, but his worst fears regarding Lucy's return hadn't materialised, which was an enormous relief to him.

Despite only getting to bed after midnight, and even though he'd consumed a little more pinotage than he should have, Carmichael felt re-energised following a good night's sleep, when even Penny's rhythmic snoring didn't seem to have disturbed him.

With his aircon on low and the volume on the radio turned up loud, Carmichael's thoughts turned to the three issues he and his team still had to resolve:

Why did Richard kill Wall?
Why did Richard attack Faye?
How can they stop Faye protecting Richard?

He trusted Rachel to tackle the last one, but as for the first two, he knew he'd either need Cox to start talking or, more likely, he and the team needed to do a lot more digging and to think more laterally than they had up until now.

Without any deliberation whatsoever he allocated himself the cerebral assignment and earmarked Watson and Lucy to focus on the grunt work, as he called it, a logical and obvious division of work in his view.

With his thoughts moving on to the detail of the job in hand, Carmichael decided to drop in to see Mary Price on his way into the station, to see if she could shed any light on where her older sister might have gone to have Richard. If it were the Bakewell region of Derbyshire, that could not have been a random choice by Harriet's parents. And even if Mary wasn't totally sure where the birth took place, she might be able to provide some sort of help in knowing where they should be looking.

* * *

Lucy's mood couldn't have been more contrasting. She'd been stewing over Carmichael's parting comments to her all of Thursday evening, which didn't make her the greatest company; a point Calum had made her aware of on several occasions and in no uncertain terms.

Her first week back at Kirkwood, in her eyes, was not

going well at all. It seemed so different there now, with the steady, dependable Cooper not around and with Rachel, the young pretender, hanging on Carmichael's every word, the whole atmosphere in the team had changed from what she'd remembered; and she hated it.

As for Carmichael, who on the face of it was the same, her relationship with him wasn't what it was. He no longer seemed so imposing and in control as she remembered, and with what had gone on between her and Carmichael in America, on that evening and in the morning after, she didn't see him in the same light anymore. In fact, apart from Watson, who hadn't changed one iota, everything at Kirkwood was different: and mostly for the worst.

However, Carmichael was still her boss and to ensure he had no further reason to have another go at her, Lucy had risen early and made it into the station by seven-thirty, which she was confident would be earlier than Watson, almost certainly earlier than Carmichael and probably golden girl, Rachel, too.

So, at eight-fifteen and eight-thirty respectively, when Rachel then Watson arrived, Lucy was already deeply absorbed in her given task of finding out more about Richard Cox, when he was known as Richard Purnell.

"The boss not in yet?" enquired Watson as he sat down at his desk, placing in front of him the beaker of steaming coffee and bacon roll he'd bought from the canteen on his way up.

Lucy shook her head. "Not so far," she replied curtly, keeping her head buried into her computer.

Rachel checked her watch.

"I might head over to the hospital and take over from PC Twamley. The poor girl got given the night shift last night, so I expect by now she'll be keen to get home and get her head down."

"Have fun," replied Watson flippantly, his mouth half full of bacon roll.

"Yep, have a good one," added Lucy, her eyes still fixed on her screen.

Rachel grabbed her bag and rushed away. "See you later," she remarked as she disappeared out through the door.

* * *

It only occurred to Carmichael just as he was ringing Mary Price's doorbell that she may have been on her way to work. However, he was in luck. Within a matter of seconds Mary opened the door, her face pale and tired-looking.

"Has something happened to Richard?" Mary asked as soon as she saw it was Carmichael. "He didn't come home last night and he's not answering his messages."

Carmichael nodded. "He's safe but he's in custody," Carmichael replied. "I'm sorry to have to tell you that we believe Richard is responsible for Tim Wall's murder."

Mary looked crestfallen but strangely did not offer any argument in Richard's defence. "That's terrible," she muttered, her eyes glazing over and her head gently shaking from left to right.

"I wanted to ask you about when Harriet had Richard," continued Carmichael. "Do you have any idea where your sister would have gone to have him?"

Still clearly shaken by what Carmichael had told her, Mary shook her head even more vigorously. "Not a clue," she replied.

Carmichael paused. "Did your parents have any connection with Derbyshire?" he asked.

Mary looked up into Carmichael's blue eyes.

"That's where Mum was from," replied Mary. "She was born and bred in Buxton. I still had an auntie who lived that way, until she passed away last year."

Delighted to have established a link, Carmichael nodded. "Thanks Mary," he replied. "That's all I needed to know."

Mary remained at her door while Carmichael made his exit down the drive and into his car. Then, with a last disconsolate shake of her head, Mary went back inside and closed the door behind her.

Chapter 93

"Buxton," Carmichael announced enthusiastically as he burst into the incident room.

Watson and Lucy looked up from their respective computer screens.

"I've just been speaking to Mary Price again and she told me her mum was from Buxton," he continued. "So, I think there's a good chance that's where she'd have sent Harriet to have her baby."

"I'll get on to the nearest government adoption agency," Lucy remarked.

"What about Barnardo's?" Carmichael asked. "Have they got back to you?"

Lucy shook her head. "Not yet, but Marc's onto that."

"Just spoke with them now," Watson piped up. "They've nothing on any male adoption at around that time with the surname Price, Cox or Purnell."

Carmichael paused for a few seconds before continuing.

"Whilst driving here this morning, I've been trying to work out what motive Richard had for killing Wall and also why it was he attacked Faye," he remarked. "After all, he'd bought Wall that expensive whiskey and that suggests to me that he wanted to impress him rather than to harm him."

By their expressions both Lucy and Watson seemed to agree.

"Have you a theory?" Lucy asked.

Carmichael shook his head. "No," he replied despairingly, "but if I'm right, something must have gone terribly wrong when Cox met his father."

"So, what's the plan for this morning?" Watson asked.

"I suggest one of you stays here and keeps digging into Cox's adoption," Carmichael replied, "and one of you comes with me to talk with him again."

Carmichael looked over at his two sergeants to see who would ask to join him first.

"Who wants to join me?" he asked, when neither said anything.

"You go, Marc," Lucy said, her head turned in his direction. "I'm happy to finish this off."

Stunned but delighted to get out of the boring task of scouring for information on Cox's past without even a fight, Watson sprang to his feet.

"That suits me," he replied chirpily.

Lucy turned her attention back to the screen in front of her, not looking at Carmichael for even a split second.

"Great," remarked Carmichael who started walking to the door. "Let's get on with it then, Marc."

Carmichael allowed Watson to exit the room first, before turning back to face Lucy.

"If you discover anything you think I should know about, interrupt us," he told her. "I'm not expecting Cox to be any more cooperative today than he was yesterday so we'll probably need all the help we can get."

Lucy looked over from her desk. "Will do, sir," she replied, before turning her attention once more back to her computer screen.

* * *

Rachel was pleased to find Faye sitting up in bed and looking significantly better than she had the evening before. According to what PC Twamley had told her, before she'd left to go home, Faye hadn't stirred once until she'd been woken at six-thirty by the nurse, who wanted to get her up and ready in time for Dr Borchini's morning round.

"You look tons better, Faye," Rachel told her, her smile wide and welcoming.

"I feel so much better," replied Faye with a smile on her face, too. "Almost human again."

* * *

As soon as she was alone in the incident room, Lucy reached for her bag and took out the brown envelope she'd written before she'd gone to bed the evening before. She tapped the sealed envelope against her chin a couple of times, before getting up from her desk and striding over to Carmichael's small room.

Lucy walked the few paces inside, placed the envelope in the middle of the desk, face up, with the words *'Private and Confidential. FAO Inspector Carmichael'* in full view.

Lucy glanced briefly at the envelope one last time before turning on her heels, leaving Carmichael's office and going back to her desk.

Chapter 94

Richard Cox and his brief had positioned themselves in the same places as they'd occupied the day before, when Carmichael and Watson entered interview room 1.

"Did you have a good night's sleep?" Carmichael enquired.

Cox remained silent; his arms folded tightly against his chest.

"Before we talk about your involvement in the murder of Timothy Wall and the attack on Faye Hemmingway, I'd like to ask you a bit more about your childhood growing up in Derbyshire," began Carmichael, his piercing blue eyes transfixed on his subject, watching intently for any sign that his new tack might be having an effect.

However, Carmichael was disappointed, as Cox remained totally impassive.

"You were born in Buxton, I believe," continued Carmichael, unperturbed. "That's right isn't it?"

* * *

Although she was keen to grill Faye about her attack, Rachel decided to adopt a more patient approach. Faye had yet to be seen by Dr Borchini, so Rachel's strategy was to avoid talking about the attack at all for the time being and to build their relationship even more, while they waited together.

"What's the food like here?" Rachel asked.

Faye smiled. "Breakfast was fine," she replied. "Mind you, I was starving and it's hard to mess up cereal and toast, I suppose."

Rachel laughed. "I suppose so," she remarked. "Although my boyfriend did a good job at burning the toast this morning. Black smoke all over my kitchen and the smoke alarm peeping away at seven wasn't much fun, I can tell you."

Faye smiled again. "Do you live together?" she asked.

Rachel shook her head and opened her eyes wide. "God, no," she replied. "I love him to bits, but I'm not sure I'd want to live with him permanently. He's far too messy about the place."

They both laughed.

"His apartment is a tip," Rachel continued. "He shares with a mate from his work, who's probably the messiest of the two, but Matt's definitely not house proud."

Faye stared forward. "I'd love Richard to move in with me," she remarked wistfully. "He's staying in lodgings at the moment, but I'm hoping we'll move in together soon."

Rachel maintained her smile but felt a little uneasy. Faye seemed totally oblivious to Richard's predicament; completely unaware that Richard wasn't going to be sharing with anyone for quite some time, other than maybe another convicted criminal in a prison cell.

* * *

Lucy hit the jackpot almost as soon as she started to revisit the adoptions with Buxton as the most probable place of the birth. Within minutes of providing the administrator with the details, she came back with a result.

"Can you email me over the paperwork?" Lucy requested, before giving the woman at the end of the line her email address.

With the call over, Lucy leaned back in her chair and cupped her hands behind her head, a broad smile emblazoned across her face. Despite Carmichael's insistence on her interrupting him if she made any sort of breakthrough, Lucy decided to hang fire. She wanted to get all the paperwork through before she shared her discovery with Carmichael and the rest of the team.

* * *

Carmichael soldiered on for forty minutes with Richard Cox.

Having asked about his life in Buxton and the jobs he'd had in Bakewell, Carmichael had moved on to ask about his thinking behind coming to Kirkwood. After each question he'd paused to allow Cox to answer, only to receive either silence or occasionally a monotone 'no comment'. However, Carmichael persevered, and even, at times, looked like he was enjoying the ludicrous scenario.

He then asked Cox how he'd found Mary Price, how he got on with Adrian Hope at Mullion and Thorpe and finally, how he'd met Faye Hemmingway. Again, either silence or 'no comment' was all that Carmichael could get out of the man across the table.

"The bottom line here," Carmichael eventually announced, "as I'm sure Mr Fairfax will have already told you, is that you're not going to get off with this, Richard. You're going away for quite a considerable time. However, the court might feel inclined to mitigate that sentence if they knew the circumstances of the meeting you had with Timothy Wall."

Carmichael paused and looked directly at Cox, who seemed as disinterested as he had during the rest of the interview.

"I believe you genuinely went to meet your father, hoping he'd be keen to build a proper relationship with you," Carmichael continued. "You strike me as a smart guy, Richard, so I'm sure the possibility of him being a little hesitant in embracing you to his bosom is something you'd have considered, maybe even expected. But I'm sure that you went there in friendship and certainly not with the intention to kill him. Buying him that expensive bottle of whiskey proves that. However, something went terribly wrong and as a result, you hit him with that paperweight and your father died. Isn't that true?"

For a split second, Carmichael thought Cox was going to speak, but he didn't.

"The thing is, Richard," Carmichael continued, "if you go on refusing to cooperate and persist in not telling us what actually happened, then almost certainly, it will mean a lengthier sentence for you. It won't take the best barrister in the country to convince the court you went to Wall's office hell-bent on killing him, if you continue to say nothing. So, why don't you do yourself a favour and give your side of the story."

Carmichael looked almost pleadingly at Cox, but to no avail. Cox remained expressionless and seemingly unmoved by what Carmichael had to say.

"No comment," Cox eventually replied.

Chapter 95

Lucy was about to go down to the interview room when Carmichael and Watson suddenly emerged through the incident room door.

"How did you get on?" she asked.

Carmichael shook his head. "He's being as uncooperative as before," he replied. "How about you?"

Lucy smiled. "You guys have saved my legs. I was just about to come down and give you the good news," she replied.

From the enthusiastic look in her eyes and the triumphant expression on her face, Carmichael and Watson knew she'd got something important to tell them.

* * *

For the next three hours the incident room was a hive of activity. The whiteboard had been wiped clean and, based upon what Lucy had unearthed from Derbyshire, a new set of information had been written, this time more legibly, in Lucy's neat hand.

Carmichael, Watson and Lucy had then discussed and agreed what more they needed to do and exactly who should do what. They then got on with their tasks as they pieced together, layer after layer, information about the birth of Harriet and Timothy Wall's baby thirty years before, the child's adoption and, most illuminating of all, Richard's life before he arrived in Kirkwood.

When they'd finished, they studied the whiteboard, astonished but also delighted by what they'd uncovered that morning.

"I think it's time to have one more discussion with Richard," Carmichael finally announced. "And this time I'd like you both to be in on it."

With their wholehearted agreement, Lucy and Watson stood up and headed towards the door.

"Can you both make sure that Cox and his brief are ready," he remarked. "I'm going to hang on here for a little while. I need to update Rachel, so she knows what's happening."

"Will do," replied Watson, who followed Lucy out into the corridor, leaving his boss to make the call.

Carmichael dialled Rachel's mobile as he was walking into his office and sat down waiting for her to answer.

As soon as he was seated, he noticed the envelope on his desk, marked private and confidential and for his attention.

"How's Faye?" he asked as soon as Rachel answered the call.

"She's fine," replied Rachel. "The specialist saw her earlier and they might release her later today."

"That's great news," remarked Carmichael, who at the same time picked up the envelope. "I need you to be aware that Lucy's located the adoption details and we've dug up quite a lot of new information."

As he updated Rachel on the morning's crucial developments, Carmichael fiddled with the sealed envelope in front of him, curious about its contents.

Amazed with what she was hearing, Rachel at first didn't know what to say. However, as it started to sink in, she, as her colleagues had done earlier that morning, started to make sense of what had been happening.

"That would explain why Richard's remained silent," she remarked.

"I know," replied Carmichael. "And I also have a hunch why his meeting with Wall last week turned sour so rapidly."

Rachel couldn't quite see what Carmichael was getting at but didn't ask for any clarification as her thoughts were drifting towards Faye Hemmingway in the next room.

"Faye's going to be devastated," Rachel announced.

"I know," replied Carmichael. "I'll leave it to your judgement, but I'd suggest you tell her nothing for now. Should she be discharged, remain with her at all times. We can work out how we break the news to her later."

Happy that all his team were now up to speed, Carmichael placed the envelope, still unopened, in his jacket pocket and headed away to confront Richard Cox once again. This time, however, with total confidence, knowing their latest conundrum was now all but solved.

Chapter 96

Richard Cox and his brief, Mr Fairfax, sat silently across the table from Carmichael, who on this occasion was flanked by Lucy to his left and Watson on his right.

"Before we start," Carmichael began, "I want to update you both on what I and my officers have been up to since we last spoke."

Richard folded his arms tightly in front of his chest, while Mr Fairfax scribbled a note on the pad he held in his left hand.

Carmichael paused and looked over at the two men opposite, firstly at Mr Fairfax then at Cox.

"We've been very busy," he continued. "DS Martin has spoken with the adoption agency in Buxton, who have sent her the details of the child Harriet Price gave birth to almost thirty years ago. She's also been in contact with the local government offices in Bakewell where you were employed in IT, when you still went by the name Richard Purnell."

As he finished, Carmichael turned his head to face Lucy for a few seconds, who was smiling at Cox.

"What you've found out has been very illuminating, hasn't it, DS Martin."

"It certainly has, sir," replied Lucy, her eyes not flinching away from Cox.

Carmichael then turned his head round to face Watson.

"And DS Watson here has been busy looking into your time employed, again in IT, with an engineering company called Thomas Mallings. He's also managed to talk on the phone with your father, Neil, and I think it's fair to say that Neil's not the proudest father we've ever come across. Is that a fair assessment, DS Watson?"

Watson nodded. "I'd say so," he replied.

"Given that we now know much more than we did earlier," continued Carmichael, "don't you think it's high time you started to talk to us, Richard?"

It was clear from the expression on Cox's face that he knew the game was up.

"Your team appear to have been very busy," he replied calmly. "But I've never pretended to be anything other than who I am, and surely, you're not going to start trying to pin these trumped-up charges on me, based upon things from my past. I don't think that will hold up in court, Inspector Carmichael."

As he spoke, Cox looked back at Carmichael, his expression a strange mixture of arrogance and relief.

Carmichael smiled. "You are of course, right about that," he conceded. "However, the past has a big part to play in this case; as well you know."

Unfolding his arms, Cox leaned back in his chair and placed his hands behind his head.

"Come on then, Carmichael, tell us what you've got," he said cockily, as if he saw his predicament as a game of little significance; and in a tone that clearly irritated Carmichael.

"Very well," Carmichael remarked, his face now serious and his eyes displaying a level of annoyance. "This is what we now know."

Carmichael paused for a few seconds before continuing.

"Harriet Price was brought to Buxton by her mother thirty years ago," Carmichael announced in a clear but emotionless voice. "She'd fallen pregnant by Timothy Wall and her mother took her to Derbyshire so that she could have the child and it could be adopted, without anyone back in Lancashire knowing. She chose Buxton as it was where she'd been brought up and she had a sister there, who no doubt helped her and young Harriet through an exceedingly difficult time."

Carmichael again paused for a few seconds.

"In that March, the child was born and was given up for adoption," continued Carmichael, "and fortunately went to a good loving home. Harriet then went home to Lancashire and a few years later she married a man called Justin Stockley."

Carmichael stopped for a few seconds and took a sip of water from the plastic cup in front of him.

"About twenty-five years later, a young man called Richard Purnell started to work at the government offices in Bakewell, not far from Buxton, as an IT officer," Carmichael remarked. "That's you, Richard. And in that job, you had access to a lot of confidential information including the adoption records for the whole region. In normal circumstances having access to this sort of information isn't a major problem, unless of course those with access are dishonest, which is unfortunately what you are, isn't it, Richard? You're also unreliable, too, which according to your old boss at the government offices is why you were eventually let go. I've no way of knowing whether you'd used the information you could access on adoptions before you were let go, but once you had left it must have been gold dust to you, and we know for sure you then started to use it for your own ends."

"Prove it," Richard remarked.

Carmichael continued. "Well, we know you blackmailed a senior manager at Thomas Mallings into giving you a job, on a ridiculously high salary, with some information you had on her about a child she'd had adopted years before. We spoke to her earlier and she told us about that little scam. Had she not finally decided that she'd had enough and had the courage to tell her husband what was going on, you'd probably still be blackmailing her now. I believe her husband is a big chap, who gave you a good hiding and told your father about what you'd been doing. As a result, you were forced to leave that job and the area. That must have been very annoying for you."

The smug expression on Richard Cox's face had now totally evaporated, and he shuffled nervously in his chair.

"We know this is all true, as your father also confirmed it to us," continued Carmichael, who turned his head to face Watson as he spoke. "And what was it he said about Richard?"

Watson looked at his notebook, so that he could relay the quote accurately.

"He called Richard a pathological liar, a conman and an embarrassment," he read out loudly.

"Not the greatest reference," Carmichael added sarcastically. "He also confirmed that you weren't adopted. Isn't that right DS Watson?"

"Absolutely, sir," Watson acknowledged. "His exact words were, 'I wish he was adopted then at least I could say he's not my flesh and blood, but sadly, he's mine'."

Carmichael looked across at Cox, his face stern and unfriendly.

"Which brings us nicely to the scam in hand," he remarked. "Your current attempt to con Mary Price, Faye Hemmingway and, of course, Timothy Wall."

Cox was now extremely agitated. He was unable to remain still, shuffling in his chair and wringing his hands as if they were continually becoming wet with sweat.

"When did you come up with the idea of trying to convince people you were Harriet Price and Timothy Wall's son?" Carmichael asked. "And what did you expect to achieve from such a scam?"

Carmichael stared at Cox, but he remained tight-lipped.

"Maybe that wasn't his original plan," interjected Lucy. "Maybe Richard was just looking to repeat the first scam and try to blackmail Harriet about putting her baby up for adoption. After all, Richard wouldn't have known about Harriet having died, until he got here."

By the expression on Cox's face, Carmichael realised Lucy may have hit upon something.

"That makes perfect sense," he remarked enthusiastically. "You were just following the same scam as at Thomas Mallings, but then you changed it when you found out Harriet was dead. Was it when you met Mary you decided to pretend to be the baby? Did her naïve belief that you were the baby persuade you to change your strategy?"

"You tell me," replied Cox forcefully. "You two appear to be the smart ones."

"I reckon it was," continued Carmichael. "And poor Mary, who was so keen for you to be her beloved sister's boy must have fed you with so much information that you felt confident you could pull it off. I bet you thought you'd hit the jackpot when you met Mary Price. She even helped you get a job here and allowed you to stay in her house."

A wry smile appeared on Cox's face. "She's such a gullible cow," he remarked. "Quite frankly, she deserved it."

"And what about Faye?" Lucy asked. "Did she deserve it, too? Because you spotted her as a potential way to get to Timothy Wall, didn't you?"

Arrogantly, Cox retained a fixed smile, shrugged his shoulders but said nothing.

"Of course he did," added Carmichael. "And poor Faye fell for you."

"It's my magnetic personality," remarked Cox, quite clearly indifferent to any pain he'd caused Faye.

"But she didn't seem to know about you wanting to meet

410

Wall and she wasn't aware that you were planning to pretend to be his son," continued Carmichael. "Not initially anyway. Did you actually tell her the lie about being Wall's son?"

"I bet he did," Lucy added. "But I'd guess it was probably as late as yesterday, when Faye was in hospital."

Once more, Cox shrugged his shoulders and smiled. "It's good to know you guys don't know everything yet," he remarked facetiously.

"No, but we will once Faye comes to her senses, stops lying for you and starts telling us the truth," Watson remarked.

"DS Watson's right isn't he?" Carmichael remarked. "Faye's not going to carry on protecting you once she knows the whole truth about you."

Cox just kept smiling, an egotistical smile of someone who wasn't worried about Faye deserting him.

However, Carmichael wasn't fazed in the slightest by Cox's bravado.

"I didn't mention what I did this morning did I, Richard," he remarked calmly.

Cox shrugged his shoulders, as if to suggest he wasn't bothered.

"Well, your father told DS Watson something else that was really interesting," Carmichael added. "Something I followed up. He told him that you were married and had a child. A young girl."

At the mention of his marriage and child, Cox's expression changed dramatically.

"I wonder what Faye will make of that," Watson added with a broad smile. "I don't expect you've bothered to tell her about your wife and daughter, have you, Richard? She'll not want to carry on lying for you when she knows you're married with a child."

It was obvious from Cox's expression that he wasn't best pleased.

"Well, as I said," continued Carmichael. "I spoke with your wife, Mandy, about forty minutes ago. She seems genuinely nice. However, she appears to have an almost identical opinion of you as your father. Do you know what she told me?"

"No, but I'm sure you're keen to tell me," replied Cox through gritted teeth. Carmichael smiled. "She told me that you're a fraud, a cheat, a serial liar, a lousy husband and an awful father. She also said that you had a short fuse and a vicious temper. All in all, I got the impression she doesn't like you very much."

Cox lunged across the desk at Carmichael. And had he not been grabbed by Mr Fairfax and Watson, would have almost certainly reached his intended target.

"Please calm down, Richard," Mr Fairfax insisted as his client shrugged off his and Watson's restraining arms and slowly slumped back in his seat.

Carmichael kept smiling. "Now you've got that out of your system, why don't we talk again about last Friday evening when you met Timothy Wall," he said calmly.

"I'm not saying anything more," shouted Cox. "As far as I'm concerned this interview is over."

"Then for Mr Fairfax's benefit, let me outline exactly what I think happened, since you arrived here in Kirkwood, and particularly on Friday evening," Carmichael remarked.

To demonstrate he wasn't going to take any further part in the interview, Richard Cox turned his chair ninety degrees, so it was facing the side wall with his back to Fairfax and his gaze now away from Carmichael and his two sergeants. As if to further emphasise his defiance, he folded his arms tight against his chest once more.

Carmichael ignored Richard's bizarre, childlike antics and started to explain what he believed had happened on Friday to Fairfax, knowing full well that Cox would be listening.

"Having met with Mary Price and, as DS Martin suggested, having changed his initial plan to a new one, pretending to be Timothy Wall's son, I think your client sought out Faye and started a relationship with her in order to get close to him," Carmichael announced. "Just as Mary had been useful to Richard in telling him all about her sister and her relationship with Wall, Faye was also valuable to him. For example, she must have told him about the expensive Irish whiskey Wall liked. And, even more helpfully, she had keys to the office, which I think he took advantage of, too. I suspect he's made copies of those keys, which no doubt we'll find either at Mary's house or at his work."

"Being with Faye so much, it would have been easy for him to take her keys and get the duplicate set made," Lucy added.

"Anyway," continued Carmichael, "having gained the trust of both Mary then Faye, over a number of weeks, I believe your client felt able to execute his new plan last Friday." Carmichael paused before continuing. "I think Richard did two things early on Friday morning. The first was to use a copy of Faye's keys to get access to the office before anyone had arrived. Once inside, I think he opened the fire exit and wedged it ajar, then made off. I think he decided to use the fire exit as a means of entry on Friday evening so he wouldn't accidently bump into Faye. With it being tucked away down the corridor, I also suspect he was confident it being open wouldn't have been spotted during the day. We've not had chance to check any CCTV footage in the area for early Friday morning, but I'm sure when we do, we'll see Richard in the vicinity of the office before Wall arrived."

Carmichael paused for a moment and looked across at Richard, who remained silent, his eyes still focused on the bare wall.

Carmichael turned his head back and made eye contact again with Mr Fairfax.

"The second thing he did," Carmichael continued, "was to call the office when he knew Faye wouldn't yet have arrived and make the appointment to meet Wall that evening, at a time after Faye had left to go to The Lamb. I think the name Haverstock-Price he used was some sort of joke he'd thought up, maybe to see if Wall was smart enough to work out who he was. Perhaps your client may share his reasoning for that with us at some stage later."

Richard turned his head slowly, to catch Carmichael's eye for a moment, but said nothing.

"So, with his access sorted and an appointment set for a time when he knew Faye would have left for the evening, Richard was then able to enter the office unseen and confront Wall, safe in the knowledge that they'd be alone. And as the icing on the cake, and as a gesture of friendship from a loving son, he buys Wall the bottle of Gelston's fifteen-year-old Irish whiskey; the whiskey that Faye must have told him her boss loved so much."

Carmichael looked over at Richard Cox, who was still pretending not to listen. "How am I doing so far?" he enquired.

Cox remained silent, so Carmichael continued. "So, coming in via the open fire exit he enters the office and confronts Timothy Wall. We cannot know exactly what Richard said, but he clearly gives Wall the bottle, which he must have accepted willingly as he opened it and poured himself a glass. But then things started to go wrong. An argument then ensued; we know that because a witness has stated he heard one of them saying to the other that he should be ashamed of himself and that his behaviour was disgraceful. Initially I thought it was Richard who had said those words, referring to Wall, the inference being that he hadn't accepted him as his son or acknowledged his responsibility as a father.

However, now I think those words were spoken not by Richard but by Wall. It was Richard who was the disgraceful one, for trying to pull off his outrageous scam."

Carmichael paused again and took another sip of water.

"You see, when Richard told Wall that he was his son, Wall didn't react as he'd expected," Carmichael announced with a glint of delight in his eyes. "Isn't that right, Richard?"

Cox turned his chair to face Carmichael and stared menacingly in his direction.

"I think that rather than being shocked at the news he had a son he'd never known about, I think it's likely that Wall wanted to test you, to see if you were telling him the truth," continued Carmichael. "Isn't that what happened?"

Richard leaned forward in his chair, his gaze never wavering from Carmichael, and hatred written all over his face.

"You see, based upon what DS Martin discovered this morning, I now know that Wall did know about the baby," Carmichael added. "Mary Price was wrong about Harriet not telling him all those years ago."

Carmichael looked directly into Richard's angry eyes. "Do you know why I know that?" he enquired.

Richard sat back in his chair. He knew the game was over.

"It was the birth records DS Martin was given earlier," Carmichael continued. "They gave the actual date when the child was born. The 30th of March 1992."

Carmichael smiled at Richard who stared back with venom in his eyes.

"Or more commonly written as three, zero, zero, three, nine, two," Carmichael added. "Exactly the same number that Wall kept on a scrap of paper under his writing pad in his office, which was coincidentally the combination to his safe at home." Carmichael smiled once more. "Once I saw that date, I knew Wall was aware he had a son, why else would he have the child's birth date as his safe combination?" remarked Carmichael. "I think Wall asked you what your date of birth was when you met him on Friday."

Richard didn't reply, but by the look on his face, it was clear that Carmichael's assumption was correct.

"And what did you tell him?" Carmichael asked. "I bet it wasn't the 30th of March was it, because I imagine you hadn't expected to be asked for that piece of information, as according to what Mary Price had told you, Wall didn't know about the child. So, I bet when he asked you that it threw you completely."

Richard lunged across the table again. However, this time he was too quick for anyone to stop him, and in a split-second he'd managed to catch hold of Carmichael by the throat.

Watson and Lucy sprang to Carmichael's aid, joined a few seconds later by PC Dyer, who'd been stationed by the door. Together the three officers wrestled the cursing prisoner to the floor before placing him in handcuffs and hauling him back to his feet.

"You think you're so smart," shouted Richard, his mad, angry eyes bulging in their sockets. "Just like Wall did, but I'll have you, too, Carmichael."

Shaken but unharmed, Carmichael stood up, put his right hand to his neck and took a couple of steps backwards.

"Take him to the cells," he instructed Watson and Dyer. "This interview is now well and truly over."

Chapter 97

Carmichael sat calmly alone in his office with a beaker of water in his hand. Although he was unhurt, he was still a little shaken from the sudden attack he'd experienced thirty minutes earlier in interview room 1.

With Watson and Lucy downstairs adding assault to Richard Cox's charge sheet and Rachel still at the hospital with Faye Hemmingway, Carmichael suddenly remembered the envelope he'd found on his desk earlier that morning.

After extracting it from his jacket, he slit the envelope open and pulled out the single sheet of paper from inside.

He didn't notice Lucy enter the office, until the sound of the door shutting behind her made him look up, by which time he'd finished reading the short letter.

"So, you're leaving us," Carmichael said, Lucy's letter of resignation still in his hand.

"Yes," Lucy replied. "Calum's now got his promotion in the Labour Party, so he'll be spending more time in London from now on and I want to be with him."

Carmichael nodded. "Doesn't it make more sense for you to simply get yourself a transfer?" he asked.

Lucy shook her head. "No," she replied, "I'm quitting the force altogether. To be honest my heart's not in it anymore."

Carmichael frowned. "But you're a good officer and you've a promising career in front of you."

Lucy smiled and shook her head. "No, Rachel's a good officer," she replied firmly. "A bit like I was when I was a DC, but I'm not anymore."

"I don't agree," Carmichael remarked.

Lucy shook her head again. "I just don't want to do this anymore," she explained.

Carmichael's expression remained one of bewilderment, so Lucy felt she needed to elaborate.

"I've been unsettled at work for a while, but it dawned on me when I went with Rachel up to Newcastle the other day," Lucy said. "She was everything I used to be. She was organised, structured, intuitive and keen as mustard. And, to my shame, she infuriated me. But I've thought about it since and I realised that I wasn't really annoyed with her, or even myself, the simple truth is that I don't want to be a police officer anymore. My life has moved on and I've got different things I want to do."

Carmichael's first thought on hearing this was that what she probably meant was she wanted to have children, but he didn't dare say so. He just nodded.

"I see," he replied. "Well I wish you all the best, Lucy and I hope whatever you do decide to do works out for you."

By the look in her eyes, Carmichael could see Lucy was relieved that he wasn't going to try and persuade her to change her mind, which he guessed she'd probably half expected him to do.

"Thank you, sir," she remarked, before forcing a smile.

"About what happened in America," Carmichael heard himself saying. "I behaved badly and..."

Before Carmichael had a chance to continue, Lucy held up her hand to get him to stop.

"What happened in America is in the past," she remarked in a firm assured voice. "It happened, and although I guess neither of us are particularly proud of that episode, we've both moved on and as far as I'm concerned it's ancient history. That incident had no part to play in my decision to leave the force."

Relieved that Lucy had cut him short and appeared, like him, to want to draw a line under Winston Salem, Carmichael simply nodded.

Lucy turned on her heels and departed, leaving Carmichael alone in his office.

After watching Lucy go, Carmichael sat quietly for a few minutes before he folded up her resignation letter and placed it to the side of his desk.

Chapter 98

Leaving Lucy and Watson at the station tidying up the loose ends of the case, Carmichael decided to head over to the hospital to find Rachel and see how Faye was doing.

When he arrived, Faye was sat up on her bed, dressed and appeared ready to leave.

"Faye's been discharged," Rachel remarked as she walked over to meet Carmichael at the door. "We're just waiting for the pharmacist to dispense her medication."

"Have you spoken to her?" Carmichael asked in a hushed voice.

Rachel nodded. "I had to," she replied, almost apologetically. "She wouldn't stop asking what was going on."

"And how did she take it?" he asked, clearly a little louder than he'd wanted.

"I'm furious," announced Faye at the top of her voice. "What a bastard!"

Rachel, whose back was still to Faye, pulled a face that suggested Faye's remark may have been an understatement.

"She's very, very unhappy," Rachel mouthed.

Carmichael smiled, nodded, walked across to Faye and sat down next to her.

"I'm sorry about everything, Faye," he said sympathetically. "But the main thing is that you're safe and

Richard's not going to be bothering you or anyone else for a very long time."

"Good," Faye exclaimed. "And to think I believed him when he told me he hadn't killed Tim. What sort of idiot am I?"

Carmichael smiled. "Trusting and believing someone doesn't make you a fool," he remarked.

Faye seemed to feel a bit better after hearing that from Carmichael.

"I promise you I had no idea about him killing Tim," she insisted. "And I genuinely couldn't remember, when Rachel initially asked me about who'd attacked me, but eventually it did all come back to me and I should have told you then."

Carmichael nodded, to try and reassure Faye but also keep her talking.

"But when he told me he wouldn't do it again I believed him," continued Faye. "So, I lied; and I'm truly sorry for that."

"That's fine," Carmichael replied supportively. "The important thing is that you're now telling us the truth."

Faye shook her head gently from side to side. "He said he loved me," she muttered angrily, "but he's already married and has a child. What an idiot I've been."

Carmichael put a reassuring hand on Faye's arm. "So, why did Richard attack you?" he asked.

Faye shrugged her shoulders. "I'm not totally sure," she confessed. "One minute we were talking about him joining me to run the detective agency, the next he hit me and then put his hands around my neck and was squeezing so hard."

"And you don't know what caused him to turn on you?" Carmichael enquired.

Faye stared at the floor and gently shook her head as she tried desperately to remember.

"I think I said something about us having to celebrate and he…" Faye's voice tailed off as she struggled to recall the exact details but was clearly still finding it painful to bring the assault back into her thoughts.

"It was the whiskey," she then said with some bewilderment in her voice. "I said we'll have to go to the pub to celebrate, but Richard said he had a better idea and opened the drawer, where Tim kept his whiskey bottle. I asked him what he was doing. It was then his expression changed and he became violent."

Carmichael looked across at Rachel.

"Had you talked to Richard about Tim's passion for good whiskey?" he asked.

Faye shrugged her shoulders. "Richard asked me a bit about Tim early on in our relationship and I told him he liked good whiskey."

"And did you mention he liked Gelston's fifteen-year-old Irish whiskey?" Carmichael asked.

Faye looked down at the floor and nodded gently.

"I think I may have done," she replied, her response meek and vague.

Carmichael saw no need to quiz Faye any further and moved his attention over to Rachel.

"I assume you will be taking Faye home?" he enquired.

Rachel smiled and nodded. "Absolutely," she replied. "And I'll stay with her until her parents arrive. They live in France and they're driving back to be with her. They should be in Kirkwood at around five this afternoon."

"In that case I'll leave you both," announced Carmichael, who smiled warmly at Faye before getting to his feet.

As he walked to the door, Carmichael signalled with his head for Rachel to join him.

"Is everything alright with you?" he asked.

Rachel nodded. "Yes," she replied. "And what about everything back at the station?"

"Yes," Carmichael confirmed. "Lucy and Marc are sorting out the charge sheet for Cox, and tying up the rest of the loose ends, but at last I think we've just about got everything sorted."

"That's good," remarked Rachel, who had a slightly perplexed expression on her face, which Carmichael noticed immediately.

"You look like you've got something on your mind," Carmichael said, his eyebrows raised, and brow furrowed.

"I may be a bit dim," replied Rachel, "but what I don't get is how Richard managed to attack Faye when he was only in the office a few minutes."

Carmichael smiled and nodded. "I've asked Marc to check the CCTV footage around Wall's office on Wednesday afternoon," he replied. "I think when he was seen entering Wall's office by all those witnesses, it was the second time he'd been up there that afternoon."

Rachel nodded. "So, the assault happened the first time he went in and he came back later to give himself an alibi."

Carmichael nodded. "That's my theory," he replied.

"How devious," remarked Rachel. "But I guess he would have used the fire exit the first time to get in and out, so we may not see him on any CCTV in the area."

Carmichael shook his head. "I suspect he left via the fire exit, so he wasn't seen," he replied. "But I think he'll have entered via the main staircase. Remember the fire exit will have been closed to the outside and he wasn't planning to attack Faye, so he didn't have any need to conceal his entry. I may have it totally wrong, but I'm expecting Marc to find some CCTV footage from the vicinity that shows he was in the area around the front of the building earlier than we thought at first."

Rachel shook her head. "He's cunning, that's for sure," she remarked.

As Rachel considered what Carmichael had just told her, she looked across at the forlorn figure of Faye, perched on the bed, with eyes aimlessly focused on the floor.

"I'll see you back at the station later," Carmichael remarked, before giving Rachel a warm smile, and then heading away.

Chapter 99

Carmichael had one last thing he wanted to do before returning to Kirkwood Police Station. Having parked his car outside Tim Wall's house, he walked down the path to the front door, with Wall's now infamous red book under his arm.

It had been a few days since he'd last been inside the house and he'd forgotten what a state it had been left in following Fat Malc's unsuccessful attempt to find those damaging photos Marcus Rigby had taken of Shelley Baybutt.

As he stepped gingerly over the various items still strewn all over the floor, Carmichael suddenly, out the corner of his eye, saw Simon Baybutt's distinctive white car pull up outside next to his black BMW.

Moving over to the window, he saw Cassie Wilson lean across and kiss Simon before getting out of the car. As soon as she'd clambered out, Carmichael then noticed Shelley Baybutt get out of the seat behind her dad and walk around the back of the white Tesla towards the front passenger door. Before she climbed into the front seat, Shelley smiled then waved at Cassie, who waved back. Cassie then watched as the gleaming white car sped off.

Once it was out of sight, Cassie walked down the path to the front door, and put her key in the lock.

Not wanting to startle her, Carmichael shouted through to Cassie as she entered the tiny hallway.

"Hello Ms Wilson," he said in a loud voice. "It's Inspector Carmichael, I'm in the front room."

By the expression on her face when she entered the lounge, it was clear Cassie hadn't expected to meet anyone.

"My God, what a mess," she remarked when she saw the state of the place. "Tim would have been mortified to see his house in such a state. He was so house proud and tidy."

Carmichael raised his eyebrows.

"The good news is we don't think anything was taken," he remarked. "And although it's a mess, I'm not sure much, if anything has actually been broken."

Cassie nodded. "I thought I'd better just make sure it's OK," she explained. "As it's now mine."

Carmichael nodded. "I just came back to drop this off," he remarked, holding up the red book.

Cassie shook her head. "I hadn't thought about his book," she remarked. "Is that mine, too?"

Carmichael handed it over to her. "I think it's classed as part of the house contents." he replied. "We don't need it for evidence, so it's yours to do with as you please."

Cassie opened it up and flicked through some of the pages.

"It's going to have to go," she concluded after only seeing three or four entries. "By any standards, this is just plain wrong."

Carmichael couldn't help but snigger. "I know," he replied.

Cassie turned to the last entry, about her. "I suppose I should feel honoured that I got straight tens," she remarked.

"And you got his house in the will, too," added Carmichael. "So, he obviously did like you a lot."

Cassie nodded. "I suppose so," she remarked, before throwing the book down onto the settee. "The weird thing is, if I'd scored him, he'd have probably got a nine for his personality, but as for looks and the other one, sixes at best."

Carmichael shrugged his shoulders. "I never knew Tim Wall," he replied. "But I expect he'd have been a little put out to know that."

Cassie laughed loudly. "Mortified, I would imagine."

Carmichael paused for a few seconds before changing the subject.

"I saw you arrive with Simon and his daughter," he said. "So, I take it you've told her about your relationship?"

"Yes," responded Cassie. "And she's absolutely fine with it. To be honest I'm not sure why Simon was so concerned."

"I'm pleased it's all OK," Carmichael added.

"Well, regarding me and Simon, it's fine with Shelley," continued Cassie. "With regards to Shelley's foray into the world of risqué photographic poses, it's not quite so with Simon."

"Ah," Carmichael replied. "So, Simon knows, does he?"

"Oh, yes," continued Cassie. "And he's not best pleased with her, with Trevor, or with me, as it happens."

Carmichael frowned. "I get it as far as Shelley is concerned and I suppose he's probably a bit miffed with Trevor for covering it up and paying Tim to keep him quiet, but how come you're in the bad books?"

Cassie pulled a guilty-looking expression.

"I happened to say, in an attempt to try and take the heat out of things, that it's not that uncommon for women to allow these sorts of photos to be taken," she explained. "Which, on reflection, was not my smartest ever moment, as he now thinks that I'm not only condoning what Shelley let that little creep do, but that I might have done something similar myself."

Carmichael grinned. "I see," he replied.

"So, I'm currently tiptoeing on eggshells as far as Shelley and her dad are concerned," Cassie added. "But he'll get over it. Well, I hope he does."

Carmichael nodded again and headed towards the door.

"I'll be off," he said. "We think we have Tim Wall's murderer in custody, who's also the person who beat up Faye so badly," he said. "So, I need to get back to the station."

As he walked past her, Cassie grabbed hold of Carmichael's arm.

"I bitterly regret slapping Faye on Wednesday," she remarked. "I have no idea what came over me. But it was inexcusable."

"It was," he replied, with no attempt to allow her any mitigation. "It was common assault, and you may well have to go to court as a result. However, Faye has corroborated your version of events and we are confident that you did just slap her face once, so hopefully it won't be too onerous for you, but it's largely out of my hands now and up to the CPS and, if it goes that far, the courts."

"So, do you think it will go to court?" Cassie asked.

Carmichael shrugged his shoulders. "I couldn't say," he replied, even though, in his heart, he doubted it would.

Although Cassie was clearly concerned about the potential repercussions of her assault on Faye Hemmingway, she was able to force a smile as Carmichael moved away and opened the front door.

"Oh," Cassie suddenly exclaimed as Carmichael was just about to depart. "I forgot to thank you for finding Debra Poulter."

Carmichael turned. "Have they now spoken?" he asked.

"They did more than that," Cassie added. "Debra, or rather Jennifer as she now calls herself, and her boyfriend went over to see Mrs Poulter yesterday evening. She rang me last night at about ten o'clock after they'd left. She was so overjoyed."

Carmichael smiled. "I'm glad to hear that there's been a happy ending to that one," he remarked. "But the credit has to go to Tim Wall, not me. He was the one that tracked Mrs Poulter's daughter down. And for free, too."

Cassie smiled broadly. "Yes, we need to give him a ten for that one, don't we, Inspector."

"We certainly do," replied Carmichael before finally leaving Cassie alone in her house.

Chapter 100

With Faye Hemmingway handed over into the safe arms of her parents, Rachel returned to Kirkwood Police Station, just in time to see Lucy in the car park about to clamber into her car.

"You off then?" Rachel shouted over.

Lucy turned and smiled. "You could say that," she replied, her answer deliberately ambiguous.

Rachel walked slowly over to within a few feet of Lucy.

"You may as well know," continued Lucy, "I've handed in my notice."

"What!" exclaimed Rachel. "Why?"

Lucy shrugged her shoulders. "To be honest I've been thinking about it for a while. I had hoped that by coming back here I'd get back the enthusiasm I had for the job when I was here before. But during these past few days, I've come to realise that I want to do something else. Calum is going to be in London a lot more from now on and quite frankly, I just don't want to be in the force anymore."

Rachel was astounded at what Lucy had just told her.

"How did Carmichael take it?" she enquired.

Lucy shrugged her shoulders nonchalantly. "Like you and Marc, he was surprised," she replied. "But I've explained my reasons to him, and he understands."

"Right," remarked Rachel, who didn't know what else to say.

Lucy smiled. "I'm not sure how long they'll want me to carry on before I can go," she added. "So, I guess I'll still see you around, but I just thought you should know."

Rachel nodded. "Well, thanks for telling me," she replied.

Lucy smiled again, climbed into her car and started the engine. However, before the car started moving, she wound down the window.

"I never asked you," she said, "are you in a relationship?"

Rachel frowned as she tried to work out why Lucy would ask her that, particularly at that moment.

"Yes, I am," Rachel replied. "Why do you ask?"

"No reason really," remarked Lucy. "I just think it's always better when you've got someone you can bounce things off, away from the station, especially for us female officers. Serious relationships also come in handy, too, when you have to deter those unwanted advances from other officers."

Without elaborating any further, Lucy wound up her window and her car slowly glided out of the car park.

As her car exited through the gates, Lucy smiled to herself as she watched Rachel, in her rear-view mirror, standing perfectly still, her young colleague clearly in shock.

* * *

"So, Lucy's leaving us?" Rachel proclaimed to Watson when she arrived at the incident room. "I just spoke with her before she drove away."

Watson looked up from his desk with a look of bewilderment on his face.

"Yep, she's quit," he replied succinctly. "She just told me, too."

"But don't you think that's weird?" replied Rachel. "She's only been back here a week, why quit now?"

"Search me," Watson replied, who was clearly as shocked as Rachel.

"Has something happened between her and Carmichael?" Rachel asked.

Watson shrugged his shoulders. "Lucy says it's because she and Calum are going to have to be in London quite a bit from now on, with him now being given a new position in the party."

"She told me that, too," replied Rachel. "Do you buy that?"

Watson shook his head. "No way," he remarked. "I think she's realised that you're Carmichael's number one girl now, and she can't take it."

. Rachel shook her head disparagingly. "You never give up, do you?" she remarked.

Watson smiled. "Well, it's the best theory I can think of."

"No, I think something's happened between her and Carmichael," Rachel said eagerly. "Whether it was this week, or when she was here before, there's something not right between them two."

Watson shrugged his shoulders.

"Well, the upshot is that it's now down to just you and yours truly to get the paperwork sorted on this case."

Rachel remained baffled, not just by Lucy's sudden departure, but also the comments she'd made prior to driving away. However, she decided there was little point in prolonging the discussion about Lucy with Watson any further. She knew that she'd get little sense out of him and anyway, it was obvious he had no idea why Lucy had really resigned.

"So, where is the boss?" Rachel asked, suddenly realising what Watson had said and seeing Carmichael's office door was open and the room empty.

Watson rolled his eyes. "Now that the case is solved, the great Hercule Poirot has taken himself off home early," he replied scathingly. "He said he'd be back in the morning but has left it to us minions to make sure the paperwork is all in order and to tie up the loose ends."

"Like what?" Rachel asked.

"Like checking the CCTV footage in the vicinity of Wall's office from last Friday morning, to see if we can see Richard Cox approaching the agency before they opened," replied Watson. "And also, checking it again for Wednesday afternoon to see if he entered the office earlier than the time we already know about. Then there's finding the set of keys Carmichael thinks Cox used to gain access."

Rachel puffed out her cheeks. "I suppose they're all my jobs," she remarked woefully.

Watson smiled. "Right in one," he replied.

"And while I'm doing that, what are you going to be doing?" Rachel asked.

Watson's smile evaporated instantly.

"My job is to discover whether we have a duty to find the real offspring of Tim Wall and Harriet Price to let him know what's been going on," Watson replied despairingly.

"I guess that's a good point," Rachel remarked.

"We think we don't," added Watson. "But, as usual, Carmichael wants to be sure and it's yours truly who's been given that job. So, I'd say you've got off lightly."

Feeling mentally exhausted, Rachel sighed, walked over to her desk and sat down.

She'd only just made herself comfortable when her mobile rang.

"DC Dalton," Rachel said as she put the phone to her ear.

"Hello, this is Sara-Jane Turnbull," the strong Geordie accent at the other end of the line announced. "I'm going to be picking up Brian from Manchester Airport in the morning and I just wanted to make sure that you didn't drop me in it with him, as you'd promised you wouldn't."

Rachel's eyes widened and her throat went dry, as she desperately tried to recall exactly what it was she'd said on her call with Sara-Jane's boyfriend on Tuesday.

Chapter 101

After a pleasant, straightforward and uneventful journey home, to his surprise, Carmichael discovered the whole of his family, plus the partners of his eldest two children, gathered in the back garden enjoying a few cold drinks in the warm evening sunshine.

"You're earlier than I'd expected," remarked Penny as she saw her husband walking towards the sunbed she was reclining on.

Carmichael smiled. "The privilege of rank," he replied, seconds before planting a huge kiss on his wife's forehead.

"I take it the good mood means you've solved your case?" Penny remarked.

Carmichael's smile widened. "Spot on," he replied, regurgitating a phrase frequently used by his eldest daughter's partner. "All done and dusted."

Penny sat up and swung her legs over the side of the sunbed so that she was sitting more upright and there was room for her husband to join her.

"So, what was the outcome?" she enquired eagerly.

Carmichael gently shook his head.

"It's complicated," he replied, resting his hand on her leg and kissing her once again. "I'll fill you in later, after I've had a drink and something to eat."

His eyes then scoured the area to try and spy any sight of his favourite wine, but to no avail.

"Here you go, Dad," remarked Jemma, his eldest daughter, who'd crept up behind him with an exceptionally large glass of pinotage poured from one of the bottles he'd bought from Mr Dod. "Is that what you're looking for?"

Carmichael smiled. "What service," he remarked with a grin.

* * *

Three hours later, after several glasses of pinotage along with far too much of the Chinese takeaway they'd ordered from 'The House of the Orient' and having been abandoned by the younger family members and their partners, Penny and Carmichael sat quietly alone under their large red sunshade.

"So, it was the boyfriend," Penny remarked.

Carmichael took another sip of the wine before nodding. "Yes," he replied. "It was Richard Cox, or rather, Richard Purnell, to be precise."

"Why?" Penny asked.

"His initial idea was to blackmail Harriet Stockley about giving away her child, but when he found out she'd died, he latched on to her sister, Mary Price. He then changed his plan, deciding instead to pass himself off as the child to Tim Wall, the father," replied Carmichael. "A child he thought Wall didn't know anything about. Problem is, when he changed his plan, he didn't do his homework properly and it turns out that not only did Wall know he had a son by Harriet, but he also knew the child's date of birth; he used it as his safe combination."

Penny nodded. "I do that for a lot of my PIN numbers," she confessed.

Carmichael smiled. "Well, that was his downfall when he met with Wall," he continued. "And a mistake that scuppered his scam and sadly cost Tim Wall his life."

Penny frowned and shook her head. "So, he wasn't that bright," she concluded.

Carmichael laughed. "Clearly not," he concurred.

"But why kill Wall?" Penny asked. "And why did he hang around afterwards?"

Carmichael nodded. "Both good questions," he replied. "And as he's keeping tight-lipped, ones we may never know the answers to. However, what we do know is that Richard has got a really short fuse and when cornered, he's prone to turn nasty. I reckon that's what happened with Tim Wall last Friday evening, and with Faye when he thought, wrongly as it now appears, that she'd rumbled him as Wall's murderer. I saw a bit of it earlier today in the interview room. Had it not been for PC Dyer, Lucy and Watson, he might have done me some damage, too."

Penny never liked to think about her husband getting close to violent situations but had accepted it was a hazard of Carmichael's job. Nevertheless, she wasn't too thrilled to hear what had gone on that afternoon.

"But why did he hang around after he'd killed Wall?" she asked again.

"He'd have quickly attracted attention to himself if he'd done a runner on Friday," Carmichael replied. "And I suspect, having arranged for Faye to be out of the way at the pub, so he could meet Wall alone, he probably realised that he had a perfect alibi. And it almost worked, too."

Penny nodded slowly. "So, maybe he's not that stupid after all," she remarked.

Carmichael took another sip of wine but didn't respond, his mind clearly starting to drift off elsewhere.

"And how's Lucy settling in?" Penny asked.

"She's not," replied Carmichael bluntly. "She's decided she wants to leave the force and has handed in her notice."

"Really," remarked Penny. "What's she going to do?"

"Relocate to London with Calum," replied Carmichael. "He's now got some big party job, so he needs to be there more, and she wants to be with him."

"I see," remarked Penny, who was stunned by the news, but mightily relieved, too.

They sat quietly for a few seconds before Penny spoke again.

"And what about Wall?" she asked. "You said that you weren't sure whether he was a saint or a sinner. Have you come to a conclusion?"

Carmichael shook his head.

"If you ask Lucy or Rachel, or many of the women he dated and who knew about his penchant to give his ex-girlfriends scores out of ten, then unanimously they'd say he was a chauvinist and would judge him accordingly," he replied. "And given he wasn't averse to blackmailing people either, on the face of it you'd have to deduce that he wasn't the most pleasant person around. But there are other people, including both the women he had worked with at the detective agency, other women he'd dated, and people he'd helped through his work, many of whom he didn't charge a penny, who'd have a totally contrary opinion. He also gave a lot of time and money to charity."

Penny exhaled deeply. "But what about you?" she asked, keen to get Carmichael to commit himself.

"Neither, I suppose," he replied. "He was clearly not someone I'd want one of our daughters to get within a million miles of, and I wouldn't trust him as far as I could throw him, but I don't think he was evil. I'd say he was immature, and his behaviour was more than a bit shady at times, but fundamentally I'd say Tim Wall was harmless."

Penny frowned. "Harmless," she repeated, her tone one of disbelief. "From how you've described him, I have to side with Lucy and Rachel," she announced. "I don't like the sound of him or his murky little world one bit. He sounds an immoral, obnoxious, evil man."

Carmichael shrugged his shoulders before taking another sip of his wine and staring out across the fields.

"I'm not so sure," he replied. "Immoral? Sometimes. Obnoxious? Certainly, he was to some people, but he wasn't evil. Richard Cox is the evil one. He's the one who was calculating. He's the one who really did use people and he's the one with the short fuse, capable of murder. No, if pushed, I'd conclude that Tim Wall was like most of us."

"What do you mean by that?" Penny enquired.

Carmichael looked across at his wife. "Not perfect by any stretch of the imagination, but certainly not all bad," he replied.

"Like all of us," Penny remarked firmly. "Speak for yourself, Steve Carmichael."

Carmichael, his eyes still on Penny, raised his glass high into the air.

"When I say all of us, that's present company excepted," he conceded with a broad smile. "Obviously, that just goes without saying."